Praise for the thrilling romances of
Kasey Michaels

THE HOMECOMING

"A tale of love and passion. . . . A fast-paced plot and the history of the Lenape tribe, told with poignancy and sensitivity. . . . Splendid and worth the read."
—*Rendezvous*

"Intriguing. . . . Michaels provides vivid description and authentic historical detail. . . . This colonial romance with a dash of English elegance and a touch of Irish sass is an uncommon mix. . . ."
—*Library Journal*

"Kasey Michaels' obvious adoration for Pennsylvania's history glows within the pages of *The Homecoming*. Readers will be fascinated by the colorful details, marvelous characters, and the exciting adventure and passion. . . ."
—Kathe Robin, *Romantic Times*

Books by Kasey Michaels

The Passion of an Angel
The Secrets of the Heart
The Illusions of Love
A Masquerade in the Moonlight
The Bride of the Unicorn
The Legacy of the Rose
The Homecoming
The Untamed

Published by POCKET BOOKS

Kasey Michaels

THE UNTAMED

POCKET STAR BOOKS
New York   London   Toronto   Sydney   Tokyo   Singapore

This book is a work of fiction. Names, characters, places and incidents are products of the author's imagination or are used fictitiously. Any resemblance to actual events or locales or persons, living or dead, is entirely coincidental.

An *Original* Publication of POCKET BOOKS

A Pocket Star Book published by
POCKET BOOKS, a division of Simon & Schuster Inc.
1230 Avenue of the Americas, New York, NY 10020

ISBN: 0-671-50115-1

First Pocket Books printing November 1996

10 9 8 7 6 5 4 3 2 1

POCKET STAR BOOKS and colophon are registered
trademarks of Simon & Schuster Inc.

Cover art by Lina Levy

Printed in the U.S.A.

A student's best friend is a good teacher.

My life has been blessed by five of the best: Marjorie Lazarus, William Piff, Ranald MacAdam, John Durishin, and William Helfrich. They gave me a love of reading, of writing, of history. They made me angry; they made me think. They awakened me to the world.

This book—every book I write—belongs in part to them.

Happy the man, and happy he alone,
who can call today his own:
he who, secure within, can say,
tomorrow, do thy worst, for I have liv'd today.

—John Dryden

PROLOGUE

1763

A Violent Land . . .

Would that I were under the cliffs,
in the secret hiding-places of the rocks,
that Zeus might change me to a winged bird.
— Euripides

And if I perish, I perish.
— Esther 4:16

New Eden

❦

"COME HERE TO ME, EILEEN, AND WE'LL BE WATCHING GOD'S great sun set together. The sky's as faerie pink as our sweet Mary Catherine's lips, and a multitude of birds are singing us their good-nights. And look—here's our own two fine, strapping sons, traipsing up the hill, back from the village in good time just as they promised. They've got themselves a bit to go yet, but even from here I can see their cheeks stretched with sugar plums. Glory be! Could that be the bolt of fancy plaid cloth you've been pining for tucked up under our Joseph's arm? It's a glorious sight you're missing, sweet Eileen, don't you know, rubbing at those pots."

Eileen Cassidy frowned and put down the heavy cast iron pot she had been scrubbing. She hastily dried her hands on her apron as she walked to the open doorway of the barn that housed not only her family but the farm animals as well, and would until Daniel could spare the time to build them the fine new house he had promised her when they left county Clare to seek their fortune in this new, untamed land.

She rested her head against her husband's shoulder. "It's a pretty picture you paint with your sweet blarney, Daniel Cassidy," she said, smiling. "And who was it lied and whispered in your ear that I've been pining for a scrap of cloth, plaid or otherwise?"

Brighid Cassidy, just turned sixteen, and the oldest of Daniel and Eileen's four children, scooped up her sister, Mary Catherine, and followed her mother to the doorway. "Oh, would you listen to her, Da, pretending not to know what it is you're talking about. And after spending a good ten minutes visiting that same bolt of cloth each time we go into Mr. Benjamin Rudolph's store. It's a new dress she wants for when Uncle Sean and Cousin Bryna come."

Eileen shook her head, her fair cheeks blushing as pink as the sky—as pink as her little Mary Catherine's sweet lips—and admitted the truth. "But I didn't need it, Daniel, truly I didn't. Not with us so penny pinched. How wonderful it will be when Michael comes with the money to pay the quitrent on our warrant and we can patent our land." She laid her head against her husband's shoulder once more, sighing. "Our land, Daniel. Is there not a beautiful sound in those two sweet words? Nearly as beautiful as this lovely sunset."

Daniel didn't answer her, his body suddenly stiff and tense beside her. She lifted her head and looked out over the land they had cleared, the few acres they had so far carved out of the dense forest that made up the majority of this area of the Pennsylvania colony so hopefully christened New Eden. Joseph and Michael must have seen something, too, for they had stopped a good fifty yards from the barn and were looking to their left, into the dense undergrowth. "What is it, Daniel? What do you see?"

"Indians. At least six. There, in the trees. Haven't seen these particular fellows before," Daniel said tersely, reaching for the weapon he kept propped against the wall just inside the door, then seemingly changed his mind. "Savage-looking beasts, don't you know, but harmless enough I'll

4

wager, for all Rudolph says. I'll go out to meet them, Eileen, to show we mean no harm. You and the girls stay here."

Eileen looked to her boys, so near to the barn and yet still disconcertingly distant, and then to her husband, who stood just beside her, tall, straight, and appearing utterly fearless. She remembered the brace of dueling pistols their nearest neighbor, Dominick Crown, had pressed upon her only a few short weeks ago, and the horrific instructions he had imparted to her against her wishes, against all her motherly instincts. But surely Dominick had been overreacting, as everyone in New Eden said—seeing demons where there were none. Surely Daniel was right to offer a friendly welcome rather than combativeness. Dear Virgin, please let him be right.

Eileen began to tremble, then willed herself to swallow down her panic, her impulse to scream. "Offer them some food, Daniel," she heard herself say, taking Mary Catherine from Brighid's arms and motioning for her older daughter to fetch some of that day's fresh loaves from the cabinet. "Daniel, I—"

"I know, darlin'," he said soothingly, kissing her cheek and then Mary Catherine's as well as the five-year-old reached up to grab at his shoulders with her chubby fingers. "But this is our land now. If we'll be staying, it's best we begin as we plan going on. And Daniel Cassidy is not one to bar his door and shut out his neighbors, white or red." His smile faded. "Especially with our own two boys still out there."

Eileen nodded and stepped back to watch as her husband, his stride long and confident, walked down the slight slope toward the half-dozen Indians who had now moved fully into the clearing. Eileen drew her breath in sharply. She had seen Indians before: Dominick Crown's friend Lokwelend and his son and daughter. They didn't wear painted marks on their faces. Who were these men, these strangers? And what did they want?

Daniel raised a hand to their unexpected visitors, shouting out a cheery "A thousand welcomes to you! And a fine

5

evening it is for a bit of visiting!" At the same time, he unhurriedly motioned with his other hand for Joseph and Michael to come to him.

Eileen held her breath and maintained her own smile with a steely determination, wishing the boys inside with her. Wishing Daniel inside with his family. Wishing the stout wooden door closed tight and bolted. Wishing all of the Cassidys safely back in county Clare, still dreaming of their new home in America.

Brighid left the loaves on the table and returned to stand beside her mother. She leaned around the doorjamb to peer outside. "Should Da be doing this, do you think, making these Indians as welcome as the flowers in May? Mr. Rudolph says the Lenni Lenape are nothing more than ignorant savages, no better than wild bears, and we should shoot them all as soon as look at them."

"Benjamin Rudolph would have us shoot everybody, child, for he's a mean, narrow man." Eileen turned to Brighid for a moment, hoping to ease the girl's fears with a reassuring smile.

Neither woman saw the war club that suddenly, unerringly, sliced through the dusk-dimmed air and brought Daniel Cassidy down, his forehead split open like an overripe melon. Eileen only looked to her husband, saw him sprawled on his back on the packed brown earth, as she heard her boys scream out in panic: "Da! *Da!*"

"Sweet holy mother! *Daniel!* Brighid—they've killed your da! Dear, good Jesus, no! *Daniel!*"

"There's no time!" Brighid grabbed at her mother's arm as Eileen instinctively made to rush to her husband's side and pulled her back inside the barn. "Michael! Joseph!" Brighid shouted, her voice holding an icy command far beyond her age and experience. "Run, boys! This way! *Run!*"

The Indians began to yell now as well after being so silent, after killing so silently. They added their fierce voices to the sudden, strident cacophony of sound that had nothing to do with faerie-pink sunsets or brightly chirping birds. Bloodcurdling screams reverberated in Eileen's chest and rooted her to the floor, no longer able to move, no longer able to think. She looked on, as if caught in a dream, while the boys dropped their packages and prepared to defend themselves.

The report of Daniel's rifle being discharged close beside her made Eileen flinch, even as a part of her mutely cheered the fall of one of the Indians. But only one. Five more remained, and it would take Brighid precious time to reload.

"Run, boys!" Brighid commanded yet again, standing the rifle on its hilt as she measured powder and charge. "Mama, tell them to keep running."

But it was too late for running. Eileen knew that, just as Brighid must know it. Just as Michael and Joseph, for all their youth and innocence, must know it.

The boys halted a heartbreaking thirty yards from the barn and lifted their childish weapons—more toys than weapons, fashioned for them by Lokwelend's son, Pematalli—only to have them torn from their hands by their attackers. Eileen watched, unbelieving, as her babies were thrown to the ground, still loudly crying for their da, for her, as if they'd had a nightmare and were calling out for comfort. Their agonized cries were terrible but blessedly brief.

And then the Indians were on the move again, heading straight for the barn. Eileen reacted at last. She was awash in disbelief, stunned, her happiness destroyed in an instant, her only thoughts those of anguish and terror over what had happened. What could still happen. Mary Catherine began to struggle and cry in her mother's fiercely clutching arms. Too late to protect her from the horrific sight, Eileen belatedly turned the child's head against her bosom.

Mary Catherine's cries reminded Eileen that even if Daniel and her boys were gone, she still had the remainder of her precious family to protect. She resolutely closed the door on the carnage, stifling her sobs, and threw home the bolt even as she ordered Brighid to shut the heavy shutters on the single window. "Stick the rifle through the gun slot and shoot yourself another one, Brighid, while I hide Mary Kate," she ordered, willing herself to concentrate on her girls and not the horror outside her door.

Eileen pressed a kiss against Mary Catherine's bright red curls. She traced the sign of the cross on the child's forehead with her thumb, then bent and slid her youngest daughter under the bed, pushing her back as far as she could, all the way to the rough wooden wall. "Not a word, Mary Catherine," she warned as sternly as she could. "You hear me? Stay under here until I come back for you. As you love your mother, sweet baby, not a word, not a sound!"

The child nodded, her eyes already wide with the shock of what she had seen. Eileen whispered a quick prayer, then lowered the coverlet, hiding Mary Catherine from sight.

"Mama, hurry—they're still coming!" Brighid screamed to her mother, sliding the barrel of the rifle through the slot in the shutters even as Eileen rose, stumbled over to a nearby shelf, and picked up the rosewood box containing Dominick Crown's loaned dueling pistols. "Oh, why, Mama? In God's name, *why?*"

"I don't know, Brighid," Eileen answered at last, her hands shaking as she stood at the table and fought to load both the pistols. Late at night, while the children were sleeping, Daniel had taught her how. "Just in case, darlin', like Dominick told us," he had said. Daniel had taught her how. Like Dominick Crown, he had told her why.

She just hadn't believed either of them, that's all. Even now, with Daniel murdered, with her babies butchered before her eyes, she could not believe it. Surely the savages had enough of killing by now? Surely they'd go away and leave them in peace, leave them to bury their dead?

"Filthy bastards! They're after Da's hair!"

Eileen flinched when she heard the report of the rifle as Brighid fired again. She knew the next shots should be hers—one fired into her older daughter's brain, another into Mary Catherine's.

But could she do it?

The crash of axes hitting the door, the piercing war

whoops of the savages ringing inside her ears, nearly undid Eileen. She had to fight to recall how to load the pistols, could barely cudgel her panicked brain into remembering Daniel's instructions. Her entire body shook. She bit through her bottom lip to hold back her screams.

Now that Brighid had fired again, there would probably not be time to reload the rifle. Not that it mattered. She didn't possess the strength of will it would take to shoot her own babies with the dueling pistols, then either reload the rifle or one of the pistols and dispatch herself to hell. Murder her own children? Commit the unforgivable sin of suicide? No. Her Lord's teachings were too ingrained, her hope of heaven, of being reunited with Daniel and her boys for eternity, too dear to her.

Daniel, she implored her beloved husband silently. *I can't do this. Forgive me, my love. I simply cannot do this. There must be another way.*

A sure, certain calm washed over her. What happened to her would happen. She would not, could not, murder hope. The pistol ball she was holding fell from her suddenly steady fingers and rolled under the bed.

Eileen laid the pistol in her lap, refusing to consider it further. She extracted her rosary from her pocket and looked to her older daughter. Brighid had picked up a carving knife and was turned toward the door that was already half kicked in. The girl's expression was resolute and remarkably brave for all that tears streamed down her pale cheeks.

Eileen greedily drank in the beauty of this first child of her heart. Brighid's was a beauty that had been there since birth but was just now blossoming into a true wonder of fair skin, bright green eyes, and a glorious fall of midnight dark curls. And she was as purely beautiful within as she was on the surface. Brighid deserved a future. Both her girls deserved a future.

The wood holding the lock gave way and one of the grotesquely painted savages crashed through the doorway, then stopped as he saw the two women. "Brighid!" Eileen called out, gaining her daughter's attention for a split second. "Da said they sometimes take children as captives—"

"Never!" Brighid shouted, brandishing the knife with one hand as she loosed a bit of crockery toward the savage's head with the other. The Indian ducked his head out of the way and remained where he was, probably shocked to see this fiery-eyed demon whose expression held not fear, but naked hatred and loathing.

"Cling to your life, my darling!" Eileen was unable to look away as the savage yelled and raised his bloody ax. "You are never a slave if your mind is free! Lay down the knife!"

Eileen Cassidy then rose to her knees, using her own body to block the savages from the bed, from Mary Catherine. Her lips barely moved as she held the rosary and began to recite: "Holy Mary, mother of God, pray for us sinners . . . now and at the hour of our death—"

BOOK ONE

1768

Confrontation

The greatest griefs are those we cause ourselves.
— Sophocles

CHAPTER 1

THE SUN SHONE DOWN BRIGHTLY AS PHILIP CROWN, EARL OF Ashford and reluctant savior of damsels in distress, guided his weary mount along the dusty groove of a footpath leading toward a small encampment of tepees and rude tents outside the gates of mighty Fort Pitt.

"This is where they're keeping the returned captives, Lokwelend?" he asked of his companion, the elderly Lenni Lenape who rode beside him, holding the lead rope of the extra mount they had brought with them from New Eden. "Hardly seems fitting unless they're all lousy with lice or some such thing."

Lokwelend grunted. Lokwelend grunted a lot, Philip had decided. At least the Indian had for the past three weeks, the time it had taken for the two men to cross nearly from one end of the colony of Pennsylvania to the other. When he wasn't quoting long dead Greeks and Romans, which Philip had seen as a splendid joke, before they'd been just the two

13

of them, alone together, traveling through the wilderness between outposts for weeks.

"To your people, Little Crown, the captives are White Indians. They are Lenape, no matter what the color of their skins," Lokwelend said now. "These people did not come here willingly, and the whites inside the fort fear them as enemies. For many years the Night Fire has been a Lenape, and she might not agree to go with us."

Philip smiled, shaking his head. "You think so, do you? And would you be willing to be the one who says as much to my dear aunt Bryna when we return to Pleasant Hill without her cousin, now that she has hope Brighid may have at last been found? Wasn't having her shoot at you once enough for you? Why, the way I heard the story told, Bryna singed your feathers and came within a whisker of blowing your head right off. That was before she learned to love you or my uncle Dominick, of course."

"You have too long a memory for so young a man," Lokwelend answered as the soldier he had spoken to earlier motioned for them to approach. "Here, they are lining up the captives for our inspection. Like cattle at a sale. Nipawi Gischuch will not thank you for this humiliation. If she is even here."

"It would please me immensely, Lokwelend, if you would stop referring to Brighid Cassidy by that name."

Lokwelend grunted again, then shrugged eloquently. Sometimes Philip couldn't decide between considering the Indian as a Greek oracle or as a damned Frenchman, speaking more with his gestures than his mouth. "It is who she is, Little Crown. She is Nipawi Gischuch, the Night Fire, just as her cousin is the Bright Fire. Such it will always be. A name cannot change what is inside."

Philip gave up the argument. He only dismounted while Lokwelend, who unlike himself had previously met Bryna's cousin and could thus identify her, got on with the business of finding the girl so that they could all go inside the fort and find a wet bottle and dry beds.

The captives had been herded into a ragged single line along the pathway, standing with their heads bowed, their collective posture defeated. Philip flinched in reflected embarrassment at his government's treatment of his fellow human beings. Like cattle at a sale . . .

These, Philip knew, were the last known Lenape captives, the men, women, and children who had fled Pennsylvania with their captors five years before, having formed new bonds, new relationships with the Indians that superseded those they had left behind.

There were young mothers standing in the dust, half-breed children sitting at their feet. A redheaded man dressed all in deerskins was chained to a wagon wheel, obviously not overjoyed to have been returned to the white man's world. And, behind them, standing just outside the tents and tepees, were Indians, young and old. They were already weeping, pulling at their hair and clothing, sure that this time, with this new inspection, their particular loved ones were about to be separated from them forever.

Some of the captives had been living with the Lenape for more than a decade. Long enough for a young child to forget his natural parents, much too long to conceive of a separation from their adopted families, the only families they remembered. If, indeed, they had any relatives remaining after the particular raid that had left them not dead, but adopted to replace a child, mother, or brother lost to the white man's war. Many had married into the tribe that had captured them and were content in their new lives. White Indians, as Lokwelend had said they were called.

Returning the captives and their half-white children to civilization had seemed a practical, even laudable, idea when the last treaty had been signed and the edict had come down from the government. Seeing this coldly pragmatic solution in practice made Philip shiver with distaste.

Lokwelend's warning that he would not be greeted with effusive thanks for "rescuing" Brighid Cassidy sounded more logical now. His mission seemed less noble than when he had agreed to—how had he said it? Oh, yes, he remembered. He had volunteered to "go Brighid hunting, the moment misplaced, recalcitrant Irish maidens are in season, of course."

For the five years since making that promise to Bryna Cassidy Crown, Philip had traveled throughout the colonies, even returned to England for a few months, his offer more than half forgotten. Until the long arm of the government had reached out and found the last of its once-loyal, captive subjects and demanded they be brought home.

Philip had been visiting at Pleasant Hill once more at the time of the news, and Bryna hadn't hesitated a moment to remind him of his promise. Dominick couldn't leave. Not with Bryna once more with child and with all the responsibilities Dominick had, both at his estate and in the town of New Eden, where he remained its most prominent citizen.

Leaving Philip to make good on his rashly spoken promise. Leaving Philip to be the one who got to ride on horseback across the width of the colony with the grunting, shrugging, bear-grease-smelling, Greek-quoting Lokwelend, who swore he could recognize Brighid Cassidy no matter how many years had passed.

The sound of weeping brought Philip back to the moment at hand. "Let's get this over with, Lokwelend," he urged quietly, "before the soldiers decide to silence a few mouths with their rifle butts." He accepted and held the reins of all three horses as the Indian began walking down the long line, looking intently into each young woman's face.

Lokwelend had known Brighid Cassidy when her family first came from Ireland to settle in New Eden. It had been Lokwelend who, at Bryna Cassidy Crown's request, had searched for the girl several months after her capture by a raiding war party. And it had been Lokwelend who had found Brighid, then left her behind with her new Lenape family, returning to New Eden empty-handed.

But full of sage sayings and obscure reasons, no doubt, Philip thought ruefully as he watched the Indian's slow progress.

No more than a third of the way down the line, Lokwelend halted in front of a particular young woman.

"Palli áal, Grandfather," the woman begged plaintively, Philip's limited knowledge of the language still encompassing the translation of that particular phrase. "Go away," the female had said. He tilted his head to one side, beginning to be interested.

Lokwelend mumbled something in reply, then bowed his head, saying quietly, *"Itah!* I say, good be to you, Nipawi Gischuch. When last we met, you told me of your wish to remain with your new family. I had promised the Bright Fire only that I would find you, and so I left you again as you asked, without breaking my word. The Bright Fire learns quickly and was more pointed in her request this time. She wants the sister of her heart to come home. As her friend and as the friend of Crown, I could not refuse her. I ask you to forgive me."

The young woman sighed, keeping her chin lowered.

Lokwelend grunted, stepped back a pace, and pointed to the young woman as he stared levelly at Philip, his dark eyes silently imploring the younger man to measure his words well. "This is she, Little Crown. Before you stands the Night Fire, the one I have told you about, the one you call Brighid Cassidy."

"Are you sure?" Philip leaned forward slightly to get a better look at the girl. Her hands were bound in front of her, unlike those of the other women, as if this one particular woman might prove dangerous if untied. Her skin, what he could see of it, was as dark as either birth or Mother Nature could make it and glowed from the usual Lenape application of sunflower oil meant to keep her safe from sunburn while working in the fields. Her black hair, slick with bear grease that could tame any tendency to curl, hung nearly to her waist in long, thick braids.

Tall and slim, she wore a fringed, deerskin wrap skirt that fell to her knees over deerskin leggings and soft-soled moccasins. A man's blue cotton shirt was tied at her waist with a striped length of material. Colored beading decorated her clothing, a band of beads sewn to a thin strip of leather encircled her forehead. She looked about as Irish, as white, as Lokwelend, clad in a kilt, would appear Scottish.

Philip, a tall, broad-shouldered English peer with shoulder-length hair the color of liquid sunlight, a man dressed in comfortable deerskins yet carrying an English walking stick—and not for a moment considering his own confusing appearance—laughed out loud. Then, speaking in the slightly amused, cultured tones of London, again so unusual an occurrence here, in the middle of a wilderness, he said advisedly, "Time to reach into your pouch and pull out those spectacles of yours, Lokwelend. Look at her. That's no white woman."

"You want this one?" the soldier interrupted, walking up to the young woman. "Be glad to get shed of her if you do. We had to tie her up after she bit Corporal Manton. Damn near took his ear off as a matter of fact. Here, I'll give you a better look-see."

So saying, the soldier grabbed at the girl's braids and roughly pulled back her head. Philip, his good humor quickly leaving him, found himself looking into a pair of frightened, yet excruciatingly lovely aquamarine eyes, their whites startling against deeply tanned skin. "God's teeth, I don't believe it," he swore quietly as something tightened deep in his gut. "Those Cassidy eyes. So many ways to be green. Excuse me. I'll introduce myself. I am Philip Crown, nephew of Dominick—and your escort back to New Eden."

Brighid Cassidy looked at him for a long while, her aquamarine gaze unwavering and growing rudely assessing, infinitely hostile. Then, as the soldier released his grip on her braids, she turned her back to Philip, exposing the wooden cradleboard strapped to her shoulders and the sleeping child tied to the board.

She turned around once more to face Philip again, her expression now more than hostile, more than merely protective. Fierce. Nearly murderous. "The child is my son, Tasukamend," she quietly announced in a rusty-sounding Irish accent that carried more than a hint of Lenape

18

gruffness. "In your language, he is known as the Blameless One. And this," she continued, employing a slight inclination of her head that brought a small, wizened raisin of a Lenape woman scurrying to her side, "is my mother-in-law, Lapawin. Her son, my husband, is dead. Killed by the white man."

She took a deep, steadying breath. "Move me one step from this place without both Tasukamend and Lapawin by my side, *Geptschat,* and it's a sharp knife I'll be taking to your gullet first time you turn *your* back. Is it understanding me you are?"

Philip was nonplussed for a moment but only for a moment. *"Geptschat?"* he asked, leaning on his walking stick as he turned to Lokwelend. "That, if memory serves, would be the Lenape word for *fool,* would it not?"

Lokwelend smiled, then reached forward to untie Brighid Cassidy's hands. "We'll need a wagon, Little Crown," he said unnecessarily as Lapawin broke into raucous sobs, obviously believing she was about to be left behind.

Brighid put an arm around her mother-in-law's thin shoulders as the soldier walked away and whispered something in her ear, which seemed to silence the woman. She then smiled at Philip, displaying straight teeth as brilliantly ivory as the whites of her eyes. "And a cow, Little Crown. We must have milk for Tasukamend as I have gone dry with shock, and the cow we brought with us must remain with the other mothers. I'll be wanting us on our way before nightfall, I will. Once we're out of sight of the fort, you can let us go, and we'll be making our way back to our own people."

"The devil you will!" Philip exclaimed, wondering what great sin he had committed to find himself saddled with this trio of impossible charges—one too old, one too young, and one worlds too exotically, belligerently beautiful—not to mention Lokwelend, the grunting, quoting oracle. Was there ever such a mess? "We're leaving before nightfall all right," he bit out at last, "traveling east, all the way back to Pleasant Hill and your cousin. *All* of us."

Brighid lifted her chin a fraction. She seemed to be feeling stronger and more sure of herself by the minute. "Very well, Little Crown. I hadn't really believed otherwise. But I warn you now, I do not wish to return to New Eden, and I will do my level best to make every step of that trip a living hell for you."

"Yes. I'll just wager you will," Philip said dryly. "Lokwelend, remain with the women if you please. I'm off to purchase a wagon—and a cow." He took one last look at those amazing aquamarine eyes before deftly swinging the ebony walking stick up and onto his shoulder, turning smartly on his heel, and heading for the fort. *I've got to make Lokwelend stop calling me Little Crown,* he decided as he walked. *The girl finds the name entirely too amusing.*

Brighid sat quietly on the uncomfortable wagon seat, refusing to cry as the man called Philip Crown sat beside her and guided the lurching, dipping wagon along the rutted dirt roadway. Crying would do her no good. Besides, Lapawin had been doing enough weeping for the three of them. For the past two hours the old woman had keened and howled. She had wept so long and so hard that she now noisily snored in exhaustion in the back of the rudely jolting wagon, a sleeping Tasukamend beside her.

But Brighid refused to cry. She was going back. Against her will and contrary to her wishes, she was going back while the remainder of her tribe, as unwelcome in the Ohio territory as they had been in Pennsylvania, moved once more to the West. Every turn of the wagon wheels made the distance between them greater, until that distance would open into a wide, deep chasm she could never cross.

All of her friends gone. Her family scattered. Wingenund, her dear friend and sister, buried beside the White River. Wulapen's body lying somewhere, she'd never know just where, unprotected from the ravages of wild animals, his bones bleaching in the sun, his hair hanging on some Iroquois belt or in an English trading post. She didn't know who had killed him, who to hate. So she hated everyone.

She had no one now, no one save Lapawin and Tasuka-mend. She'd had a mother once. A father. Two wonderful brothers. She'd had a sister. But they, too, were all gone from her these last five long years. Lokwelend had told her about their fates not four months after the raid that had swept her from New Eden and into a new, frightening, ultimately welcoming world.

Until the moment Lokwelend had said the words, that lifetime ago when he had searched her out the first time she'd seen Fort Pitt on her way west, Brighid had believed all of her family to be dead. She'd had no other choice but to accept their deaths, as she could remember little more than playing with her baby sister, Mary Catherine, as her father moved to the doorway of their small living quarters and began talking of sunsets and plaid cloth. Of the raid itself, of what had happened after her father had gotten to the doorway, she remembered nothing.

It had been Wingenund who had nursed her back from a serious head injury during those first days. Wingenund who had explained that their captors had cut a path of death and destruction through New Eden, sold their captives to Lapawin and other Lenape a week later, and then moved on. All Brighid had left of her family were happy memories and, thanks to Lokwelend, the comforting knowledge that young Mary Catherine was still alive and safe and living with her cousin, Bryna, in the glory that was Pleasant Hill.

Brighid could have gone back then. Home to Mary Catherine. To her cousin Bryna. Home to the memories that eluded her yet filled her with some nebulous, crippling fear, as if recovering her memory of the raid and the days that had followed it held more danger than answers. Home to taint Mary Catherine with her presence. For a woman captive, be she gone four months or five years, was naturally assumed to have been violated by savage, dirty Indians, so that she was tainted, less a woman, and a definite embarrassment both to her remaining family and her whole community.

With Lapawin, with Wingenund, Brighid had felt safe;

safe from her hidden memories, her nameless fears. She had felt loved. And she had felt *necessary*. If Mary Catherine had needed her, Brighid would have gone back. But she would not go back only to humiliate the child with the stigma of her "soiled" presence.

No, there had been no reason to go back five years ago. There was less than no reason for her return now. Better to starve with the ragged remnants of her small tribe as they moved ever westward than to return to New Eden, where she would soon outwear her welcome and taint Mary Catherine's future with her presence. Better to die with her people than return to a place where she could never belong. And if it weren't for Tasukamend and Lapawin, who depended upon her, she would have found a way to escape long before Philip Crown could come and get her.

For she had no future now. Nobody wanted a woman of one and twenty who had lived with savages for more than five years. No one wanted a half-breed child, especially a man-child, and she would never give up Tasukamend. Bryna would say she wanted her, but after the thrill of the reunion of the two cousins, what would there be for either of them? Not when she was Nipawi Gischuch, wife of Wulapen. Not when she bore such hatred of the white man in her heart.

"This won't work, you know," she said flatly as the roadway widened, signaling their approach to some small frontier hamlet—and none too soon, for it was rapidly growing fully dark, when only the moon and Lokwelend would be able to guide them. "They won't let me in their inns, and I wouldn't stay there if they did. I'd suffocate beneath a roof, I swear it."

Philip Crown turned his head toward her, his smile so naturally pleasant that she had to look away from him. "You'll stay where I put you, Miss Cassidy, and like it. And while I'll admit that you and your small company don't smell especially wonderful, I'll wager that my money will be as good at the upcoming inn as it was on my way out here."

Brighid, angered, turned back to look him up and down, then sniffed. "And you smell even less appealing. You smell English to the marrow. *Little Crown*. And it's a proper name, I'm thinking, as you're no more than half the Dominick Crown I remember. What are you then, the toad-eating relative? Playing fetch and carry at a rich woman's whims? That's what our Bryna is now, isn't she? A rich woman? Rich Bryna Crown, of Pleasant Hill. Never lived with the chickens, our Bryna didn't, even when her nimble-fingered, cardsharping da had not a feather of his own to fly with. I'll be no more than an embarrassment to her, you know."

"This is how you talk about a woman who has done everything but move heaven and hell to get you back? God, but you're a pleasant little bitch, aren't you?" Philip remarked, nodding to Lokwelend as the Indian spurred his horse into a fast trot, taking him ahead of the wagon to guide the way. "I suppose telling you that I am actually Philip Crown, earl of Ashford and sole male heir to the marquess of Playden and the Sussex estate called Playden Court—along with several other properties whose names and locations I won't bore you with right now—would do no more than convince you that I am a liar as well as a toad-eating poor relative?"

Brighid looked at him for a long, assessing moment, taking in his clothing, his accent, his infuriating good humor. "An earl, is it?" she commented at last. "Well, of course you are." She then exaggeratedly rolled her eyes heavenward and spoke to the darkening sky. "And isn't that just like Cousin Bryna? Sending off a madman to fetch a fool! For it's a fool I must be to stay sitting here beside this poor, deluded fellow who thinks himself to be such a mass of grandeur. You're as much the misfit as me, aren't you?"

She watched, astonished, as Philip Crown threw back his head and laughed out loud, clearly amused rather than insulted by her intentional sarcasm. "Oh, lady! Bryna won't be able to deny I've brought her the right Brighid Cassidy," he said when he'd recovered his composure. "In your own way, you're going to be every inch the handful your cousin is and more, aren't you? And if I turn my back on you between here and Pleasant Hill, I'll deserve that knife in my gullet, I swear to God, I will!"

All have not the gift of martyrdom.
—John Dryden

CHAPTER 2

Philip set the brake and looked up at the sign hanging over the inn door. The Weary Traveler. Good description, unfortunate building. Sprawling, crooked in its top floor, and probably choked to its rafters with drinking, singing, unwelcoming farmers, trappers, and tradesmen. He could already hear a chorus of strident voices destroying a perfectly good sea chant.

Even as he watched, the front door opened, spilling yellow light, more raucous sound, and a drunken trapper onto the packed dirt. "And stay out, yer bloody lout!" a growling barn door of a man ordered from the threshold, his fists jammed on either side of his three-foot-wide waist. "We gots respectable folks in here wot don't take ta yer foul mouth!"

"Charming," Philip drawled as the trapper lurched to his feet, grabbed at his crotch, pushed his hips forward in the direction of the innkeeper, then staggered off down the street to the next inn of this two-inn hamlet. "I do so delight in encountering an establishment with such pleasant *ambiance* when traveling, don't you, Miss Cassidy?"

"You also enjoy hearing the sound of your own voice, don't you, Little Crown?" Brighid countered, turning about slightly and motioning for the slowly waking Lapawin to remain in the wagon. "Wulapen, my husband, could go for days without uttering a single word."

"That's understandable. From what little I've learned of you so far, Miss Cassidy, the poor fellow was probably afraid to open his mouth," Philip remarked pleasantly, then hopped down from the wagon, flexing his stiff knees. "Lokwelend, stay here and guard the ladies, if you will. I'll go arrange for our rooms."

Brighid quickly clambered down after him. "Wait! I'm coming with you."

"The devil you are," he answered with an assured laugh, then realized that unless he tied her to the wagon wheel he had no way of stopping her. He ran a hand through his hair, poking inside his brain for something politic to say, then realized that tact would be completely wasted on the young woman. So thinking, he went with blunt honesty. "Look, Miss Cassidy—Brighid. This won't work. You look like a bloody squaw. We wouldn't get past the common room."

She tipped her head to one side, suddenly appearing much more Irish than Lenape. "Oh, so it's admitting the truth at last you are, is it? Well, good. I told you I won't be staying under any white man's roof."

"You will if you'll let me alone long enough to arrange it. Two rooms, a private dining room. Enough coins greasing the proper palms. If I take you all in by the back entrance, no one but the innkeeper will be the wiser."

The minute the words were out of his mouth, Philip regretted them.

"Sneak us in the back door? That would be your grand plan? Is that how you traveled with Lokwelend? And he allowed it?" Brighid turned to the Indian, who was standing beside the wagon now, his back deliberately turned on

Lapawin, who seemed to be eyeing him assessingly. "Is this what the proud Lenape have come to, Grandfather? Playing the white man's slave? Is staying on this land worth such humiliation?"

" 'Yet do I hold that mortal foolish who strives against the stress of necessity.' "

Brighid's frown was comical when she turned back to Philip as if for an explanation of Lokwelend's response.

"Euripides," he told her, shrugging. "You'll get used to it. God knows I've had to. But Lokwelend has a point, Miss Cassidy, although I think you might understand it more if I just say that needs must when the devil drives. Now, are you going to let me go secure us a private dining room and some dinner, or are you going to stand here in the dirt and be foolish?"

As if also asked for her opinion, Lapawin leaned over the side of the wagon and growled out something that, Philip supposed, must have roughly translated to "What's the problem? Let's eat!" Brighid shot her a quelling look—Lord knew it would have quelled him if she'd looked at *him* that way—and then motioned for him to enter the inn.

"Needs must when the devil drives," he muttered beneath his breath as he pushed open the door, ducked his head under the low lintel, and blinked, trying to become accustomed to the light of a half-dozen lanterns. "Innkeeper!" he called out imperiously above the din coming from the common room as he banged the flat of his hand against the scarred desk that was the only bit of furnishing in the small hallway. "I require assistance if you please!"

The barn door appeared from the back of the building, wiping his hands on a greasy leather apron as he looked from Philip to Brighid, at which time he misplaced his welcoming smile. "Don't serve no squaws in 'ere," he pronounced shortly, turning to return to his customers.

"The lady is white," Philip blurted out. And none too tactfully, he thought a moment later as he heard his own words echoing in the hallway. "A captive," he continued in explanation, "just returned from long years in the West."

"Even worse," the innkeeper pronounced, spitting toward a small brass pot in the corner, appearing unconcerned that his aim was wide of the mark. "Sinners, all o'em. That's why they was taken in the first place, yer know. Ta pay fer their woeful transgressions. It's God's own punishment fer their wicked ways, and so says every preacher I ever heard, an' I won't have no Jezebels in m'house with decent folk. Now, get gone wi' yer both, or feel the back of m'hand."

Philip took a single quick step forward. "Now, look here, my good man, I'll have you know that—" he began angrily, only to have Brighid cut him off.

"That's it, boyo," she said in clearly understood and thoroughly damning English. "Tell him what you told me, why don't you? Tell him you're a great and powerful English earl. Tell him you've got gold enough jingling in your deep pockets right now to buy this putrid tinter box and put him and his whole wretched family out in the street. Tell him—"

"Would you shut up!" Philip growled under his breath as he took hold of Brighid's elbow and all but flung her back out into the street, slamming the door behind him. "Idiot! Why not just hand me over to be murdered in my bed?"

She shook off his hand. "There's no time for chitchat, Little Crown. You have to hie yourself down the street and get us some food from that other inn. We have several miles to be putting between ourselves and this hellhole before we'll sleep safe."

"No thanks to you and your flapping tongue," Philip countered, knowing she was right—and knowing she was perfectly aware of what she'd done. "And we'll be sleeping out-of-doors tonight, which is just what you wanted. Are you happy now?"

"Happy as a leprechaun with his pot o'gold tucked tight beneath his arm," she answered with a bright grin, climbing back onto the wagon seat, giving him a maddening view of her derriere as the deerskin skirt pulled tight over her shapely bottom. She picked up the reins and released the brake. "You'll learn, Little Crown, that I invariably get what I want. And right now I've a hankering for some thick pink ham and a crusty loaf if you don't mind, as it's been dogs' years since I've had a bite of either. A bit of cheese wouldn't come amiss either, now that I think on it. Don't frown, Little Crown, I *did* warn you. We'll meet you at the bottom of the street."

Philip looked to Lokwelend, remembering that he'd had Brighid Cassidy in his grasp once and lost her. He calculated how far a wagon, two women, a child, and a cow could travel in the time it would take him to procure food for them and shook his head. Why borrow trouble? "Yes, Brighid," he said, making up his mind. "You'll meet me at the edge of the village." Reaching into the wagon, he lifted out the sleeping child, cradleboard and all, and started off down the street, muttering words he hoped the child too young to remember.

And on the seventh day, He rested. The familiar Bible passage ran through Philip's head as he sank onto a large rock beside the babbling stream. "Of course, God could go that long without a rest. He only had Adam and Eve and a conniving snake to deal with. If he'd had Brighid Cassidy," he said, picking up a flat pebble and skipping it across the surface of the water, "he would have had to take a break along about Wednesday."

Which Philip would have done, except that he had wanted to keep moving, praying that somehow the miles would magically disappear between Fort Pitt and New Eden, so that he could be shed of his responsibility. No, responsibility was too tame a word. He picked up another pebble as he searched his tired mind for a better term. *Obligation? Commitment? Burden?*

"Penance," he pronounced at last, grimacing as he spoke. "That's what it is. Penance. I've committed some dastardly, long-forgotten sin, and now I'm being punished. There's no other explanation."

Tuesday, the cow he had traded the extra horse for went

lame. Wednesday, the damn thing died on him. It died on purpose just to torment him. He was convinced of that fact. So he'd bought a goat at the next farm they'd come to. A goat that, his manner and disposition strangely resembling that of Miss Brighid Cassidy, took an instant dislike to him. The cursed animal had butted him, all but tearing the seat out of his deerskins. Which had made it necessary for Lapawin to sew them for him as he hid behind a tree, far enough away to be private, close enough to hear Brighid Cassidy's every girlish giggle at his predicament.

The woman was a menace. Too uncivilized to know that she should keep her mouth shut, her opinions to herself, and her eyes downcast like a lady should do, she also took every opportunity that presented itself to show him up as the dandified, useless Englisher. What she did, Philip had long ago decided, either consciously or unconsciously, was behave like a man, believing herself capable of all a man's freedoms, all a man's tendency to think for herself and make up her own mind.

Lokwelend said that most Indian women were like Brighid. Strong. Independent. Outspoken. No wonder the Lenape went to war. It had to be less stressful than remaining at home with their wives. And a hatchet to the head had to be a kinder death than to wither away slowly, watching one's manhood be trampled on by a headstrong, opinionated, outspoken, generally disagreeable woman!

Not that Philip was alone in his travails. Lokwelend was coming in for enough problems of his own to make him give up Greek poets and take up swearing. On only their second night on the trail, as they sat around the campfire, Brighid had translated for Philip questions Lapawin had shot rapid-fire at the usually loquacious but suddenly, unusually, taciturn Lenape.

"Why you have a scalp lock, old man? Do you fight old wars in your sleep, kicking your hind leg and whimpering like a dog dreaming of a rabbit?" had been her first question, one which Lokwelend had ignored.

"Do you have a house?" Brighid had further translated

her mother-in-law's words, beginning to giggle lightheartedly as Lokwelend shifted uncomfortably on the ground.

"Do you have many blankets?" had been the next question after Lokwelend had signified with a curt nod that, yes, he did indeed possess a house. A second nod seemed to indicate that he had blankets. Philip decided then and there that Lokwelend also had a problem.

"Do you have a woman?" Brighid had whispered to Philip next, confirming his suspicions, adding, "Now she'll go in for the kill." Which Lapawin did with her final question, delivered with a gap-toothed smile that nearly split her raisin face.

"Do you *want* a woman?" Brighid translated, barely able to restrain her laughter as Lokwelend bolted from the clearing as if all the yapping hounds of Dante's Inferno were after his soul.

Yes, Lokwelend was keeping far out in front of the wagon these days, blazing a trail through already cleared paths, spending any free time off in the woods, hunting. Hiding was more like it, but Philip had refrained from teasing the man, considering the fact that he'd probably take off, leaving Philip to find his way back to New Eden through Virginia or some such thing.

Philip had already learned from Brighid that Lapawin was Lenape for "rich again," which is what the enterprising old biddy definitely preferred. She'd had three husbands, burying two of them, divorcing the third, and she had once been a wealthy woman—at least by Lenape standards. So wealthy, she had bought her son a white wife five years ago. So powerful within her tribe that she had been able to protect that wife from insult and attack by those who might not wish that white outsider in their midst.

All of that changed, Philip had also learned, when Wulapen and the rest of the tribe had joined forces with several other tribes bent on ridding the colonies of the Yankwi menace. First to go had been Lapawin's lands, her fields of corn and squash and wheat, as circumstances had forced them out of their homes and put them on the run.

Her horses had gone next. Then her blankets. And then her son. Lapawin had been left alone with only the white woman and her grandson to care for. The two women had followed after the tribe, with no man to help them with their burdens, nothing with which to trade for victuals. They had boiled maple bark for food when the hunters returned empty-handed. But they had not starved. Brighid had been adamant about that. The tribe had taken care of them as best they could.

Until the Yankwis came to talk peace. Then a few of the desperate mothers had pulled Brighid out of her hiding place and made the white men take her away. There would be two less mouths to feed if she and the child were gone. Three, counting Lapawin. It wasn't, Brighid had told Philip, that the tribe didn't want them. It simply couldn't afford to keep them, to feed them.

"We all had to think of our survival, Little Crown," she had told him as they rode side by side on the wagon seat, passing the time by speaking of this and that. "We were better off with the English, and my people were made lighter in their burden as they traveled westward. I do not feel hatred for those who turned me over to the Yankwis. It'd be far more to their blame and mine if Tasukamend had starved. My milk had dried, you see."

"You've mentioned that before, yes," Philip had told her, squirming uncomfortably now as he had then, still finding it difficult to think of Brighid as a mother. Picturing her as wife to a Lenape was even more impossible.

Except at night. At night, Philip had found, it was more than possible to see Brighid as Wulapen's squaw. Lying on mounds of animal skins, her head thrown back as a dark, brawny savage ministered to her slim body . . . his mouth on her breasts . . . his fingers sliding between her thighs . . . her hands reaching up, clutching at him, giving herself to him . . .

"I need a drink," Philip announced to the uninhabited countryside, rising from the rock and looking about as if he expected an inn to materialize in the near distance. "I need a drink, I need a real bed, and I need a docile, conformable, *quiet* woman. Not necessarily in that order."

And then he heard it. Splashing. Coming from around the bend, downstream of where he had been sitting. Could it be a bear? That's all he needed. A bear. Maybe a couple of cubs for Mama Bear to feel protective of—so protective, she'd take a bite out of him without so much as a second thought.

He debated about returning to the small camp, where Brighid had soured something in his spleen by yet again quietly organizing all five of them so neatly and effortlessly. Watching her, he'd felt as useless as a wart on the king's nose. Which was why he'd struck out into the woods in the first place. He knew his way around London, a card table, the dance floor, and a beautiful woman. He knew less than nothing about survival in the wilds of Pennsylvania. As she had pointed out, he was a misfit. No, he wasn't ready to go back to the camp. He was in no mood to be made to feel inferior again.

All right, so he wasn't a woodsman. He couldn't build a fire half so well as Brighid. He couldn't skin a rabbit if he had twice the time and a surgeon's scalpel. His expertise in the area of lean-tos could be squashed into a thimble with space left over for everything he knew about predicting tonight's weather by sniffing the breeze and still leaving room for the damn goat. That didn't mean he had to stand around, watching, as she competently wove a pile of grass into a miniature Taj Mahal or calculated how long it would be before they'd see rain—and looking so damn appealing as she performed her small miracles.

With his pride guiding him and blinding him, Philip picked up his walking stick and struck off in the direction of the splashing, half-prepared to sacrifice himself to the bear gods, if there were any such things. Anything to rid himself of his growing frustrations, his uncomfortable feelings of inadequacy, his swirling anger that he refused to direct toward himself.

He'd gone no more than fifty feet downstream when it at last occurred to him that it was not splashing bears he heard now, but the sounds of a woman singing. A small, fairly evil smile lit his features as he began to move slowly, stealthily, through the trees.

It had to be Brighid at the stream. Brighid washing out dirty nappies or building a dam out of small tree branches she'd gnawed herself, like a bloody beaver or whatever. Brighid. Alone. Unsuspecting. He could sneak up behind her as she crouched on the bank, give her a little push with the tip of his walking stick, and be back in the trees before he heard the sound of her splash.

Not that she would drown. The stream wasn't deep enough for drowning the insufferable chit, more was the pity. And hell's bells, it wasn't as if the woman couldn't do with a small bath.

"Stop it, Philip, old man," he whispered to himself. "You're an English gentleman. A peer of the realm. You shouldn't even have such thoughts." Then he smiled. "But she has been *begging* for me to get a little of my own back, especially after telling me yesterday that I couldn't make it out of a thicket at noon with a map and a trail of bread crumbs to follow."

Caught between an admittedly juvenile need to get some of his own back against this beautiful Irish thorn in his side and his better judgment, Philip continued forward, deciding that the least he could do was to take a small peek and see if it were even possible to sneak up on the woman. Which, he was to tell himself later, was probably why, as he pushed a fir branch to one side and got his first look at the stream from his new vantage point, he felt a twinge of disappointment to see that Brighid was already in the stream. A heartbeat and quick blink later, his disappointment had evaporated, leaving him to stand there, dumbstruck, the fir branch smacking him smartly in the face as he unconsciously released it.

Brighid was in the stream all right. As was the infant, Tasukamend. They both were laughing. And they both were quite naked. Naked as they day they'd been born—although Brighid's form had certainly blossomed with age, reminding him of another reason he disliked her so—she was simply too appealing to him.

He watched as she held the child high against her shoulder, the infant's chubby fists digging into her unbound hair as she dipped him in and out of the water up to his chin with each downward bend of her knees.

Christ, but she was beautiful! Savage. Elemental. Yet completely female. Her skin was the color of honey, as if she stripped to the buff often, exposing herself to the sun, which she probably did, heathen that she was. Her hair, that night-black curtain she kept bound in braids, was hanging in long, damp curls, covering her beyond her waist, hiding some of her, revealing snatches of her that kept Philip from taking more than a single deep breath before he swallowed, finding his throat dry and tight.

As he watched—he could no more turn away than he could condemn himself for watching—Brighid turned her back to him, revealing the smallest, trimmest waist he'd ever seen and a flare of hip that had him clutching the fir branch for support as his knees nearly buckled beneath him.

She held Tasukamend at arm's length, his feet kicking out as he giggled, and began to sing in clear, lilting tones:

In the town of Kilkinny there dwelt a fair maid,
Oh, in the town of Kilkinny there dwelt a fair mai-
aid;
She had cheeks like the roses—and hair of the same,
And a mouth like ripe strawberries drown'd in cream.

And then, before Philip could slink away, a man in considerable physical pain and mental anguish, she turned about to face him—he, who thought he could not be seen—and inquired sweetly, "Would you be wanting to hear another verse, Little Crown, or is the one enough?"

The fir branch slapped him in the face yet again, a punishment he felt sure he deserved, before he decided that he was not only embarrassed, he was angry. Very, very angry!

"You knew I was here?" he asked, pushing away the branch with such force that it booted him in the back a moment later as he walked toward the creek bank. "You *knew?*"

Using the child, the waist-deep water, and the curtain of her hair to cover her, Brighid flashed him a smile that told him she not only wasn't afraid of him, she was laughing at him. "You're as quiet in the woods as Uncle Muldoon was staggering home to my aunt Mairead after a night at his favorite pub. Now, if you've seen enough of the White Indian squaw to satisfy your interest, it's the back of you I'd like to be seeing. It will be raining shortly after dark, so you'd best occupy yourself in making a bed under the wagon."

Philip looked up at the sunny sky, not seeing a single dark cloud anywhere, and decided that Brighid Cassidy wasn't only forward, ill-mannered, and damn near savage, she was also about as good a forecaster of rain as *his* great-uncle William, known to the family as Newgate Willie, had been adept at filching candlesticks from Playden Court. "I'll take my chances under the stars I'm sure will be shining brightly all night, Miss Cassidy, if you don't mind. As a matter of fact, I espied a lovely spot earlier, just upstream, where I believe I will spread my blanket away from Lapawin and Lokwelend, both of whom snore prodigiously loud."

"You do that, Little Crown," Brighid said, walking deliberately toward shore, a move that had Philip ducking back toward the trees—as she must have known it would, damn her eyes. "And I'll have Lokwelend fetch you some dinner to your garden spot, so that I won't have to be looking at your leering face again this day."

"What? I was *not* leering!" Philip was stung into saying, wishing himself back in England, at Covent Garden, where you could tell the ladies from the ladies of the evening with one quick, assessing look. "And you—you were flaunting yourself."

"Flaunting, is it? Really? And what were you being, then,

hiding behind a tree like some drooling *googeen*? A *gentleman*?"

Philip opened his mouth to continue the argument, then realized how stupid that would be. She was right, damn her. He had been leering. What man wouldn't? "I'll see you in the morning, Miss Cassidy," he snapped out as he employed his walking stick to give yet another push to the much-abused fir branch. *"Early* in the morning. The faster we get back to New Eden, the better I shall like it!"

"Have a good night, Little Crown," she called after him. He heard Tasukamend giggling his infant giggles again before he had gone more than another ten yards.

But they did leave the campsite early the next morning. As early as Philip had promised they would. Oversleeping had not been a problem for him as he had sat, huddled beneath a tree and his blanket, for most of the night, trying to stay out of the rain.

*To be caught without a ready answer
is worse than a defeat.*
—Irish saying

CHAPTER 3

❧

For two full days, Philip Crown bore a strange resemblance to Wulapen, not speaking a word as their small party made its way ever eastward, toward New Eden. He didn't even drive the wagon anymore, preferring to ride out in front with Lokwelend, leaving Brighid to urge the tired horses forward over bumpy roads that, in places, were little more than rutted tracks through the wilderness.

Brighid would think he had been embarrassed by their awkward confrontation at the stream if she didn't believe the infuriating man incapable of shame. But it had been shame that Brighid had felt, still felt every time she thought back to the moment she had realized that he had been watching her and had deliberately, consciously chosen to confront him with her knowledge.

It had been a stupid, silly, childish thing to do—not that she was ashamed of her human form. There had been little room for shame as her tribe had lived and worked so closely together, sharing intimacies her memories told her were not considered civilized in the world she had left behind.

With danger all around, many were the times the women had bathed together in a clear-running stream, the men of the tribe standing at the perimeter, their backs turned, their weapons at the ready, in case of attack. More than once, Brighid had caught the eye of one of the men as he had snatched a quick peek at the laughing women and children. As she had felt safe with Wulapen, with Lapawin, with Wingenund, she slowly had learned to relax and enjoy this absence of shame, delight in her moments in the stream, even to preen just a little in the admiring, respectful, sometimes longing looks of the young braves. There was an innocent joy, a new freedom, to be found with the Lenape that she had never before known in her life, and she had enjoyed this latitude of behavior.

Yet, deep in her heart, Brighid still remembered the pained modesty of her mother, Eileen, as her whole family had lived, cramped together, in the barn. She could easily recall her mother's humiliation at having to sleep jumbled in the same small cabin on the ship that had brought them to Philadelphia. Brighid had never seen her mother unclothed. She doubted her father had ever seen his wife fully naked even though she had borne him four children. For her mother, for all their straitened circumstances, had been a lady.

Which Brighid was not.

She couldn't be a lady. Not when she had lived with savages. Not when she had chosen to remain with them when she could have returned to her own people. Not when she had delighted, perhaps even reveled, in Philip Crown's astonished, admiring expression that day at the stream.

She had been sixteen when she had been taken, when her world had exploded around her. Old enough to know what is expected of a gently bred young lady. Old enough to have her language and her manners and her Christian beliefs ingrained so completely that not even five years of speaking the Lenape tongue, of living the Lenape life, could erase them. She still had her God. She still had her mind.

But she had seen another life, had lived another life, and in many ways, she preferred it. Her mother had gone where her father had led, but Wulapen had heeded his mother, for it was the matriarchy who held the purse strings. Men hunted. They made war. They wore feathers and collected scalps and smoked at the council fires. But women were the family. The bedrock. The real strength, the real power.

Would she survive this return to the white man's civilization? Would she be able to accept the strict rules, confining clothing, and constricting notions of a female's role in a white society? Could she bear to watch Tasukamend grow up to be another Daniel Cassidy, another Philip Crown?

She looked forward, boring a hole into Philip's back, as she had been doing for the past two days. He may be dressed in deerskins, but he was an Englisher down to his long blond hair and ridiculous walking stick. He spoke like an Englisher, thought like an Englisher, even rode like an Englisher, his spine ramrod straight as he sat on an Indian saddle.

Is this how Tasukamend would look in Englisher clothes? Out of place, like a china plate at a campfire or an eagle feather headdress at the king's ball? If Brighid didn't know where she belonged, how was Tasukamend ever to know where he belonged? Less than twelve moons old, there was no disguising his shock of thick black hair, coal dark eyes, or the swarthiness of his skin. Although his features were refined, more "white," they could not disguise the heritage of his father's people. No matter where he went, he would always be different. Always slightly out of place, slightly out of step.

Like her.

Brighid sucked her bottom lip into her mouth, biting back on tears that stung at her eyes. She shouldn't have come. She should have taken Tasukamend and run off into the woods when the Englishers first arrived in the camp. Better to starve with her adopted people than to suffocate with her own. Better to give Tasukamend to the women of the tribe, leave him where he was accepted as Wulapen's son, than to selfishly bring him with her to a place where they both would not be able to breathe, to think, to belong.

Philip turned his horse and rode back to the wagon. Brighid blinked rapidly to clear her thoughts, to prepare for another verbal battle if the Englishman was of the mind for one. "There are still four hours of daylight ahead of us," she told him before he could say a word, avoiding his eyes. "You cannot want to stop here."

"I stop where I want, Miss Cassidy, unless you wish to predict a snowfall before dusk, in which case, I suggest we push on to the next town," Philip responded, his jaw barely moving as he bit out the words. Oh, yes, their meeting at the stream was still very much on his mind. The memory probably bothered his sense of himself as a civilized gentleman, for she had seen the desire in his eyes, the surprise mixed with a liberal serving of interest. She hoped his own guilt choked him. Lord knew hers kept her from swallowing easily.

"Did you want something?" she responded tightly, refusing to enter into another senseless debate over the weather. After all, *she* hadn't been the one who'd stubbornly nearly drowned in that drenching downpour the other night. *She* had been warm and dry—and feeling more than a little smug about it actually.

"I want a multitude of things, Miss Cassidy. I want a clean bed, a hot meal, and your absence. However, as none of those things are available, I've come back to take Tasukamend up in front of me for a while. He rides in the wagon too much, strapped to that damnable contraption. He must get weary of seeing nothing but treetops."

Brighid felt a moment of panic, which surprised her. Why should she care if Philip wanted the child with him for a while? She looked back at Tasukamend, fearful for him, fearful of any new change, and then made up her mind. "All right. But you must hold him tightly."

"If I drop him more than twice, you can withhold my

dinner as punishment," Philip answered, still sounding angry even as he made a small joke. "Actually, if I *don't* drop him, you can reward me by withholding my dinner, as all we have left until we reach the next trading store is dried venison, which is not particularly appealing."

Brighid ignored him, stopping and setting the brake before climbing into the back of the wagon to release Tasukamend from his cradleboard. She was about to hand the child up to Philip when she suddenly had an idea. "Lokwelend can drive the wagon, can't he?" she asked as the Indian turned his horse and headed toward them, probably to see if something was wrong.

"Lapawin could drive this wagon, with those broken-down slugs we've got in the traces," Philip answered, looking at her quizzically. "Why?"

"I've a hankering to ride a horse again, that's all," Brighid said, still holding the child.

"You ride?" Philip's tone was incredulous.

"No. I'm just saying I do so that I can keep an eye on you," she shot back, bristling, although if she knew why he was able to ruffle her feathers so easily, she'd be a happier and probably wiser woman. "Of course I ride, Little Crown. I can also shoot and trap and raise a crop. Who do you think took care of us when Wulapen was away? The servants?"

Philip smiled. "How cozy. The husband goes looking for children to scalp while the little wife stays home and skins rabbits. Domestic bliss, I suppose." He turned to Lokwelend. "Miss Cassidy would like to ride your horse for a while, old man, if you don't mind?"

Lokwelend looked to the wagon and to a broadly smiling Lapawin. If he had wings, Brighid thought, he would fly up through the trees to cower behind a cloud. "Nipawi Gischuch asks much," he said at last, as Lapawin, who understood more English than she spoke, began to giggle girlishly and motion for Lokwelend to join her.

"Thank you, Grandfather, for your gift," Brighid answered.

"My stick is under the seat," Philip said as Lokwelend

and Brighid changed places. "You can always beat her soundly about the head and shoulders if she clings too tightly."

The old Indian muttered under his breath in his native tongue, making Brighid laugh, although she didn't bother translating for Philip. He was a man. He probably already understood.

And then Brighid forgot about the two old Indians, concentrating only on the exhilarating feel of solid horse-flesh beneath her, as she had when Wulapen had sat her on her first mount. She gripped the horse lightly with her knees, fighting the urge to push her heels into the mare's flanks and clear the cobwebs from her head with a brisk run. Her last mount had been so thin at the end that she could count the bones beneath its skin. Skin that she had used to make a blanket for Tasukamend after they had eaten the stringy meat toward the end of this past long, hard winter. She had boiled the horse's liver; she had fashioned small, silly-looking hand mitts for the child from the horse's ears. And she had thanked the horse for its gift each time she dug through the snow to raid its corpse to save her own life. What would the mighty earl of Ashford say if she told him all of that? Would he be horrified? She doubted he would be pleased.

"Good Lord, Miss Cassidy, I believe you're smiling," Philip said as they took their place, side by side, ahead of the wagon. "Although you ride like a man—an indulgence you'll not be allowed once we're back at Pleasant Hill—you do seem to appreciate a good piece of horseflesh."

An imp of mischief crawled into Brighid's brain to make its exit through her curved lips. "Indeed, yes, Little Crown. It is much more to my taste than field mice. So little meat on their ribs, you know."

She watched as Philip's face went deathly pale and Tasukamend nearly slipped from his suddenly loose grip. "You ate *mice?*"

Brighid slipped a hand into the pouch tied at her waist and pulled out a small strip of dried venison, popping it in her mouth to chew it soft before she could offer a bit of it to Tasukamend. "We are surrounded by food, Little Crown," she told him, employing a sweep of her arm to encompass the woods on either side of the trail. "Not all of it to my liking, but all of it better than pulling my sash tighter at my waist to squeeze away the pangs of hunger. But you wouldn't know hunger, would you, Little Crown? You know nothing of what life can hold."

"I know it can hold a hell of a lot more than mice and dried venison," he answered, sounding young and fairly wistful. "Lucretia served up a huge roasted joint of beef in the dining room of Pleasant Hill the night before I left. And then there was this lemon tart—"

"Geptschat!"

Philip's expression not only told Brighid that he understood that she had called him a fool, but that he delighted in her reaction.

"Are you so blind that all you can think of is your aristocratic belly?" she asked him, wanting to reach across the space between them and shake him into seeing the world she had just lost, the world she mourned.

"Well, to tell you the truth, I've also been waxing sentimental about a certain leather chair in Dominick's study," he answered smoothly, clearly still intent on baiting her. "But knowing the sublime comfort of stretching out on the ground, only a thin blanket separating you from the damp and any unfortunately positioned, jabbing stones, I imagine you can't appreciate my longing."

"Things," Brighid spat at him, feeling suddenly tearful. "All you speak of are *things*. You don't see the trees, the blue sky, the deer poised by the stream at dawn, its velvety antlers poking holes in the morning mist. You think of the world only when you want something from it. You know nothing of true beauty, as all you care for is yourself. I have learned to time the seasons by the bark on the trees, the fullness of the fur on the animals in the woods. I have learned the smell of winter even before the first frost. I have danced before the fire, both in thanksgiving and in preparation for war. I have watched life be born and held its hand as it died. I have *lived,* Little Crown, while you do no more than exist. I feel sorry for you."

Philip's smile had slowly faded as he listened to her. And he *had* listened, which rather surprised her, for she had spoken emotionally, not measuring her words, not really sure of what it was she wanted to say. But how could she explain the life she had lived with the Lenape? It had been burdened by hardship, yes, but it had also been wonderful, full of friends and small joys and considerable love.

"I am a fool, aren't I, Miss Cassidy, just as you said?" Philip shook his head as he looked down at Tasukamend, who had been busily gnawing on a bit of fringe from his jacket until Brighid passed him some venison. "You've had an experience few of us can imagine, let alone understand. I have to admit that there is a part of me that envies you these past five years. The freedom of going where you want, when you want, everything you own traveling with you to yet another new place, another new experience, another possible adventure. Bryna says we English carry all of England on our backs wherever we go, so that we see everything and learn nothing."

Brighid shrugged, feeling more than a little sorry for the man, but not beneath giving him one last jab. "Putting on deerskins is not the same as first slaying the deer and scraping and tanning the hide. We had little, but what we had we planted, reaped, and prepared with our own hands. I know I can survive, Little Crown, no matter what. If I learned nothing else with the Lenape, I learned my own worth. You can only open your pouch and count yours."

Philip was silent for a long time, long enough for Brighid to go from feeling satisfied with herself to wishing she hadn't been so blunt with him. After all, he had volunteered to come for her. If no one had come to Fort Pitt to claim her, she would be quite alone now, responsible for Tasukamend and Lapawin, still cut off from their tribe, and probably clubbing mice in order to feed them. He had agreed to bring Lapawin along with them, had found them a goat when the cow died, had even agreed to camp along the trail rather than make her run the gauntlet of curious and acrimonious stares at the inns. She should be thanking him, not baiting him. At the very least, she could be civil to him.

"Miss Cassidy," Philip said at last. "Brighid. May I call you Brighid? I know I've already done so a time or two without your permission, but I believed then, as now, that we have already passed beyond formalities. God knows I'd much rather have you address me as Philip than as Little Crown."

Here was her chance to be kind, to say thank you without having to push the actual words past her lips. Because she sensed that he was about to ask a favor of her and be humble in his asking, she nodded her agreement to his suggestion.

"Good, that's one awkward stumbling block behind us," he continued, his smile once more in evidence, reminding her that it was indeed a most handsome smile and that she had already warned herself against it. "Not that we've cried friends, for I doubt you would go that far. However, if you would consider taking on the role of teacher for these next few days, I would be profoundly grateful to you."

"Teacher? This is what you want from me? I don't understand."

Philip allowed Tasukamend to suck on his finger, the child having swallowed the bit of softened venison he had been chewing. Brighid tried not to notice how contented the child appeared or how comfortable and competent Philip Crown looked while holding him. "You do understand the term, Brighid?"

Her animosity came rushing back. "That I do. And a lesson or two in humility aimed at your thick head wouldn't come amiss, I'm thinking," she said, knowing she was jutting out her chin just as both Lapawin and her mother had warned her against doing but unable to restrain the impulse. She had made the best of her lot, becoming one of the women of the tribe, but she had always believed her temperament better suited for the role of warrior. "If that's what you have in mind, *Philip,* then I'd be delighted to oblige."

His response was yet another infuriating grin. "I believe I already had enough lessons in humility the other day, Brighid," he remarked with a self-depreciating laugh in his voice so that she felt her cheeks flushing in embarrassment. "What I'm asking now is that you teach me some of the things you learned these past five years."

Brighid sliced him a wary look, fairly certain she was soon going to regret ever being nice to this man. "Why?"

"I haven't the faintest idea, frankly," he admitted with almost endearing honesty. Almost. "I've been in this country twice in the past years. I visited with Dominick for nearly a year before returning to England, then traveled through the colonies at my leisure, believing I had learned a great deal about farming, about commerce, about the land and its people. I've been to Williamsburg, Boston, and many points in between. But meeting you, I realize that I have neglected more than I've observed, missed more than I've learned. You've seen an America I haven't witnessed. You've *lived* an America I cannot, frankly, even begin to imagine."

"You could apply to Lokwelend for instruction," Brighid suggested, shifting her weight on the mare's back as she struggled to shed herself of that still growing, still uncomfortable feeling that she was about to fall into a hole she herself had inadvertently dug. "I'm sure he would be happy to act as your teacher."

Philip looked back at the old Indian. "I fear I'll never understand Lokwelend," he said quietly, so quietly that Brighid had to strain to hear him. Then he looked straight at her, his blue eyes piercing, yet clouded with an old pain. "But you've lived in both worlds here in Pennsylvania, Brighid. If anyone can make me understand, it's you. If anyone can teach me what I still want—no, *need*—to know about this land, about the Lenape, it's you. Will you help me?"

"You're not talking about how to live off the land, are you, Philip? You don't want to know how I have lived, where I've lived, how I've survived. What are you asking of me?"

"You're right. I have no real curiosity about what you ate or what you wore or even how you existed, especially after that business about the mice." Philip shifted the sleeping Tasukamend into the crook of his arm, smiling down at the infant. "I want you to teach me how the Lenape *think,* how they can feel love for their enemies. Love so strong, Brighid, that you, who lived with them, who learned from them, could take a Lenape into your bed, could bear a child of the people who butchered your parents, your brothers. What I want, what I *need,* is for you to tell me how Lokwelend forgave me, how he can bear to be with me. How, after what I did, he can call me his friend."

Brighid looked to Tasukamend, suddenly fearful. She had seen nothing more of Philip Crown this past week than she had wanted to see, no more than he had chosen to show her. Now she believed she was seeing more of the man, a deeper part of him. A troubled part. A wandering, yearning, searching part of him that he usually kept hidden behind his fine words and carefree manner. "Why was it necessary for Lokwelend to forgive you? What did you do?"

"I'd rather discuss the whole of it later, once we've camped. Some things are easier spoken of in darkness if you don't mind a modicum of melodrama. Are we agreed, Brighid?"

She didn't know what to say, had no answer except to do as he asked or else spend a sleepless night berating herself for walking so blithely into his trap—and wondering just what had occurred between he and Lokwelend.

"Since I have no idea what you're talking about, I suppose I have to agree," Brighid answered at last, reining in the mare so that she and Lokwelend could trade places once more. Any joy she might have found in the afternoon had collapsed beneath the sure knowledge that she was about to experience a very unpleasant evening, one she had been manipulated into agreeing to by the very smooth, extremely devious Philip Crown. "Now, if you will hand Tasukamend to me, I will return to the wagon. I've had enough of riding for today."

You were a stranger to sorrow:
therefore Fate has cursed you.
— Euripides

CHAPTER 4

PHILIP SAT AT THE TOP OF THE SMALL RISE THAT LOOKED OUT over the valley they would leave the next morning, watching the sun set as a hawk circled above, gliding effortlessly with the shifting breeze.

Pennsylvania seemed to be a series of valleys; green, lush stretches of land formed of gently rolling hills and low, deep blue mountains that only saw snow in the winter. He had seen the Alps when he'd traveled to Europe after that last, unsatisfying visit home to Sussex, and the mountains of Pennsylvania were only hills in comparison, not that traveling over them in a wagon could be considered a simple matter.

He enjoyed this country. Enjoyed its greenness, the limitless expanse of trees, the diverse wildlife, the vistas he could see when he took the time to look. He understood the potential, had even purchased a good-sized piece of New Eden land for his own colonial estate. He knew the crops to plant, the times of the harvest, the passing of the seasons.

But he did not know the people. He was a stranger to the Germans, the Irish, the Austrians, who had come here to build new lives. His life, after all, was in Sussex, at Playden Court. His future was in England. His land here was nothing more than a prudent investment, or at least he had told himself that as he'd patented the land, then stood on a hill much like this one and tried to tamp down his feelings of pride and excitement, replacing them with notions of yield, profit, and practicality.

He'd told himself that going in with his uncle Dominick's purchase of three fine trading ships had also been no more than the result of practical thinking. After all, why should he pay to have his raw goods shipped to England when he could turn a profit at each level? And if he at times thought like a merchant while bearing the title of a gentleman, it was only because he had watched his father and grandfather fritter their money away, and he never wished to be similarly circumstanced.

Or so he told himself.

And if a small slice of his new estate happened to contain the land where they had buried Pematalli—useless, rocky land he had badgered Dominick into deeding over to him—what of it? It meant nothing. Less than nothing. Only a mere coincidence.

The whole venture was a lark, that was all—a frivolous investment that might bear fruit. New Eden was no more than a small village in the back of beyond. Yes, Dominick's estate of Pleasant Hill was a daring venture that already had grown into a near empire, and Philip wished him continued success with it. But it was only land. New Eden was only a place. His own estate was no more than a hopefully profitable gamble. He had no deep, personal ties to the colonies, no emotional involvement.

No emotional involvement?

I need to know, Philip shouted inside his head as he unconsciously drew his hands into fists. *I need to understand. Who am I kidding? Who am I trying to fool? Certainly not Lokwelend, who still calls me Little Crown, who still smiles at me indulgently and says I have much to learn.*

"Lapawin and Tasukamend are already asleep for the night in the wagon, and Lokwelend is wearing his spectacles as he squints in the firelight, reading from one of his books. We can talk now."

Philip refused to move or in any way appear startled by Brighid's sudden presence beside him, even though her ability to move so quietly and materialize so suddenly unnerved him. He swallowed once to bring some moisture into his dry mouth and moved over on the large, flat rock, giving her space to sit down beside him. "We have no more than two hours travel ahead of us in the morning before we reach a trading post, or so Lokwelend tells me. Once there, we can load enough supplies to carry us through to New Eden and be home by Saturday."

"Home," Brighid said quietly, looking westward, toward the sliver of sun that still was visible beyond the mountains. "I doubt I'll ever feel at home, Little Crown. I've traveled too far to ever find such a place again."

"I thought you had agreed to call me Philip," he reminded her, lightly touching one of her tightly bound braids and recalling how her hair had looked hanging free to below her waist. "Remember?"

She tucked her legs up under her, the supple deerskin conforming to her long thighs. She moved with the unconscious grace of a child, the freedom of a man, unbound by the constraints English society expected of a woman of one and twenty, a woman who, in a few short days, would be outfitted in panniers and hard-soled shoes—and hating every moment of it, he was sure. Would she still be so exotically appealing in silk and lace?

"I *remember* how you deliberately tricked me into making you a promise," she told him, turning her head, catching him staring at her with more than mere curiosity. She had a unique way of looking at people, he had noticed. First, she turned her eyes in the direction of the one who was speaking, and only then did she, slowly, gracefully, turn her head. It was uncanny, the way this seemingly simple, artless maneuver had the power to skewer him to the ground, letting him know that not only did he have her full attention, he had her curiosity, her searching nature—all directed at looking at him, looking through him, reading his every thought.

What did she see? What did she know? And would she share that knowledge with him?

She fascinated him. He couldn't help it. Every time he looked at her, every time he thought of her, he felt something elemental rising inside of him, coiling deep in his gut. Could that something be hope? His mind was full of hints and questions that had burned there for five long years. More and more, he felt that somehow, some way, this one woman held all the answers that had so far eluded him. But in order to get them, he would have to stop thinking of her as a desirable woman and concentrate on his single problem, which was somehow becoming two problems.

"Bryna . . ." He hesitated for a moment, clearing his throat, then stumbled into his question, the first of many questions that, at the bottom of it, remained the same single question. "You and your cousin Bryna lost family to the Lenape in the raid in which you were captured. Yet Bryna has developed an almost uncanny rapport with Lokwelend and sincerely missed him in the years he absented himself from Pleasant Hill after the last raid, when the Lenape were removed to the west. She welcomed him back this past year with opened arms and has even hired Cora, his daughter, to care for her twins."

Brighid continued to stare at him, see through him, all the way to his uncomprehending unease. "You have a prejudice against Bryna's relationship with Lokwelend and Kolachuisen—with Cora? Would you rather my cousin wasted her spirit in hating them? And for something they did not do? Do you hate all Lenape for the actions of the few?"

"No. No, I don't. I don't think so." He spread his hands, searching for words that would help explain his confusion, his seeming intolerance. "I'm not doing this well, am I? Let me try again." He took a deep breath and let it out slowly. "All right. Try this. I—I simply don't understand how Bryna can look at Lokwelend, at *any* Lenape, and not see the deaths of your family—of her relatives. We're at war, granted, not with Lokwelend himself, but with his race. And not right now, I'll also grant you, but we were, and we will be again, the more we expand our own territories to the north, to the west, and displace the Indians. We'll be killing each other again. It's inevitable."

"Love thine enemy, Philip," Brighid recited quietly, saying the same empty words he had heard in church all during his growing-up years. "But who is your enemy? For you are talking about yourself, aren't you, Little Crown, about your own troubled mind, and not about Bryna or me. Who is *your* enemy? Surely not Lokwelend? What has he done to you? No—that's not my question. Tell me, Little Crown, what have *you* done to *him?*"

Philip bent his head and studied his hands. Oh, yes. She could see right through him.

The sun slipped behind the mountains, and there was an almost instant chill in the air as the sky turned pink behind the clouds. "Five years ago, during the last raid," Philip said quietly, "I killed Lokwelend's only son. I killed Pematalli. I fought him hand to hand, and I sank my knife in his throat." He lifted his head and looked straight into Brighid's eyes, those all-seeing, all-knowing aquamarine eyes. "Even now, all these years later, knowing Pematalli was Lokwelend's son, I can't regret it. And in spite of this, or because of it, Lokwelend loves me."

"Poor Grandfather." Brighid placed a hand on Philip's forearm, and he closed his eyes as a warming sensation of comfort warred with his never-to-be-forgotten awareness of her as a desirable woman. "I played with Kolachuisen and Pematalli a lifetime ago. We were all children together. Laughing, happy. So long ago and for so short a time. I didn't ask Lokwelend about Pematalli, because he did not mention him to me. The Lenape do not speak of the dead, and I feared hurting him with memories. Tell me about this please. Tell me so that I understand. Tell me about Pematalli and how he died."

Philip lifted his head and looked out toward the other end of the valley, into the rapidly gathering gloom. But what he saw was New Eden five years ago and what he felt was the stupid excitement of a naive young man eagerly anticipating his first battle, oblivious to anything save the glory of the fight. Never considering fear. Never considering death.

"We knew the Lenape were coming," he began slowly, "or at least Dominick felt sure of it. There had been trouble— months of trouble—and it was all coming to a head in one terrible day. Dominick and I rode out to all the farms, warning the settlers to go to Fort Deshler or into New Eden, not that many of them listened."

"As Da didn't listen," Brighid said, then shook her head as Philip looked at her, surprised by the vehemence of her tone. "Now why do you suppose I said that?" she asked, smiling, the smile not quite reaching her eyes. "Please forgive my interruption. Go on."

There was something in Brighid's voice, something in her expression, that told Philip that she had her own secrets, her own private demons that haunted her. But now was not the time. First he would tell his story, and then she might feel free to relate her own. "I stopped last at Henry Turner's carriage works," he went on quickly, "but April—Mrs. Turner—and her baby daughter were there alone. Henry was a member of the local militia, you understand, and was still in New Eden." *At Benjamin Rudolph's inn with the others, availing themselves of some liquid courage,* Philip added silently. "Mrs. Turner wouldn't leave, Henry didn't come home, and the next thing I knew, it was already dark and I was stuck there for the night, nearly three miles from the safety of Pleasant Hill."

He took a deep breath, exhaling slowly. "The Lenape attacked just before dawn."

Philip closed his eyes, still able to see the scene as clearly as if it had all happened only yesterday. He remembered the unbearable tension of waiting, heard the war whoops, felt his heart pounding double time in his throat. He smelled the gunpowder as he discharged his rifle from the safety of the gun slot, felling one of the savages, then took the second rifle from April and dispatched another one, watching both of the attackers fall, knowing he had been the one to put an end to their plans of butchery. It had been terrifying. It had been exhilarating. He had felt all elemental male, protecting the female of the species.

He had thought it was over when he stepped outside to view the result of his first victory, gone to view the carnage he had wrought—the two bodies nearly naked and covered with bright, garish paint, wide, gaping holes in the center of their chests. He had stood there in the pale light of dawn, looking down into the Indians' faces, looking beyond the war paint, beyond the vacant, staring eyes, and wondered if he was older or younger than these youths who had raced toward Henry Turner's house, intent on killing everyone inside.

Like madmen they had come, risking exposure as they sprang from the trees, calling attention to their movements with their ear-piercing whoops, daring their enemy to do its worst, as if they were protected by some magic spirit. Philip had not been prone to deep thinking—he had been only one and twenty—and his life had never before seemed much more than an adventure, a game. But even then, he had known that it made no sense. No sense at all. Not then. Not now.

War was no game. And there were no winners. There had been just these two young Indian braves, sprawled in April Turner's frost-browned front garden, their life's blood seeping into the dirt. The exhilaration Philip had felt drained away just as silently, leaving him without a clear notion of what to do next. He had just been bending down to take up the first Indian's feet at the ankles, having decided to pull the bodies out of April's sight, when another war whoop murdered the silence.

Fear as cold as a February morning had slammed into his

gut at the sound, for he knew he was a good twenty yards from the safety of Henry Turner's house, a good ten yards from his empty rifle that he had propped against the fence post. He was naked, defenseless, and under attack. Pulling a large knife from the sheath at the dead Indian's waist, he whirled about, knees bent, arms wide, as ready as he knew how to be to kill again or to die.

He gave not a single thought to April Turner and her baby, to their terrible fates if he were to die. He thought not of his home in Sussex or of what his uncle Dominick's sorrow would be if he learned of his nephew's death. No. What came to his mind, the only thing that came to his mind, was to wonder how it would feel to have a knife plunge into his body. Would it hurt? Would it hurt for long? Would the savage wait until he was dead to take his hair?

And then the Indian was upon him, launching himself at Philip like a lion springing on a lamb, and Philip didn't think at all. He felt the Indian's bear-grease-slicked skin under his fingers, smelled his sweat, saw the raw hatred in deep black eyes that were no more than inches from his own. They were locked together, moving almost as one, doing a macabre dance there in the dirt, a dance of death. *"N'dellennówi!"* the savage had gritted out, his breath visible in the cold October dawn, mingling with Philip's own misted breath. *"Lennápe n'hackey!"*

"I am a man—I am of the Original People," Brighid said quietly when Philip stopped speaking, which was the only way he knew he had spoken at all. "It's strange that you should remember what Pematalli said. And then you killed him."

Philip gave a fairly sarcastic sniff and shook his head before looking at Brighid. "Killed him? Did I, Brighid? I often wonder exactly what it is that I did that day."

She frowned, clearly not understanding, just as he had been struggling for five long years to understand. "You fought. You lived, he died. What else would it be?"

"Suicide," Philip said quietly, forcing himself to smile, knowing how ridiculous he must sound. He rubbed at the back of his neck, feeling the unwelcome prickling that had been his companion for far too long, the feeling of having been not a conqueror, but a victim, of still being a victim. "The raid was over. April Turner's house was the last to be attacked before the Lenape recrossed the river. Pematalli could have gone away without my ever knowing he had been in the area. He could have shot me from the trees—I found his rifle there later, fully loaded."

He looked directly at Brighid, looked deeply into her eyes. "And then there is Lokwelend. He thanked me—*thanked me*—for giving Pematalli a warrior's death. And whenever I ask him how he can forgive me, how he can *thank* me, he calls me Little Crown and says I still have much to learn."

Brighid remained silent, sitting so still, so quiet, in the dark. Waiting. As if somehow she knew. She knew he wasn't quite finished with his story.

"Lokwelend won't explain," he said at last, his voice seeming unnaturally loud to him as the quiet between day and night had yet to be bridged by the nocturnal animals who were waiting for the eerie light of the full moon to begin their nightly hunt for food. "He said I was to wait for the Nipawi Gischuch, the Night Fire. So, Brighid Cassidy— Nipawi Gischuch—much as I hate doing it, much as it humbles me, I'll ask you again. Will you be my teacher?"

Brighid's hands, always so still when they were not weaving miracles out of dried venison or broken grasses, twisted in her lap, betraying her nervousness, as did the slight tremor in her voice when she finally spoke. "Five years ago, many of our tribe bowed to the white man and removed themselves to the Ohio. But many could not abandon this land. Knowing they would either conquer or die, they chose to fight for their land and die as warriors if they saw that the battle was lost. You gave Pematalli a warrior's death, which is doubtless what he craved. For that, Lokwelend thanks you."

"That's insane, Brighid, and you know it," Philip said shortly, feeling he had exposed himself to her, only to have to listen to nonsense. And yet . . . and yet. "That still doesn't explain why Lokwelend can stomach having me around him."

"So impatient, like all the English! Allow me to tell you a story if you please. Then, perhaps, you will understand." She was silent for a few moments, then took a deep breath before speaking, her speech patterns formal, as if she were first translating her words from Lenape to English in her head. "There were two young men, Lenape braves. Unique and, in their own ways, remarkable and worthy. They met on the outskirts of the village one day, and words were exchanged, words that ended in the death of one of them.

"The other man, distraught at what he had done, sat down beside the body and awaited his fate, which was surely death, for if he hadn't meant to kill, he had done so. No one else would strike with the tomahawk but only took the body away and left the man there, alone with his pain and sorrow. The man, not knowing what to do, for surely he must be punished, moved himself to a more public part of the village, where, once more, he lay himself on the ground in hopes that someone would gift him with the death he deserved. No one laid a hand on him. So the man took himself off to the dead warrior's residence, saying to the widow who had lost her only son, 'Woman, I have killed your son. He had insulted me, it is true, but still he was yours, and his life was valuable to you. I, therefore, now surrender myself up to your will. Direct as you will have it, and relieve me speedily from my misery.'"

Brighid looked at Philip, her eyes shining with tears, and continued: "The woman replied to the man, 'You have indeed killed my son who was dear to me. One life is already lost, but the taking of yours cannot better my situation. Give me yourself in place of my son, and all shall be wiped away.' And so the man, in his confusion and agony, rather than facing death as he had thought, found a new life with the mother of the man he had killed. This is the height and breadth of Lenape forgiveness and how it has been explained to me."

"A charming parable, I suppose." The moon and the stars

lit the night-dark sky, casting weird shadows on the ground as Philip took Brighid's hand and assisted her to her feet. "And now I'm to call Lokwelend Father? Be his comfort, his supporting prop in his old age? Sit at his feet as he spins tales of his youth and reads to me from those books of his? Take the place of his son, of the man I killed? Somehow I doubt that. And even if that's what he believes, I've been gone for a long time. Surely he's changed his mind in my absence?"

Brighid shook off his hand as she turned toward the camp. "He came back to New Eden once he could, didn't he? He waited for your return as well, didn't he? He brought you along to Fort Pitt. He calls you Little Crown—surely with some measure of affection. And, like any good parent, he is patient and willing to continue waiting until you come to him." She stopped ahead of him on the narrow path, turning to look up into his face. "So, Little Crown, what will you do now? Continue in your self-pity because Pematalli chose you as the instrument of his death, or become a worthy son to your new father?"

Philip narrowed his gaze, the better to read Brighid's expression in the near darkness. "You're serious, aren't you? You really believe this?"

"I see nothing of levity in your situation. Lenape address even strangers as friend. Those of their family or those they especially respect, those venerable men they love, they address as Father or even Grandfather, as I do with Lokwelend. As Wulapen called Lapawin Mother when she accepted him into her house as her new son."

She turned away again, only to have Philip take hold of her arm and swing her back toward him. "That story you told—it was about your husband?"

"Love thine enemy, Little Crown," Brighid recited softly as she had when this disquieting conversation first began. "Or did you think the white man invented charity and forgiveness? Lokwelend is right. You still have much to learn, much to understand. If you are to be this earl you say you are, if you're to have the welfare of many people in your hands, it is time you begin. We'll talk again tomorrow—if you'll release my arm."

"Not yet." Philip released her arm, only to take hold of her shoulders with both hands. "You didn't say anything when I told you that Lokwelend saw you in my future. That was five years ago, when I first met him. Do you believe in things like that, in the dreams of an old Indian?"

"I believe in dreams, yes," she answered, never looking away from his face. "I believe in Lokwelend's dreams and even more in my own. But it is five years too late for dreams."

"Is it, Brighid?" Philip asked, pulling her closer, lowering his mouth to hers. She tasted sweet, fresh, and young. She didn't fight him as he deepened the kiss, as he felt the flash of passion mixed with something, some sense of *knowing,* of recognition, that he could not understand.

"Brighid?" he asked as he moved slightly away from her, looking at her in confusion.

She slowly shook her head. "Please, Philip. Don't ask questions for which there can be no answers."

And then she was gone, disappearing into the dark under the trees, where neither Philip nor the moonlight could find her. Leaving Philip with a lot to think about and wondering why the night and his arms suddenly felt so empty.

> *. . . a hundred thousand welcomes.*
> — Irish saying

CHAPTER 5

❧

THE DREAM FLOATED ABOVE HER, NEARLY OUT OF REACH. THE same dream. The dream she had been having and fighting ever since she'd first struggled back to consciousness in Lapawin's longhouse, pulling herself free from the clinging tentacles of some shadowy netherworld where dreams seemed real and her new reality nothing more than a sheltering illusion.

This dream had been her first memory of her new life with the Lenape, as clear to her as any recollection of the raid on her parents' home, and the weeks following remained dim, lost to her, shadowed behind a thick and opaque veil.

There, again, in her dream stood the great stone mansion, a building of such majesty as she had never seen, much less imagined existed. High on a hill, strong, solid, impenetrable. Safety lay within those thick walls, safety and comfort and a most wondrous, healing love. As she looked up at the sprawling building, saw the sun winking off its many windows, heard the song coming from the birds nesting in the eaves, she could feel the love reach out to her, calling to her. *Home, Nipawi Gischuch. Come home.*

But how? How to get home? Because, down below, before the house, where Brighid sat fairly content, if not happy, in the sweet green grass, lay the hill. A vast, steep hill, covered in brambles, littered with twisted trees, heavy with portent, cluttered by evil and cleverly concealed traps meant to snare the unwary. The sun never reached the ground in these dark woods, and the myriad of paths leading into it disappeared into blackness within a few feet of their beginnings, only to open onto strange vistas, ugly twists in the dream.

One path, Brighid already knew, led to the barn, led back to her family. She never took that path, for she had walked it once, and it was the path of sure death, one she had explored but a single time, felt, tasted, then rejected.

Another began promisingly enough but ended as her feet sank into hot white sands before a stark, unwelcoming landscape of blinding sun and vividly striped, flat-topped hills. There was nothing for her there: no food, no bubbling streams, no bear, no deer. Nothing but the wailing of women, the sounds of trumpets in the distance, and the feel of a fully grown Tasukamend in her arms, his blood on her wrinkled, aged hands.

One path led into the mountains, climbing toward the cold and snow. When she traveled this path, eyes stared at her from behind the bare branches. Wolves howled and yapped like hungry dogs, and she ran, Tasukamend strapped to her back. The eyes didn't want her; they wanted Tasukamend. They wanted her child. She ran and ran and ran, trying to escape, only to be flung to the ground from behind, surrounded by flashing red eyes, gleaming white teeth. Whenever she had taken this path, she awoke at once, screaming.

So many paths. One led to heat and stagnant water and

squat, large-toothed monsters who ran fast on short legs, their tails whipping the ground. Another wound all the way to the big blue water where the sun sets and with its setting would, she knew, come an end to all dreams. Yet another wended its way toward a small wooden house marring a flat plain on the windswept edge of nowhere, surrounded by nothing, yet filled with lights and sad-eyed, laughing, painted women who beckoned for her to join them, become one of them. "We all must eat, ducks," the women told her.

None of the paths she had yet discovered led to the great stone mansion. Brighid knew this after years of the dream, so she had given up walking them, contenting herself by sitting in the sweet grass of the meadow and staring up at the house, waiting. For so many years . . . waiting. She woke from these dreams no longer screaming or crying but merely unsatisfied, yearning for something, for someone— her mind and heart full of vague longings and more questions than answers.

Except for tonight. For tonight someone new had entered her dream. A man astride a great white horse. He rode into the meadow, pulling his mount to a plunging, stamping halt in front of her. Full of impatience was this faceless, near-formless man, his entire posture speaking of his anxiety to move on without her. "Yonder lies my home, and if I am to reach it, I must travel my pathways alone. Go away, Nipawi Gischuch. There is no place in my home for you. What I find, I find on my own!"

And with that, not even sparing time for a final salute, the man wheeled the stallion around, pulling him up to his hind legs, and plunged into the woods. But he had taken the wrong path, the one leading to the barn—to the past, hers or his, she could not be sure. She should follow after him, warn him. Because, for all his belligerence, for all his braggadocio, she felt drawn to this man, drawn by pity, drawn by love. If she cared at all, she should follow him. But not there. Please. Not back there, back to the beginning of her sorrow.

Brighid woke to hear herself calling out, *"No!* I won't go back! You can't make me!"

"We're less than two days from Pleasant Hill. Isn't it a little late for such dramatics?"

Brighid pushed the dream from her consciousness. Would he always be present when she was at her most vulnerable? She took refuge in anger. "Go away, Little Crown. Hens who cackle before sunrise have their necks wrung."

He put out a hand to help her to her feet. "A bit of Lenape wisdom, that, I suppose. Now come on. Tasukamend smells like a bear after a long winter—if that's poetic enough for you—and he'll need cleaning before we move on to the trading post."

"Daniel," Brighid said flatly. "His name is Daniel."

She watched as Philip frowned, then looked to the child, who was squirming in Lapawin's embrace. "Daniel, is it—after your father, I suppose? Well, that will make things easier once we're back in New Eden. And what, may I ask, brought this on?"

" 'Yet do I hold that mortal foolish who strives against the stress of necessity,' " Brighid quoted tersely, brushing past him, turning back to add, "Euripides, I believe, if I remember correctly. Oh, and you'd be wise to be closing your mouth before a fly lands in it, Little Crown. You wanted a teacher. Does that mean the teacher herself can't still learn? For Tasu—for *Daniel's* sake, and only for his, I have heeded the words of Lokwelend, and I am learning. Will you learn as well?"

He pushed at his long blond hair, raking it away from his forehead with long fingers. "I'll feel like a fool. What if he laughs at me? What if he tells me I can't hold a candle to Pematalli's ghost?"

"I'm surprised such a brave man as yourself ever ventured out of London," Brighid replied, wishing he'd go away. The dream was still too close. He was still too close. The memory of his kiss was still too close. "Or are you content to be always Little Crown?"

She watched as Philip looked toward Lokwelend, who was putting the horses in their traces. "All right, damn it. I'll try it. I owe the man that much. But if you're wrong—"

"If I'm wrong, you will still be an earl, still the son of a marquess, still the silly Englisher in his deerskins, searching everywhere and finding nothing. But if I am right—"

"If you're right, I might sleep better than I have these past five years," Philip ended for her. Then he smiled, looking so boyish, so earnest, that she longed to reach out and brush his cheek with the back of her hand. "Wish me luck?"

"Luck is not necessary to the pure of heart. Put your ghosts and your guilt to rest, Philip. Give my grandfather back his son. Pematalli. Do you know what that name means? 'Always there.' Let Always There live again in you, through you. You've fought it long enough."

She watched as Philip Crown, earl of Ashford, heir to Playden Court, crossed the small clearing. He stopped beside Lokwelend and assisted him with the horses. Then, in tones so low she could not hear the words, he began to talk. Lokwelend finished with the horses before nodding to Philip, at which time they clasped forearms, sealing what had to be a new bond between them.

The two men stood together for a long moment while Brighid blinked back tears, then separated, Lokwelend walking off swiftly toward the trees, his back ramrod straight, Philip returning to her, a rather bemused look on his face.

"My new father tells his son that he is no longer Little Crown, but Tauwún," he told her, his usually clear blue eyes clouded with emotion, feelings he attempted to disguise behind a rather sheepish grin. "Tauwún. That's rather nice, don't you think? What does it mean? All these Lenape names mean something."

Brighid shot a quick look toward the old Indian, but he had already disappeared. Drat the man! "Um . . . ," she began, searching for a lie, then fell silent once more. She might as well tell the truth. "The Lenape mostly give names after animals or times of day or seasons. But those names are not always forever. As the child grows, both in size and wisdom, his name might change to reflect better who he now is or his accomplishments—even his expected mission."

"And?"

Brighid would rather eat field mice for the next fortnight than say any more. "Yours is definitely full of meaning, many meanings. I must go see to Daniel."

He took hold of her elbow, his eyes no longer clouded, but clear and sharp and intensely interested. "Tell me, Brighid. Tell me now."

"Open the door!" she nearly shouted, rushing her speech. "Tauwún means 'open the door.' Lokwelend has already begun his own lessons." *But to whom is he giving them?* she thought, fighting back tears of her own. *To Philip Crown—or to me?*

"Open the door?" He looked puzzled for a moment, then slightly chagrined, then threw back his head and laughed aloud. "You get Night Fire, and I get Open the Door? What in bloody hell is that supposed to mean?"

"That is for you to figure out, Tauwún. For you to figure out. Now let me go, or we won't reach the trading post before we're forced to dip into the dried venison once more."

Philip wrinkled his nose comically. "You have a point. Very well, we'll leave this for another time." But he didn't release her arm—he had the most irritating habit of holding her to a spot she wanted to vacate. "Just one more thing, Brighid," he said quietly, no trace of either amusement or chagrin remaining in his tone. "I want to thank you. I still don't quite know what is going on, but I do know I'm feeling remarkably good about it." And with that, he bent and kissed her forehead before stepping back a pace and looking deeply into her eyes. "Thank you, Nipawi Gischuch. You're a good teacher."

She stood quite still after he'd gone, unable to raise her

hand to wipe away the touch of his lips . . . or even to merely explore the spot where they had been, where a most discomfiting sensation lingered, unexpected, unwanted, and yet—as with their first kiss—instinctively understood.

Dominick would have his nephew's liver on a spit if he knew what Philip was thinking as he rode ahead of the wagon, able to recognize the landscape near Pleasant Hill for the past five miles or more. And Philip knew it. He'd known it from the moment that soldier had pulled back Brighid Cassidy's bowed head and he'd first looked into those damning aquamarine eyes. From the moment he had kissed her in the woods. Oh, yes. His liver. On a spit. And then fed to him.

Because he'd spent the past three weeks wondering what it would be like to touch Brighid Cassidy, to lie with her in the soft grass. Each night he'd imagined her in his arms, soft and pliant, yet full of white hot fire. Night fire. Meant to both illuminate and hide, the way her night-dark hair had both covered and accented her physical beauty the day he'd discovered her in the stream.

Awake, she was all he thought about; asleep, she was all he dreamed of. She was like a fire in his blood, a fire and a sickness.

For she was not a part of his future, which lay far away from New Eden, worlds removed from this benighted civilization that was, at best, only a sad echo of the sophistication of Playden Court, where he would raise his family of proper English lords and ladies, mothered by their proper English mother, who would give them the credit-ability, the easy entry into London society, that he and his sister had lacked.

Not a mother who chewed dried venison, then transferred it from her mouth to that of her half-breed son. Not a wife who ate mice and bathed in streams or whose accomplishments numbered not water painting and harp playing but grass weaving and deer-skinning.

Not, in her own way, a woman like his mother, like Dominick's mother, who didn't fit, had never fit, into a proper English household. Not a child like his sister, who had been damned by her birth, by her strong resemblance to her mother's family, to a life on the fringes of society—an ostracism his sex, title, and new fortune had saved him from. None of which meant anything, as Philip reminded himself again and again, because Brighid Cassidy would never see Playden Court, would never be introduced in society, would never even, he was sure, leave New Eden.

So, if Dominick were to skewer him, it would be because of what he did to Brighid Cassidy here, in New Eden. Which would be—what? To hold her, to kiss her, . . . to bed her? To fill her head with hopes, dreams, that had no chance of fruition? Knowing full well that she was Bryna's cousin? Knowing full well that there would never be a marriage between them as there would have to be if he dared to bed a "proper" female, an innocent virgin? Knowing full well that everyone else would think he was just treating her as they supposed her to be: a fallen woman, a soulless, soiled dove who had opened her heart and her legs to the savage Lenape who had slaughtered the majority of her family?

"Thinking again, Tauwún? Thinking is good for a man. Unless the thoughts disturb."

Philip shifted on the saddle and looked at Lokwelend. His "father." The man who had waited all these years for a stupid young idiot to come to him, so that they could both be whole again. For as long as the old man lived, no matter whether Philip was in New Eden or Sussex, he knew Lokwelend's well-being would always be his concern, his duty, his pleasure. And never again would his memories be his penance. "I'm merely dreaming of the end of this journey and my bed, Father, and how happy I will be to see them both."

"Your journey has been long, my son, but it is far from over," Lokwelend said as he motioned with his arm for Brighid, who was driving the wagon, to follow as they turned onto a new road: the long, private drive that led to Pleasant Hill. "As Nipawi Gischuch's journey is just now beginning."

"I cannot make Brighid Cassidy's well-being my concern, Father," Philip bit out tersely, deciding that, at times, Lokwelend could be as subtle as a wet rag whacked across the face. "Even if I wanted to, which I most sincerely do not. I made a promise to Bryna, a promise that I'd bring her cousin home. Now that I've done it, I am clear of the whole thing, I wash my hands of it. And not a word from you about Pilate if you were planning on saying anything. I've no interest in your interpretation of the scriptures."

"'A wise man prefers the sweet taste of his own silence to that of fouling his mouth with a lie,'" Lokwelend answered and wheeled his horse around to ride back to the wagon, leaving Philip feeling as if he'd just turned five and been scolded for fibbing about the frog in his nanny's bed.

He did have great sympathy for Brighid. She must feel like she was being led into the lion's den to be served up as dinner. Lord knew Bryna would all but eat her alive with kisses and questions and—if Philip knew anything at all about his uncle's lovely young wife—then turn on him, demanding to know why her cousin was still dressed in Lenape garb. He'd already decided he would have no need to answer that question as, no matter that he really didn't know Brighid, he had already learned that she had no difficulty in opening her mouth to state her opinion on most any matter.

And I want to be standing clear once those two lovely Irish ladies get over their first flush of greetings and have to live with each other, he thought, smiling as a turn in the roadway revealed his first sight of Pleasant Hill. Built on high ground, above a long, sweeping expanse of well-scythed lawn, its drive lined with oaks, Pleasant Hill resembled nothing more than a prosperous English manor house, its deep gray stone, white wood accents, and heavily dormered third floor reminding Philip of the fine homes he had seen in Sussex on his last visit home.

Dominick had added two wings to the structure in the past five years, one on each side of the house for balance, and had enlarged the kitchens to the delight of his housekeeper, Lucretia. An immense glass succession house stood behind and to the left of the west wing, home to Bryna's increasingly exotic collection of flowers and fruit trees, and the stables had doubled in size, as Dominick's collection of prime horseflesh had trebled.

Difficult to believe that in the midst of what was still a raw, new land, anyone would take the time and effort to establish such an outstanding outpost of English civilization, but Dominick had come to New Eden to build a dynasty, and Philip's uncle did nothing by half measures. But then, Philip mused, neither did Bryna. Hadn't her firstborn turned out to be look-alike twins—Roarke and Nicholas—who, at the tender age of four, had already mastered their first ponies and turned Lucretia's dark, kinky hair to a startling white?

To say nothing of the havoc the terrible twins had wreaked on Lucas, Dominick's very English, very proper butler. They hid his butler's keys in the sugar bin. They tied all the doors shut with cords from the draperies. They dipped his every wig in ink, so that he had given up his last pretense of proper butler ways and tossed the powder pot to the back of his closet, where the twins found it and powdered themselves head to toe before hiding behind a door and leaping out to scream like banshees, startling poor Lucas, so he said, out of ten years' growth.

But Lucas loved Roarke and Nicholas, probably even more now that Cora had returned and been brought into the house to act as their nurse. Philip knew that the shy, quiet Lucas had loved Lokwelend's daughter for a long time, and he and Dominick had been thoroughly enjoying the butler's many excuses to visit the nursery floor since Cora's return—only to leave again with sticky fingerprints marring the hose on his spindly shanked legs.

Philip smiled, all his thoughts pleasant, warm, actually bordering on mellow. He would have a house like this soon, once the construction, nearly completed, ended on his own estate not two miles from Pleasant Hill. And someday, he would have Playden Court—four times the size of Pleasant Hill and steeped in the memories of countless generations of Crowns and their sometimes happy, sometimes clouded lives.

Difficult as he found it to believe, Philip actually longed for Playden Court, seeing it in his mind's eye not as it was now, but how it had been, how it appeared in the watercolor he would hang over his new hearth, how he would make it again. Once his father cocked up his toes. Once he, Philip, was the marquess and the steady drain on the estate's resources was plugged. For now, for a while, he would live here, in New Eden, where he felt comfortable. But someday, someday, he would go home.

And Brighid Cassidy would remain in New Eden . . .

"Philip, you've done it! Dominick, Lucas, come quickly! It's Philip! Lucretia, fetch Mary Kate! Hurry!"

Bryna's voice broke into his thoughts, and he looked up to see his uncle's wife dropping her basket of flowers and making her way down the wide stone steps of Pleasant Hill, her skirts held high above her ankles, her step as graceful as ever, even encumbered by her advancing pregnancy. She was as beautiful now as she had been the first day he'd seen her; perhaps even more so, as motherhood had rounded her a little, smoothing out a few of her youthful edges, giving a new warmth to her smile, even more of a glow to her pale, intensely lovely, smoky-green eyes. But the bright flame of her hair hadn't changed, nor had the clear, milky glow of her skin.

And yet . . . and yet for the first time in his memory, Philip's heart didn't catch in his throat at the sight of her. He smiled, because he loved her, but he didn't ache, because he wasn't in love with her, stupidly, foolishly, impossibly in love with his uncle's wife. Not anymore.

When had that happened?

He turned in his saddle and watched as Brighid urged the

weary horses up the drive, her chin held ridiculously high, her outlandish Lenape garb suddenly seeming so much more serviceable than the full skirts that hampered Bryna from moving as she wished.

"Brighid! *Brighid!* Oh, Philip, it's her! It's our own Brighid!"

"Stay where you are, Bryna," he called out warningly as she seemed ready to race down the drive to meet the wagon, drawing his mount to a halt just beside the porch and handing the reins to a young boy who ran to take them. "She's not about to bolt now unless you scare her off with all your caterwauling." He bent down and kissed the woman's cheeks, allowing himself to be hugged as Bryna sniffled and laughed and generally babbled that he was the best and most brilliant of all creatures for having brought her cousin home to her.

Bryna had a stranglehold on his neck, one that she released only as the wagon came to a halt beside them, at which point she deserted him as if she had suddenly spied out a diamond as large as a robin's egg in the grass.

For the next few minutes, chaos reigned in the drive in front of Pleasant Hill, and Philip forgot that what he had wanted most was a quick trip to Dominick's study and the decanters that waited there. He stood to one side, grinning foolishly as the cousins embraced and cried, then embraced again. He accepted Dominick's firm, backslapping welcome. He covered his ears when Gilhooley, Dominick's large, boisterous dog, skidded around the corner to join loudly in the celebration. He laughed out loud as Lapawin, who had been sleeping in the back of the wagon, awoke, looked to see what all the commotion was about, called out, *"Aiiiii!"* and then buried her head under the blanket, as if hiding her top half could make the rest of her, including her stuck-up rump, disappear.

Brighid was passed from Bryna to Dominick to a widely smiling Lucretia and back again, being hugged, kissed, and clucked over. Philip soon gave up trying to understand a word that was said, feeling content to see that Lokwelend, his new father, had recourse to wipe at his suspiciously moist eyes with a large checked handkerchief.

Suddenly, a mighty wail was heard from the back of the wagon, at which time all conversation stopped.

"Was—was that a baby? Gilhooley, hush!" Bryna demanded, looking first to Brighid, then to Dominick, who quickly took her hand. "Brighid?" she asked again, tipping her head to one side as she sliced her questioning gaze toward the wagon and to Lapawin, who had resurfaced once more. "Never tell me that's a baby. And who, precisely, is *that?*"

Brighid's spine went stiff even as her chin lifted again and her eyes narrowed to glittering slits. Philip momentarily considered taking refuge behind his uncle, then quickly stepped forward to explain. "Bryna, your cousin has a son. A wonderful little boy named Daniel, after your uncle. Lapawin is the boy's grandmother. Isn't that grand? You sent me off in the hopes of fetching back one, and I brought you three. And a goat," he added lamely as he stepped back a pace, wishing himself somewhere far, far away.

Bryna didn't let him down, thank God. She continued to look blank for a moment, then grabbed Brighid again, kissing her on both cheeks. "A baby!" She turned to Dominick and kissed him as well, probably just for good measure. "Dominick, isn't it wonderful? Brighid has brought us a *baby*. We have a whole new family!"

Philip looked at Brighid, who was staring at him, and lifted an eyebrow at her. *See?* that eyebrow said, *I told you it would be all right.* "Why don't you have Lapawin hand Daniel down to you, Brighid, so everyone can see him?" he suggested quietly before realizing that Brighid had not been looking at him but *past* him, toward the top of the steps, and her face had gone deadly white beneath her sun-kissed skin.

"Mary Catherine," he said quietly, turning to see the child standing almost completely behind one of the pillars, clutching it with both hands, only her face and the hem of her dress visible. He smiled, because he had a great fondness for the child and he knew that she was the direct opposite of both Bryna and Brighid. Shy, quiet almost to a fault, the ten-year-old Mary Catherine was no match for her more gregarious sister and cousin and was probably feeling more than a little overwhelmed by all the commotion.

He took three steps in her direction and held out his hand, motioning for her to join them. "Come along, Mary Catherine. Your sister wants to see you. You don't want to spend all day hiding back there, do you?"

Brighid came to stand just slightly behind him, her arms at her sides, her smile tentative, probably attempting to keep her exotically clad self looking as nonthreatening as possible. "Well now, would you look how you've grown, Mary Kate. Do you remember me at all? It's your own Bridie. Imagine that I used to carry you from place to place like my own sweet doll. I couldn't be lifting you now, could I?"

The child's bottom lip began to tremble even as her hands balled into fists around the pillar. "Go away," she said quietly, her clear green eyes shining with tears, her mop of curly red hair almost dancing in place as her whole body shook with sudden fury. "You're bad. You left me. You left Mama. I don't want you here. Just go away."

Philip thought he could feel Brighid's heart breaking inside his own chest. "Now, Mary Kate, my little sweetheart," he scolded softly, hoping not to spook the child into running back into the house.

"I hate her!" The words seemed to explode from the little girl's body, stopping all speech.

"Mary Catherine Cassidy, we've been all over this before. You don't mean that," Bryna scolded quickly, already bustling toward the steps, Gilhooley at her heels.

"Do so! And God hates her, too! That's why He let something terrible happen to her! To punish her!" the child exclaimed, then whirled around and disappeared through the open doorway just as Gilhooley began to bark again—madly, frantically—then take off at a run toward the side of the house.

"Gilhooley!" Dominick Crown called after the animal. "Would you for the love of heaven shut—*my God!*"

Cora, Lokwelend's daughter, appeared from behind the shrubs, her bodice and one sleeve torn, her face swollen and bruised. She cried out to her father, then collapsed, unconscious, to the ground.

Everyone ran to Cora's side, leaving Brighid and Philip to stand together on the drive, forgotten. Brighid's expression was bleak as she looked from the open, empty doorway to the wagon, where a crying Lapawin held an equally unhappy Daniel. "And it's a grand day, this, don't you think, Tauwún? How could I have been so silly as to have dreaded it?"

"It will get better, Brighid," Philip heard himself say, knowing he sounded as erudite as the village idiot.

Brighid's laugh was hollow, mocking. "Well, it can hardly get worse, now can it, Tauwún?"

BOOK TWO

Compromise

Had I been present at the Creation,
I would have given some useful hints
for the better ordering of the universe.
—Alfonso the Wise,
king of Castile

What hath night to do with sleep?
— *John Milton*

CHAPTER 6

"DANIEL STILL DOES NOT REST WELL IN HIS NEW SURROUNDINGS," Cora said quietly as she entered the darkened nursery, where Brighid sat with the child, rocking him to sleep, as she had done every night since coming to Pleasant Hill.

"My son misses his cradleboard," Brighid answered with a tired smile as Daniel snuggled close, his breath warm and sweet upon her cheek. "He misses the times I hung the board from the branch of a tree and the breeze and birdsong lulled him to sleep. He misses the nearness of his grandmother, who snores in her soft feather bed, taking to the white man's ways with an ease that amuses yet disgusts. How are you tonight, Kolachuisen? Your bruises are healing well."

"I am well enough, Brighid. Better if you were to call me Cora, as I have asked."

Brighid felt her cheeks flush, partly in embarrassment that she had displeased her friend, half in chagrin that her friend tried so diligently to be what she was not, what she could never be. She rose carefully so as not to wake the sleeping child and laid him in his cot, keeping the blanket wrapped tightly around him, as he liked, then motioned for Cora to follow her out of the room.

"Forgive me for my error, Cora," she said as she shut the door behind them, then smiled and nodded to Halfrida, the nursery maid Bryna had just hired to help Cora in her expanded duties. "Shall we go outside to talk? I have questions I have waited to ask."

"I have answers I have longed to give," Cora told her, flashing the wide smile Brighid remembered from the time they had spent together a lifetime ago, when the Cassidys had first come to New Eden. "Hallie, why don't you peek in on the twins one last time, then go to bed? I will return soon to sleep here in the schoolroom, as usual, between the little devils and our restless Daniel."

Hallie, keeping her eyes averted from both women, merely nodded, then stayed where she was, where she would probably be when Cora came back to shoo her off once more.

"She likes reading the children's books, you understand," Cora said as she and Brighid slipped down the back stairs and out into the gardens. "It still delights her to know that she remembers how to read, even if it's only a little bit."

Brighid shook her head in the darkness, her heart aching for Hallie, only seventeen, whose eight-year captivity had been not nearly so tolerable as her own. She'd been sold more than once, moved from tribe to tribe, the last of which had tattooed markings all over her forehead and cheeks to keep her from fleeing, as her captors had assumed she would be too embarrassed to go back to her people disfigured. Bryna had seen Hallie in New Eden and immediately taken her in, using Daniel's presence in the nursery as her excuse. That was Bryna's way: gathering the world to her tender heart while never admitting that she had any softness about her.

"Hallie also remembers her last name," Brighid said coldly, "for all the good it does her. Bryna says her family took one look at her face and turned her away. She'd be earning her living on her back, like Silky Wattson, if my cousin hadn't rescued her. As I would also be, I suppose."

"You see your cousin doing charity, which you resent. Cannot you see her acts coming from her great love for you? Can you not bend, sister of my heart, not even a little?"

Brighid looked at her childhood friend, dressed all in blue gingham, her thick black hair drawn back in a bun, her dark skin and broad nose giving the lie to the outer trappings she wore, intending to blend in with the new world that had displaced all she had once known. "Will I take off my deerskins, you mean, don't you, *Cora?* Will I loosen my braids and squeeze my feet into tight shoes and walk around with small cages tied to my hips beneath my skirts for the sake of fashion? What good are cages, Cora, except to trap small animals and fish? You are what you are, my friend, and I am what my life has made me. Nipawi Gischuch, wife of Wulapen, mother of Tasukamend. I need no tattoos to remind people who I am, where I have been. And I need no cages to tell me that I am more captive now than I have ever been. My own sister . . ." Her voice trailed off and she took a deep breath to steady herself.

"And you're as stubborn now as you were that day at the stream when you insisted to Pematalli that he teach you to swim," Cora said, sitting down on a nearby bench, arranging her "cages," her panniers, about her. "You nearly drowned that day, you know, and lived only to have your mother chase you all the way home, batting at your behind with her broom."

Brighid sank, cross-legged, to the soft ground and lapsed into the Lenape tongue, which still seemed more comfortable to her than her native English. "I remember," she said, gratefully smiling up at her old friend. "We were all so free then, weren't we? No hatred, no divisions, no notion that we were so dangerously different from each other. I would have gladly stayed in county Clare had I realized that finding our own home would displace you from yours. We had no right, Cora. No right at all. We destroyed you, and in doing so, we destroyed ourselves."

Cora looked out over the darkened landscape, acres of formal gardens that were Bryna's pride and joy. "Once, deer roamed this hillside. Beaver built their dams in the streams, and bear nursed their young. Now the beaver have gone beyond the mountains and farther, and the deer hide from us in fear, knowing we take not for our own needs, but for the sport of killing and for profit. I have not seen a bear in two seasons. I envy you your life of these past five years and have only fond memories of my time in the Ohio, before we were allowed to return here."

"And yet you came back. You stay. You and Lokwelend both. Why?"

"Where am I to go, Nipawi Gischuch? The Ohio will not be ours much longer. Already we are being pushed to leave. Will we fight and die there or go westward again and again, from where our grandfathers tell us we first came? Back to the desert, to the mountains, to the sea—always with the white man following after, pushing—to live our end at our beginning? No, my friend. There is no safe place for the Lenape. In my heart, this is my land, and I have chosen to be moved no more. Outside, I try to make it easier to fit in. If dressing in these clothes and cutting my braids are what are needed to remain on my native soil, then I will do it and gladly."

She pressed her clasped hands to her heart. "But on the inside, I am Lenape. What lives *here* cannot be touched and will be passed on to my children and their children's children. I am Lenni Lenape. I am of the Original People. Pematalli chose to die, his bones forever in the earth of his grandfathers, always a reminder to those who come that he, Always There, was here first, will always be here. I chose to live, to survive, to remember, to teach."

"And if that man comes at you again?"

Cora closed her eyes, her hands twisting together in her lap. "There will always be hatred and ignorance. I cannot stop that. I cannot hide from it, as Hallie hides her sad face in the nursery. Nor will I court it, as Silky Wattson does each time she walks into the woods with another man in exchange for a dram of gin."

"Lucas Deems was very upset when he saw you," Brighid said, trying to lighten the mood, which had grown uncomfortably somber. "Anyone would think Dominick's starchy butler was topsy-turvy in love with you."

"Lucas is a good man, yet timid and unsure. He has little confidence in his own worth and still suffers an old hurt that keeps him from giving his heart without fear of new pain. But I will wait for him—for a while." Cora's wide grin lit her face. "He was upset, wasn't he?"

"You were beaten and nearly raped, Cora—of course he was upset. If you hadn't had your knife, you could have been killed! As Dominick tells us, this man has killed before," Brighid countered, angry once more as she remembered Cora's condition when she had stumbled onto the drive and fainted. "Tell me again what happened, what the man said. Perhaps it would give some clue as to who he is."

"I do not care who he is. I already know *what* he is. He is evil, speaking the words of your God while doing the work of your devil. He fears Lenape men so works his evil on their women, who he calls whores. He is weak as well as evil."

Brighid persisted, for she did care who the man was, the man who had nearly raped her friend, who might be the same man responsible for the deaths of other women elsewhere in the colony. "He came at you from behind in the woods while you were out walking. He covered your head with a sack and flung you to the ground, then began telling you how 'evil' you were and how he would *purge* you of your sins. Is that right? And you didn't see him at all? Couldn't tell the size of him when you struggled with him?"

"A knife measures only the thickness of the skin, not the

height and breadth of the man," Cora answered. "I cut him on the thigh, I believe, as he used both his hands on me while I lay on the ground to hit me, to tear at my clothes, to punish me for my heathen blood, my heathen ways. I cannot tell you more, Brighid, any more than I could tell Dominick or my father. He was big and strong and mean."

She smiled as she stood up, looking down at Brighid. "And he squealed like a pig when I sank my blade into him, then ran off like a hobbled rabbit. It has been more than a week, without word coming to us of another attack, since that returned female captive was murdered in Easton. He's probably miles and miles from here, never to return. Everyone is worrying for nothing. It's over, Brighid. Let it go. Let us return to what I have said, what you have so carefully pointed out, then shied from as my answers struck too closely to your own pain. But first, you must remember this, Brighid: We are what we have been born and cannot change what is inside."

Brighid felt her chin go up and deliberately lowered it. "I don't want to listen to this, Cora. Our situations are not the same."

"Aren't they, Brighid? If I am Lenape in my heart, you are a white woman in yours. Try as you wish, Brighid Cassidy, you cannot forget the world you were born to, lived in, and loved before you were taken. Deerskins and braids cannot disguise you any more than gingham can change me. Only fools who judge solely with their hopes or fears believe that or are comforted by such silliness. As those in New Eden who smile at me in my gingham, who take comfort in my 'outside,' are silly. As they will fear and resent you in your deerskins. Now are you coming inside?"

Brighid shook her head, feeling more than a little weary, more than a little confused, and more than a little angry—with herself or with Cora, she wasn't sure. "No, Daniel won't wake again. I think I'll stay out here awhile longer. I breathe freer here."

"You're going to sleep here again, aren't you?" Cora

asked, tilting her head toward the bench she had been sitting on, silently indicating the small bundle of blankets Brighid had rolled up and hidden beneath it. "You're a stubborn woman, Nipawi Gischuch, and you pain your cousin's heart."

"As her soft bed pains my back," Brighid responded without rancor. "As her airless rooms smother me. As my own idleness wearies me but will not let me sleep. Now, good night to you, Pretty Bluebird. For so you will always be in my heart. Kolachuisen, the pretty bluebird. You still do your best to sing your sweet song, though your wings have been clipped. I still seek the fire of the night, though my moon has been dimmed. But I will think of all you've said. I will try to be better for Daniel's sake, if not my own. As Lapawin has told me, we are women, and we do as we must to survive."

She *was* here. He could sense her presence, damn her, feel the tension in the still night air. Was there no escaping the woman, not even in the gardens at midnight? And if he had wanted to escape her, why had he come here?

"Brighid?" he called out softly. "I know you're about somewhere. Bryna complained to me that you creep out to sleep in the gardens, but I only half believed her. Answer me before I trip over you."

Her voice came to him, full of amusement. "You're not within ten feet of me, Tauwún, not that I didn't hear you coming from fifty. The moon is full if you'll but open your eyes. If Wulapen had suffered your sad lack of stealth on the hunt, we all would have starved years ago."

Philip followed the sound of Brighid's voice, at last able to make out the bench, and the darker bundle on the ground that had to be her. He sat down, doing his best to keep a rein on his temper. "You're not going to give it up, are you, Brighid? Even with the chance that Cora's attacker could be close by. Tell me, how difficult is it to find ways to weave the past five years into every conversation, nearly every damn sentence you utter? You use those years to beat Bryna over the head, and I find it totally unfair. Remember, it wasn't her fault that you were taken."

Brighid stirred, sitting up and tossing back the blanket that had been covering her. He could see her eyes flashing in the moonlight. She was right: There was more than enough light if one really looked. "It's Bryna's fault that I have been returned, Tauwún, don't you forget that. I don't. For the joy of reunion, she dragged you and I both partway across the world, and now that I'm here, she has no idea what to do with me. I'm like a pet to be patted on the head. It's the messes I make that she never considered and refuses to face. Or did she send you to clean that up as well?"

Philip pinched the bridge of his nose between his thumb and forefinger, attempting to squeeze back his frustration that had been growing at a steady rate all week, for nearly a month, from the moment he'd first seen this complicated, infuriating woman. "Christ, but you're stubborn. It was the Lenape who turned you over to the English soldiers, not Bryna. You could have been rejected like Hallie, you know—turned away by your own family. You could have been left outside Fort Pitt, nobody coming to claim you at all, so that you ended up saddled with a child and an old woman to feed and only one way to support yourself."

"I know that."

His laugh was hollow, mocking. The woman was like an annoying rash he tried and failed to keep from scratching. "You *know* that? Really? And that explains your show of gratitude, I suppose. Gratitude that extends to refusing to speak to your own sister?"

Brighid stood, folded the blankets she had been lying on, and sat down beside him. When she spoke again, her voice was low, sad, and devoid of belligerence. "I'm dead to her, while all her painful memories are alive again and full of hatred."

Philip turned on the bench and grabbed hold of Brighid's shoulders. "Would you stop prosing on so formally, like a damned Indian?" he exclaimed, giving her a rough shake, suddenly even more angry with her than he had imagined possible. "You're Irish, for God's sake—not Lenape. Say what's on your mind and no more of this deep talk that, in the end, is nothing but another way of hiding."

She didn't try to escape his grip but only smiled at him, so that he knew he wasn't going to like what she said next. And when she opened her mouth again and that deliberate brogue came out, he knew she wasn't about to soothe his misgivings. "So, it's plain talking you'd be looking for, Philip Crown, is it? Well, then, I'll talk to you plain. I hate you. I hate Bryna's charity, I hate Pleasant Hill, I hate this land—this once happy land where an innocent like Cora can't be who she is and is persecuted even as she tries to fit in. Or didn't Dominick explain to you that this man who tried to kill Cora only attacks Lenape women or white captives returned from the West? And he kills in God's name, Philip, I am sure. Just as Mary Catherine curses me in the name of the Lord."

"Brighid—"

"No! I'm begun, Philip, and now I'll finish. I also hate myself for being so weak and soft as to remain here. I hang freshly cut grasses above the soft bed in my room and breathe deeply of their sweetness, trying to pretend I'm back with my people. My ears ring with dinner table talk of repealed Stamp Acts and the rights of the colonies—and you're wrong, Tauwún, to say that the English king deserves unquestioning loyalty and I mightily wish you would shut your mouth and listen to Dominick, who at least talks sense. I choke on your rich food, which I could get to my mouth a good sight sooner if I didn't have to be changing forks every five seconds, whenever Bryna politely clears her throat to warn me that I'm using the wrong one. I have a closet full of ridiculous clothes that have more laces and ties than a good fishing net, and if I could sell them all, I could feed my small tribe for a year on the proceeds."

Philip was beginning to feel very uncomfortable. "That's enough, Brighid," he said warningly, wishing she'd stop.

"No, Tauwún, it's not enough. You have knocked on the door, and I, your *teacher*, have opened it. It's the bold truth you want, and it's the bold truth you'll be getting. My sister thinks I deserted her, leaving our mother and her to die, and I can't remember if I did or not. There must be some good reason why I can't remember, why I don't want to remember the raid or those first days following it, when I was lost in the woods with my captors. Memories Wingenund begged me not to think of. And yet, not all of my memory is gone, even those parts that make my heart ever heavier. Everywhere I turn, everywhere I look, I'm reminded of what it was before, who I was before, a life and time even young Mary Kate knows can never be the same again."

"Your parents and brothers are gone, it's true, but—"

"Would you be silent? Because, terrible as those hurts are, they are old heartaches, and I have learned to live with them, even as they rise to batter at me again and again. I have not yet told you the worst of it. *You,* Philip Crown— you're the worst of it. It's truth you want, I'll give you truth. *You* are my problem. Living under the same roof, *sleeping* under the same roof. More than the forks, more than those blasted panniers, more than my fears and pains of the past, I want *you* gone. I don't want you, I couldn't have you if I did, and I'll be damned if I'd live in England if you asked me, because I know you'll be leaving here one day. So why don't you go now and leave me alone? Go! Go to your precious England, go to the devil. Just *go!*"

Philip sat very still, keeping his hands on Brighid's slim shoulders, stunned by both the length of her tirade and its blunt, shocking conclusion. "Well," he said after an awkward pause during which Brighid continued to glare at him, daring him to speak, "I suppose I asked for that, didn't I? Except that last bit, of course. Exactly what did it mean, if I might beg you to elaborate?"

Now she did pull away from him, leaving him alone on the bench as she stood up, prepared, he thought, to bolt into the darkness, out of the way of the moonlight that brightened this area of the gardens.

He hastened to rise, taking hold of her elbow as she stood with her back turned to him. "Don't run away now,

Brighid," he said softly, pulling her toward him so that her back rested against his chest and he could feel her stiffen, then relax into him. "And no more talk of Mary Catherine or Bryna or correct forks for now, all right? Let's push the door open a little wider, shall we? Let's talk about what's really bothering you—what's bothering me, although I've not been honest enough to admit it."

She sighed, the sound hitching in her throat—surely not catching on a sob, for Nipawi Gischuch never cried—then spoke again. "All those days and nights on the road from Fort Pitt you watched me. As I watched you. I knew you were at the stream that day. Knew before you were there and shamelessly waited for you. Wanted to watch you as you watched me. I knew you, Tauwún, before I ever saw you at Fort Pitt, even if I hadn't yet dreamed you. And you knew me, had been warned of me by Lokwelend's dreams, by Lokwelend's words," she said quietly, so quietly that he had to strain to hear her. "You kissed me—and you recognized me—as I recognized you. But it is hopeless. You don't want to touch me because I was once Wulapen's wife. And you can't touch me because Dominick would kill you if you did. What I was forbids you, what I have become repels you. So where does that leave us, Philip Crown? Where does that leave us? With me taking my blankets to the gardens and you prowling Dominick's study half the night, drinking yourself into a dreamless sleep?"

He pulled her closer against him, stroking her arms from shoulder to elbow as he rested his chin against the side of her throat. His senses spun with her nearness, her truths, her depressingly accurate assessment of their damnable, damning situation. "You don't miss much, do you, Brighid?"

"I've watched Wulapen with . . . when he looked at me," she told him tonelessly. "I know the face of desire."

"And do you know merely the face, Brighid Cassidy, or the desire as well? Was it desire you felt when we kissed, desire you feel now?" he asked, daring to press his lips against the soft skin beneath her ear. "Did you lie to me before? When you first looked at me and recognized me, was it because you had seen me in your dreams?"

Her body stiffened once more. "When I first saw you, it was not in my dreams, but in the smoke from the fire, late at night, while Lapawin and Tasukamend slept and my hunger kept me awake. I saw your long, fair hair, your face floating upward with the smoke. Your searching blue eyes. All of you. Laughing, teasing. Too close, and always out of reach."

She swung around to face him, her fingertips digging into his forearms. "I thought it was my hunger deceiving me. Or the vision of what my death would be, the face of the one who would find my small family and kill us. I didn't know then that life could be more painful than death."

"And is this painful, Brighid? For this is life," he said gruffly, daring to crush her hard against him, pulling back her head by the simple expediency of taking hold of her braids, then capturing her mouth with his own. He wasn't gentle, because he didn't feel gentle. She didn't need gentle. She was no innocent girl but a fully flowered woman, a mother, and, once, a wife. She had plainly stated her wants, her needs. He was hungry for her, so he fed. His thirst raged, so he drank. Searching, finding, taking. Being made hungry for more. And never, never, realizing that after a first encouraging response she had gone stiff under his assault.

His head was spinning. She was everything he had wanted all these weeks, from the first moment he'd looked into those wise, flashing aquamarine eyes. She wanted him, too. Man to woman, woman to man. Now, here, in the moonlight.

He pressed his roused manhood against her thigh, showing her his need. He drew her closer, closer, stroking her back, capturing one firm breast beneath his fingers. His need grew and grew, carelessly banishing thoughts of Dominick's sure wrath, deliberately pushing out all memory of the man she had laid with, made Daniel with . . .

"Geptschat!" Brighid cried out, pulling back and sharply bringing up her knee so that the next thing Philip knew he was curled up at her feet, fighting a crippling nausea, his

arms wrapped tightly around his own body, lightning bolts flashing behind his closed eyes. "Who now is the savage?"

He looked up at her, saw her rapidly rising and falling breasts, recognized the anger in her clenched fists—and winced at the fear in her eyes.

"I'm sorry, Brighid," he gasped out, feeling lower than he had ever felt in his life. Base. And incredibly clumsy. Stupid. "I'm so very sorry."

"So am I, Tauwûn. So am I. You tried to wipe Wulapen from my memory and your own with the force of your will, your body. This is a door we shouldn't have attempted to open, for a beast lives behind it."

Philip painfully made his way to his feet, needing to make use of the bench in order to rise. "A damned cad, more like," he said, pushing back his hair that had fallen onto his face. "Where did you learn that nasty little trick? I probably won't be able to walk straight for a week."

Brighid looked at him for long moments, then shook her head and smiled. "Will you take me to my family's graves tomorrow, Philip?" she asked, her quick change of mood and subject both surprising and baffling him.

"You want *me* to take you there? After what just happened? Why?"

Her smile broadened. "Because I know I'm now safer with you than I would be with Father Finnegan, the old parish priest in county Clare. With this one door shut, another may open. Now we can, if you wish, perhaps even become friends. Will you take me there? It's time I face more of my demons. The forks and petticoats can wait for another time."

"We can leave at nine and have Lucretia pack us a lunch," he answered distractedly, speaking quickly before she could see the folly of her logic. The "door" between them was far from shut. It had been damn near blown off its hinges. "We'll visit the graves and then drive somewhere else and have a picnic. Perhaps I'll even show you my house."

"Agreed," she answered, picking up her blankets. "I'm going to give Bryna's soft bed another chance. I suggest you sit here a while longer until the blood returns to your brain, which is where it belongs. Allowing it to go anywhere else will only cause us both pain."

"Brighid Cassidy," Philip whispered into the darkness when she was gone, "you're a hard woman. But that hint of softness you can't hide in those eyes of yours is probably just enough to keep me dreaming of miracles all night long."

O Memory! thou fond deceiver.
— *Oliver Goldsmith*

CHAPTER 7

꧁ꕥ꧂

SHE SAT IN THE MEADOW, CONTENT TO LOOK AT THE GREAT *house from afar, waiting for the horseman to come again. Which path would he choose this time? Because he could not have perished on the path to her parents' home. He was like her now, locked inside this riddle of a dream until, separately or together, each found their way out.*

Perhaps tonight he would take the path that led to the short-legged monster. She'd rather like that, as he might be able to give the monster a name, give that still, hot, stagnant land a name. At least it would no longer be a mystery, even if it remained a puzzle.

She began tapping the side of her foot against the ground, growing impatient for him to appear. And then he was there. The man astride his great white horse. He rode into the meadow as now he did every night, pulling his mount to a plunging, stamping halt in front of her. His impatience swept over her, banishing her own comfort, angering her slightly, because he was such a stubborn, persistent man. Even more stubborn than she. She squinted up at him, trying to see his face, but it remained hidden from her.

"Still here, woman?" he called out sharply, fighting his spirited mount. "Have you no sense of adventure? Then stay there. It's better that way. He travels best who travels light."

She smiled as he rode into the dark trees, not fearful of his fate, knowing he had chosen the path that led to the short-legged monster . . .

She woke up, still smiling . . . confident she would see him again tonight, wondering if he would be able to give her monster a name.

"Da's barn burned down? When?"

"Not quite a year after the raid that took your family," Philip said rather tersely as he turned the wagon onto the rough track that led to what had once been the Cassidy farm. "Dominick refused to rebuild it."

Brighid asked another question, foolishly hoping to fill her mind with inconsequential things, thus keeping herself from concentrating on what she would soon see. The graves of her family. The beginning, but never the end, of her long journey. Still, a first step that had to be taken. The memories had been knocking at the door to her mind for five long years. It was time to let the first few of them in.

Philip stopped the horses at the entrance to the clearing, set the brake with his foot. "Dominick had invited the local militia here to practice their drilling," he said, his tone so impersonal that Brighid instinctively knew what he would say next still pained him terribly. "We made a party of it. Fiddlers, food, everything. Most all of New Eden showed up, including the village dolt, Jonah Newton."

"Newton?" Brighid shook her head, her braids slapping against her deerskin-covered back. "I don't remember him. Was he simpleminded?"

"He was a troublemaking bastard," Philip gritted out from between clenched teeth. *"Him,* Benjamin Rudolph and his witch of a wife, and a monster named Renton

Frey—all of them dead these past four years, since the last Lenape raid. And none of them missed."

"Benjamin Rudolph? He and his wife were the innkeepers in New Eden, weren't they? I do remember them. Horrible people and brazen cheats in their store, although their daughter was sweet. Alice, I think. Yes—Alice. She walked with a limp. Goodness, I had quite forgotten her. She must be a wife and mother by now. Philip? What's wrong? Are you thinking about the fire? Please tell me about it."

She watched as a muscle twitched along his finely chiseled jawline. "Late in the afternoon that day, Newton—or one of his drunken cronies—took a pipe into the barn. The whole place was dry as tinder. Alice and her friend, the Traxells' youngest boy, had stolen off into the barn by themselves for a while, and both were killed in the fire. I—I carried her out. She shouldn't have died that way. A few months earlier, she'd come to live with Bryna and Dominick—another of Bryna's charitable projects, I'd guess you'd say—and then she was dead. Just when she was learning to be happy, she died. We buried her here, next to your family."

Brighid let out her breath in a rush, not knowing what to say or how to say it. "You should have told me," she said at last. "I wouldn't have made you come here if I'd known."

He flashed her a quick smile so that the shadows fled his eyes and he looked young and almost happy again, the way she liked him best—and least. Because sometimes his smiles were real, and sometimes he hid behind them. He was hiding behind one of them now. "It was a long time ago, Brighid. Now come on," he said, hopping down from the wagon and holding up a hand to assist her to the ground. "Let's go visit for a while, and then we'll ride over to my estate and have that picnic. Lokwelend came to Pleasant Hill to tell me my newest purchase arrived this morning, and I'm eager to see it."

Brighid reached for Philip's hand and, a moment later,

felt herself being lifted at the waist and swung high in the air before he put her down. She reached back onto the wagon seat for the flowers she had cut in Bryna's garden and didn't draw away when Philip took her hand and led her up the hill.

Steeling herself to the job at hand, she purposely cleared her thoughts of the everyday and deliberately opened her mind to the past, the way Lapawin had prepared her.

"Da cleared this land himself," she said, smiling in memory, eagerly looking around as they walked. Memories were coming to her, but they were old ones, happy ones, memories she had treasured these past five years. "He and the boys, although they were too young to do more than hold the horse's head and shout encouragement as Da worked to pull another tree stump from the ground."

Then, for no good reason she could think of, she stopped, looking toward the ruins of the barn, still a good fifty yards away, then at the grass at her feet.

The grass was wet and dark with blood. She could see it. She could feel it seeping through the soles of her moccasins. She could smell it, taste it. Didn't Philip see it, too?

She was suddenly cold, although the morning was warm. "They died here," she said quietly, almost in a whisper, as her first memory of that long-ago evening came to her in quick, vivid flashes, branding themselves against the back of her eyes. "Sweet Virgin, it's Michael and Joseph. They died just here, on this very spot. I can feel their fear."

She dropped the flowers and wrenched her hand free of Philip's, covering her ears. "I can hear them screaming. Screaming."

She sensed Philip's hand on her chin, lifting her face toward his. With a mighty effort, she opened her eyes. Mercifully, the visions cleared, and she saw him, saw his concerned expression, the horrific tableau of her young brothers being thrown to the ground, surrounded by painted savages, splintering and, mercifully, vanishing.

"You may not be ready for this yet, Brighid," Philip said

kindly. "Come on. Your memories will wait for another day."

"No, Tauwún," she told him as bravely as she could. "If I had stayed with the Lenape, the memories would still have been here, waiting for me. It is time to put them and my family to rest." *No matter what the cost,* she added silently, striking out toward the ruins once more, her mind still deliberately open, seeking, searching for answers. The stone end walls, blackened by smoke, rose eerily against a backdrop of trees, the center of the barn a jumble of charred wood and weeds that snaked around the beams like concealing green fingers.

As she walked on, the memories came down the hill to meet her, drawing her in one by one, and she began to speak out loud without knowing she did.

"I'll finish here, Mama, and put Mary Catherine in her nightgown. You go stand with Da and watch for the boys."

A smile tickled at the corners of her mouth. "Oh, would you listen to her, Da, pretending not to know what it is you're talking about. And after spending a good ten minutes visiting that same bolt of cloth each time we go into Mr. Benjamin Rudolph's store. It's a new dress she wants for when Uncle Sean and Cousin Bryna come."

She reached the top of the long rise, all the way to the broad, flat stone that marked what had once been the entrance to the family's side of the barn, and turned, looking back the way she and Philip had come.

She squinted as she peered down the hill, seeing her brothers, Michael with his jaw stuffed with sugared candies, Joseph carrying her mother's plaid cloth wrapped in paper under his arm. Her wee brothers. How she had loved them. She smiled and lifted her hand in a welcoming wave, but they hadn't seen her yet. They had stopped walking and were looking into the trees.

She was handing Mary Catherine to her mother now, and watching her da walk out of the barn, his rifle still leaning against the doorjamb.

Should she go to the boys? She was the eldest, sometimes believing herself older than her parents, wiser in the ways of the world. Not so simple, never so trusting. Her heart was pounding. Faster the memories came, tumbling over each other, each worse than the last. And she saw and heard it all.

The boys screamed again, as she had heard them earlier, calling for their parents, then were silent. Her da, her silly, simple, gullible da, lay sprawled on the ground, his head split open.

"Stupid, stupid man! Now look what you've done! I *hate* you for trusting!"

She could see her mother kneeling beside the bed, her rosary in her hands, a pistol in her lap. "Why are you praying? Praying won't help. Damn your bloody beads! Would you die like a sheep awaiting the slaughter? Would you die like Da, bidding death a good welcome? Load the pistols, Mama. For the love of God, load the pistols!"

She dropped her hands to her sides, then balled them into fists and began pounding on Philip's chest, although she wasn't aware that he was even there. All she could feel was hatred and disappointment. All she could do was to rail at the futility, the insanity of it all. "Ah, Joseph!" Brighid cried out, wildly sobbing in her grief, her anger. "Little Michael! Da! Oh, *Da!* Look what your wild dreams have done to us!"

She could see the bear grease slick on the savages' dark skin as they burst through the door, inhale their sweat with every ragged breath, smell her brothers' blood that stained their hands. She could see her father's scalp, dripping as it dangled from a large fist. One of the Indians went for Mama, lifting her head by her hair as he slid a knife across her throat. Brighid moaned in agony as a bright crimson stream hit her pristine white apron, then launched herself at the closest savage, a kitchen knife raised above her head, intent on taking at least one more of the murdering bastards into hell with her . . .

And there the memories stopped. Her fists stilled, no longer beating impotently against an enemy larger and stronger than herself, but desperately holding onto the safe haven she sought, the refuge her tortured spirit craved.

Brighid collapsed against the strength that surrounded her, burying her head against Philip's hard chest, and sobbed. She felt his arms go around her back, sweep beneath her knees, and allowed herself to be lifted, to be carried away from the ruins, away from the pathetic row of weathered crosses, back down the hill to a sheltered place beneath the trees, away from the memories that were worse than no memory at all.

He didn't like her this quiet. For as much as he had wished her silent back at the barn, when she had looked beyond him with flat, frightened eyes, had called out in her anguish, when she had gone so far away from him into a past that could only hurt her, he wanted her to talk to him now.

She'd cried for a long time, deep, shuddering sobs that sliced through him like shards of broken glass, then slipped off into the woods by herself for a while, not returning until she had gone to the stream and scrubbed at her face with the cold, clear water.

"Thank you, Tauwún, for opening that door," she'd said simply, her expression telling him that he'd better keep his own silence unless he wanted her to disappear again. "Now, shall we go see your fine house?"

Because it was easier than fighting her, he had agreed.

He halfheartedly flicked the reins, not really caring that the horses kept up their slow meandering walk along the deserted roadway. "You can't hate him for not taking his rifle with him, you know," he said at last, believing he'd discovered the reason for Brighid's reluctance to remember what had happened the day of the raid. "Your brothers were outside, still far from the house. He had to play the welcoming host, at least until he got the boys safely inside. That took a tremendous amount of courage."

She looked at him in that disconcerting way she had: first sliding those all-seeing aquamarine eyes toward him and only then turning her head, skewering him to the seat. "Daniel Cassidy was a fool, Philip. A misguided, trusting dreamer. My mother was a weak, hopeful martyr. And I loved them both very, very much."

Philip nodded. "Yes, you did. You loved them so much that you closed your mind to their deaths and to the anger you felt against both of them for having allowed themselves to die."

Her smile flashed briefly, then died. "Now who is prosing on like a damned Lenape? Perhaps you are spending too much time with your new father?" she asked, turning forward once more, just as Philip's nearly completed estate house came into view. "My, my, you are an ambitious sort, Lord Ashford, aren't you? This place is nearly as large as Dominick's Pleasant Hill."

"I enjoy comfort," he answered, feeling decidedly uncomfortable. The woman sitting beside him had lived close to the raw for five long years, whereas he considered a four-course meal served on the finest plate the norm. They had so little in common, so few shared experiences, such different dreams, such disparate futures.

A smart man would remember that and stop thinking about a few angry admissions in a dark garden, an explosive interlude that had kept his blood hot all night, with no real hope of it cooling any time soon. "I consider this place an investment. The colonies are growing at a furious rate. When my—when I go back to Sussex, I'll install a manager here to look after my interests, and Dominick will oversee him. And I do plan to visit again, whenever I am able."

Her smile unnerved him further. "Not if Lokwelend's dreams are correct. When you leave, it will be for a considerable time. No one can exist for long with divided loyalties, and Lokwelend says the enemy will not be the Lenape in the coming years. He sees a new enemy. A new conflict. And all the faces are white."

Philip set the brake with his foot as he turned to Brighid. "That sounds more like Dominick's dream than Lokwelend's," he snapped angrily, looking up at the front of his house, at the gray fieldstone walls, the still unpainted columns, the windows he'd had transported in from Philadelphia. "The crown has every right to collect taxes, no matter what those idiots in the Massachusetts Colony say to the contrary. But it's a long way from grumbling about the Declaratory Act to sedition, Brighid. The colonists would be nowhere without the British army, the British might."

"True enough, I suppose," she answered as he helped her down from the wagon. "I would not be here if not for the British might, now would I? But you've seen this land, Philip. How rich it is, how vast. The small dog does not tell the large one when to bark, not for long. Or do you forget that I'm Irish and my people have heard the English dog bark, felt the English dog bite? Now," she added with gentle teasing in her voice, "show me this great pride of yours and tell me when you will be leaving Pleasant Hill to come to it. It's planning a wee celebration I am for the day you are out from underfoot."

He laid a hand on her shoulder, relieved when she didn't flinch. "I apologize again for last night, Brighid—" he began only to have her cut him off.

"I am taking my journey, as you are following your own path. We shut a door last night that should never have been opened, Tauwún," she reminded him, her eyes searching his, silently pleading. "For your own sake, it would be best to leave it closed."

"I don't think I can, Brighid," he admitted honestly, his fingers tightening on her shoulder. "I'm not that strong. Are you?"

"I have to be," she said, bending her knees slightly so that she could step out from beneath his grip. "I've said too many good-byes. At the end of the day, you'd be no more than another one. Now please show me your grand house, and then we'll have that picnic."

He followed her up the half-round flight of steps, then stepped in front of her to insert a large key in the front door. "It's nearly done, except for the last of the painting outside, the delivery of wall coverings for three of the bedchambers, and a few bits of furniture. Bryna picked most of it. Then I'll have to see about hiring a staff. With any luck, I'll be settled in by the end of summer."

Standing back, he watched as Brighid crossed the threshold, feeling his chest swell with the pride of ownership as she looked up at the chandelier he'd ordered all the way from England. For the most part, he'd let Bryna have her head in the decoration, bowing to her sense of color, of style. But the chandelier had been his choice. Whenever he saw it, he was reminded of the one that hung in the foyer at Playden Court, and he remembered that someday, someday . . .

He followed behind Brighid as she quickly swept through the downstairs rooms, lifting dust covers to show her the furniture that lay hidden beneath, pointing out the fine view from the mostly glass morning room, laughing as she exclaimed over the harp standing in the corner of the small music room.

"What a mass of grandeur, Lord Ashford," she said as they retraced their steps to the foyer and she put a hand on the carved banister, prepared to mount the curved staircase to the upper floor. "You've a definite appetite for the finer things." She started up the stairs, stopping halfway and turning back to smile down at him, her eyes dancing with mischief as if she were a child sneaking about in a fairyland. "I feel very much out of place in my deerskins. A woman needs a rich brocade gown to grace these stairs, its train sweeping along the carpet, diamonds glittering at her throat and in her ears. And you, sir. Where are your satins, your fine linens?"

"Dominick has successfully blended his two worlds, Brighid," Philip reminded her as he watched her step onto the landing that led to a square hall and four large bedchambers. "I don't see why I should have any problem."

"No, you don't, do you?" She peeked into the first open doorway, a room stuffed with scaffolding and buckets and the smell of raw wood and damp plaster. "You don't yet see that Dominick Crown has made his choice, and his choice is Pleasant Hill. His choice is with this new land. He is free to take the best of his old world and this one and blend them into a comfortable whole. But you, Lord Ashford, don't have Dominick's freedom. Your title calls to you, your responsibilities bind you to a single world. No matter how you strain at the ties, no matter how you occupy and indulge yourself while you wait for your destiny."

She was about to enter his bedchamber, the single upstairs room that was ready for occupancy. He put out his hand, taking hold of her arm just above the elbow, and turned her toward him. "You may be right about me. But what about *your* destiny, Brighid? How do you see that? Do you plan to spend the rest of your life fighting to remain Nipawi Gischuch, or are you ready to move on? You've remembered the raid now, remembered how you came to live as you did these past five years. But five years isn't a lifetime, Brighid. You've got your entire life ahead of you. Which will you pick: the world you were born into or the one that was forced on you?"

They were so close. Too close. He could almost hear her heartbeat. "I don't know, Tauwún," she told him softly, laying her palm against his cheek, searing his skin with her gentle touch. "I've tried to imagine the future, but whenever I look, I cannot see beyond you."

He raised his hand to cover hers. "And you've seen that my future doesn't include you. That it can't include you. Is that what this is all about, Brighid? That, much as I want this—we both want this—there *is* no future for us?"

"Yes, Tauwún," she answered steadily, her eyes bright, her smile tremulous, both beautiful and sad. "But for all I have tried to tell you otherwise, for all I have attempted to lie to myself, there *is* still today. If we want it."

"You planned this," he said as everything suddenly became clear to him. He dropped his hands to her waist, pulling her closer. "This isn't any sort of Lenape fortune-telling. This is pure Brighid Cassidy. You laid out all your objections one by one, both the mystical and the practical, so that I'd know just what this is costing you—costing us both—then turned them all on their heads. My God, woman, I think you're seducing me! Well, I'll be damned."

"I imagine we both will, Tauwún," she replied, pressing her hands against his chest, her touch light yet driving the breath from his lungs. Her voice dropped to a near whisper. "But I cannot imagine myself any less damned without you."

He took a deep, steadying breath that did little to calm him. "I can't make any promises, Brighid, because they'd all be lies."

"The truth is painful enough. Lies would only hurt me more."

"Then it's the truth I'll give you, Brighid. I do want you. I want to kiss you, to hold your fire, to die inside you, knowing I'll only be half alive without you. I fight a new battle inside myself each time I look at you."

He gazed down at her for another long, desperate moment, then banished any last tearing shred of gentlemanly honor to the farthest recesses of his brain. Swooping her willing body into his arms, he crossed the threshold to his bedchamber, the door slamming back against the wall, and took her into his bed, into his world, if only for the moment.

Her mouth was warm and inviting, opening at the first touch of his tongue. He lay half on her, half off her, their hands between them, struggling with their deerskins that branded her the widow of a Lenape warrior and him the foolish Englisher who wanted only to hide from his fate. Skin met skin, and the fire built. His mouth skimmed her long throat, the soft sun-kissed skin above her breasts, the creaminess of her belly.

Her hands clutched at his shoulders, drawing him down to her again and again, giving him her sweet breasts, allowing him the slick silkiness between her thighs. She rose up to him with each new foray, each new landscape mapped and charted by his fingers, his mouth, teeth, and tongue.

This was desire at its most basic. Mutual need at its most elemental. He didn't give her time to think, didn't allow himself time to regret. Their passion had been too intense, too close to the surface not to break free all at once, full-blown and ready to explode.

He rose above her one last time, giving her a single heartbeat in time to change her mind, to beg him to stop, and then plunged deep between her thighs, filling her with a single stroke. "Sweet Christ," he breathed as a small alarm began to peal in his brain, warring with his passion, a passion that told him he'd only imagined what he'd believed he'd felt.

And then, as Brighid began to move beneath him, he pushed all misgivings from his consciousness and allowed that passion to rule. He covered her mouth once more, mimicking his thrusts with his tongue, taking them both higher, higher . . . deeper, deeper . . . losing himself in her until she cried out his name and he held her close as he took her over the edge with him into the unknown.

Any man may make a mistake,
but none but a fool will continue in it.
— *Cicero*

CHAPTER 8

"I RODE OVER TO YOUR NEW HOUSE LATE YESTERDAY MORNING, Philip," Dominick said as the two men sat together in the study at Pleasant Hill, going over accounts. Philip had learned a lot about estate management from his stepuncle and could now read the entries as easily as he could his own name. "That was one of my wagons tied up out front, I believe?"

Philip looked up from the ledger he had been writing in, careful to keep his expression interested but not too interested. "I took Brighid to see the house," he said evenly. "Why didn't you stop in?"

"I had Roarke and Nicholas with me and wasn't sure what I might be interrupting," Dominick answered, sitting back in his chair, holding a silver letter opener balanced between his fingertips. "Philip, I'm rather enjoying watching you and my wife's cousin dance. You light sparks off each other whenever you're within fifty yards of each other and have done from the first if Lokwelend can be believed.

But if you were to hurt her, treat her with any less respect than you would any young woman, well, I'd probably have to serve your head up on a platter to Bryna. She'd accept nothing less."

Philip closed the ledger with a snap, then sat back in his own chair, looking across the desk at Dominick. "You have a rather unique way of asking a man his intentions."

"We're in a rather unique situation," Dominick answered, his tone still conversational although the air fairly crackled with tension. "You're my nephew, and Brighid is my ward."

"Hardly your ward, Uncle. She's one and twenty and has been on her own for quite some time."

Dominick sat up, bracing his elbows on the desk. "All right. I'll put it another way. Brighid, like Mary Catherine, like young Daniel, is my responsibility. And I don't take my responsibilities lightly."

"And you're frightened to death of Bryna," Philip added, grinning, trying to reduce the tension. "As am I. Don't worry, Brighid and I know exactly what we're doing."

"Oh, I sincerely doubt that. She knows you'll eventually be returning to Playden Court? Returning to find yourself a proper English wife who will bring her impeccable birth and breeding to help rebuild the Crown name after my father and yours did their damnedest to destroy it? Or have you forgotten both our mothers and the folly of trying to fit people into roles they are not prepared to perform? Brighid barely knows who she is. She certainly can't know what she wants."

Philip's mind flashed back to the preceding day. To Brighid lying beneath him, reaching up to him, taking, giving. "And that's where you'd be wrong, Uncle," Philip said tersely, rising to go to the drinks table and pour himself a glass of wine. "Brighid Cassidy knows precisely what she wants and isn't exactly shy in going after it." He turned to face his uncle, his friend, before he could quite banish the delight and confusion mingled in his eyes. "I've never met anyone like her before in my life."

"She was the wife of a savage, living in conditions we can only imagine. She's the mother of a half-breed son. She saw her family slaughtered in front of her eyes. She crossed an ocean from Ireland to New Eden but has no conception of London or the savages she'd meet there—the English *ton,* who slice just as deeply with their tongues as the Lenape do with their knives. You can't take her back with you, Philip, not as confused and conflicted as she is now. It would kill her. And you can't stay here."

Philip didn't want to hear this. He didn't want to think about it, about the day he would have to go. For years, he had dreamed of the day he would walk into Playden Court and begin restoring it to the glory that once reigned there. For years he had isolated himself from his beloved home, unable to witness the shambles his father was making of the place, unwilling to watch his mother sliding daily further into her drunkenness. For so long, he had been biding his time, cursing time for moving so slowly. Now he cursed it because it would eventually pass.

"I believe my father intends to live forever," he said at last, trying to smile and failing. "In the meantime, I have my lands here. Brighid would be comfortable at my estate, more comfortable than she is here. She and Bryna are each too strong willed to share a roof for long. Brighid needs her own house. And when I have to . . . when I'm gone, she can still live there. I'll—I'll visit . . ." His voice trailed off, as speaking the words made them real, no longer nebulous imaginings, and he immediately saw how cold his plans were, how selfish. "Damn it, Dominick, what a bastard I am! What am I going to do?"

Dominick stood up and walked around the desk to lay a hand on Philip's shoulder. "Long ago, when I was dealing with another headstrong Irish miss, I was very agreeably maneuvered into providing settlements for both Brighid and Mary Catherine. Bryna made sure I was extremely generous, God love her. Neither of the Cassidy girls are penniless and could live quite comfortably on the income from those settlements. Mary Catherine is as dear to me as my own daughter would be, and she'd be better off here, with Bryna. That's not the case with Brighid, I'm afraid."

"Go on," Philip said, the muscles in his jaw tensing.

"I have every intention of going on, Philip, much as I can see you don't want to hear what I'm going to say. Brighid and Daniel and their history are known throughout New Eden. I don't think you completely comprehend the fullness of that yet, Philip. Daniel doesn't stand a chance here once he's an adult, not if the current mood against the Lenape prevails, and Brighid faces an uphill battle to be accepted. And there's still that damnable business about this man— or, for all we know, *more* than one man—who is traveling around the colony, attacking Lenape women and returned captives. First in Easton and now here with Cora and another murder last week in Lancaster I hadn't told you about. Another female captive recently returned from Fort Pitt. I'm afraid for Brighid, frankly. She insists on traveling around the countryside on her own, which makes her an easy target for any idiot who believes she's a threat, or whatever in hell he's thinking. So, much as Bryna hates the idea, we've discussed buying a house for Brighid and setting her up there. Somewhere far away from here but where Brighid would feel at home."

Philip sliced his uncle a suspicious look. "Where?"

"County Clare," Dominick said, then went to the drinks table and poured himself a glass. "She's safe enough here with us right now if we all keep a close guard on her. But we're thinking of sending Brighid home if she'll go. Together we can fashion some farradiddle about her having rescued an Indian boy from certain death and then adopting him after the loss of her family. I suppose the old woman would go with them. Can you see Lapawin in Ireland?"

He turned back to Philip. "Christ, man, I don't know what to do, what's going to be right for Brighid and Daniel. But I do know one thing. Brighid has enough on her plate as it is. She can't be made to deal with the problems she'd have as Philip Crown's whore, either here or in Ireland. Or haven't you thought ahead to what it would be like for her while you're here and, most especially, after you've gone? How she'd live between your little *visits,* which would grow more and more infrequent as you became more involved with Playden Court and the children you'd have and the social world your English wife would expect? Is that what you want for Brighid? Doesn't she have enough to deal with as it is?"

"Christ!" Philip collapsed into his chair once more, disgusted with himself. "What a hell of a mess! But she won't willingly go back to Ireland, Dominick, of that I'm certain. And if she can't stay here, then I'll just have to take her to England with me, get her away from the idiots, the bigotry. God knows I can understand what it's like to face such blind stupidity. There are *gentlemen* who still cut me dead in London because I'm half Jewish. I mean it, Dominick—why don't I just marry her and have done with it?"

Dominick sat down on a corner of the desk. "A better idea, I believe, would be just to stay clear of her, let her find her own feet. You're a man, Philip. You can handle what happens to you in London, and your title and fortune will always allow you entrée into society. But your shared ancestry has served to turn your sister into a bitter, unhappy girl—you've told me as much yourself, many times. Much as I'd like to believe in happy endings, much as you'd be there for Brighid, can you really take the chance of something similar happening to her?"

Brighid stood in front of the mirror, her small nose wrinkled in disgust. The muslin camisole wasn't so terribly bad, but the laced corset and whalebone panniers were, if not precisely tight, *confining*—in a way her Lenape clothes were not. Why would anyone, given the choice, willingly truss themselves up like a wild turkey ready for the spit when it was so totally unnecessary? But Philip might like to see her in something other than her deerskins. And he had to be much more familiar with unlacing a woman's corset than he was with stripping her of leggings . . .

"Oh, to have such a tiny waist again," Bryna Cassidy said longingly from her bed, which was where she had been the past week after fainting at the dinner table. Her first pregnancy had gone smoothly, a fact she had not appreciated until the miscarriage she'd suffered two years ago, and neither she nor Dominick were taking any chances with this baby. "Now stop making faces, Brighid, or it might freeze that way. At least that's what our mothers told us. Cora, help Brighid into her gown before she changes her mind."

Brighid turned to look at her cousin, who sat propped against a half-dozen pillows, an opened tin of candies on the bedspread beside her. "I'm only doing this so that I can help out at the store without sending the ladies screaming into the street," she not entirely untruthfully reminded her cousin, who was the proud proprietress of Crown's Inn and Stores in New Eden. "Cora said you were planning on getting up this afternoon to go check on the latest shipment from Easton. You're a stubborn woman, Bryna Crown, without a lick of sense."

"I'm totally hopeless," Bryna agreed, popping a sugarplum into her mouth and not quite hiding her smile of triumph as she did so. "And how nice that Philip has volunteered to drive you. Why, he just can't seem to do enough for you, can he?"

Brighid sliced a look at Cora, who kept her own eyes focused on the carpet. Heaven help her! Bryna was playing at matchmaker! And how better to do the thing than to find a way to shove her unsuspecting cousin into a corset and gown, so that Philip might see her not as a returned captive, but as a woman. A desirable woman. Perhaps even a more than slightly civilized woman.

Now it was Brighid's turn to smile, which she did as she bent her knees and allowed Cora to drop the deep brown linen dress over her head. If Bryna already knew how Philip saw her, how much of her he'd seen . . .

"Pull down the hem, Cora," Bryna ordered affably, "it's all twisted. Lace the bodice over the chemise, making sure it's snug. There! Now stand back and let me see. Oh, my, Brighid, you have filled out since last I saw you, haven't you? I never would have known it, seeing you in those deerskins. Cora, perhaps we might loosen the laces a tad. That's quite a bit of her charms my dear cousin is showing. And she'll need a shawl for cover if not for comfort. I know just the thing—"

"You get right back in that bed, Bryna Crown!" Brighid commanded as her cousin's tiny bare feet peeked out from under the thrown-back covers, already heading for the edge of the mattress. "I think we can handle this, Cora and I. You always did believe you should be in charge of all of us. Of all of the world, if memory serves. Now how do I look? I feel ridiculous."

"Look in the mirror and see for yourself, my love," Bryna announced, subsiding against the pillows once more. "Although I do wish you'd reconsider the braids. With your skin still so dark from the sun? I don't know. Cora, do you think we made a bad choice? Perhaps a soft blue rather than the brown?"

"*I* chose the brown if you'll recall. Push another inch, Cousin, and I'll go back to my deerskins," Brighid warned as she turned to face the mirror once more, nearly toppling to the floor as she forgot that her feet were now encased in fairly hard, heeled shoes. She hated to admit it, and wouldn't, but she looked rather silly in her braids now that she was wearing English dress. "Enough of this. I'm off to play shopkeeper for the afternoon. Cora, you said Daniel was asleep?"

"He was running the schoolroom all morning after you left for your bath," Cora answered, shaking her head even as she grinned. "I don't know how you kept him tied to the cradleboard as long as you did, so eager he is to be up and about. And if he puts one more thing in his mouth, Nicholas and Roarke will have his head. He nearly chewed an arm off one of their favorite soldiers."

"He's getting new teeth, I think, which will soon give him more than his grandmother can claim," Brighid said, giving a last two-handed upward tug at her chemise, wishing it covered more of her bosom. "Wulapen's son does his father credit. I'll be back before he wants his dinner, I promise."

"Take your time, Brighid," Bryna called after her as she opened the door to the hallway. "You and Philip have a nice afternoon."

Brighid turned to her cousin, rolling her eyes. "You're impossible, Bryna. And so are your notions. Cora, be sure she naps. The woman is far less apt to think up more trouble for me if she's unconscious."

"The Schmidts own Rudolph's Inn and Stores now, turning the place into a tavern and inn," Philip was saying, keeping up the running commentary he'd begun the moment Brighid had appeared in the foyer at Pleasant Hill, ready for her first trip to New Eden. "They're nice people, and Dominick sees them more as fellow business owners than rivals. Jonah Newton's widow married James Kleppinger before Jonah was three months in his grave, and they both run the tannery now. Henry Turner and his wife April have three more children, and he hasn't been near a drop of ale since the last raid. The Traxells moved west after the fire in the barn, but Elijah Kester is still here. He said he remembered you. Good man, Elijah. He's the smitty, and—"

"You're not going to say anything, are you?" Brighid interrupted when she could stand no more. "Nothing about yesterday, nothing about my dress—nothing! Are you ashamed of what happened? Are you embarrassed by the way I look today, reminding you that I am a white woman and not a squaw you can take and then forget?"

Philip pulled the team to a halt just before the first buildings that made up New Eden. "What do you want me to say, Brighid?" he asked in a low voice, looking not so much angry as he did exasperated. "We made love yesterday, and we both enjoyed it as I recall. As I also recall, you initiated the experience. With no strings attached, no promises. Or are you changing the rules now? Because if you are, I'm certainly open to suggestions."

She looked at him for a long moment, remembering how his eyes had looked clouded with passion, remembering the feel of his lips against her own. "We made no promises," she agreed quietly, then faced front once more, looking down the hard-packed dirt street and seeing nothing. Like her life. A long, long road that led to nothing. "But you could have at least commented on my dress."

"Should I tell you that I spent all of last night dreaming about what happened between us yesterday afternoon, reliving each moment, my guts twisting with the need to be with you again today? Would you feel better to know that my title, my ancestral home, my duties and responsibilities, all of them pale into insignificance compared to a single moment spent in your arms? If I admit that all I want to do is to throw you into the back of this wagon and ravish you for the next several hours in ways that would shock and amaze us both, well, would any of that help?"

She tipped her head to one side and grinned, deliberately baiting him. "Yes, Tauwûn, that would be very helpful. But do you like my dress?"

"Yes, damn it! I love your bloody dress! I'd like it a damn sight more if it were lying on the floor next to my bed. But that's not going to happen, Brighid. God help me, it's never going to happen. We made a mistake yesterday, one that can't be repeated. Do you understand?"

Brighid had to remember how to breathe. One moment she had been teasing him, enjoying his frustration, and the next he had taken her heart and crushed it. "Why? Because of Wulapen? Because I disgust you? Because you disgust yourself, touching a body that was touched by a savage with the blood of slain white children on his hands? In the clear light of day, Lord Ashford, is your disgust more powerful than your passion?"

She felt him take hold of her hand and didn't have the strength to pull away. "I may hate myself, but do you really have that low an opinion of me, too, Brighid?" he asked, and she bit her lip to hold back a sob as she heard the hurt in his voice.

"No," she answered simply. "No, Tauwún, you may not like that I was Wulapen's wife, but you would never turn away from me on that account alone. So what is it? Can't we simply enjoy each other for the time we have? I haven't asked for more, and I won't."

He ran a hand through his hair, cursing beneath his breath. "This is neither the time nor—"

"You aren't leaving yet, are you?" she broke in suddenly, just as the thought hit her. She had been alone before, both in body and spirit, but she'd never known such fear. "I know you have to leave someday, but surely not so soon."

"I should go," he said, shaking his head. "If I were any sort of a man, I'd leave Dominick in charge of my estate and board the first ship leaving Philadelphia. But I can't leave. Not yet and not because of my estate. I can't leave you even though I know I should. Dominick said—"

"Dominick said?" Brighid's eyes narrowed as she glared at Philip. She should have known! "And just what did Dominick say?"

"Dominick pointed out everything that I already knew, Brighid, everything I so conveniently forgot yesterday afternoon and a few other things you and I already discussed. You have enough to deal with, fitting in here in New Eden, picking up the threads of your life—or even starting life over again somewhere else—without me complicating things."

"I see," Brighid said, and she did, although it was obvious Dominick and Bryna hadn't thoroughly discussed the matter with each other, not with Bryna's blatant matchmaking still going on. Now *that* was an interlude between her headstrong cousin and her calm, commonsensible husband Brighid definitely intended to miss! "Does Dominick know how late he is with his advice, or is he only guessing?"

At last, Philip smiled. "Think about it a moment, Brighid. I'm still alive, aren't I? Miserable but alive." Then he sobered. "No, he doesn't know. But he does suspect. If only there were some way to lock out the world."

"We did yesterday, if only for a few hours," Brighid pointed out, blinking to hold back tears, tears she had shed so seldom in the past five years, until her visit to the Cassidy farm, her return to some of her unhappiest memories. "I don't think I could have made it through the day without you, Philip Crown. Please don't ask me to be without you for these next weeks until I decide what's best for Daniel and myself. I told you not to lie to me, but I would ask this one promise of you. Don't make me face these next weeks alone."

"Hullo, Crown! Good day to you! What's wrong? One of your team throw a shoe?"

Brighid bent her head, hiding her tear-bright eyes as Philip greeted Elijah Kester, a large man astride an even larger horse that he was returning to one of the local farmers. "The horses are fine. I was just pointing out the changes in our grand metropolis to Miss Cassidy here before we rode in," Philip explained. "That's all, Elijah. You remember Brighid's family, don't you?"

"That I do," Kester said, tipping his hat to Brighid as she looked up at him, his homely face taking on a sympathetic frown. "Miss Mary Catherine is a pure joy and must be that tickled to see you home, so say both the missus and m'self. And don't listen to none of those who say you should have stayed away." He flushed deep red as if ashamed that he'd let his tongue run away with him and hurriedly looked to Philip. "How's Missus Crown doing? Haven't seen her in the village for more than a week."

"She's fine, Elijah, if a little tired," Philip answered, taking up the reins and releasing the brake. "We're going to the inn now to check on things for her. Which we'd better be doing, for she'll want a full accounting. Good seeing you, Elijah."

Brighid remained silent for the minute or two it took to reach the Crown Inn and Stores, then waited on the wagon seat as Philip hopped down to tie up the team, taking the opportunity to look up and down the wide street at the people who wandered along it, going about their daily business.

She felt as if the distance between the wagon and the rough wooden flagway was the length of a Lenape gauntlet that she was being dared to run. If she made it to the end without crying out or falling to the ground beneath the blows, would she be accepted? Or would her spirit break under the assault? Philip could have no idea what she faced, no notion of just how terrified she was, just how much she needed him beside her right now.

Five years, she realized, had brought a multitude of changes to the small village she remembered. Besides Dominick's sprawling building, there was now a small apothecary shop across the street and what looked to be a tailor's beside it. Peering between the tailor's and the silversmith's shop, she saw that another street had been added to the village, little more than a dirt track lined with small houses that probably served as homes to the few residents who made their livings not farming, but in supplying the everyday to those who did.

Quite the bustling metropolis, she decided, especially when she made out the sign on a small stone building standing by itself on the second street. New Eden had itself a gaolhouse! Interesting. With few Lenape left to kill or fleece, the colonists must have turned to committing their crimes against their fellow white men.

"Ready to run the gauntlet of Bryna's instructions on how to unpack boxes and load shelves?"

Brighid started at Philip's laughing use of the word and looked down to see him standing beside the wagon, his arms raised to assist her from the seat. She struggled to keep a tight rein on her composure. "I—I suppose so, although I'm dreading this, and Elijah Kester's warning didn't help. Say something that will make it easier, if you can?"

"You're the most beautiful creature I've ever seen, and I

want you so much my teeth ache," Philip whispered as he lifted her from the seat, holding her close for a moment so that he could whisper the words in her ear.

Tears were dangerously close again. She allowed her hands to linger on Philip's upper arms as they stood face-to-face in the street. "Then our earlier discussion was all for nothing? We can go on as we are? I promise you, I won't push for anything more. I know what you can give and what I can give."

"Yes, Nipawi Gischuch," he said, his smile fading. "We both know each other's limits. Or we think we do."

Brighid felt his hands tighten on her waist, and she tensed as he turned his head, looking to the three women standing on the wooden flagway that ran in front of the store. "Ladies?" he asked, stepping away from her to bow in their direction. "I believe the door is unlocked, and Harold is inside to help you. Or perhaps you're waiting to say hello to Miss Cassidy here and welcome her back to New Eden?"

"We'll be doing nothing of the sort, Mr. Crown," one of the women declared, lifting her chin so that she glared at Brighid down the length of her sharp nose. "And we'll be taking our custom elsewhere until that Lenape whore and her unholy breed are removed from our midst. We're God-fearing people, Mr. Crown, and will have no truck with the Lord's damned."

Just to emphasize her point, Brighid supposed, the God-fearing woman then made a disgusting sound in her throat and sent a spray of spittle at Brighid's head.

"Ignorant bitches!" Philip growled, using his handker-chief to wipe at Brighid's cheek. "Christ, Brighid, I'm so sorry."

She was trembling both with anger and the sure knowl-edge that, had Philip not been with her, she would have launched herself at the women without a thought to any chance of injury to herself or repercussions against Dom-inick and Bryna. "Take me back to Pleasant Hill, Tauwún," she said quietly, staring at the women as they lifted their skirts and stomped back down the flagway. "Just take me back. Now."

Philip ended the afternoon as he had spent his morning: in Dominick's study. "She spat on her, Dominick! I can't believe it. The ignorant bitch *spat* on her!"

Dominick held out a glass of wine, which Philip ignored. "Take this, Philip, and stop that pacing. You're wearing a hole in my new carpet and, as it was a gift from Bryna, I shudder to think what she might do to you. Sit down, and I'll explain more of what I tried to tell you this morning. Difficult as it is to believe, there are many people, the woman you met today included, who obviously believe that white female captives were taken as punishment for some sin they'd committed against God. People like that woman in New Eden believe these captives to be Jezebels, unclean."

Philip sat down, but he waved away the glass and his uncle's explanation. "I don't want to hear any of that ridiculous tripe, Dominick. I've already *seen* what you've been trying to tell me. I just want to go upstairs, get Brighid and Daniel, and take them the hell away from New Eden. How *dare* they treat her this way?" He drew his hands into fists. "God, you don't know how hard it was for me to put her back in the wagon and bring her home. What I really wanted to do was to find Eunice Wright's spineless twit of a husband and grind his face into mulch. And I still might! How could he let a harridan like that out of the house?"

He closed his eyes, trying to regulate his breathing. "But that's not the worst of it."

Dominick took a drink out of the glass he'd offered Philip. "Deep inside, you agreed with the woman?"

Philip leaped to his feet, ready to attack his uncle. "Jesus, God, no! How could you think such a thing?"

"I don't, but I thought you'd been feeling sorry for yourself long enough. This is Brighid's pain, not yours," Dominick answered, saluting Philip with the wineglass. "So, what else? You said there's more."

"Always the uncle, is that it, Dominick? You can't forget you're the elder by seven years. Not that I've been acting like I'm out of leading strings." Philip ran a hand through his hair, remembering what Brighid had done when they'd returned to Pleasant Hill. "But you're right. This isn't about me. I know what *I've* done in the face of stupidity like Eunice Wright's. It's about Brighid, how *she* reacted to the whole miserable episode."

"I doubt it was with tears or a maidenly swoon," Dominick said, taking another sip of wine. "This isn't anything I'll want to be telling Bryna, is it? I'm already worried about her health and don't plan to let her find out about Eunice Wright's little show of drama if I have to keep her tied to her bed until the baby is born."

"You won't be able to keep such news from her forever, unless Brighid lies about the bandage," Philip told Dominick as he began pacing once more, "which is just another reason to get Brighid away from Pleasant Hill, I suppose. You see, when we got back here, Hallie was outside with Daniel. Brighid hadn't spoken, not all the way home. She just sat beside me, her hands curled into tight fists, all stony and silent. Then she saw Daniel. She went to him and, still without a word, took a knife out of her pocket—God, the woman carries a knife like other women carry lace handkerchiefs—and ran its edge clear across her palm. Then," he closed his eyes for a moment, able to see the scene once more, "she pressed the wound against Daniel's forehead, swearing with her blood that she'll keep him safe forever, no matter what the cost. I'll tell you, Dominick, I've never been so shocked or impressed in my life."

"And you're still entertaining the notion of taking her to England? Presenting her at court? Wouldn't that simply be changing one miserable existence for another? What would your sister say, Philip? Really. What do you think Lilith would say?"

"I know what you're trying to do, playing the devil's advocate. But it won't work," Philip ground out, then turned on his heels and headed for the door that led into the gardens.

"I just want you to *think,* Philip," Dominick called after him. "Think of what is best for Brighid. Eunice Wright showed you only one side of the challenges Brighid faces. She spreads her evil with words. But somewhere out there, someone else is spreading *his* evil, feeding his hate, with a knife. There's nothing else for it. Brighid has to go back to Ireland."

"No! No, she's not going anywhere. Not yet." Philip stopped, his hand on the door latch, his back to his uncle. "I was a selfish, ignorant child when I first came to New Eden five years ago, Dominick, and haven't grown too much since then, much to my shame. But that's over. Pematalli's death was only a test and only the beginning. Brighid's *my* concern now, Dominick, as Bryna is yours. She needs me, and I won't abandon her. So just shut up, all right?" He opened the door, then turned back to look at his uncle. "Just shut the bloody hell up!"

*He knew the things that were and the things
that would be and the things that had been before.*
— Homer

CHAPTER 9

❧

AFTER A NEAR-SLEEPLESS NIGHT, BRIGHID ROSE AT DAWN AND,
with the Indian's permission, spent an hour in Lokwelend's
sweathouse, ladling water over hot stones and breathing
deep of the mind-cleansing vapors, then walked, nearly
naked, into the cool stream outside, seeking invigoration
after the relaxing interlude. And she did feel calmer as she
dressed in her comfortable deerskins and made her way
back along the path to Lokwelend's cabin, more able to cope
with the impotent fury that had done its best to infect her
soul.

"*Itah,* Grandfather," she said in his native language as
she sat herself cross-legged on the ground across from the
elderly Lenape. She had known he would be here, waiting
for her, willing to share a silence, willing to speak if she so
desired. Unlike Philip or her cousin Bryna, who would be
more than eager to speak, to rant and rave and expound,
telling her just what she ought to do.

Lokwelend closed the book he had been reading and unwound the wire spectacles from his ears. "I thank you for the loan of your sweathouse, Grandfather," she continued, savoring the Lenape words she only felt free to speak with him and Lapawin. Such a simple language. So basic, yet so eloquent, so easy to employ to say what was in her heart. She wondered what her friend would do if she went to him, put her head on his shoulder, and cried out the remainder of her sorrows. "I now feel free of that foolish woman. Clean once more."

Lokwelend nodded. "But not yet sure of your direction. This will take more time. Tauwún was here earlier, seeking you. He will return soon. You would do best to avoid him this day, Nipawi Gischuch. His blood has not yet cooled. It is good to act with the head while listening to the heart. My son follows only his anger right now, which has little to do with either, and can only lead to rash acts and sorrow for everyone. And you do not yet fully trust him. As you do not trust your grandfather."

Brighid let her gaze slide away toward the trees. "I don't know what you mean, Grandfather," she said, wishing her pulse wasn't pounding in her ears. For her, lying was difficult in any language. "I have always trusted you. I came with you from Fort Pitt, did I not?"

Lokwelend's smile was wise and sad. "You had no choice, Nipawi Gischuch. Your light could no longer shine with the Lenape. I would not have agreed to seek you if I believed otherwise."

"I miss my old life, Grandfather," she said quietly, picking up a stick and poking it in the dying fire. "It was never easy but never hard. Without the interference of the Yankwi, the Lenape life is a most innocent, pleasant existence. Here, everything is complicated, and I must think all the time. How much simpler it was to live each day as it came to me and not have to worry about the future. Time was, I worried how to fill Tasukamend's small belly. Now I wonder how I will fill his life."

"Wulapen's son will grow tall and strong and wise,"

Lokwelend said as he meticulously filled his pipe, then lit it with a stick from the fire. "I have seen this. But he has a long, sometimes difficult road to travel and needs the truth to guide him. Will you hide the truth from him as you have from your family, from Tauwún? This will make the path more difficult for young Tasukamend, for everyone."

Brighid swallowed down hard on the sudden lump in her throat. "You know? How do you know?" Then she shook her head, smiling sadly. "I am a foolish infant to ask such a question. My grandfather knows everything."

"You hide the truth to protect the child. It is understandable."

"I made a promise . . . ," she began quickly, then allowed her explanation to die away to a sigh as she picked at the white cloth bandage that wrapped around her hand. For Lokwelend, for her grandfather, she could do no less than be honest. "Wingenund's Yankwi name was Johanna, Grandfather, and she was the first wife of Wulapen. His beloved wife and the sister of my heart. Tasukamend, the Blameless One, is their son. There were two more, a boy and a girl, whose names I cannot speak without pain. I buried them with Wingenund, before we came to Fort Pitt."

Lokwelend sucked on his pipe in silence.

"I was the second wife of Wulapen, taken only because one of the braves wanted me. Lapawin had chosen me as her daughter, and the brave was not kind. Still, it was awkward. So Wulapen took my hand at the urging of his mother and led me into the longhouse. It was an innocent deceit, no more. I slept beside Wingenund and Wulapen. I heard the laughter in their lovemaking. I helped ease their children into the world. I was happy within my family. I was needed. And I didn't have to think about all that I had lost."

She looked at Lokwelend, tears standing bright in her eyes. "Tasukamend is mine, Grandfather. He is my life. I have lost my family, both of my families, and my white sister no longer wants me. I will not give my son to Johanna's miserable Yankwi husband as the king's law dictates, as everyone would say would be best for me. I made a promise to Johanna that I would raise Tasukamend as my own."

"It is your promise and your secret, Nipawi Gischuch," the old Indian said, laying down his pipe. "But the time will come when secrets must be told. I trust you to know that time, for I will not always be here."

Brighid rubbed trembling fingers over her cheeks, wiping away her tears, concentrating on Lokwelend's words. "What have you seen, Grandfather?"

"In this book," he said, patting the volume in his lap, "the wise chief named Euripides says, 'God, these old men! How they pray for death! How heavy they find this life in the slow drag of days! And yet, when Death comes near them, you will not find one who will rise and walk with him, not one whose years are still a burden to him.' But the wise chief is wrong. For the first time, Nipawi Gischuch, I have seen Death come near and feel ready to rise and walk with him. Do not keep me here too much longer by your foolishness, you and Tauwún both. Pematalli waits for me, where the deer are plentiful and old bones feel young once more. It will soon be time for me to go."

Brighid squared her shoulders, refusing to give in to foolish tears, fighting down the urge to contradict Lokwelend in his melancholy message, for that would show disrespect. "I will miss my grandfather, and I will honor his memory all my days."

"Honor me now, Nipawi Gischuch, and listen to what I say. My dreams are very close. You have enemies, but two most of all. You must beware the pale stranger. And you must also beware he who speaks of the white man's God for his own ends. I have seen these men, and they are coming soon. You, like Tauwún, stand alone before a dark woods, with monsters on all sides ready to rip at your heart. Only together will the light of your combined spirits lead you on the correct pathway home. Help him, Nipawi Gischuch. Tauwún's world did not prepare him for you, and he struggles to understand."

Lokwelend picked up his book once more, then said to

her in English, "Open the door, Brighid Cassidy. Open the door."

Lokwelend was still alone when Philip returned to the log house beside the stream. He wished his Lenape father would agree to move to his new estate, but the man was proving stubborn. As a matter of fact, the man was the most stubborn creature Philip had ever met. And the most confounding. Like now, when he motioned for Philip to sit, ignoring his question as to Brighid's whereabouts, and then remained silent for nearly a quarter hour, staring into the fire, puffing on his pipe.

Quiet reflection was not one of Philip's strong suits, especially now, when he wanted nothing more than to find Brighid, sit her down—tie her down if he had to—and tell her that she had to leave New Eden with him. Now. Today. Before anyone could cause her any more pain. Before he could think through to the end of it, beyond the immediate, and find reasons that would make a mockery of his impulsive solution.

But he would remain silent until Lokwelend was ready to speak. Brighid had taught him some of the Lenape's deep regard for their elders on the ride back from Fort Pitt, told him of the respect the tribe showed their parents and all the old people who had lived so long and knew so much. She had told him how the warriors would take the old men along on the hunt, even when they were past such exercise, carrying them on their backs if necessary. They would position these old hunters in the woods, then be sure to drive the game past them so that they might be in on the kill. Never would one of the elders go hungry, even if it meant that the grown men and women had to do with half rations. All the children of the camp gathered at the feet of these elders, listening to their stories again and again, learning from them, bowing to their judgment, showing them deference in both word and deed.

Philip did his best to show such respect now, even as he

burned to demand answers from his new father. Answers he was sure only Lokwelend knew.

"A maiden saw a lovely flower in the woods, one she had never seen before in this woods, and longed to take it home," Lokwelend said at last. "She pinched it between her fingers, severing the stem, and took the flower to her longhouse and hid it away, for its beauty was hers, and she was not about to share it or expose it to any who would hurt it. But the flower wilted and died, for all that the maiden fed it water and talked to it and praised its beauty."

Flowers? What the devil did flowers have to do with Brighid? With what had happened yesterday? With what he had determined to do today? Philip spread his hands in frustration. "I don't understand, Father."

Lokwelend packed his pipe again, then relit it with a stick from the fire. "So the maiden went back into the woods," he continued. "This time she dropped to her knees and dug the whole plant out of the soil, even though it was not so beautiful without its flower, and its leaves were prickly and hurt her, nearly bringing her to despair that she could be doing what was right. She carefully carried the plant back to the village. She gave the plant to the whole village to enjoy, even though some laughed and some turned away in disgust, their fingers cut by the sharp leaves. But she was stubborn, and she persevered. She planted her treasure in the sun. She watered the roots. She praised it. She protected the plant from the careless feet of the village children, from the hungry rabbits who would devour it with their sharp teeth. She gave the plant time and love and patience. And the plant grew. And the many flowers it brought forth were the most beautiful of all, admired and loved by everyone."

Philip bent his head, rubbing at the back of his neck. "Roots," he said, smiling ruefully, believing he understood. "I can't take Brighid to England by cutting her in half, can I, taking only what I find beautiful and leaving the rest? She's not just a pretty flower. She's all of the many parts of her, and if she isn't accepted for all that she is, she'll wilt and die. I can't hide her away from this world or mine, not if I expect her to thrive." He smiled again. "That's good, Father. Very good. But Brighid's flower can't bloom here in New Eden, roots or no roots. What happened yesterday proves that."

"Then you must learn to accept all of her, Tauwún," Lokwelend said, passing him the pipe. "You believe she is like you, and in many ways she is, but she is the Nipawi Gischuch, and she has suffered much you cannot yet know. You must praise and nurture, and *you* must suffer all that is needed to be done to bring her into her full flower. To want is not enough. To admire is not enough. To protect is not enough. These are all good things, yes, but first, my son, you must *understand*, as the maiden understood. And to do that will take patience. More than you believe you possess. But I believe my son Tauwún will not fail, because his heart is good."

Philip stayed very still for a long time. He and Lokwelend shared the pipe between them before he spoke again, before he could trust the steadiness of his voice enough to speak again. "Pematalli was a fortunate son to have had your great wisdom for all of his life. It is my deepest honor that you allow me to call you Father."

Brighid stood at the edge of the cliff, looking out over the valley. So green. So beautiful. So deceptively peaceful. Behind her, Pematalli's grave was indistinguishable from the remainder of the hillside, which was covered in long grass that waved in the soft breeze.

Safe. Protected from those who would desecrate this holy place.

Lokwelend needed no reminder of where his son's body lay, would always be, beneath the sweet grass, resting forever in the rich earth of his beloved country.

Already this hill was called Lenape Hill, the cliff Lenape Cliff. Part of the hillside had broken away three years ago, Bryna had told her, severed by a lightning strike during a fierce October storm. October. The same month as the last raid, the same month Pematalli had died. There were those who now said they saw the weather-chiseled bust of an Indian chief in the outcrop of limestone slabs on the cliff face, swore they could distinguish a nose, chin, high cheekbones, a flat brow above fierce, all-seeing eyes.

Always There. Pematalli's name. Pematalli's home. Pematalli's destiny.

But not hers. Not as long as she was Nipawi Gischuch. The Night Fire.

Kolachuisen, like her brother, and in her own way, had also chosen to stay here, outwardly taking on the white man's clothes, the white man's speech, the white man's God. She tried her best to blend in, to become invisible, to hide behind a comforting, conformable exterior that eased the fears of the white man. To tame the savage was laudable, the tamed savage acceptable. Domesticated. Safe.

But the civilized turned savage was not acceptable. Like mad, desperate Silky Wattson. Like poor, tattooed Hallie. Like Nipawi Gischuch and her half-breed son. They did not so easily disappear behind a prudent facade. Their history kept them too visible, too different. It was one thing to be born a Lenape; it was another thing entirely to be a white woman who lived with the Lenape.

Whore. Jezebel. One of God's damned. Taken by savages because of her sins.

That is what New Eden thought of her. Her and her reluctant "sisters," two of whom were dead now, murdered for their "crime."

Even Mary Catherine had heaped more shame upon her, believing she had not only chosen to stay with the Lenape, but that she had chosen to go with them in the first place, leaving her mother and sister to die.

Of all the pain Brighid suffered, Mary Catherine's cruel words had cut deepest and refused to heal. Even now, now that Brighid at last remembered at least some of what had happened that terrible evening.

No, she could not stay here. Not as Nipawi Gischuch, the Night Fire, the white squaw widow of Wulapen.

And yet, as Brighid Cassidy, she had nowhere else to go.

Only Philip Crown would leave. Only Philip, who had not entered her dream to be with her—as she had hoped, as Lokwelend still believed—but who only presented another path that led nowhere. She would miss him when he was gone. Miss him as a friend. Miss him as someone, if only her life had been different, whom she could love.

Did love.

Would always love.

She turned away from the view of Philip's fine estate house that nestled below, tucked beneath the cliff, surrounded by trees and serenaded by the river that lay beyond, glinting silver in the sunlight. Dropping to her knees in her grass-green linen gown, she picked up the packet containing her deerskins, her moccasins, and, opening it, placed it in the hole she had dug. She then raised her hands to her hair and removed the strips of leather holding her braids. She tugged her fingers through the twisted locks, loosening them, allowing the dark tresses to fall free to below her waist.

Barely able to see beyond her tears, she tied her hair once more, at a spot several inches below her shoulders. With her knife, she sawed through the fist-thick rope of hair just above the leather strip, then placed the cut hair in the bundle. Lastly, she removed the beads from her neck, beads Johanna had strung for her, and reverently laid them with the rest, tying the bundle shut with another length of leather.

"We cannot go back, Wingenund," she said quietly as she filled the hole with dirt and covered it with leaves and bits of grass, hiding it from curious eyes until the woods reclaimed its own. "For Tasukamend, I will attempt to do as Kolachuisen has done and pray your son will grow to find the same peace she seeks. Today, so that the child might live, Nipawi Gischuch has died. She will remain here, with Pematalli, her heart lying deep in the earth. But it is not enough for a name to change. Lives have to change as well. Because of her love for Daniel, Brighid Cassidy cannot run away anymore. Like Cora—for Daniel—she takes her stand here."

Brighid's left heel was rubbed nearly raw by the time she had washed her hands and face at the river and then walked the distance back to Philip's estate in her new hard shoes. Her legs felt hampered by her petticoats, so that her step was made smaller, her journey longer. Her hair, falling in loose curls over her shoulders, some of it sticking to the damp skin of her neck, was tossed by the breeze and seemed more an annoyance than what her mother had often called her crowning glory.

It never would have occurred to her that, with her trim waist, wild ebony curls, dark-lashed aquamarine eyes, and rather wistful expression, she painted a living picture that was wildly, exotically, heartbreakingly beautiful.

She stopped at the bottom of the wide gravel drive, remembering her first visit to Philip's fine house. How it had begun. How it had ended.

Lapawin had been wrong. Brighid's time spent on horseback, her long hours of labor in the fields, neither had been sufficient to weaken her membrane to the point where there had been no telltale ripping when Philip had entered her. But it had been a gamble she had taken, a gamble she had won, even if she had nearly bitten through the soft, inner flesh of her bottom lip before the pain eased and all she felt was the passion rising, spiraling above the hurt.

She knew, Brighid Cassidy knew, that what she had done was wrong. Unacceptable in the white man's world. But she had lived in the Lenape world for five years. She had listened to Johanna and Wulapen whispering in the dark, laughing in the dark, loving in the dark. Mating, lovemaking, whatever name was put to the act, seemed a natural progression between a man and a woman, a wondrous beauty and not a sin to be hidden away, not an expression of need, of love, to be withheld because of convention or any demand for ceremonies, for promises that might never be kept.

Could never be kept.

She had needed to be held after her trip to the home she had shared with her first family, in the wake of the memories that had washed over her, battered her, made her yearn to reach out, to be comforted. To forget again if only for a little while. She had desired Philip as he had desired her. There was so little in this world for her; surely a few stolen moments of happiness before a lifetime of solitude was not so unforgivable.

And she could not feel that she had acted only out of her own selfish need. Philip had also been in need of comfort, of some release from worry, tension, guilt. As they both were today. If she knew nothing else, she knew that.

The sound of hoofbeats traveling fast in her direction made her turn in time to see a single mount and rider pounding across the cleared, not yet planted fields. Before she could see his face, his flowing blond hair, she knew the rider was Philip. Just as she knew the white stallion was the horse in her dream. She felt her heart stop, then begin to beat again, shakily, all fluttering wings, like a small, frightened bird she'd once held between her hands.

Philip pulled the horse to a plunging, hoof-pawing stop just in front of her. "What are you doing here?" he asked, only his considerable skills keeping the horse under control. "I've been looking for you for two days. Lokwelend's close as a clam, and Dominick just keeps saying you are where you are, and that is obviously where you want to be."

She could only stand there and stare. "You . . . you ride a roan. Wh-where did you get that horse?"

Philip reached forward to pat the thick white mane, obviously proud of his new possession. "Pegasus? I saw him in Virginia before I came back to New Eden, and had to have him. He's Arabian, smuggled out of the country and brought here, which is another way of saying he cost me the earth. It took a while, but he arrived the other day, and he's a fine start to my breeding plans." He looked at Brighid, tipping his head to one side, assessing her, his eyes seeming to feed on her even as he tried to hide behind a friendly smile. "You look very nice, Brighid."

"Thank you."

The friendly smile disappeared as his eyes flashed blue fire. "You know you shouldn't be abroad alone. Damn it, Brighid, I've been going out of my mind! We have to talk."

"I'm safe enough on my own, Philip," she said, shaking her head, pushing the breeze-stung hair out of her eyes. "And no, we don't have to talk, for there is nothing left to say." She reached up her hand to him. "But we'll get to your bedchamber faster if you take me up behind you."

"Get to my—" He broke off, stabbing his fingers through his own near shoulder-length hair. "Christ on a crutch, Brighid, we can't . . . Oh, *hell!*" He reached down his hand, and she grabbed onto his wrist as he did hers, pulling her up in front of him in one fluid move that set Pegasus to dancing in a circle before Philip could turn him toward the house.

There were no dark woods here, no twisting paths that led nowhere. Just the smooth drive up to the house and the long curving staircase that led to Philip's bedchamber. He carried her all the way, his arms strong around her as she rained kisses on his cheeks, his bared throat.

And when he laid her down on his bed, as she looked up at him, beyond him, just before his mouth came down to claim hers and she shut her eyes in the ecstasy of it all, she smiled as she saw the thick bundle of sweet grass he had hung from the ceiling.

"This is wrong, Brighid. Wrong," he whispered against her ear even as his hands moved to loosen the ties holding her bodice, to lower her chemise, allowing her breasts to tumble free, to be cupped in his palms, to be caressed and teased and finally worshiped by his hands, by his intense seeking mouth.

"This is the only *right* thing we have, Philip," she murmured into his hair, slipping her hands inside his shirt, branding his skin with her heat. She moved her hands to his sides, feeling the involuntary ripple of muscle, and pressed her head back against the pillows as he suckled at her breasts, his tongue sending invisible wires of tension to tie into delicious knots in her lower belly and at the same time loosening the painful bonds of responsibility, of loneliness, of isolation that held her taut in their grip.

She felt warm and fluid, as free-running as a woodland stream, as graceful as a hawk soaring on the wing, as secure as a child held in strong arms after waking from a nightmare. This room had become her haven, her safety. This man, her only freedom. These moments, her only happiness.

Through a haze of sensation, she felt the remainder of her constricting clothing leaving her, falling away, releasing her from the purposely donned cocoon of civilization and transporting her fully into the world of sensation, of awareness, of crystal-clear perception, a place where all that mattered was the moment and all that existed was this time, this place, this man.

He touched her everywhere, and she allowed it. She touched him everywhere. And wanted more.

And he gave, even as he took. His fingers found her, opened her, explored her, draining her of strength while filling her with a need so elemental that she felt no shame, no shame as her legs fell apart and he took with his mouth all that his fingers had prepared for him.

She rode each new crest, reveled in the building heat, the wanton giving that brought such searing rewards, the long, tumbling release that had her crying out his name.

She drew him back up to her with frantic hands, still hungry for all that she had been satisfied. As she held him, then urged him into a slow roll onto his back, her kisses thanked, gave, and still yearned to take. He was her golden god. The fine hair on his body, that light sprinkling of golden dust that drew her lips against his chest, urged her to trace the glorious pathway it mapped toward his flat belly and beyond.

She slid down his body until her hands rested on his thighs, until she could see all of him, see his need, and glory in it. She acted out of instinct, out of love, out of a deep need to show him how precious he was to her. All of him. She felt the tension building in her again, a different, never before felt but still recognizable power that only intensified at his guttural "Brighid. Dear God, Brighid!"

And then she was on her back once more, feeling her legs being lifted high, high on his shoulders, as he drove into her with one powerful lunge; burying himself in her, grinding against her, then retreating for a moment, only to return, faster, harder, deeper.

"Yes, Philip, yes," she pleaded, not realizing she had spoken. "Oh, God, please. Yes!"

She knew how he felt, for she was a part of him now, as he was a part of her. Civilization shredded into a distant memory, stripped away like cobwebs concealing a deeper, rawer, wilder world. Their needs, elemental, were all that mattered; their private universe was absolute, and it was as vast as it was small. Wrapped in sensation, stroked into a white-hot heat, their bodies melted together, re-formed into one, and then exploded, rocketing them outward, beyond the ties of the earth, past the boundaries that defined, the rules that restricted.

Again and again, for the length of that single desperate afternoon, they fought the world with their lovemaking. They went to war armed with lengthy kisses, endless embraces, some gentle, some frantic, some so tender they made her weep, some so shattering she could find no words.

Until she found the wrong ones.

"You'll leave one day."

"I have no choice."

"I can't go with you."

And the world came crashing back, breaking down the door, entering, knife in hand, to destroy.

Philip rolled away, presenting Brighid with his ramrod-stiff back as he sat on the edge of the bed, looking out the window at the slowly setting sun. "Get dressed, Brighid," he said dully. "I'll take you home."

She bit her lip, refusing to cry. "I have no home."

"So you say."

"Please, Tauwún—"

He grabbed at his deerskin shirt and flung it across the room. "Don't call me that! God damn it, Brighid, don't call me that! You want to forget for a while? Forget your responsibilities, your limitations? Well, so do I. Damn it, *so do I!*"

She opened her mouth to answer him but stopped when she heard Dominick's voice calling to Philip from the foyer. "I'll stay here," she said quickly as both of them reached for their clothing.

"Do that," Philip bit out shortly, running his hands through his hair before taking a deep breath and opening the door, telling his uncle he'd be right down.

After Philip had quickly dressed and gone downstairs, Brighid struggled with the laces and ties that had become tangled by impatient fingers even as she moved, barefoot, to the opened door to listen to the conversation taking place below her. She could hear easily, both Dominick and Philip's voices echoing in the empty house.

"She's here, isn't she?" Dominick asked, and Brighid flinched at the cold steel evident in his tone.

"You'd ask a gentleman to compromise a lady?" Philip's drawling voice was calm, nonchalant, almost joking, far removed, Brighid knew, from the tension he must be feeling.

"God's blood, Philip, I've no time for this. Bryna wants her home now. There's been another killing."

Brighid leaned closer to the door, her knees suddenly weak, then tiptoed out onto the balcony, careful to keep out of sight even as she could look down on the two men.

"Another returned captive?" Philip asked, voicing her questions for her. "Where? When?"

Dominick ran a hand through his hair, looking distracted and faintly ill. "A thirty-year-old woman in Easton, another white woman captive who'd just been returned from Fort Pitt. Raped, then strangled. And like the other victims, the woman had a cross carved into her forehead."

"Jesus! And you think—"

"Just bring Brighid home, Philip, all right? Bryna's half out of her mind with worry. Oh, and one more thing, Nephew—"

Brighid clapped her hands to her mouth as Dominick's fist shot out and Philip landed on his back on the foyer floor.

"I suppose I deserve that," Philip remarked, rubbing at his chin but making no move to rise up and strike a blow of his own.

"Sometimes it takes more than words to knock some sense into a thick head," Dominick said, putting down a hand to help his nephew to his feet. "I hope you know what you're doing, spinning daydreams where love conquers all without thought of what Brighid brings to your union, what you bring to her, what you're risking."

"Did you know what you were doing, what you were risking? Remember, Lokwelend named them both," Philip replied as he walked his uncle to the door. "The woman upstairs is Nipawi Gischuch, Dominick. The Night Fire. What would you have risked for Bryna, for the Bright Fire? What would you have given for an hour in her arms?"

Brighid saw Dominick's rueful smile. "Every penny I hold and every one I hoped to have. My life. My soul. God help you, Philip. I don't know how this will end, but your life will never be the same."

BOOK THREE

Consequences

> Badness you can get easily, in quantity:
> the road is smooth, and it lies close by.
> But in front of excellence the immortal gods
> have put sweat, and long and steep is the way to it,
> and rough at first. But when you come to the top,
> then it is easy, even though it is hard.
> —Hesiod

So little in his purse,
so much upon his back.
—Joseph Hall, bishop of Norwich

CHAPTER 10

NEW EDEN WAS RESTRICTING. PLEASANT HILL WAS STIFLING. Locked inside its four walls, let outside only with a keeper—no freer than a hound on a leash—Brighid spent the next week unconsciously making everyone else in the house as uncomfortable as a nettle jammed beneath a fingernail.

She didn't complain. She didn't rant and rave about her new confinement. She didn't even, much to Philip's surprise, attempt to sneak out into the gardens with her blankets to sleep where she could see the stars.

What she did was to sit, stoic as Lokwelend. Very still. Very quiet.

She spoke when spoken to.

She looked to Bryna at the table, to be sure to use the correct fork.

She sewed moccasins for both Philip and Dominick, then decorated them with colored beads.

She allowed Cora to even out the uneven lengths of her hair, and now wore it softly combed back from her face and secured at her nape with a wide ribbon that matched whatever gown she had chosen for the day.

And proving to everyone that they were all correct to be living in uneasy expectation of a certain explosion that would come soon, very soon, she quietly, politely, excused herself from any room Philip Crown entered.

Only in the nursery, in the long hours she spent with Daniel and Lapawin, was Brighid the least bit animated. Only at night, in her dreams, was she more confined than when awake . . .

"What are you still doing here, woman?" the horseman asked her, demanded of her nightly. *"Come with me now, or go away. Leave me in peace!"*

"My path has been chosen for me, and it ends here," she always answered him from her place in the deep grass, motioning with her hand at the objects that now surrounded her. Thimbles. Spinster caps trimmed with modest lace. An apron, rusty with dried blood. A child's toy soldier, broken and long forgotten by its owner. Her father's stiff, dried scalp. An opened book of sermons, its pages fluttering in the breeze. "Here I will stay, and grow old."

And the horseman had cursed bitterly, and ridden away, off on his own adventures. But she knew he would be back the next night, when she closed her eyes again. He was stubborn, as stubborn as she. She still did not know if she considered that certain return a blessing or yet another curse on her life. She only knew she would be devastated if he grew disgusted and did not return to hound her again and again and again. For she had been alone in her dream for much too long.

"He won't let you stay, you know," the horseman had said last night as the dream took another turn. He looked over his shoulder, into the distance, where a shadowy figure stood, knee deep in a murky swamp.

"Who is that man? Why is he in my dream? Why are you in my dream?"

The white stallion reared onto its back legs, its hooves pawing the air. "You do not know him? You should, Nipawi Gischuch. He is Death, and he is coming for you."

She looked again, and the dark man had moved nearer, so that his putrid stench, caught by the breeze, slipped insidiously into her nostrils. She dared more questions. "And you? Why can't I see your face? Are you really Tauwún?"

"I am who and what you make of me," the rider had told her, anger still in his tone, along with the hint of something softer, something very close to love. "There are many destinies, depending on the choices you make. Everything, Nipawi Gischuch, is what you make of it."

Everything is what you make of it. The words haunted Brighid, waking and sleeping. She longed to go to Lokwelend, to ask him to interpret her dream, but he had gone off alone, telling Dominick that he had "preparations to make." When Dominick had repeated this at the dinner table, he had looked pointedly at Brighid, who knew what that meant. Lokwelend was in the woods, talking with the Great One, making his sacrifices, saying his farewells to the trees and the bears and the paths he had walked as a youth. Dominick's eyes had pleaded for her to remain silent, as Bryna's love for Lokwelend would have sent her into a whirlwind of protest and denial and ended with an impassioned order to have Lokwelend found and brought to her at once so that she could argue him out of dying.

How Brighid envied her cousin. Bryna was never confused, never unsure. Her path was always the correct one, and she would brook no opposition to her plans for the correct ordering of the universe. Only with Dominick and the twins did she bend, becoming the soft, loving creature whose gentle ways never ceased to surprise Brighid when she heard her cousin say, "Yes, darling," when Dominick suggested it was time for her to lie down for a nap, time for her to leave the kitchens to Lucretia and the gardening to the estate workers.

If the petite, strong-willed Bryna had found herself a captive of the Lenape, she would have organized schooling for the children, devised a more efficient division of labor for the women, and bullied her way into a seat at the chiefs' council. Within a fortnight. And they would have loved her for it.

Instead, Brighid had bent with the prevailing wind, numbed by her losses, seeking shelter, not change, finding it easier to embrace what was left to her than to fight for anything better. But she had been happy. Hadn't she?

Yes. Yes, she had.

Until Philip Crown's face had appeared in the smoke from the cooking fire.

Until Philip Crown had strolled into her life, wearing deerskins and carrying an ebony walking stick, scattering her thoughts, bringing her to anger and more—awakening her from a five-year emotional slumber during which time she had somehow left her girlhood behind and grown into a woman she still didn't recognize or understand.

Until Tauwún had ridden into her dream on his white horse, prodding at her, yelling at her, telling her to leave him alone even as he asked her to go with him.

Until Philip Crown had gazed at her in passion, had taken her to his bed, made her look inside the frightened, displaced child who had somehow grown into a woman . . . a woman who wanted, a woman who needed, a woman who desired.

How she hated him for rousing her from the waking dream that had become her safe, comfortable, day-to-day existence. How she loved him for bringing her back to life.

How she would miss him when he was gone.

He had to leave. It had been wrong of her to use him, to hold him, to seek the promise the passion in his eyes held for her. She had needed his arms around her, needed memories of something other than death, of loss, of pain, needed something to look forward to besides the long, empty road that would eventually lead to a spinster's grave. She had wanted, if just for a little while, to know for herself what had made Johanna so content with Wulapen, so happy in the dark.

But that interlude was now over, shattered not only by the necessary realization that neither fit in the other's life, but by the silent threat of a madman. Brighid knew, as everyone knew, that Cora's attacker had to be the same man who was killing the returned captives. *God's damned.* That's how Brighid and her fellow female captives were described in the churches, by good housewives in the streets of New Eden. And now someone had taken it into his head to send these misfits all to hell.

She'd never be free. Free of the stigma. Free of her memories, even those still hidden from her. Free to choose her own path. Free to love . . .

"Bridie?"

Brighid tensed on the window seat where she had been sitting for the past hour, looking out over the grounds, contemplating her future, and seeing only the boundaries of the prison the madman had made for her, the world had made for her. "Mary Catherine?" She turned her head slowly, fearing that she had imagined her sister's voice, imagined that she had called her Bridie, as she had done a lifetime ago when they both had been young and innocent.

The child came more fully into the room, dragging her feet, her hands behind her back, her head bowed. Her wild curls had tamed somewhat over the years, the color more golden red than carrot orange, and her features were those of their brothers, Michael and Joseph: rounded cheeks, button nose, huge saucer eyes. Brighid had been the only dark-haired Cassidy child, a throwback, her father had teased, to the time the Armada had shipwrecked off the Irish coast and the survivors had been assimilated into the Irish life, welcomed into more than a few Irish beds.

Brighid didn't speak, didn't realize she was holding her breath, apprehensive of what Mary Catherine might do, what she might say, fearing her next words might even be more hurtful than those she had flung at her that first day, the only time the shy, almost reclusive child had spoken directly to her.

Mary Catherine lifted her head, her clear green eyes

shining with unshed tears as she looked at Brighid. "Cousin Philip told me what happened that terrible day. How bravely you fought. I didn't know. There was so much noise, Bridie. And then it was all so quiet. It was quiet for a long time. I was quiet for a very long time."

"I know, love," Brighid said, swinging around on the window seat so that she could put her feet on the floor. "They told me how good you were. How you kept quiet the way Mama had asked you to. How you stayed under the bed, out of sight. You did just right. Just right."

Only Mary Catherine had stayed silent too long, still obeying her mother's last request the first time Dominick Crown had come to the barn to find and bury the Cassidy family. She had stayed silent all through that first night and into the next day, when Dominick had returned to find her still tucked under the bed, wild-eyed with terror. Months later, Bryna's pleading hadn't prompted the child to speak, not her begging nor her bullying nor her steely determination. Not until Bryna had realized that Mary Catherine had been keeping her last promise to her mother. Only then had the child spoken again and at last begun to heal.

If Brighid carried scars, so did her little sister, who had spent a night and a day lying silent, staring, within five feet of the blood-stained spot where their mother's body had fallen.

Mary Catherine lifted a trembling hand to her face and wiped at her tears, roughly scrubbing them from her cheeks. "I'm going to be one of the Lord's brides one day, Bridie," she announced as simply as she might have said that, yes, please, she would like peas with her dinner. "When I'm old enough, Bryna says, I may go back to Ireland if I want and be with the holy sisters in the convent near our old village. If I'm still of the same mind, Bryna says. I will be."

Brighid eased the tip of her tongue around the edges of her dry lips. "I see. Mama would have liked that, Mary Kate, if it's truly what you want. And she'd be so very proud. If you've had the calling. But, Mary Kate, you're only ten years old. How can you know?"

Mary Catherine's smile was beatific, lighting the room. "I know, Bridie. I know. Because I've been tempted by the devil. Tempted to believe that our Lord is a harsh God, passing judgment, allowing me to use His name to pass judgments of my own. Like that man, that man who would kill you." She took several more steps forward, bringing her hands in front of her, folding them together over the rosary she held in one of them. "I was wrong, Bridie. That man is wrong. I—I love you very much, Bridie. I don't want you to die."

"I have no intention of dying, Mary Kate," Brighid told her solemnly, choosing her words with care. "I don't have your faith anymore, and I haven't been gifted with your clear vision. I don't know where my life is going or where I will end up some day. But I do know that I am not about to die because of someone else's notion of who and what I am. I make you that promise on the souls of our parents, Mary Kate. Our parents, who offered themselves up to death so bravely that their children might live."

Only then did Mary Catherine seem to be the ten-year-old child she was—a bit of the five-year-old Brighid remembered—as her face crumpled and she ran into Brighid's embrace to cry, to be held, to be comforted, to welcome her sister home.

"I don't know what I'm going to do with her," Philip said, falling into a chair in Dominick's study, a snifter of brandy all but forgotten in his right hand. "She won't talk to me; she won't even look at me." He lifted his head and glared at his uncle. "I'd give it all up for her, Dominick. I swear it. My title, Playden Court, everything. But she'd only hate me for it, saying I'd turned my back on my destiny or some such drivel."

Dominick replaced his pen in its holder and sat back in his chair, gazing levelly at his half nephew. "Are you sure she won't go back to England with you?"

Philip eyed him owlishly. "Pardon me, I don't believe I

heard that question aright. Aren't you the one who said Brighid would never be happy in England? That if we know nothing else, we have learned something from the lessons learned watching our own mothers."

"That was before I realized just how much Brighid's life is in danger here in New Eden. And," Dominick added, shaking his head, "before I knew what the two of you were doing. Bryna would have you both before a priest so fast your heads would spin if I told her. Which I won't," he added hastily as Philip opened his mouth to protest. "Brighid isn't a child, but a woman grown and already a mother. She knew what she was doing."

"We both knew what we were doing, Dominick," Philip said shortly, then took a drink from the snifter. "Or we thought we did. We were wrong." He ran a hand through his hair while searching his mind for words to ask what would seem a stupid question, no matter how he phrased it. "Dominick," he began at last, "I have a question for you, one my own checkered experience doesn't cover. What is it like to bed a virgin?"

Dominick shook his head. "Now I'm the one who must ask if I've heard aright. What is it *like?*"

"Yes, damn it, what is it like?! Aren't they skittish, shy? Don't they cry out in pain? I mean . . ." His voice and his anger faded away, leaving him feeling years too young and brick stupid.

Dominick looked at him for a long, unsettling time. "Wishful thinking, Nephew?" he asked at last, obviously seeing much more than Philip had wanted to reveal. "Or were you simply clumsy?"

Philip felt himself flushing to the roots of his hair. "Never mind. The woman's got me turned inside out, so that I don't know what I'm saying anymore."

"You may not know what you're saying, Philip," Dominick continued, "however, what you're thinking is obvious every time Brighid enters a room. I've made Bryna promise to go back to bed for another week, if only to keep her from seeing too much each time you and Brighid are together. Although she still harbors the notion that the two of you suit each other perfectly and is, I believe, secretly humoring me while she makes wedding plans. Which is probably better than having her mounting imaginary hunts for that madman who is running about, strangling returned captives."

"Raping and strangling them," Philip pointed out tightly, grateful for the change of subject, despite its morbid turn. "And carving crosses in their foreheads? I questioned Cora again yesterday about what had happened to her. She said her attacker kept muttering something about *cleansing* her. I think she was only a target because she is a Lenape dressed in English clothing. That and she was handy, walking alone in the woods the way she was. And I blame the clergy for all of it, Dominick. They keep preaching this poison about white women being taken by the Lenape as punishment for their sins. How *unclean* they are. It was bad enough when that bitch spit on Brighid. Now we've got some misguided idiot roaming the countryside, killing these poor women and thinking, I suppose, that raping them first cleanses their bodies, or some such drivel, before he gives their souls back to God by killing them. Isn't that wonderful, Dominick— and positively gothic? The wrath of God right here in New Eden. It makes me sick!"

"You've given this a lot of thought, haven't you, Philip?" Dominick asked, and Philip took another drink, the brandy sour in his mouth.

"You had to understand Renton Frey before you hunted him down five years ago. Before you killed him for what he'd done to the Lenape, what he had threatened with Bryna. What did Lokwelend teach you? Know your enemy. Understand his strengths and weaknesses. And have no weaknesses of your own."

Dominick stood up and went to the window, standing with his back to the room, looking out over the gardens. "I had a weakness, Philip. My love for Bryna. Concern for her kept me from acting until it was almost too late—until it *was* too late for the people who died in the raids Frey provoked. That same love finally made me reckless, and I acted like a raw youth out for vengeance."

He turned to look at Philip once more. "But I'm still glad I killed him. I'm still glad he's dead. I understand what you're feeling, what you want to do. Right now, your greatest weakness lies inside yourself and inside Brighid. Until the two of you have fought and tamed your own demons, it would be foolish to believe that you're sufficiently armed to go hunting for this madman."

Philip leaned forward and very carefully placed the empty snifter on his uncle's desk, knowing that, otherwise, he would fling the thing at the wall. "What do you want me to do, Dominick? Stay here all day, guarding a woman who already has a half-dozen guards? Sit at the table with a woman who won't look at me? Sleep under the same roof as the woman who was in my bed only a week ago and not go to her, not touch her? Christ, Dominick, I'm going out of my mind!"

"She's trying to protect you," Dominick explained, coming across the room to sit himself down on a corner of the desk.

"Protect me? Protect me from what? From the killer?"

"No, from yourself, I'd imagine, and, just as you've already said, from any misguided notions you might have about staying here and giving up your title or trying to take her back to Sussex with you, knowing that Daniel's presence and her history would have the gossips slicing your name to ribbons."

Philip's laugh was hollow. "And that's where you're wrong, Dominick. We've touched on this before, and I've been giving it a good deal of thought over the past week without coming up with any answers. So why don't you tell me why, Dominick. Give me a reason I haven't considered and discarded by myself. Tell me why I should worry about protecting my *name.* The great Crown name? Or maybe you're thinking about the so circumspect Crowns themselves? And who, pray tell, would they be? The widowed grandfather who married an Irish heiress to replenish his coffers, then kept her locked up at Playden Court, delighting in telling the *ton* that she was mad? The father who cold-bloodedly married the daughter of the moneylender he owed a small fortune to in order to stay out of the Fleet? Or me, the half-Jewish heir, whose beautiful sister amuses herself whoring her body all over London? Would you be talking about those Crowns, Dominick? Would Brighid be worried about those Crowns? Dear God, yes—they could barely survive another blotch on their so pristine escutcheon."

"Have you told any of this to Brighid?" Dominick asked, going to the drinks table and pouring himself a glass of wine, so that Philip regretted his hasty speech and how it must have hurt his half uncle, who had loved his Irish mother very much.

"No," Philip said, rising as Lucas knocked on the door, then entered to stand silently, waiting for an invitation to speak. "Only you and I have discussed it and mostly from the standpoint that bringing yet another rather unconventional bride to Playden Court, to London's ballrooms, might be disastrous for the bride, not for us. And I've figured out that I don't give a tinker's damn about any of it. All I want is Brighid. Everything else will just have to be worked out later."

Philip then whirled around to face the butler. *"What?* Lucas, stop wringing your hands as if the world will end any moment. What in hell is the matter, man?"

Lucas Deems looked from one Crown to the other, then swallowed down hard as if what he was about to say was sticking in his craw and he had to fight his way around it in order to speak. "It's him, my lords," he said at last, tears standing in his eyes. "It's the marquess."

"He's dead?" Philip asked, believing Lucas had brought in the mail pouch and then taken some liberty with a missive that had arrived from Sussex. But that didn't make sense. For one, Lucas was the perfect servant and respected his employer's privacy. For another, if Philip's father was dead, Lucas Deems wouldn't be crying. He'd be dancing a jig.

"No, more's the pity," Lucas grumbled just loud enough to be heard, then seemed to remember that he was a proper English butler. Pulling himself up stiffly, he announced: "The marquess of Playden, my lords, along with his daughter, Lady Lilith, await your pleasure in the foyer."

Brighid was already in the upstairs hallway, safely hidden behind the turn in the stairs, able to lean forward a smidgen and peer through the balustrades. She remained where she was, out of sight, preferring to listen, to watch, without being seen.

Her bedchamber was located at the front of the house, so that she had heard wheels crunching on the gravel drive and gone to the window in time to see a large black traveling coach pulling up at the front door. Pushing back the curtains, she had watched, only mildly interested, as the coachman hopped down from the box, opened the door, and pulled down the steps so that whoever was inside could negotiate the distance between coach and drive without the inelegant necessity of having to make a jump for it.

Brighid hadn't seen a coach like this since the Cassidy family disembarked in Philadelphia so many years ago, and she wondered if this particular coach had made the long journey to Pleasant Hill from that great distance. She noted the amount of baggage strapped both to the boot and the roof and supposed that, whoever was inside, they planned a prolonged stay, which—knowing her cousin and her love of company—would probably cheer Bryna no end.

But from the moment the bottom half of an ornate bamboo cane had become visible, then was employed to give the strapping young coachman a smart rap across his bent back, presumably for not moving quickly enough to suit his passenger, Brighid's total interest was caught and held. The cane had been closely followed by the emergence of a single male leg clad in a highly polished, buckled shoe;

ivory clocked stockings; and robin's egg blue satin breeches banded just at the knee.

While Brighid was trying to assimilate all of this outlandish splendor, the passenger had managed to extricate his exquisite self completely from the cavernous interior of the coach, to stand on the drive, his tricorn hat tucked beneath one arm, his right hand lifted to his face, delicately patting at his upper lip with the lace-edged handkerchief he held clutched in his beringed paw. Yet, dazzled as she was by the man's foaming lace jabot, the patches on his thin cheeks, the twin circles of rouge that rendered him a near clown, the elaborate full-bottomed wig, the pale blue, large-cuffed jacket, she could not fail to recognize the resemblance between this London exquisite and her own Philip Crown.

The man was as tall as Philip, carried himself with much the same though highly exaggerated grace, had the same fine aristocratic nose.

Which set him very much in contrast to the young woman who extended her hand to the coachman when the exquisite failed to assist her. She ignored the drawn-down steps in order to lightly hop to the ground, grabbing onto the man's other arm as well for balance and giving the coachman a tongue-swallowing glimpse of her high, outrageously exposed breasts before she lifted her hands and "settled" her obvious pride and joy back where they belonged.

There wasn't much Brighid could discern about the woman other than that her hair was full, high, and generously powdered and that her deep rose gown was full and low cut and made of the finest silk. She stayed on the drive even after the man had ascended the stairs and disappeared from view, looking up at the house with a highly amused smile on her breathtakingly lovely face, then snapped open a fan and allowed the coachman to escort her.

Before the pair disappeared beneath the portico, Brighid saw the young woman reach behind the coachman and give his buttocks a pinch.

Sure that their guests were the marquess of Playden and

his daughter, Lady Lilith Crown—for no man would treat his mistress so cavalierly—Brighid had then raced to her mirror, patted at her hair, and smoothed her gown before realizing that she was behaving more like Brighid Cassidy than the Night Fire, and then hastened out into the hallway to skid to a stop at the railing, hunker down onto her knees, and watch the show.

Bryna had given her some information about Philip's family, explaining that Dominick's father had been married twice, Dominick being the child of the second union, with his older half brother, Giles, being the heir. It was Giles who had brought disgrace to the family, not by marrying for money, but by marrying a Jewess for her cent-percenter father's money.

If Philip had been born first, according to Bryna, there would have been no second visit to the marriage bed. But Lilith had been the firstborn, and by the time Philip had appeared, Giles's unhappy wife had discovered the lovely escape to be found in the bottom of a bottle of gin. Both children had been raised by a succession of governesses and tutors, their father off in the fleshpots of London, their mother secluded in her rooms, drunk, and surrounded by fat orange cats. Philip, Bryna had explained, hadn't so much left home to see the world the moment he'd gained his majority as he had run away, hoping to escape the world he lived in.

All this, Brighid had decided in this past week, only reinforced her belief that the last thing Philip Crown, heir to the marquess of Playden, needed was an unsuitable wife. He had enough on his plate as it was without the Lenape whore and her half-breed son.

And now his father had come to Pleasant Hill, the home Philip had run to, the family he had adopted as his own. Why? And for the love of heaven—why now?

Below her, barely within her sight, the new arrivals stood in the foyer, unattended by Lucas, who was probably even now notifying Dominick of his visitors.

"It's rather lovely in a bucolic sort of way, don't you

154

think?" Lady Lilith drawled, looking up at the chandelier, so that Brighid quickly shrank back behind the wall. "I had no idea Uncle Dominick was faring so well. In fact, dear Papa, I can almost hear you grinding your teeth at your much younger brother's good fortune. So at variance with your own decades-long run of bad luck."

"I should have followed my instincts and drowned you in a bucket the day you were born," the marquess of Playden remarked almost affably, and Brighid leaned forward once more in time to see the man's painted features extend themselves into a similarly artificial smile as he held out his manicured hand, nearly covered by a full yard of dripping lace, and cooed, "My son! My son! How it warms my heart to see you again. Aren't you dashing in those animal skins. So very, um, *colonial*. And Dominick, good brother! I could weep with joy at this long-anticipated reunion. Lilith! Don't dawdle, child. Go kiss your brother and uncle."

"Stay where you are, Lilith, if you please," Philip ordered coldly as he entered the foyer, his blond head visible now beneath the chandelier. "Father? What in bloody hell are you doing here? And a better question: What will it take to have you leave again?"

Brighid watched, fascinated, as Giles Crown's faded blue eyes came alive with malice. "Still the angry young cub, I see," he bit out, then turned his attention to Dominick, who was standing out of her line of sight. "Tongue still cleaved to the roof of your mouth, Brother Gollumpus? How droll. The years pass but little changes. Will you welcome me, do you think—*if* you think—or will you wait until my back is turned, then strike me from behind. Old habits die hard, they say."

"Oh, if that isn't above everything wonderful," Lady Lilith said, rolling her exotic black eyes. "Cross an ocean, spend a week on the road sleeping on damp sheets and choking down the most inedible food and then insult your only hope of having a roof over our heads tonight. May I kneel at your feet, dear sire, to listen to and learn more of your infinite wisdom?"

"You've enough daylight to make it back to New Eden without difficulty. I'll give you a written message to my man, Harold, and you may have use of two bedchambers and a private dining room at my inn," Dominick said at last. "Philip can visit with you there tomorrow if he so chooses."

"Nonsense!" Bryna declared loudly from just behind Brighid, giving the younger woman a start, for she hadn't known her cousin could move so silently. She looked up as Bryna brushed past her, sailing down the sweeping staircase in her burgundy dressing gown, looking as regal as any queen. "Dominick Crown, would you have me branded a poor hostess?" she continued as she approached her "guests," extending her hand for the marquess's kiss. "Please excuse my tardiness, but I have just now been apprised of your arrival. I do believe a second coach has only now arrived, carrying your personal servants? Yes, yes, how lovely. Dominick, have Lucas prepare rooms for the marquess and your niece."

"Gracious lady," Giles drawled as Bryna tugged her hand free of the man's grasp, "I am in your debt."

"Yes," Bryna answered, her tone suddenly as cold as a viper's heart, and Brighid put a hand over her own mouth to keep from betraying her presence by laughing out loud. "Yes, my lord, you most certainly are in my debt." She slipped into a broad Irish brogue, obviously employed for effect, just as Brighid was prone to do. "And if you'd be thinking to forget that fact for a moment, if you'd be planning to upset me or mine in the slightest, it will delight me no end to have the pair of you pretty, painted posturers tossed out on your ears."

While Giles glared and Lilith tittered behind her fan, Bryna drew herself up to her not very impressive height and continued: "For now, I want you here, as I'm not allowed to travel into New Eden in my somewhat delicate condition, and refuse to miss a moment of what already appears to have all the makings of a most splendid farce." She turned to smile blightingly at her husband. "Dominick, my love? I have your approval?"

"It doesn't appear as if you need it, but yes, you have my approval. Philip?"

Brighid's pride in her cousin's mettle as well as her delighted smile faded as she watched Philip brush past his father without a word and slam out the front door, clearly in a high temper.

> *Time will explain it all.*
> *— Euripides*

CHAPTER 11

BRIGHID SAT IN THE DRAWING ROOM AT PLEASANT HILL AS THE
setting sun glinted off the windows, her hands demurely
folded in her lap, watching, deliberately attempting to keep
herself invisible, uninteresting, not worthy of attention—or
investigation. For Bryna had been correct; the visit of the
marquess of Playden and his daughter to Pleasant Hill held
all the makings of a splendid farce. Or a melodrama, better
to watch from the wings rather than to be dragged onto the
stage to participate.

Philip, who would have seemed by his earlier behavior to
be perfectly cast as the angry, sulking scion of this strange
troupe of players, appeared to have been improved by his
absence from the house these past four hours. Because he
was *not* the same Philip Crown who had grown to his
majority at Playden Court, obviously both ashamed of and
confused by his strange sire. He was a man now, seasoned
by life, and he must have remembered that fact after his

first, furious reaction to his father's unexpected and definitely unwelcome arrival. It was Philip, Brighid saw with some satisfaction, who shone in the Crown drawing room tonight and his father who faded into the woodwork, old and defeated, weak and pathetic in his heavy-handed sarcasm that could not override the fear in his eyes.

Brighid was proud of Philip as he sat beside Bryna, looking almost unbearably handsome in his custom-tailored satins, his blond hair tied back severely in a queue, his eyelids at half-mast as he smiled, listening to his sister's brilliantly cutting recitation of the latest *ton* gossip. Oh, yes. Philip was his own man now. She was glad he knew it.

Lady Lilith's easy mention of titled lords and ladies, her well-drawn verbal caricatures of their failings, petty triumphs, and amusing peccadilloes—all delivered with accompanying facial grimaces and arch smiles—had long since reduced Bryna to searching for her handkerchief to wipe tears of mirth from her eyes, and even Brighid had been hard-pressed to hold back a giggle as Lady Lilith finished her story about the duke of Norfolk, called the Jockey of Norfolk by his cronies.

"Philip, you also know how prodigiously *fat* our poor Jockey is," Lady Lilith said before taking another healthy sip of sherry. "And how very badly he stinks? Why, the only time the servants can wash him is when he gets so drunk as to be insensible, so that his man can strip his body and give him a good scrub. Well, the way I heard it, one day Jockey was at his club, complaining to all who would listen, lamenting his terrible rheumatism and his fear of ever finding a cure for his malady. So some wit—I never did learn who—cheekily shouted out from the back of the room: 'Pray, my lord, did you ever try a *clean shirt?*'"

As the beautiful woman—for as lovely as Lady Lilith was, she was also a full year older than Philip, closer to thirty than twenty, and no shy, retiring girl—launched into another story centering on a certain "Lady H" and her scandalous liaison with her second footman, Brighid turned her attention to the marquess of Playden. He was standing before the fireplace, one elbow propped on the mantel, a glass of port dangling from his fingertips, looking over the exquisitely decorated room with the coolly measuring eye of a racetrack tout. But still, behind the painted sophistication, Brighid could smell the man's desperation.

The resemblance between Philip and his father was unmistakable, unable to be ignored or denied. The same blue eyes and finely drawn sable brows. The same high-bridged, straight nose. The same tall, broad-shouldered frame.

But there the similarities ended, for the older man wore his age—and his failings—on his once handsome face for all to see. Clearly the marquess had led a most dissolute life, his handsomeness no match for the lines around his eyes, the pouches beneath them. The corners of his mouth dipped toward his chin, as if a lifetime of sophisticated sneering had weighed them down, carving deep slashes on either side of his lips, his nose.

Most pathetic was the fight the man was waging against his age and his past, a battle fought with paltry weapons of powder and rouge and patches. His skin was unnaturally pale, both from the powder and, Brighid suspected, small doses of arsenic Bryna told her she had read many *ton* exquisites used to whiten their skin. His full white wig did nothing to bring a hint of healthfulness to his face, and his blond satin evening clothes only drained him more, so that he appeared as if shrouded by morning mist or a damp fog.

Only his lips and cheeks had color, accented by the burgundy patches on his face. The single other contrast was the black taffeta affair called a Solitaire, a ribbon that he wore tied to his wig in a bow at the back, the ends brought to the front over his white cravat and tied in yet a second bow under his chin. The whole thing was so confining the marquess had to move his head and upper body all together or not at all. And when he did move, although his form seemed thin enough, Brighid could hear the telltale creaking of a whalebone corset.

Brighid felt some pity for the man, only thirteen years the

senior of his half brother, Dominick—according to what Bryna had told her earlier—yet looking old enough to be his father. There was positively no familial resemblance between the two men other than their aristocratic noses, which must be a distinguishing Crown characteristic, and likewise no familial affection between them if their earlier conversation in the foyer was any indication.

No, there was little love lost between father and son, brother and brother, which seemed sad to Brighid, who had so little family of her own left to her. Very sad.

Brighid wondered where Dominick was now, for Lucas would be calling them all in to dinner shortly and it wasn't like her cousin's husband to be tardy. Almost before she could complete the thought, Dominick walked into the room, looking most splendid in his own evening clothes. He greeted the ladies, acknowledged his half brother with a curt nod, and asked Philip to join him in his study.

Bryna was instantly on the alert, as was Brighid. "Is something wrong, Dominick?" Bryna asked, struggling to rise from the couch, her new bulk making the maneuver somewhat difficult. "You look upset."

"Mayhap one of his pigs died," the marquess drawled, then finished his drink in a single swallow. "God, Dominick, you call that a cravat? You have been gone from London too long. Not that you ever fit there either," he ended almost under his breath as he made another trip to the drinks table, his third in the past twenty minutes.

"Now, Papa, if you drink your dinner, you'll end by falling facedown in the pudding," Lady Lilith crooned sweetly as she extracted a small gilt-edged folding mirror from her reticule and smiled at her reflection. "Again," she added, throwing a wink at Brighid, who was caught between revulsion and a grudging respect for this woman who held her unlovable father in such open contempt.

"While you'd skip dinner entirely to go tip yourself over on your back in the stables in the desperate hope one of the grooms is as well hung as the horses he tends," the marquess bit out coldly. Then, as Lady Lilith clicked the mirror shut, he smiled evilly. "As usual."

Philip stood up, looking from his father to his sister, clearly torn between slapping them both silly and wondering if they'd just go away if he snapped his fingers and wished hard enough for a miracle. "Ladies, if you'll excuse us? Dominick?" he said at last, turning to follow his uncle out of the room.

Bryna subsided onto the couch once more, obviously knowing her duty lay with entertaining her guests. "Brighid?" she inquired sweetly, giving her cousin a look that Brighid could have read in the dark. "Would you be a dear and fetch my shawl? I feel a chill in the air, which is not the least unusual, considering that Dominick persists in leaving windows open throughout the downstairs until after dark. Oh, the shawl is not in my bedchamber actually. I believe I left it in the morning room."

"Of course, Bryna," Brighid answered, already on her way out of the room, headed for the morning room and the door that led out into the gardens. If she hurried, she could be outside Dominick's open window in the study before she missed a single word of what he had to say to Philip.

"Thanks for rescuing me, Dominick," Philip said, subsiding into a chair in the study, sliding down to sit on the bottom of his spine, his legs flung out straight in front of him. "I apologize yet again for their presence. Lilith's amusing enough if she'd only cover her bosom, but my father draws all the air out of a room. God, did you see that rouge on his cheeks? It's pathetic! Just when I think he can't get any worse—"

"I've only a few moments ago received a visit from Elijah Kester, Philip," Dominick interrupted sharply. "Some children found poor Silky Wattson's body this afternoon in that stand of trees behind the gaolhouse. It appears she took one too many walks into the woods for the price of a dram."

Philip leaped to his feet in one abrupt movement, his senses immediately alert, his sister and father forgotten. "Raped?"

Dominick nodded. "But our madman progresses. This

time the cross was carved into his victim's chest. Deeply—
all the way to her heart, which is missing, in case you were
about to ask. And Elijah thinks she was still alive when the
bloody bastard did it, in much the same way as the Lenape
dispatched Jonah Newton if you'll remember. Her hands
and legs were bound, a rag stuffed in her mouth to keep her
silent. Elijah says her eyes were still open and full of the
agonies of the damned. He's not a particularly eloquent
man, Elijah, but this shook him badly."

"Sweet Jesus," Philip breathed, sitting down once more.

"Elijah also says they now believe the killer to be a
Lenape because of the brutality of the murder, I suppose,
and he wanted to know where Lokwelend was last night,"
Dominick ended, pouring them both a glass of wine.

"You told him that's bunk, I imagine," Philip said,
dragging his hands through his hair, forgetting that he was
dressed as a gentleman this evening as he tried to block out
a mental picture of Brighid lying in the dirt, her body
soaked in her own blood, her beautiful aquamarine eyes
open and staring. "Dominick?" he asked, looking up at his
uncle when the man didn't answer. "You did tell them,
didn't you?"

Dominick handed him a glass. "Of course I did," he said
shortly, downing his own wine. "I also reminded him that
Cora was attacked. That seemed to satisfy him, although I
don't know about the rest of the citizens of New Eden. It
has been five years since the last raid, but memories run
deep. And Brighid's return to the area, hers and Hallie's,
have ripped the scabs from more than one old heartache. Or
did you forget that Eunice Wright's sister died in that raid?
Her and more than twenty others. The thought of a white
man committing these murders upset them, but if they
could point to a Lenape as the killer—well, that would be
acceptable in some twisted way. Elijah told me a few of the
men are already saying it isn't a cross that's been carved on
the bodies, but some heathen Lenape symbol. Ignorant
fools!"

Philip put down his glass, its contents untouched, and

began to pace the length of the carpet. "I've got to get her away from New Eden, Dominick, from the colony, maybe even out of the country."

"She won't leave. Like her cousin, Brighid isn't the sort to run away. Although her enforced confinement here at Pleasant Hill, with all of us watching her like hawks, is killing her by inches."

"Then I'll change her mind. She can't stay here," Philip said, already mentally juggling all his obligations: the nearly completed estate, the unexpected arrival of his father and sister, how he would transport an unwilling Brighid, a young child, and an old Lenape woman across the ocean.

"And what about Lokwelend? Can you really want to leave him? He says he's dying, you know."

Philip's eyes were bleak when he turned them on Dominick. "I know. It's impossible for me to leave him now," he said quietly, the sudden pain in his chest nearly robbing him of his breath. "My father is dying, whereas that painted mummer posing in your drawing room will probably live another twenty years. I——" He broke off, believing he saw movement beyond his uncle's shoulder, outside the window, a flash of yellow the shade of Brighid's gown.

He put a finger to his lips as he stepped past his uncle and pressed himself against the wall so that he could peek outside without being seen. Then he walked back to the center of the room. "We'll talk about this later, Dominick, when I've had time to think. For now, we'd better go rescue Brighid and your wife before Giles tries to seduce them or Lilith regales them with the story of her bare-breasted ride through the park with the earl of Beresford at the reins of his sporting carriage."

Dominick sliced a quick look toward the gardens, then voiced his agreement with Philip's plan, the two men leaving the study together only for Philip to turn back, moving as quietly as possible, heading for the door that led outside. He then pulled the door open quickly, stepped out, and grinned down at Brighid, who was tiptoeing past the door.

"Lovely evening for eavesdropping, don't you think?" he fairly cooed, then neatly sidestepped the kick she'd aimed at his shins and grabbed at her arm, dragging her into the gardens with him, not coming to a halt until they were halfway down the long hill, well out of sight of the house.

"Stop, you fool!" Brighid commanded, tugging away from him, trying to loosen his grip on her arm. "I'm coming out of my shoes. And the grass is wet, which will ruin the hem of my gown."

Philip smiled, his eyes feasting on her, taking in her flushed cheeks, her rapidly rising and falling bosom so beautifully framed by the ivory lace on her bodice. "Now there's something I once despaired of ever hearing: Brighid Cassidy concerned for her pretty gown. And you look truly lovely again tonight, Brighid, as usual. Domesticated if not tamed."

She tugged against him one more time, and this time he let her go. "Flattered as I am by your words, Philip, they are not the ones I want to hear right now," she said, showing him that the week of behaving herself, of avoiding him, had definitely come to an end.

Philip instantly sobered. "How much did you hear?"

"Enough," she answered tightly, avoiding his eyes. "We're going to have to find this monster, Philip. Find him and put him down the way Wulapen put down a mad dog that wandered into our village."

"*We* don't have to do anything of the sort," he countered, taking hold of her hands and bringing them to his lips, unable to be with her and not touch her. "*You* have to stay here, where you're safe. *I* will put down the mad dog."

She shook her head so that her curls, which he knew to be warm to the touch, danced on her bare shoulders. She could be any English or Irish maiden now, although much more beautiful than most—made even more beautiful by the clear intelligence that showed in her aquamarine eyes, the hint of excitement, and the promise of passion that elevated her far beyond any woman he'd met, ever hoped to meet. "You won't find him on your own, Philip, because he isn't looking for you. He's looking for me, for Hallie. Only a fool goes fishing without first baiting his hook."

"Oh, good, good," Philip said, shaking his head in the hope of warding off the sudden slam of temper that made him want to shake *her* instead. "More Lenape wisdom, no doubt. So what is it you're suggesting, Brighid—that I use you as bait? Use you as I would a few enticing kernels of sweet yellow corn on a hook? Stake you out in the middle of a meadow as I would a bleating goat, hoping to attract a hungry bear?"

Her smile dazzled him. "You are a fast learner, Tauwún," she said, stepping closer to him, laying a hand on his chest, her fingers playing with the lace of his jabot, her scent teasing with his power to concentrate. "I suggest we begin with another trip to New Eden tomorrow. Bryna tells me there are some lovely ribbons at her store that I might like to see. Strange as it might seem, I am beginning to very much enjoy English clothes. I especially like the way you look at me when I'm dressed in them."

Philip closed his eyes, laughing silently, amazed once again with the woman who could hear anything as horrific as the details of Silky Wattson's barbaric death and not have run screaming into the night. Or fainted dead away. "Take you into New Eden with a madman on the loose? Not on your life, Brighid. Not on your life. It's insane."

"Not half as insane as locking me up here at Pleasant Hill for however long it takes to capture an animal who won't rest until he's killed every female captive that's been returned to the area. Bryna says there must be at least twenty of us spread from here to Lancaster. He's *here* now, Philip, right here in New Eden. We have to give him a reason to linger. Seeing me in New Eden, with Daniel in my arms, should be more than enough to keep him close."

"There has to be another way," Philip persisted, unwilling to see the logic in Brighid's plan, one she must have been considering all of this past week.

"And what would that be, Philip? I can't leave here, and

neither can you. Not now. Not with your father and sister here. Not with Lokwelend preparing to leave us. Who will carry him to Pematalli's side with the ceremony he deserves? Who will help Cora say the Lenape words over him as Lapawin wails and laments, proving his greatness, showing our great despair at his loss? Who will bring food to the grave for the next weeks until our grandfather has safely passed on to his greatest happiness? We cannot allow Cora to do all of this herself. Lokwelend has need of his son, his granddaughter, and I will not abandon him, as you will not abandon him. We must settle this business with the madman, the monster walking among us, so that Lokwelend's heart is not troubled and he may leave us with peace in his heart."

Philip stepped away from her, spreading his hands impotently. "Just when I think I'm making progress, just when I begin to believe you truly want to recapture your life as it was before you were taken, you turn into a Lenape on me again, going all stiff and formal and damn near cryptic. I'm forever off balance, Brighid, never knowing who you are, what it is you want."

"I can't be who I was born, and I can't forget who I've been these past five years. I want to find a way to take the two halves of me, Philip, and make them into a new whole, a whole I can live with, that Daniel can live with. But it's hard, Philip, when the only time I feel the least bit whole is when I'm lying with you."

He drew her fully into his arms, pressing her head against his chest, resting his chin on her hair, not wanting her passion right now as much as he just wanted to feel her, close, warm, safe within his grasp. "Always so honest, thank God. Christ, Brighid, but I've missed you. Missed you in my arms. We seem to go from one complication to another, don't we?" he asked, staring out over the gardens, watching dusk slowly turning to a velvet, moonlit night.

"The madman is a problem, Philip, yes," she said, snuggling against him. "But your father is more than that.

For good or ill, he has helped to shape your life, and I believe I have to understand him in order to know you better. Will you please tell me about him?"

Philip kissed her hair, then led her to a nearby bench and sat down beside her. "I wouldn't know where to begin," he said, smiling ruefully as he dredged up a mental picture of how his father had appeared tonight in the drawing room. "He's the part of *my* life, my history, that you've never seen, Brighid. You're not the only one trying to make a new whole out of two very disparate halves."

"Then let's begin slowly at the beginning the way you let me begin by taking me back to the barn." Brighid picked up his hand and laid it against her cheek for a moment before pressing a kiss into his palm. "I'd like to know why Dominick, that calm, steady man who is able to control my nearly uncontrollable cousin with ease, seems at a complete loss in dealing with his own half brother. There's something hanging between them, some unfinished business. I'm sure of it."

Philip grimaced. "You're right. I would have to start at the beginning for you to understand fully, begin with my grandfather," he said at last, knowing it was more than time for explanations if Brighid was to ever learn about the Crowns, about how he had come to be in New Eden at all. Only then could she make a decision as to whether he, the man who truly loved her, could figure in the future she wanted so desperately to build for Daniel and herself.

"You probably already know that Dominick and Giles—my esteemed father—are half brothers," he began, looking at her while she nodded. "Giles was already in his teens when his mother died and my grandfather married again, both for the money his Irish bride would bring him and to further solidify the Crown line. An heir and a spare, as it's said, especially since Giles was sickly as a child. Giles hated Dominick from the beginning—strong, sturdy Dominick—who quickly grew to be worlds better at sports, was loved by the servants, had a natural talent for riding, fencing, whatever the challenge. But for all his baiting of him, I understand that Dominick never defended himself until the day Giles insulted Dominick's mother in his presence. Then it took three footmen to pry him off my father. Giles never forgave him for that."

"Bryna says Dominick is like the dog we had long ago in county Clare," Brighid commented quietly. "He had a huge heart. He allowed us children to ride him like a pony and was as sweet and docile as could be until some of the village boys cornered my brothers. Never heard a bark out of that dog, someone told Da. He just bit."

Philip's mind filled with the memory of how Dominick had reacted when Bryna's life had been threatened. "You're right, Brighid. Dominick's just like that dog. But Giles saw him as being stupid, slow, and not worthy of the Crown name. Once Giles had married at eighteen—bracketing himself to the daughter of a Jewish moneylender from London in order to cancel his debts—even my grandfather began to see Dominick as superfluous. He was taken out of school completely by the time he was halfway through his teens, made to work on the estate, and treated with outward contempt. A clumsy Irish gollumpus, Giles is fond of saying."

"Yes," Brighid said. "I heard him say that today in the foyer." When Philip looked at her in surprise, she tilted her chin and continued firmly, "I'm sometimes better at eavesdropping than I was this evening."

Philip smiled, shaking his head. "It was your gown, Brighid. Deerskins are much better suited to eavesdropping. Never wear bright yellow when skulking around in the gardens. But to continue—Giles wasn't happy in his marriage, if you don't mind some understatement, and even less happy that Lilith was born first. His father-in-law, a crafty man, held most of my mother's funds in reserve until I was born, as his greatest desire was to see a half-Jewish peer of the realm. I never met with him above a few times when I went to London on my own, as my mother had long since decided that the only person she hated worse than the Crowns—Lilith and I included—was her father, who had only hoped to launch his daughter in society. I regret not getting to know him better, for he was a fine man in his own way and I'm proud to have his blood in my veins if only to hopefully dilute some of the Crown meanness."

Brighid rested her head against his shoulder, and he took a deep breath, then went on.

"In the end, he willed all of his rather immense fortune directly to me, with small stipends for my mother and sister. I believe he'd hoped I'd cut quite a dash in society, the way Giles had done until his marriage. His father-in-law, you understand, kept him on a very short leash after the marriage, doling out funds piecemeal rather than letting him have and most probably gamble away all his money at once. Giles still spends his life waiting for his quarterly allowance, then making mad dashes to London that always end in more debt and a return to Playden Court."

It was difficult to continue, as the story did not get prettier. "It was, I understand, a particularly bad run of luck at the tables that sent him back to Playden Court about a dozen years ago. Both Dominick's mother and mine were in residence—Dominick's mother branded as mad by my grandfather and my mother locked in her rooms, lost in drink, as she has been since my birth. Lilith, who had to have been only fifteen by that time, had just been told there'd be no come-out in London for her, and she'd run off with one of the grooms, believing she could make a fine living on the stage. She was back within a fortnight, ruined, and has been doing her best to continue ruining herself ever since, although her taste now runs to bedding wealthy peers, who reward her with jewels such as those hanging around her neck tonight. Playden Court has not treated its women well, Brighid."

He fell silent again, remembering his discussions with Dominick, remembering how the fate of the Crown women—along with his own experiences in society as a half-Jewish peer—had been one of the reasons taking Brighid to England had seemed such a distant hope, one that could easily end with her unhappiness. But neither Dominick's mother, his own mother, nor his sister had been loved. Brighid was loved. He, Philip, would never allow anything to happen to her, would never allow anyone either inside or outside the family to hurt her. Never!

"Dominick was already all but running the estate at not quite twenty-one," he went on at last, "while my Crown grandfather nursed his gout, so that Giles was left to amuse himself as best he could until his next quarter's allowance arrived from London. It wasn't a happy household.

"Anyway, Giles discovered some amusement at last in the form of harassing Polly Rosebud, Dominick's mother's personal maid, who was betrothed to our butler, Deems— our own Lucas Deems." Philip rubbed at the back of his neck, avoiding Brighid's interested gaze, trying to find some more delicate way of saying what he had to tell her now. "One morning Polly was found in the attic rooms she was preparing for Lucas and herself after their marriage. She had most obviously been assaulted—and she had hanged herself rather than face Lucas with what she must have seen as her disgrace."

He closed his eyes at Brighid's sharply indrawn breath. "Oh, poor Lucas," she said sorrowfully. "I didn't know. No wonder he's under Cora's feet these last weeks every time she turns around. He must be terrified for her."

"Yes. Yes, I suppose he is," Philip said, then pushed on with his story. "Giles accused Dominick of the attack on Polly and our grandfather backed him, threatening to destroy his second son, publicly disown him, throw him off Crown land or some such thing—perhaps even find a way to have him arrested. Dominick was set to leave England under a cloud so that his mother could be spared any more heartache, when he balked and decided to confront Giles with his suspicions. Giles admitted to *seducing* Polly, as he saw the thing, and Dominick hit him. He hit him hard, and Giles went down, striking his head on the hearth. Everything happened quickly after that: my grandfather calling

Dominick a murderer as Giles lay there senseless, Dominick's quick departure for the colonies on the next tide, obeying his mother's plea that he outrun the hangman.

"It was nearly two years later before Dominick found out that Giles's head was harder than anyone had supposed, but by then he had settled here in New Eden and decided he'd had enough of England, enough of being Lord Dominick. He built this house for his mother, hoping she'd join him, but she died before he could talk her into the journey. She was Irish, remember, and devoutly Catholic, and felt she couldn't desert her marriage vows, no matter how hollow they were."

He took Brighid's hand in his. "If it hadn't been for Bryna, I don't know if Dominick would have survived when I came here five years ago and told him about his mother's death."

"And you came here to see your uncle—or to escape your father?" Brighid asked quietly, and he knew yet again that she saw more, much more, than any woman he'd ever met.

"My mother's father died within two months of my reaching my majority, leaving me his fortune and guaranteeing that Giles would hound me hourly for funds. He was the marquess in all but name by then, as my grandfather was growing weaker by the day. Giles was systematically running Playden Court further into debt, stripping the very walls of the estate to finance his townhouse in London, his nightly trips to the gaming hells. I couldn't stay there and watch, so I came here, for I'd always admired Dominick, admired him more for having the good sense to leave Playden Court—much as he loved it, much as I love it."

He hesitated for a moment, reliving that earlier time. "I arrived here in time to kill Lokwelend's son. After that, I drifted about for a few years, touring the colonies, learning about new farming practices, returning to Playden Court for a while, then running back here, where my true family waited."

He pulled Brighid closer, slipping an arm around her shoulders. "And I returned just in time to travel to Fort Pitt and find you. In a strange, convoluted way, Giles and my grandfather were responsible for both Dominick's and my happiness."

"And your unhappiness," Brighid said, sighing. "And the English call the Lenape savages. You can only be grateful, Tauwún, that you finally found your real father, one who truly loves and needs you. You can't desert him now."

Philip pulled slightly away from her to smile down in her face. "Lenape squaw or Irish miss—you certainly know where to aim your knife, don't you, Brighid? No, I can't leave Lokwelend, much as I want to take you and Daniel and leave the colonies on the next ship departing for England. Although a heavy purse will probably be enough to rid Pleasant Hill of Giles and my sister, which would be one problem solved."

"Which brings us full circle," she pointed out, rising from the bench and smoothing down her gown. "We have to find this madman, Philip. The Lenape are very indulgent of those who have misplaced their minds as long as they aren't harmful. But this man is dangerous and must be put down, as the Lenape would put him down, as a favor to his tortured soul. Neither of us can allow his crimes to be blamed on the Lenape or stand back and do nothing while more women die."

"And then, Brighid? Will you go to England with me then? You and Daniel both?" His grin was only partially forced and most definitely nervous as he uttered his back-handed proposal. "Will you marry me? Now? Tomorrow? Next week?"

"I won't pretend to be surprised by your question as I imagine a finely bred lady might." She took his hand, their fingers intertwining, as their lives were entwined, leading him back toward the house to where his father waited, ready to complicate his life further. "But I can't marry you, Philip," she told him quietly. "Not yet. You've opened your doors as Lokwelend hoped you would, letting out the past, letting in the truth, settling all your old ghosts, and I thank you for your honesty. I'm not so strong. Not yet."

He stopped on the path and pulled her around to face him. "Then I'll stay here. The hell with Playden Court, the hell with my title." Then he frowned, his mind slowly taking in all that she had said. "You're not strong enough? For what? For *truth?* What are you afraid of, Brighid? What is it you aren't telling me?"

A single tear slipped out from beneath her lashes as she closed her eyes. "You know I had been unable to remember the . . . that day at our farm. You helped me, made me face my memories so that I could put them away where they belonged. But the raid wasn't all I'd forgotten, all I still cannot remember. The entire week after the raid is still a huge blank slate to me, and I don't know why. Something is still hidden from me, Philip, something that frightens me in the night, that keeps me locked inside a dream I can't escape. Something I believe Lokwelend sees but won't discuss with me."

"So we're back to Lokwelend, back to Lenape dreams and prophecies," Philip said, feeling frustrated by Brighid's stubborn belief in this business of opening doors and following fates. "I don't believe in dreams, Brighid. I believe in what I feel for you. The love I feel for you."

She reached up a hand and touched his cheek. "Poor Philip. You once asked me if you were in my dreams, and you are. You're the best part of them. But the madman is in them with us now, too, and I have to get him out or force him to help me remember what I have chosen to forget, what I'm too afraid, perhaps even too ashamed, to remember. Only then will I be able to come to you as I want to. Only then—when I'm sure of who I am, *what* I am. I don't know why, but I feel that the man, this killer, holds the answer to all my questions, all my fears."

She opened her eyes, looking up at him from their tear-drenched aquamarine depths. "Try to understand, Philip. Please, if you love me, and I believe you do, give me this time. I cannot come to you as your wife until I can bring *all* of myself to you. Until I know I'm free to choose a path."

Philip wanted to argue, but he could see that Brighid,

although upset, was also determined. "I'll agree to wait, my darling, if you'll only promise to remember that no matter what you finally remember there is no shame in anything you had to do to stay alive. Do you understand that?"

"I wish I could believe that," she whispered, and he wrapped his arms tightly around her, feeling the soft shuddering of her body as she bit back a sob. They stood that way for a long time, locked together, one of them eager to face the future, the other still hopelessly trapped by her past.

*The haft of the arrow had been feathered
with one of the eagle's own plumes.
We often give our enemies the means
of our own destruction.*
—Aesop

CHAPTER 12

❧❧❧

SHE WAS ON THE HUNT, JUST AS SHE WAS BEING HUNTED.
Dressed in her mud brown gown rather than her deerskins,
Daniel in her arms rather than strapped to his cradleboard,
she sat on the wagon seat, her chin held high, and allowed
Philip to drive her along the main street of New Eden,
advertising her presence, flaunting her vulnerability.

A piece of sweet yellow corn dangling from a hook.

"Damn it," Philip said as he saw the black traveling coach
in front of Crown's Inn and Stores. "Just what this needed:
my father and sister. Did you know they were coming to
New Eden this morning?"

Brighid shook her head, painfully aware that Eunice
Wright was standing outside the smithy, glaring at her, and
unwilling to show that the woman's presence bothered her.
"Did you think they should ask your permission before
setting foot outside Pleasant Hill?" she asked, wishing
Philip could forget his annoying relatives, knowing that

would be impossible. Easier to ignore a nail in one's shoe on a five-mile walk than to forget those two flamboyant creatures.

"Hardly," Philip answered shortly. "If the man had ever thought to come to me for permission before doing anything, he'd still be in Sussex, hiding from his creditors. He's really in deep this time and needs thirty thousand pounds to stay out of prison when he goes back to London. Did I tell you that? A small price to be rid of him if I thought he wouldn't be clamoring for more within six months."

Brighid turned to goggle at him, Eunice Wright forgotten for the moment. "Thirty thousand pounds? That's a fortune! Surely you aren't going to give it to him?"

Philip turned the wagon at the corner so that he could tie the horses up behind the inn, where Harold would load it with the provisions Bryna had asked for. "I'll end up giving it to him one way or the other, Brighid. For the past five years, I've had a man in London buying up anything my dear father is looking to sell. Paintings. Sculptures. Silver plate. Anything the old reprobate can lash to his coach and transport to London. I have it all in storage, awaiting the day I'm master of Playden Court. I already own the mortgages he put on the estate."

Brighid shook her head. "You're a strange man, Philip Crown," she said as she allowed him to take Daniel from her so she could descend from the wagon. "For all you deny it, you must love Playden Court very much."

"I love *you* very much, Brighid Cassidy," he said simply, handing Daniel to her once more, warming her heart with his easy admission even as she wished he wouldn't push at her with his affection, use it as a weapon against her inability to make a commitment to him. "Playden Court is my duty. But you're right. It's also my home. And someday, if you'll ever let me convince you, it can be yours as well."

"You are the persistent one, aren't you, Philip?" she tossed at him over her shoulder with what she hoped was tolerant amusement. She was already on her way back to the corner and the main street, where she and Philip and Daniel were about to "take the air." Like a goat tied to stake in the middle of a meadow.

"Let me carry him if you won't let him walk," Philip said as they stepped onto the flagway, heading for the front door to Crown's. "He's growing so much his little shoes are hitting at your knees with each step you take." He held out his arms, and Daniel grinned, struggling to go into them. "See? He wants me to put him on my shoulders, like I did this morning."

Brighid passed the child over, reluctantly, happy that Daniel felt comfortable with Philip, glad that Philip seemed to enjoy the boy, and yet fearful of watching this new relationship begin if it might end with the eventual return of her memory of those dark days after the raid, days Johanna had begged her to forget. "I was going to let him walk, you know. Between you and Cora, Daniel's feet will never touch the ground," she said gruffly. "Now that he's seen the world from up there, he won't settle for crawling or stuttering around on his own still unsteady legs."

And then she laughed as Daniel took two great fistfuls of Philip's blond hair and tugged on them as he would the reins on a horse. "Oh, yes, I see who the master is in this relationship. But as you're enjoying it so much, I think I'll give him a peppermint stick once we're inside, then let you carry him again once his fingers are all sticky."

"You're an evil woman, Brighid Cassidy." Philip bent his knees in order to enter the store without hitting the child's head against the doorjamb, Brighid entering ahead of him, still smiling, almost forgetful of the real reason they had come to New Eden today. For if only for these few moments, she had felt as if the three of them were a family out for a day's amusement. A real family, the way her parents had been, the way Bryna and Dominick and their children were now.

But the feeling fled and her smile faded as she saw the marquess of Playden and his daughter standing inside the store, looking as splendidly colorful and as out of place as peacocks in a chicken house: his lordship dressed all in shades of light green, Lady Lilith patently overdressed in blue taffeta, more than a half-dozen rose-red bows marching the length of her stomacher, with yet another bow tied tightly around her slim throat.

"Well, well, well, Lilith, would you look at your brother?" the marquess piped up, raising a small single eyeglass as if to inspect his son's appearance. "The very picture of rustic domesticity, wouldn't you agree? Wearing wild animal skins and toting a half-breed 'round his shoulders like an ornamental wrap. And just to balance the picture, we've got the White Indian squaw. I had no idea, Miss Cassidy, of your rather flamboyant background until a Mrs. Wright broadened my education a few minutes ago. We must have us a small coze once we're back at my brother's humble abode. I should like above all things to hear of your travails, and Lilith, I'm convinced, would be amused to learn of any titillating eccentricities savages might employ in their lovemaking. Isn't that right, Lilith? Or perhaps you could tell us that, Philip? Surely you must already be privy to Miss Cassidy's—um—*accomplishments?*"

Philip handed Daniel to Brighid and stepped in front of her, clearly longing to shut up his father with one well-placed punch to his painted lips, only to have Lilith declare quickly: "Philip, he's not worth it, you know. Brighid, my dear, won't you step outside with me and bear me company as I cross the street to that quaint little haberdashery I saw when we first drove into town? There was a bonnet in the window I would dearly love to try on."

Brighid looked to Philip, aware that he was holding himself silent only through sheer force of will, and decided that Lilith might know better than she how to handle this extremely uncomfortable situation. "I'd be happy to join you, Lady Lilith," she said quickly, already heading for the door. "Philip? Will you come with us?"

He was still glaring at his father, who was still posing,

dangling the single eyeglass from the riband that held it around his neck, his painted smile nothing short of triumphant. "Go on, Brighid," Philip said tightly. "I'll give Harold Bryna's order and join you in a few minutes."

"My dearest papa, who knows nothing of subtlety," Lady Lilith explained, slipping a companionable arm through Brighid's as they crossed the dirt street, "has just given my brother a lesson in the cost of withholding the few pennies Papa desires before he'll agree to leave this benighted village. If Philip doesn't kill him first, you understand. I'm only sorry he felt it necessary to include you in his nastiness. Although I must say, his speech was rather inspired, considering it was so impromptu. Did you really spread your legs for a savage? Well, I suppose you did, seeing as how you've got that adorable little bastard on your hip. How delicious! Tell me—was there only the one savage, or did they pass you around among them, like a dish of comfits?"

Brighid didn't know whether to laugh or cry or slap the silly woman senseless. So this is what would happen if she went to London? Which was worse? To be spat on in New Eden or to be drooled over in London, seen as a highly intriguing oddity, to be asked to tea so that she could recite the horrors of her capture for a gaggle of giggling, salivating "ladies"?

"They taught me how to cut out a tongue and then feed it back to my victim, *Geptschat,*" Brighid told her coldly, glaring at the woman through slitted eyes. "I can kill more ways than you have sold your body. Remember that tonight as you lay your head on your pillow."

Lady Lilith's trill of laughter took Brighid totally by surprise and destroyed her ill humor. "Oh, you *are* precious, aren't you!" she exclaimed, holding onto Brighid's arm even more tightly as they climbed the rough wooden flagway to the door of the haberdashery. "You must pay me no nevermind, as I'm a sad rattle, but I will delight in telling Papa of your prowess just to watch him blanch. Now come along. My uncle Dominick was so kind as to tell me I might put any purchases on his bill, and I believe we *both* deserve new bonnets."

Philip placed the mug of ale in front of his father, then sat down across the table from him. "And what, pray tell, is this swill?" the marquess asked, squinting into the mug. "Is there no wine?"

"Drink it, and be happy I don't fling both mugs in your face," Philip told him, still fairly amazed that he hadn't knocked his father down, then picked him up, only so that he could knock him down again. *I must be more civilized than I believe,* he thought, hiding a small, one-sided grin behind the mug as he took a sip of lukewarm ale. "Now, shall we discuss terms?"

"Terms? Don't be so crass, Philip. We are not coal merchants, bargaining over a sale. Must be your mother's moneylender blood that gives you such a love of finance. Now, now, don't frown—I meant no harm. I've already told you. I need only a trifling thirty thousand pounds. More, if you can spare it. Or would you rather your dear mother be without her gin, forced to dine not with, but *on* her beloved cats?"

Philip sat forward menacingly. It would take a larger-hearted man than himself to love Myra Crown, but she was his mother, and he knew his duty. "You've never spent a bent penny on Mother, so don't attempt to use her now to get what you want. She's my responsibility, and I've long since made sure you can't touch any of the money set aside for her care." Then he sat back and took another sip of ale. "However, after your performance of a few minutes ago next door—and remembering my moneylender blood—I believe I might be able to part with, say, *twenty* thousand pounds. If you meet my terms."

The marquess's upper lip curled into a sneer. "I know what this is about. But you can't really have feelings for that Irish slut, can you?"

"Dear me," Philip drawled, his knuckles white as he grasped the handle of the mug, "did I say twenty thousand?

I meant *ten* thousand." His eyes were blue ice as he lowered his voice, saying, "Would you like to try for five thousand, dear Father, or do you begin to understand my meaning?"

Philip watched as his father's Adam's apple climbed his throat. "I'll apologize. That is what you want, isn't it?"

Philip shook his head. "No need for that," he said, preparing to rise. "Frankly, if I were you, I'd be concerned for my hair if I were to come within ten feet of Brighid after what you said this morning. Brighid was with the Lenape for five years, Father. Despite her beauty and good manners, she is no die-away drawing room miss. When I first saw her, the soldiers had tied her up because she had damn near bitten off one of their numbers' ears. Not that you will repeat a word of that or of anything you might think you know about Brighid once you're back in society. *Now* do you understand my terms?"

"That's your price?" the marquess asked, uncrossing his legs and rising to follow Philip out of the common room of the inn. "That I keep my mouth shut about the Irish girl? Why? Surely you don't plan to—my God! Philip, are you out of your mind?"

They stepped out onto the flagway just as Lady Lilith and Brighid exited the haberdashery on the other side of the street. "I've asked Brighid to marry me, yes. And I have every intention of taking her back to Sussex with me and, eventually, to London, where you will be delighted to inform all and sundry of the *ton* of your extreme happiness with the match."

The marquess pulled a lace-edged handkerchief from his cuff and began fanning himself. "But you can't. You *can't!* I didn't come all this way just for the money. Listen to me, Philip. I've all but promised you to Lord Halliwell's daughter, Elizabeth. Halliwell's anxious for the match, seeing as how the chit is nearly at her last prayers—nearly five and twenty, you understand—but very lovely, truly. And there's a fat settlement in it for me, I mean, for *you,* Philip. For *you.* Think, man! You can't throw yourself away like I did. And at least I got some money for my trouble. This Irish girl is penniless—and an embarrassment, like Dominick's mother. Why, when you get down to it, she's no better than a whore, Philip, a savage's leavings—"

"I imagine I'm not as civilized as I thought," Philip remarked to himself as he rubbed at the knuckles on his right hand and looked down at his father, who was sprawled on the flagway, a trickle of blood at the corner of his mouth adding some welcome color to his face. "Think about what I've said, old man. When you can bring yourself to go to London to tell everyone how overjoyed you are to be welcoming your new daughter to the Crown family, we'll see how generous I can be. In the meantime, I suggest you refrain from talking at all, as you don't seem to know when to shut up once you begin to flap your jaws."

And with that, Philip started across the street, frowning again as he saw a man approaching Brighid, a Bible in his hand.

Brighid couldn't believe it, but she actually was beginning to like Lady Lilith. The woman was rather deliberately evil but deliciously so, openly rejoicing in her own fine wit and definitely out to enjoy her life as well as applying herself to rendering her father's life as difficult as possible.

Once inside the haberdashery and in tones undoubtedly meant to carry to the ears of Mrs. Collins, the owner of the small establishment, Lady Lilith had explained that her major reason for accompanying the marquess to New Eden—other than the fact that her last protector, a duke, had cocked up his toes before making a monetary provision for her—was to watch as Philip made him dance before he paid a penny of what was surely meant to be a bribe to get the man aboard the first ship heading back to England.

"I used to be afraid of that old reprobate, if you can conceive of such a thing," she'd volunteered to Brighid quite affably, "but I view him now with amused tolerance, seeing as how he has been reduced to little more than a laughable, pox-ridden wreck, Lord curse him."

From there, Lady Lilith had gone on to regale Brighid and

astound a bug-eyed Mrs. Collins with tales of her long list of titled lovers: the duke who had just so inconveniently stuck his spoon in the wall; a viscount who had made a great fuss out of setting her up in her own townhouse and being seen in public with her, only to run off with his valet; the earl who gave her an emerald necklace just for calling him Papa when he took her to bed; the secret liaison with a high government official who once sneaked her into Parliament at three in the morning to make impassioned—and fairly perverted—love to her on one of the benches.

"I've a few more years of fun left to me, I figure," she'd told Brighid as she tried on a lace hood trimmed with striped ribbon. "Then I shall most probably retire to a quaint cottage in Surrey and promise not to pen my memoirs if my dear gentlemen friends provide me with good reason not to—money, you understand. I do, as my papa so rudely announced last night, have a great affection for strapping farm lads, so I doubt I'll be lonely."

Brighid had never encountered anyone like Lady Lilith and doubted she ever would again, and she was so astounded and entertained by her never-ending chatter that she nearly forgot why she had come to New Eden in the first place. Until, that is, they stepped back out on the flagway, Lady Lilith's arms full of packages, the two of them giggling over something the older woman had said, and nearly bumped into a man walking along the flagway.

Instantly on guard, Brighid held Daniel closer as the man planted himself directly in front of them, effectively blocking their way. He didn't appear to have sought them out and appeared not only surprised to see the two women, but clearly fearful. He just stood there, figuratively bolted in place, yet seemingly prepared to run for his life if Brighid so much as said boo to him.

The man was large, with hands like hams, his florid face swelling like a balloon above his homespun shirt, which was buttoned tightly around his neck. He wore a long brown vest and matching cloth trousers above plain white stockings and scuffed black shoes. All his clothing was patched, and he had the look of a farmer whose fields had not shown a profit in many a season.

Brighid frowned, wondering why the man kept staring at her, at Daniel. Was he about to spit at her the way Eunice Wright had done? "Do I know you?" she asked at last.

"Brighid! Are you all right?" Philip called out, trotting across the dirt street, and the man turned to look at him, then looked at Brighid once more.

"I'm fine," she answered as Philip bounded onto the flagway, positioning himself between her and the strange man who still hadn't spoken.

"La, Philip, she's not about to run off with the fellow if that's what you're thinking," Lady Lilith said grumpily, depositing her packages in his arms, so that he had no choice but to take them. "Shopping gives me such a thirst. Is Papa still across the street? More importantly, is he still alive? Whoops! There he is. Now, Philip, however did our father find himself sitting on the flagway? No, no, don't tell me. I'd much rather ask him myself."

So saying, Lady Lilith walked away, her hips swaying provocatively, leaving Philip to fetch her packages home and Brighid standing with Daniel in her arms, still the subject of the stranger's quiet scrutiny.

"I said, sir," Brighid repeated, becoming increasingly uncomfortable the longer the man stood there, "do I know you?"

"You're Brighid Cassidy," the man pronounced quietly, clutching the Bible to his chest, although no longer looking quite as frightened as he had a few moments earlier. In fact, he seemed almost confident. "You are one of those taken by the heathens."

"She knows who she is, sir," Philip shot back, stepping closer to Brighid. "The question is, Who are you?"

The man only shook his head and reached out to take hold of Daniel's right hand. "Suffer the children to come to me," he intoned quietly, then lifted his eyes to Brighid's once more, his now triumphant look sending an icy shiver down her spine. "You have been sorely used, Brighid

Cassidy, as has this child been used, brought into a world not made for him," he continued as Brighid pulled Daniel's hand away from him. "Fear not. I will pray for you both."

The man then lifted his arms to the sky as he stepped back a pace, cleared his throat, and began in a loud, carrying voice: "I am the servant of God!" He spread his arms and turned fully around in a circle, talking as if to untold multitudes only he could see. "Behold His children, my brothers and sisters, and weep for them for they are sinners who know Him not! Let us pray for their redemption."

Brighid turned to Philip, her mouth suddenly dry, her every sense alive and fearful. Was this the madman? Was this the one who had killed, would kill again if he wasn't stopped? "Philip?"

"Do not look to him, dear sister," the man continued as a small group of people began to gather in the street, obviously attracted by the man's deep, carrying voice. "You must look to God, who is all loving and all forgiving."

"Oh, for the love of—now look here, my good man—" Philip began, only to have the man cut him off.

"You have been freed from the clutches of the heathen," he pronounced, using the Bible to motion to Brighid, who stood rooted to the flagway, unable to talk, to think. The man's dark eyes burned like coals, his words slamming into her, frightening her as Eunice's Wright's words had angered her. "You must justify the Lord in all that has befallen you. You have been given God's test of the elect, been punished for your iniquities, and fought the last struggle between good and evil in the wilderness. A struggle between God's chosen and the agents of the devil—the Lenni Lenape! You were taken for your sins, and you have returned from the valley of the shadows."

He reached out and took hold of Daniel's hand again, stroking the child's thumb with his forefinger. "Drop to your knees now and speak to us, Brighid Cassidy. Thank God for your safe return!"

"That tears it!" Philip exclaimed, throwing down the

packages. He grabbed at the front of the man's shirt and pushed him straight back until his spine collided sharply with the front door of Mrs. Collins's haberdashery. "All right, mister, who are you?"

"My lord!" Elijah Kester called out, stepping between Philip and the man, separating them. "Would you strike a man of God? This is Helmut Gerlach. He long ago lost his wife to the Lenape and all but gave up his farm to preach God's word to the heathens. He's a forgiving man, a good man, and he travels everywhere, speaking to whites and Indians alike, don't you, Helmut? My lord, he means no harm."

Brighid began to tremble. Helmut Gerlach? This man was Helmut Gerlach? She pulled Daniel closer against her. *Beware he who speaks of the white man's God for his own ends.* Yes, Lokwelend knew. He'd known all along. The past Brighid feared was coming closer. Closer.

Philip gave Helmut a quick, single shake, then released his hold on the man's shirt, stepping away from him before grabbing him once more, lifting him a good five inches off the ground. "Is that what you are, Helmut? A man of God? A *forgiving* man? Are you here to save Miss Cassidy with your words? Or do you do your preaching with a knife?"

"Oh, now, my lord," Elijah said, stepping forward once more. "You couldn't think Helmut here would do anything like what happened to poor Silky, do you? Why, he prayed over her for more'an hour yesterday night, didn't you, Helmut? Helmut, you didn't carve up Silky, did you?"

"God punishes, not man," Helmut pronounced quietly, rubbing at his neck, for Philip's strong grip had lifted his tight collar high on his throat, nearly shutting off his air. "Silky Wattson went to her death willingly, for she was unrepentant and would not heed the word of the Lord. I pray for her, as I pray for the Lenape heathen who struck her down. But you," he continued, turning once more to Brighid, "you have been returned to the bosom of your family, your sins forgiven if only you will embrace the Lord and reject all that is heathen. It is not too late. Give the heathen child to me, so that I might return him to his own kind when next I travel west to preach the word of God in the wilderness. Only then can you begin to do penance and find your way back to the Lord."

Brighid's hold on Daniel tightened again until the child cried out in fright. "Philip," she whispered frantically, "get this man away from me. Get him away from me now!"

"With pleasure," he bit out from between clenched teeth. "And the next time I even *think* to listen to one of your harebrained schemes, I'll have Dominick hit me over the head with something very heavy. Take Daniel and go to the wagon, you hear me?"

"Do not be afraid, Brighid Cassidy," Helmut told her as Philip grabbed hold of his elbow and quickly—and none too gently—steered him back down the flagway. "You must but pick between God's chosen and the agents of the devil. Cast off the heathen grip, be it of man or child, and open your heart to salvation!"

Brighid heard no more of Helmut Gerlach's words, for she was running, running across the street, racing for the safety of the wagon, holding Daniel close and cursing herself for having put the child in danger.

As she passed by the door to Crown Inn and Stores, she looked up briefly and straight into the mocking eyes of the marquess of Playden, his gaze sufficient to bring her to a halt. "My compliments. Better than a play, I vow, Miss Cassidy," he drawled. "Better than a play."

"Shut up, Papa," Lady Lilith admonished the man as she put an arm around Brighid's shoulders. "Can't you see she's upset?"

"I see more than you think, my little harlot," Giles remarked, setting off across the dirt street. "Now, if you'll excuse me, *ladies,* I believe I'm off to have my soul saved from perdition. Or is it that I have recognized a fellow devil in our midst, hmm?"

Lady Lilith looked across the street, past her brother, who was heading in their direction, his face, his whole demeanor, one of someone she did not, at this moment, wish to provoke. "You go with Philip now, Brighid. I'll go see what Papa is up to. Nothing good, I'm sure."

Brighid only nodded, for speech was beyond her. She hadn't been so frightened since she had awakened in Lapawin's longhouse five years ago not knowing where she was or what had happened to her. When Philip tried to take Daniel from her, she pulled away, unwilling to loosen her grip on the crying child, her eyes wide and staring.

"Brighid? Brighid, it's all right," he told her soothingly. "I don't care what Elijah says, I think we've found our madman. All Dominick and I have to do now is watch him, wait for him to trip himself up some way. But in the meantime, you're not setting foot away from Pleasant Hill, do you understand?"

She only nodded again and let Philip take her back to the estate. For the remainder of the day and for several days after that, she never left Daniel's side, staying with him in the nursery, sleeping on the floor beside his small cot, her hand clasped around the knife in her pocket.

You cannot teach a crab to walk straight.
— *Aristophanes*

CHAPTER 13

"GERLACH WON'T MAKE A MOVE IN ANY DIRECTION," PHILIP complained to Dominick as the two men walked along the path that led to Lokwelend's cabin beside the stream. "He just sits on the porch outside the inn, preaching to anyone who is so unlucky as to wander by. Which, of course, means he's onto us."

"I agree," Dominick answered, breaking off a branch that had encroached onto the well-worn path between Pleasant Hill and the Lenape cabin. "Did you know Gerlach's wife died in the same raid in which Brighid was taken? I haven't told the ladies any of this—anything about the man's wife—but I rode out to Gerlach's farm yesterday afternoon while you took your turn haunting the common room, and the place is run-down, clearly neglected. But I found the woman's grave, and it is well marked, well tended, unlike the rest of the place. I rode back into New Eden, and Elijah told me the Lenape took their time with her, torturing her for hours until Gerlach returned from wherever in hell he was doing his preaching to scare them off. He stumbled into New Eden more than a week after the raid all but out of his mind, saying how he'd had to bury her in pieces."

Philip shook his head. "That doesn't make sense, Dominick, and we both know it. We helped bury most of those killed in the raids. The Lenape barely took time to scalp half of them, they were moving so fast. Why would they pay so much attention to one woman?"

"Gerlach preaches, remember? Maybe he stepped on some Lenape toes while he was going about, waving his Bible, so his wife was singled out for special treatment, the same as Jonah Newton and the Rudolphs were. God knows this man Gerlach has gotten on your nerves."

"Only because of the way Brighid reacted to him," Philip said, remembering the stark terror in Brighid's eyes when Gerlach had touched Daniel, the way she had all but curled in on herself since then, staying in the child's room with only Mary Catherine and Cora for company, hiding herself away from almost everyone else. "I'm half afraid she's planning to take Daniel and run away. She was angry, determined, when Eunice Wright went after her, but this time it's different. She's afraid, frightened half out of her mind—as if she could lose Daniel, which is ridiculous."

"Have you talked to her at all? Bryna has tried, but Brighid keeps avoiding her. And that's no easy trick, as we both know how determined my wife can be, even now, confined to her bed for most of the day."

"Actually, what little communication I've had with Brighid has been through Lilith. The two of them have struck up some sort of friendship, if you can believe it. The only reason I haven't prevailed upon you to throw both she and my father out is that Lilith is being on her best behavior— sitting with Brighid in the garden and spending long hours in the nursery with Hallie, of all people. She must see them as fellow social outcasts or something. Lilith says I'm to give Brighid time—whatever in hell that means, for nothing's going to change until we unmask Gerlach and have him locked up. I tell you, Dominick, between Brighid, Gerlach, and my esteemed father, I'm about at the end of my tether."

They exited the woods, stepping into the clearing in front of Lokwelend's cabin. "You're not the only one, Philip," Dominick said as Lucas walked out of the cabin to shake a small rug in the breeze. "Lucas has all but moved in with Lokwelend, refusing to stay under the same roof with my brother, not that I blame him. I'm amazed at my own patience."

Philip looked at his uncle, who had so many reasons to hate the marquess of Playden. "No more amazed than I am that you allow Giles to stay at Pleasant Hill. I promise you, my own house will be completed within another week. I'll have them moved there the moment the last piece of necessary furniture is in place."

Dominick shook his head. "No rush, I promise you. I've been happily surprised to find that I don't actively hate the man anymore. Despise him, yes. Even pity him a little, for the sad wreck he has become. And, no, don't look at me as if I'm some painted saint. I'll never forget what he's done to me or forgive it. Some things are beyond forgiveness. But if we're to live, Philip, if we're to have any life at all, we have to move on. Bryna taught me that." And then he smiled. "Besides, if you're amazed by Lilith's friendship with Brighid, I'm intrigued by Giles's growing association with Gerlach. It's always better to keep one's enemies close, where they can be watched."

Philip looked at him curiously. "You still consider Giles an enemy? As you've just said, he's a mere wreck of a man, a shadow of what he was. Surely he can't hurt you, hurt any of us? He's just a wretched old buffoon, uncomfortable to deal with but harmless, like a defanged tiger."

"Harmless? Is he? Is he really?" Dominick asked blandly, and Philip frowned, respectful of his uncle's opinion, thinking again of the dog that never barked, and freshly determined to keep a closer eye on his father and the man's seeming friendship with Helmut Gerlach.

Lucas waved the men a hello and came to greet them, saying, "How nice of you to visit, my lords. He's still lying on his cot, as he has since his return to Pleasant Hill, looking as fit as any of us and eating with twice my appetite. I don't understand. Why does he think he's dying?"

"A good question, Lucas. I'm beginning to question it myself. What does Cora say?" Dominick asked as they approached the cabin door.

Lucas shrugged his shoulders. "Less than Lokwelend, my lords," he said, betraying his chagrin that the woman he loved was being so difficult. "What little I do understand seems to point to the notion that Lokwelend wants to set his 'house' in order before he goes to sleep, as Cora puts it. And then she mutters something in her own language and looks at me as if I'm thick as a plank."

"Thick as a plank, is it?" Philip threw back his head and laughed, then slung an arm across the butler's shoulders. "Lucas, my man, I think it's time you went to Lokwelend and the two of you had a small chat. Or do you plan to worship Cora from afar forever?"

The butler looked up at Philip and then to Dominick. His face flushed scarlet. "I should ask for Cora's hand in marriage? Now, while her father lies on his deathbed? Do you really think so?"

"Yes, my nephew really thinks so," Dominick said, hesitating outside the cabin door. "And so do I. But is Lokwelend really on his deathbed? Therein, I believe, may lay the rub, if you don't mind a little poetry. Philip, I've been thinking about this for a few days, although I've hesitated to say anything, believing it to be my own wishful thinking that prompted my suspicions. That and the fact that the Lenape, for all their stoicism, have a great love of drama and playacting. Do you believe your *father* may be playing a trick on Lucas, on all of us."

Philip frowned, considering Dominick's words, then addressed Lucas once more. "Eats twice what you do, you say? Tell me this, Lucas—has he been reading from his damned books as well?"

The butler nodded furiously. "And he downed a venison steak last night bigger than his plate. But, my lords, surely you aren't saying that—"

"Oh, yes, we are!" Philip exploded, caught between wanting to choke Lokwelend and falling at the man's feet, rejoicing. "Dominick, I think you're right. We've all been hoodwinked by a crafty old Lenape. We haven't listened well to his cryptic lessons, haven't moved fast enough to suit him, so maybe he's trying to scare us into doing what he sees as right. In other words, if we won't settle our lives on our own, he'll push us into it, knowing we'd want his last days to be happy. Goad Lucas here into asking for Cora's hand, keep Brighid and me close until we settle things between us, and—I'm willing to wager—keep himself safe from Lapawin's wiles while he's at it. Why, the sneaky, conniving rascal, he's not dying at all! By God, Dominick, what do you say to that?"

By way of answer, Dominick sat himself down on the ground and laughed until he had to wipe at his eyes, Philip joining him after a few moments, the two of them so overcome by mirth that finally Lokwelend appeared in the doorway, looking down at the two of them. "A man would ask only a peaceful death, my children. Or is that too much for you to give?"

Philip toppled completely onto the dirt, lying on his back as he looked up at his Lenape father. "Oh, you're going to die, all right, old man. Brighid's going to have your liver on a spit," he warned, laughing almost too hard to speak, "and Bryna, if she finds out what you've been up to, will help her to carve it out first with a dull spoon."

"Be silent, you young fools. Would you see me sharing a blanket with that old woman?" Lokwelend looked to his left and then to his right, probably to see if Lapawin was within hearing distance. He then threw off the woolen shawl he'd had draped around his shoulders and motioned for Philip and Dominick to follow him to the small campfire, which they did, still laughing and dusting each other off before they sat down again, trying to compose themselves while Lokwelend produced his pipe from under his shirt.

Philip sobered first, looking to Lokwelend as the old man lit his pipe and drew on it deeply, smiling in contentment as smoke rose to encircle his iron-gray head. "Why, my father? Surely you didn't have us all climbing through hoops just to keep yourself safe from one toothless old squaw? Besides, I doubt she'll give up her feather bed at Pleasant Hill for any dozen of your blankets."

"So you say, my son," Lokwelend answered, keeping the pipe tucked into the corner of his mouth. "I am not so sure. Now, tell me, have you discovered the enemy? Have you given the Nipawi Gischuch's dream monster a name?"

"So, Father, Brighid is right. You do see into her dreams." He hesitated a moment, then said, "His name is Helmut Gerlach," looking to Dominick, who nodded his agreement. He didn't bother to ask Lokwelend how he knew what they had been about, how he knew that they, too, were on the hunt for Brighid's "monster," for the old Indian knew everything. "He's the one who has been killing the returned captives. We're convinced of it, not that we can prove a thing."

"You draw closer, Tauwún, but the full truth is still hidden from you, because you still will not look. Before the murders, the Nipawi Gischuch's monster already haunted her dreams, even if she only felt his menace without seeing him. He has kept her rooted in the past, afraid to take more than a single step toward the future. Do you not ask yourself why?"

Philip ran his fingers through his hair, wishing that just this once Lokwelend would speak to him in something other than riddles. "Because he knows something she can't remember? Because he's the killer? I don't understand. Are you saying Gerlach isn't our man? That there are *two* monsters, as you call them?"

"Think, my son. It is possible for a single evil to take on several forms. Do we fear the knife or the man holding it?

How does he use his weapon and when, for what reason? To punish or to hide? To feed his madness or to conceal an even greater evil? Or both? Open the door, my son. I grow weary of waiting."

"As I grow weary of puzzles," Philip bit out angrily, picking up a small stone and winging it toward the creek.

"You're not being especially helpful, my friend," Dominick agreed, taking the pipe as Lokwelend offered it to him. "Philip has more than enough on his plate as it is. Surely you know that his father has arrived here from across the water?"

Lokwelend nodded. "Lucas has told me what I already knew, what I had seen in a dream I had while I walked alone in the woods. The pale man. He is mischief and a fool, and his daughter is most happy when she is the most trouble, although her heart is good. Pity the one, and pity the other. They cannot help who they are."

"They both *enjoy* who they are," Philip said, knowing his tone sounded harsh. "And you knew they were coming to Pleasant Hill? If you see so damned much, my father, could you not warn me of just *some* of what you see? It seems only fair."

Lokwelend took back the pipe and sat drawing on it for some moments before speaking again. "My son does not need my words to tell him that he nears the end of the path. You have opened many doors. Only one remains, a single barrier you cannot breach alone. Everything in your past, everything in your future, surrounds you now. Your trials are at hand, as are all your answers. Arm yourself with truth and love, and once the last door has been opened, my son, open your heart as well. But you must always remember that good and evil cannot dwell together in one heart and therefore should not come into contact. Destroy the evil, and welcome the good, as my friend Crown has done."

Philip slapped his hands against his thighs and stood up, looking down at Dominick. "I think I liked him better when he was lying on his blankets, playing at dying," he said, shaking his head. "Dominick, did you understand any of that?"

Dominick looked to Lokwelend, who merely nodded, silently giving his consent. "Well, Philip," he said, rising, "I'd say that Gerlach is the man we're after, but not only because he's been killing these women. Although I'll be damned if I can think of another reason, one that affects Brighid's past. As for the rest of it, I suppose you're going to have to settle Giles once and for all and anything and anyone else you might see as disturbing your life, putting evil in your heart. Which probably means"—he hesitated, looking to Lokwelend once more—"that you have more problems than just you and Brighid having things to settle between you. Do I have that all right, old friend, or is there more you've seen in your dreams?"

"The Bright Fire will be mother to a girl child before the first snow," Lokwelend said, his voice firm. "I will bounce this new little one on my knee, as I did your sons, as I will the sons and the daughter yet to come. I will see that last child before I go. I will look down at the comfort and torment of your old age, my friend, and she will be the Bright Fire born again." His smile was tinged with secret knowledge. "Tasukamend has much to look forward to and much to fear."

Philip shook his head, caught between a grimace and a grin. "You're an arrogant son of a bitch, aren't you, my father? Would you perhaps agree to coming along the next time I wish to lay down a bet at cards? You'd come in damn handy, I'll wager."

"I know nothing of cards except to feel certain to avoid them as the Lenape should avoid the strong spirits your people have pressed upon us," Lokwelend said, returning Philip's smile.

And then he grew solemn, looking off into the distance. "Send Lucas to me now, my friend. He has something to say to me, and I have much to say to him. Philip, my son, it made my heart heavy to trick you, but Nipawi Gischuch would have gone if I had not kept her close with my small deception. I ask you to continue my lie a little longer. She needs to be here, my son, and not only to help herself. My people need her here. I only hope I have not made a mistake, been too selfish. For I see much danger around her as the evil forces gather and move closer. Soon, very soon, she will have to choose her path.

"Now go fetch Lucas to me, for I will say no more."

Brighid missed Philip so much she ached with it. Ached to have his arms around her, ached to feel his strength, and feed on it, take a measure of it as her own.

For she was afraid. More afraid than she had ever been in her life. All but paralyzed by her fears, by her lies, by the silence she had kept so long. Too long.

Helmut Gerlach.

How she had hoped never to hear that name again.

She tucked the sleeping Daniel in his cot and reluctantly left the nursery, having already gained Hallie's promise to remain with the boy all through the night. She closed the door to the nursery and stood in the hallway for a moment, pressing her hands against the small of her back, wishing she could relax her muscles if not her mind.

"There you are, our own little White Indian," the marquess of Playden purred from just behind her, shaking Brighid out of her own thoughts so that she cursed herself silently for not being more aware, more alert. Time was— and such a short time ago—that she would have heard the man approach. Smelled him. But her senses were dull, her thoughts all turned inward, and she was more the young, frightened Brighid Cassidy now than she ever had been the confident, capable Nipawi Gischuch.

"My lord," she responded carefully. "Are you looking for Lilith? She was here earlier, playing at snakes and ladders with Mary Catherine, but I believe she has already gone to dress for dinner. As must I," she concluded, anxious to be away. She couldn't help it. Ever since the first day he had arrived at Pleasant Hill, she could not look at Philip's father without remembering Lokwelend's warning: beware the pale stranger. Although she hadn't really needed Lokwelend's warning to know that this man wished much for her, none of it good.

"Lilith? Now why would I be looking for her?" the marquess answered smoothly, taking hold of Brighid's arm just above her elbow and steering her down the hall as if she were incapable of finding her way on her own. "I have spent the past eight and twenty years trying to shake her loose, abominable little trollop that she is. If she were a man or my mistress, I'd be proud to claim her, for she's so amoral as to be a delight. As it is," he continued, shrugging, "I can only amuse myself, hoping she'll succumb to a healthy dose of the clap."

"I believe she wishes the same fate for you." Brighid tried to pull her arm free, longing to go to her chamber and wash the evil of this unnatural father from her skin, for she could feel his malevolence through the material of her gown. "Now, if you'll excuse me—"

"Not just yet, my fine young savage," Playden persisted, his manicured nails digging into her soft flesh as he roughly pulled her around the corner into the wing holding Bryna and Dominick's suite of rooms. "I have something to show you."

She could have escaped him. She could have kicked at his shins or bitten his hand. She could have drawn her knife and threatened to slit him from gullet to groin. But he was Philip's father. And Bryna was probably nearby in her chamber, readying herself for the single trip downstairs Dominick allowed her every day. "Very well," she said tightly, no longer fighting him. "But let go of my arm, my lord, as this little savage is feeling a strong desire to notch your nose and ears."

The marquess looked down at her, clearly amused. "How droll, Miss Cassidy," he remarked, stopping in front of the outer door leading to Dominick's dressing room and placing his hand on the latch. "I almost believe it would tickle me to have you in London if it weren't for the fact that amusement almost always pales when one is attempting to outrun one's creditors. Now, shall we proceed? I've already ascertained that the gollumpus is nowhere about."

He depressed the latch and all but shoved Brighid inside the oblong dressing room. She halted a few feet inside the chamber, whirling about to glare at the marquess, barely cognizant of the furnishings behind her: the dressing table, the cabinets holding Dominick's clothing, the tub that would be moved into the bedchamber and placed before the fireplace whenever the master or mistress wished to bathe.

"My son has told me of his insane desire to wed you, Miss Cassidy," Playden began, walking past her to the dressing table, picking up a ruby stud from a tray that sat there and rotating it between his fingertips. "This, of course, will not do. He is already all but betrothed, you know. To a most suitable young lady of considerable wealth and high social standing. Oh, you look shocked. My, my, I didn't mean to upset you. Didn't Philip tell you? Naughty, naughty boy. But, then, men will say most anything to get a woman into bed, won't they? He tells me you're a most energetic lay, by the by. That is so fortunate, as most whores are much more practiced than enthusiastic."

"Philip wouldn't tell you the time of day," Brighid bit out, moving toward the door, only to have Playden leap in front of her, barring her way.

"Oh, no, no, no, Miss Cassidy," he told her, his smile bringing a sour taste into her mouth. "You see, I believe you have a genuine affection for my son. In fact, I am counting fairly heavily on it. Would you like to see what he would be giving up for you? What even the gollumpus can't forget?"

Brighid swallowed down the bile that threatened to choke her. "I still don't know what you're talking about."

"Then turn around, Miss Brighid Cassidy. Turn around, White Indian, little slut, little inconvenience. Turn around and see the albatross that hangs around all our necks. Turn around and see the treasure we all covet, the prize the gollumpus could never win, the holy grail of the Crowns that calls Philip back to England. See the siren who rules his heart even if—for the moment—you rule his body. Turn around, little bitch. See your competition and know that you can never win!"

Before the marquess had finished speaking, before she turned around, looked where the man was pointing, Brighid knew. Knew what she would see. Slowly, as if imprisoned in a spell she could not escape, her heart pounding inside her skull, locked beside the scream she held trapped in her throat, her movements slowed and beyond her control, she turned and looked at the far wall, at the ornately framed painting that hung between the two tall windows.

There, captured on a huge canvas, stood the great stone mansion in her dream. High on a hill, it stood, strong, solid, impenetrable. Safety lay within those thick walls, safety and comfort and a most wondrous, healing love. As she looked up at the canvas, the painting came to life, so that she saw the sun winking off its many windows, heard the song coming from the birds nesting in the eaves, and felt the love reach out to her, calling to her. *Home, Nipawi Gischuch. Come home.*

She did feel the love. She longed to embrace the unspoken offer of safety.

"I should have known," she whispered quietly, the painting beginning to blur before her tear-wet eyes. "From the beginning, I should have known." With her tears came a further blurring of the painting, so that the twisted trees of the dark woods replaced the sweeping lawns, obscured the long drive leading to the main entrance, raised an impenetrable wall of danger and blind paths that barred her from the house. Barred her way to happiness, to comfort, to love. But there *was* a path, and if only for a moment, she had seen it. A way existed, no matter how well it was hidden.

At last, she knew there was more than hope. There was a chance. This could be her home if she could only find her way, choose the correct path.

She could see the horseman approach, hear the impatience in his voice, the words he had spoken in her dreams coming to her quickly, jumbled, tripping over each other, changing now, as the dream had changed, as her life and circumstances had changed, the angry words, the denials, all winnowing down into a single, clear message that at last made sense. *"Yonder lies my home. Have you no sense of adventure? There are many destinies depending on the choices you make. Everything, Nipawi Gischuch, is what you make of it . . ."* And then the horseman's voice, Philip's beloved voice, gentled as he added, *"Come with me, my love. Come home."*

Playden's low-pitched growl was very close to her ear. She could smell his wine-scented breath as he spoke. "Now do you understand, little bitch? You can never have him. Never make him happy. He's already owned, body and soul."

"No." Brighid breathed the word through a smile. "No, you're wrong. I know my destination now, old man, and it isn't to remain here, locked inside my own fears. All I must find is the correct path. And the strength to take it. You can't hurt me or Philip anymore."

She turned to face the marquess, no longer Brighid Cassidy, no longer Nipawi Gischuch, but a new whole made up of bits and pieces of all the child she had been, all the woman she had become. "You've lost, old man," she told him, feeling a strength and resolve that had almost been hers, that she'd believed lost to her the moment she had heard Helmut Gerlach's name. "Just as you've done all of your miserable, hate-filled life. You have lost."

The marquess stepped back a pace, his eyes narrowed to slits, his teeth bared over his rouged lips. "Have I, little bitch? Have I really? Do you believe me stupid? Or you'd like to think, perhaps, that I would mellow in my old age? Develop a pure nature as I toddle toward my grave? Gain a compassionate heart as my one last hope of heaven? That I would hear what I've heard, what I've bought and paid for with my son's miserly allowance, and not use it to my advantage? Even my son has hoped for less. He'd know I would never turn my back on the habits of a lifetime. And now, little bitch, let me prove it to you. Helmut Gerlach, my new, carefully cultivated friend and confidante, awaits you in the gardens, full of questions about someone by the name of Johanna and about your time in the camp of those heathens who kidnapped you both. You do take my meaning, don't you?"

Brighid swayed where she stood, reeling as if the marquess had struck her, all her new courage slipping from her grasp. All her new hope draining away.

"Tsk-tsk. I should be ashamed of myself, enjoying this moment so much," the marquess drawled, taking out his snuff box and dipping his thumb and forefinger into it. "I had almost hoped the painting would be enough to make you realize how unworthy you are of aspiring to marriage with my son, for I can be kind if it suits me. But evil suits me better, don't you think? Or did you believe I would be so foolish as to count on that damn pile of stones as my only winning card? After traveling so far? And when so much is at stake?"

He leaned closer so that she backed up another step, feeling sick at her stomach. "Ignorant chit, shame on you for underestimating me, underestimating my capacity for mischief and intrigue, which I consider my supreme accomplishment. And now I've trumped your ace, haven't I? Most soundly by the look on your face. My proud son will never forgive such a deception, being made to look the fool. As for the rest of it? Well, my dear, dear girl. *No one* will forgive that. So run along now, little bitch, little savage, little *loser*. It wouldn't do to keep my good friend Helmut waiting. He has so much to say to you. And a little favor to ask as well, I believe. You'd do well to listen carefully. Otherwise, if Philip or your cousin, for instance, were to learn of—well, I'll just leave all that to your imagination, shall I?"

Philip! Brighid screamed inside her head as she left the marquess where he stood and raced toward the servant stairs leading to the kitchens. *Oh, Philip, forgive me! I've left it too late! Too late!*

She slipped through the kitchens while Lucretia had her back to the room, stirring a pot of some wonderfully smelling soup, its rich aroma only serving to make Brighid's stomach pinch together in pain. She eased herself through the doorway, only then stopping to regain her breath, to put some sort of rein on her whirling emotions, to begin to think.

She had to reach inside herself and find some semblance of calm, some measure of strength. Surely men like Helmut Gerlach could smell fear, would know how to capitalize on it. Her fingers closed around the hilt of the knife in her pocket as she took a deep, steadying breath and started down the wide center path of the two-acre gardens, her knees stiff, her breathing still betrayingly swift and shallow.

He'd be near the bottom of the gardens, where the fruit trees grew, where he could find concealment. He'd wait there, hidden, watching for her, then leap out at her, grinning, delighting in frightening her.

She wouldn't give him that satisfaction.

She was nearing the end of the gardens, already on the flat land approaching the woods, the path to Lokwelend's cabin, when Gerlach made his appearance to her right, jumping up like a jack-in-the-box from behind a large berry bush, his smile feral, his dark eyes blazing like hot, reddened coals.

"This way!" he commanded, his voice barely more audible than a whisper, yet filled with command, with menace. "And don't look back! Someone may be watching from the windows."

Brighid was no lamb being led to the slaughter. She knew Philip and Dominick believed Helmut Gerlach to be the one who had attacked Cora, who had butchered Silky Wattson. But even if they were right, even if he was the murderer, he wasn't here to kill. He was here to destroy her in another way. But how? And why?

She forced a smile as she followed Gerlach down the narrow side path for a carefully measured ten paces, then stopped. "So, *Geptschat*. What do you want? To pray over me again?"

He turned to look at her, wetting his already moist lips, rubbing his large hands together like a man contemplating a most satisfying dinner. His grin widened as he nearly danced in his glee. All he lacked were horns and a tail, for the man was Satan incarnate. A dangerous evil monster, who smelled of death and worse. "Good. His lordship left it to me, just the way I asked. I want the child, Brighid Cassidy. I want Johanna's child."

Brighid's bottom lip began to tremble, and she bit at the soft inner skin to hide her reaction to hearing her friend's name on this man's twisted lips. "You're wrong. Daniel is *my* son, Gerlach. I know no Johanna."

"Liar! The child's the devil's spawn! I saw the mark, the mark on his thumb. Our own child had the same mark, our own puling infant, who was born both a girl and dead— totally useless to me, the way Johanna was useless to me. Weak. Godless. Johanna had the same mark. The devil's mark. That boy is Johanna's, and I want him. There are uses, you understand, even for devil children. And then you're to disappear, leave New Eden as his lordship wants. We both get what we want!"

Brighid swallowed over the lump in her throat. Daniel did have a mark on the back of his thumb, a small slash of darker skin no more than an inch long and half as wide. Johanna's thumb had been similarly marked, as had been her other children. Johanna had laughed when Wulapen had remarked on the distinctive birthmark, calling it her only legacy. Now, each night, before she tucked Daniel into his cot, Brighid kissed that mark and sent up a prayer for Johanna, for her good friend who had entrusted her last, greatest legacy to her.

And Gerlach had held Daniel's hand, had seen the mark. *Because you took him to New Eden!* she condemned herself silently. *Because you wanted to dangle some bait and ended by catching yourself and Daniel on this madman's hook! Like the eagle, you have feathered the arrow of your own destruction.* But even as she screamed inside her head, even as she wanted to deny Gerlach's words, she stood silent. Unmoving. Unblinking. Refusing to respond.

"Not going to lie any more, huh? Good. Now, listen well. The way I see it, Johanna owes me a child. There's this family near Easton. Lost their only daughter in the raids and moved away but not too far away—in case their daughter was still alive. Broke their hearts when she wasn't among those herded to Fort Pitt. But if they had a child? If I could bring them a child? Tell them it's their own dear daughter's? The stupid sot is dripping with money, and I ought to know, seeing as how he's given me plenty of it over the years to help him find his daughter."

"You're out of your mind," Brighid said at last, beginning to back away from the man. "All right. I'll admit it, for there's no sense in denying it anymore: Daniel is Johanna's child. But she told me what you were like. She told me how cruel you were, how merciless. And I promised her as she lay dying that you'd never have Daniel, that no one would ever know he was your wife's son. She thought you'd take him and hate him and use him as your slave. But you're even more vile than that. You'd *sell* him? You'd sell Johanna's son? I'd see him dead first!"

Gerlach's hand shot out and grabbed onto her arm as he pulled her close against him, his face inches from hers, his eyes narrowed to slivers of ugly black hate, yet hot with the madness that burned inside him. For the first time she was frightened for her own safety, Daniel forgotten for the moment. "You don't remember, do you? But *I* remember! The Lord has blessed his servant yet again! I tried to get to Fort Pitt first in case either of you were there, but that cursed Englishman beat me to it. And I couldn't remember your name. Only your face. Only those damnable, damning eyes. When I came upon you by mistake in New Eden, when I saw the little half-breed, when I saw that you didn't know . . ."

"Let me go, Gerlach, or I'll hurt you," Brighid said, her free hand tightening around the knife in her pocket. But he didn't seem capable of hearing any other than his own words, spoken to her but seemingly meant for himself.

"I had a plan. From the beginning, I had a plan." He pulled her even closer, squeezing her throat with one large, hamlike hand, shutting off her air, closing down her brain, paralyzing her with his stench, his evil. "But now I've learned to enjoy it," he continued, his spittle searing her cheeks. "Even now that I know you're the one. You're the one, the one with those damned, damning eyes."

She pried his fingers loose, as he seemed to have no notion that he was choking her, then stared at him. Dumbly. Mutely. Her mind racing.

What did Gerlach remember? What did he know that she had forgotten? Lights flashed behind Brighid's eyes as she closed them tight, attempting to hide from Gerlach's leering grin. As on the day Philip had taken her to her parents' farm, the lights splintered into quick, dreadful scenes. Only these were not scenes of her family, of the day they died. These were different, horrifying in another way, filled with faceless men and women, painted savages.

The screams of the damned echoed in her ears. Fire in the night, a blazing campfire, throwing weird shadows, turning this wretched spot of earth into a living hell. The smell of strong liquor everywhere. A woman's brokenhearted sobbing as she was carried on the shoulders of three Indian warriors, then thrown to the ground beside the fire, her clothing cut away from her as the savages laughed and laughed . . .

Her eyes shot open wide. "It was awful," she said quietly, her voice little more than a whisper. "And it went on and on and on." Her voice gained strength and volume. "Where, Gerlach? When? After I was captured? Yes, surely after I was captured, before I woke up in Lapawin's longhouse." She grasped at his sleeves, shaking him. "What happened? *Tell me!* How do you know?"

Her eyes closed once more, she saw a man who'd been lashed to a tree, dying the death of a thousand small cuts, his agonized cries slowly dying away into unintelligible moans . . .

Gerlach's wild laugh exploded the horrible image. "Well, now, look at that. Look at your face! How about that? The high and mighty marquess was wrong. You do remember some of it. Good. Do you remember what you did? Any of it? *I* do. I remember *all* of it. I know, and now his lordship knows. God's damned! *Murderess!* Disappear, Brighid Cassidy. Disappear, or everyone will know. They will all condemn you, as God has forsaken you. Give me the boy so that he isn't tainted by your sins."

"It wasn't me," Brighid whispered brokenly as the last of the images splintered, disappeared. "It couldn't have been me. I would never hurt anyone like that! I was there, yes, but it wasn't me." She looked at Gerlach again, trying to understand. "What happened?" she begged again. "You say you know. How do you know? Tell me what happened!"

"In two days, to give me time to prepare," he gritted out, shifting his eyes in the direction of the house, so that she knew he had heard something. Someone was coming. "Friday, at noon, at the Indian's sweathouse. Bring the child, Brighid Cassidy, or everyone will know. Disappear, and save their memories. Stay, and destroy them all."

And then he was gone, running down the path, breaking through the young fruit trees at an angle, heading into the dense cover of the woods. She was left alone, trembling, knowing she had just faced the monster in her dream, and he had won. For the moment at least, both the monster and the pale stranger had won. She was still trapped. The path that led home was once more closed up.

> *One word frees us of all the weight and pain of life: that word is love.*
> — *Sophocles*

CHAPTER 14

IT IS POSSIBLE FOR A SINGLE EVIL TO TAKE ON SEVERAL FORMS. Do we fear the knife or the man holding it? How does he use his weapon and when, for what reason? To punish or to hide? To feed his madness or to conceal an even greater evil? Or both? Open the door, my son. I grow weary of waiting.

Philip's head ached from examining Lokwelend's words, turning them first this way, then that, looking for answers. And there was an answer for him locked somewhere inside the riddle, he was sure of it. But what? And where?

Gerlach was their man. He was sure of it. Everyone was certain of it. But Lokwelend had spoken as if the man did not act out of madness, but for another reason, a "greater evil." What could be a greater evil than the senseless murders of innocent women? Were the deaths the result of madness, or the madness the result of the deaths? Fear the knife—the deaths? Or fear the man—and his reasons? And what did the reasons have to do with Brighid other than the fact that she, like Silky Wattson, like the others, had been a captive of the Lenape?

Open the door. Open the door!

"What door? Where? Where does the door lead? To the mind of a madman? Or to the answers about her past that Brighid's fears won't let her see?" Philip spoke his questions to the flowers, the comforting surroundings of Bryna Crown's gardens.

He set down the glass of wine he had carried outside with him, leaving it, untouched, on a bench as he drifted down the main path of the gardens, wishing he were a wiser man, wishing his thinking was clearer, less clouded and colored by his concern for Brighid.

His need of her. His love for her. If marriage to him could keep her safe from the madman and from the secrets of her past, he would marry her tonight. If taking her away to England would help, they'd have been aboard ship by now. But Brighid had to stay here until all the "doors" were opened. In that, Philip believed his new father, believed Lokwelend's own dreams.

So Philip was giving Brighid time, as Dominick had suggested and Bryna had all but ordered. He was, on his own, determinedly looking for the answers Lokwelend hinted at and Brighid feared. And he was going quietly out of his mind.

And then she was there, a vision in her yellow gown, walking up the path toward him, coming to him out of the red-orange glare of the setting sun, staring through him, beyond him, lost inside herself as she had been for all of these past days.

"Brighid?"

She stopped walking, blinked, her eyes awash with tears. "Philip." He had heard his name on her lips many times. In many ways. In anger. In frustration. In denial. In the flare and fire of passion. But now, for the first time, she spoke his name in need. Aching, crushing need. "Oh, God, *Philip.*"

He was with her in an instant, catching her as she swayed forward into his arms, and he held her, feeling her tremble. "What is it? What happened?"

"Take me away," she whispered against his chest. "I can't go back inside that house. Not now. Not tonight. I can't face him. Daniel's safe with Cora, with Bryna. Please take me someplace we can be alone. Someplace where I can hold you and stop shaking."

"*Him?* Who are you talking about? Brighid, I don't know who—" He broke off, the image of his father as he had been a few minutes ago, smirking and preening in the drawing room, slamming into his brain. "Giles! By God, if he tried to touch you—"

"No!" she protested, pulling away from him slightly but not letting go of him, as if she needed him as an anchor, a support that would keep her from collapsing where she stood. "No, Philip, he didn't try to touch me. Not in the way you think. I didn't mean to say anything. Really. I—I just don't like the way he looks at me, that's all. And—and he told me you were as good as promised to someone in London. Is that true, Philip? Are you to be married?"

Philip let his breath go in a short, silent laugh of relief. "Is that what this is about? My desperate sire's scheme to marry me off to some heiress in order to line his own pockets? Why, Brighid, my love, I believe I'm flattered. If somewhat angry that you could believe any such drivel."

He looked down at Brighid, kissed her forehead, then drew her against him once more. "Much as you have not agreed to have me, much as you've been avoiding me these last days, I would never marry anyone else. I would much prefer to let the title pass by Dominick, who would renounce it, and to my wretched cousin Humphrey, who'd be most appreciative of the gesture, I'm sure, going to my grave wifeless and childless and still loving you. Does that satisfy you?"

He felt her head move against his chest and took the motion as a nod of agreement. Her next movement, that of slipping her hands down his back, low on his buttocks, pressing him forward against her, spoke of a different agreement, a different question. He might seldom know what Brighid was thinking, but he always knew what she wanted. God bless her.

"Take me to your house, Philip," she pleaded, moving against him, burrowing into him, like a child seeking comfort, like a woman seeking more.

She had about as much chance of being denied in her request, he thought wildly, as she had of stopping the rain with a wish. It had been so long, years too long, whole decades too long, since he had lain with her, since he had buried himself deep inside her, since they had taken their two halves and made them the only sane, coherent whole in a world that made no sense.

"Can you ride in that gown?" he breathed against her ear, his tongue searching every sweet curve, his teeth nipping at the soft skin of her earlobe, hungry to feast on her, his waiting dinner forgotten, his appetite all for the willing woman in his arms.

As she laughed softly, provocatively, he took her hand, and together, through the deepening dusk, they ran toward the stables. He saddled only the Arabian, throwing an Indian saddle of pad and blanket over the stallion's back, slipping a rope halter around the sleek neck, sliding the bit between strong, snapping teeth.

He vaulted onto the stallion from behind, using his hands on the horse's rump, then reached down a hand to Brighid, pulling her up in front of him as he had done once before. But this time Brighid didn't merely cling to him as he turned the stallion out of the yard. No, Brighid didn't cling. She wasn't the least bit passive. She was far too busy undoing his cravat, unbuttoning his waistcoat, pulling the studs from his shirt.

"Those stones aren't paste, love," he told her as the first one came free. "Oh, the devil with it!" he said, groaning as a second stud opened and her lips were against his bare chest, burning him with their heat.

He turned the stallion, plunging into the trees a mere half mile from his new house, pulling her off the horse with him almost before drawing it to a full halt, the two of them tumbling into the soft undergrowth that smelled of summer flowers and wild mint. He rolled onto his back, and she pinned him there with her hands, her kisses, seemingly caught up in a violent frenzy to possess him, to be possessed by him.

Her mouth was everywhere, kissing, biting, suckling, driving him mad. Her hands slipped between them, working at his breeches, seeking him, finding him, freeing him, even as he heard the sharp, tearing sound of ripping cloth, knowing somewhere deep in his brain that he had just destroyed her undergarments.

He was only barely aware of Pegasus nuzzling the sweet grass beside his head, then wandering off, not giving a damn if the costly stallion disappeared forever. All he could think of was Brighid. Brighid's hands, Brighid's mouth, Brighid's warm, wet body as she mounted him, as she sank onto him, enveloping him, devouring him.

She began to move slowly, teasingly, even as she worked with the laces of her bodice, loosening them so that he could pull down her chemise, gain access to her breasts as they were exposed to his eyes, his hands, pushed high and taut above the still-laced white cotton. "You asked if I could ride in this gown, Philip," she all but gasped out as he pressed her nipples between thumbs and forefingers, squeezing the hard pebbles he found, pulling on them, fighting to raise his head so that he could taste her.

"I've got my answer, don't I?" he responded breathlessly, feeling his head begin to spin as she moved once more, her knees pressed tight against his hips, her arms braced, palms down, on either side of his head, her body moving slowly, teasing him, and then more rapidly, driving him on and on and on . . .

He could sense all gentlemanly control, all link to civilization, slipping away from him, and he let it go. He allowed her to lead, to set the pace. And yet, through it all, even as the ecstasy overtook him, even as he felt her body clench and contract, even as his own body echoed her release, he knew that hers was not an act of love, but of desperation. Perhaps even of fear.

* * *

"Maybe I'm simply a wanton, a Jezebel!" Brighid exploded as she whirled to face Philip in the bedchamber of his house a scant half hour later. "Maybe I'm using you, Philip, the way Lilith uses all those men she has told me about. Did that ever occur to you? Or have you forgotten who I am, who you found that day at Fort Pitt. I'm Nipawi Gischuch, the White Indian, the Lenape whore. One of God's damned. And God only knows what I've done these past five years, who I've hurt, just to be spared, just to stay alive. I was a fool to ever believe I could forget that I'm one of His forsaken ones yet to bear witness to my sins and be forgiven!"

"Stop it, Brighid!" Philip ordered, grabbing her shoulders so that she could no longer pace, avoiding his eyes, twisting his questions into angry responses so that he might leave her alone. Leave her pain, her secrets, her fears alone. "Just stop it!"

She violently shrugged her shoulders as she raised her hands to push him away. "Always keeping me where I don't want to stay! Always looking for answers when you can't even be knowing the questions! When even I don't know all the questions. Well, I'm sorry, Philip. Sorry you ever came to Fort Pitt. Sorry I reached out to you, used you. I had no right. No right at all."

He walked over to the bed and sat down on the edge. "Do you love me?"

She raised her hands to either side of her head, her fingers spread, as if she wanted to run at him, to shake him, choke him, into silence. "That has nothing to do with anything!" she screamed at him. "I'm going back to Pleasant Hill."

But she didn't move. She just stood there, looking at him, watching as he folded his arms together across his chest. He pinned an idiotic-looking smile to his face. "But do you love me?"

"Yes, damn you!" she shot back, unable to resist him. "Yes, I love you! There! Are you happy now?"

"Delighted," he answered as he patted the space beside him. "Now, come here, and we'll talk. What happened tonight? I don't mean what happened to us in the woods, for I'd be a fool to pretend I don't know. What happened at Pleasant Hill? What *really* happened with Giles?"

She stayed where she was, knowing that if she went to him, if she sat down beside him, she'd be lost, that she was already lost. She grabbed at the reason she had used previously when they first met in the gardens. "I told you. He said you were betrothed to somebody in London."

Philip nodded. "Yes, I imagine he did. What else? God knows there has to be more to it than that lame farradiddle, although I'm sure you were crushed."

The man was too smart for her own good! Her gaze slid away from his, even as she knew she was betraying herself with the action. "Crushed, is it? Why, you're more vain than Paddy's pig! All right, so I was crushed. I felt near to dying with disappointment. Isn't that enough for you?"

His features sobered. "I don't think so, especially as my esteemed sire does nothing by half measures. I love you, Brighid. I've begged and bullied and badgered you to live with me, to marry me, to go back to England with me. No, there was more. I promise you, I won't kill him if he tried to touch you. I'll most probably maim him badly, but I won't kill him. I've too much to live for to get myself hanged now."

Panic seized her once more. Giles knew now, knew at least Gerlach's version of what she already knew about Johanna and perhaps even what knowledge remained hidden from her. Gerlach couldn't have guessed at all of it, could he? He *knew*. But how did he know? Even worse, she couldn't allow Giles to be the one who told Philip. "No! I don't want you to go to him, to say anything to him. Just let it alone, Philip. For God's sake, let it alone!"

Silence suffocated the room, filling it with stifling tension, cutting off the sweet air of truth, of communication, making it difficult to breathe, to think. She only knew she had to lie and go on lying, because the truth would not cleanse her, but condemn her as a fraud and a fake—perhaps even a murderess—while branding Philip a fool. Giles had said as much, and she agreed with him. She had left it too late, and now Philip would hate her if she told him anything but the lie he already believed, had come to accept.

"All right, Brighid," Philip said at last. "I won't say anything to him if that's what it takes to calm you. But I'm not letting you out of my sight until I boost that miserable old roué out of Pleasant Hill, which will be at first light tomorrow morning. I'm sending both he and Lilith to the inn until I can arrange transport to Philadelphia. I should have done it before this."

"Not Lilith, Philip," Brighid told him quickly, walking over to sit beside him, taking his hand in hers. "She doesn't deserve him any more than you do, than any of us do. I—I feel sorry for her."

"You're either very good or very naive, my love. Lilith makes her own rules and is most happy living by them. Rather like an elegantly groomed alley cat." He lifted her hand to his mouth, kissing each of her fingers in turn, the action sending small shivers up her arm, allowing her to relax, her secret still safe, keeping him at her side just this little while longer before he might learn of her duplicity, of her secret, of her still hidden past.

"Do you want to go back now?" Philip asked, kissing the inside of her wrist, looking at her with passion-filled eyes. "Please lie and say you don't want to go back now. Tell me you love me, Brighid. And this time, maybe you won't shout it at me."

"I love you, Philip Crown," she told him as he eased her back against the coverlet, then followed her down. "I love you, Tauwún. I love you more than my own life, my hope of heaven. Please don't ever forget that."

"Lost your manners somewhere between Playden Court and the colonies, I see," Giles said as Philip walked into the older man's bedchamber without knocking the next morning to discover his father dressed only in footed red flannel drawers and an unbuttoned white lawn shirt.

Sitting at his ease in a rather tall chair, Giles continued to look into the mirror as his man shaved him. "First you disappear, taking the cunning little Irisher with you, then you show up here this morning, smelling of sex. Such a pity we were never closer, Philip, or else you might share. I remember the times my own father and I would ride into the village to split a bottle and a few willing wenches. Wonderfully entertaining and instructive times, the only moments I didn't wish the bastard underground."

"Get out," Philip said softly, employing a motion of his head to direct the valet to the door.

"My lord?" the man questioned his master, who was only half shaved.

Giles snagged the towel hanging over the man's arm and wiped at his face with it. "Do as the uncouth earl says," he told the man, staring at Philip's reflection in the mirror. "It would appear my offspring has something stuck in his craw and, as his loving father, it is my job to extract it. But you'd best take the razor, for I don't much like the look in his eye."

"What did you say to Brighid?" Philip asked as the valet closed the door behind him, seeing no reason not to come directly to the point and knowing he wouldn't be breaking his promise to Brighid, for his father would tell him nothing, less than nothing. He only wanted the man gone, pure and simple, and he'd take his lies in place of the truth the man would never tell, anything he could use as a reason to shove the old bastard out the door.

Besides, Philip most definitely did not want to be in the same room with his sire longer than he had to, not with the man half dressed and looking every moment of his age and more. The marquess's hair, shorn very short, had grown quite thin thanks to years of wearing rubbing wigs. What hair he had left stuck up at strange angles all over his sharply planed skull of a head, the once golden blond hair now a faded yellow gray, giving him the appearance of a death's-head on a mopstick, an expression Philip had never before appreciated and did not much care for now.

As Giles unfolded his length from the chair, his too thin

arms and legs froglike appendages to the sunken chest and paunchy middle of his torso, Philip looked to his left, saw his father's dressing gown, and flung it at him, telling him to cover himself.

"Don't like looking at your future, do you, Philip?" the marquess asked, although he slipped his arms into the dressing gown and tied the sash tightly at his waist. "But no. Not you. Everything in moderation, isn't that right? It's the key to a comfortable old age—and a too long, suffocatingly boring life." He padded over to the drinks table and poured himself a glass of wine, for although it had only just gone eleven, spirits were always his liquid refreshment of choice. He kept his back turned to Philip as he poured, his tone light and sarcastic, but Philip felt fairly certain that the man's hands were shaking.

"I asked you: What did you say to Brighid last night?"

Giles turned around, the glass already emptied, and smiled at his son. "All this heat, and so early in the morning. Philip, show some restraint. What makes you think I said anything to the chit?"

"You told her I was as good as betrothed to that young woman in London."

"Ah!" Giles exclaimed, turning about to pour himself another glass, then raised it to his lips as he looked at Philip once more. "Then this conversation is redundant, isn't it? Please call my man back in here as you leave."

The glass smashed against the wall as Philip slapped it from his father's hand. "Don't push me, old man," he bit out quietly, privately shocked at the depth of animosity in which he held this man who had so reluctantly sired him. "I've already sent off a letter to my solicitor, advising him to have the funds you asked for deposited in your name, and I'm awaiting word now from Philadelphia on the cabins I've secured for your trip back to Dover. Until then, you're no longer welcome here at Pleasant Hill, do you understand? I'll tell your man to pack for you, because you're going to the inn. Now. Today. Cross me in this, speak to Brighid again, utter one word against her once you're back in

London, and I'll see that you never get another penny from me."

"How nauseatingly touching," Giles responded coolly, carefully avoiding the broken shards of glass as he returned to his chair and sat down. "And how exceedingly stupid. I know things, Philip, as I have always made it my business to travel in circles others might shun. Water seeking its own level if you understand. I know things you'd pay very much to learn. Send me to the inn, and they will remain my secrets. However, for a price?" He shrugged his shoulders. "Well, thirty thousand pounds barely begins to touch my price."

Philip immediately thought of Helmut Gerlach and his father's odd association with the man. His promise to Brighid not to push Giles for answers winged away through the opened window. "What do you know? And please, old man, don't think me above choking this information out of you."

Giles leaned forward, picked up a small silver-handled knife, and began neatly paring his nails. "Not now, Philip, as I may still be able to learn more interesting tidbits worthy of recompense. Later, say, tomorrow? That would be Friday, yes? Yes, Friday morning at this same time would be exactly right. Have a paper drawn up listing my terms. Simple terms, say one hundred thousand pounds payable upon presentation of your letter, which I shall carry on my person to London. Have the gollumpus there also, ready to witness your signature. I'll want the paper in my pocket before I depart for Philadelphia, which I will be most happy to do immediately after the paper is signed, as one inn is as uncomfortable as another and I've already become bored with New Eden. I should be on my way, your signed paper in my luggage, say, at noon? Agreed? Oh, and only if I am to remain here until then, of course, nestled in the bosom of my family. But as I know you're anxious, I will tell you one thing, all right? Consider it a gift."

He laid down the knife and smiled at Philip. "Gerlach is your man. Mad as a hatter, he is, and bound to kill again.

Tomorrow, I'll tell you why. And then, my dear besotted son, it will be up to you to decide what you will do with the information. It will be a dilemma worthy of Solomon, I promise you, and I will be that sorry to miss the outcome. Poor Philip. Poor, poor Philip."

Philip glared at the man for long moments, caught between wanting to choke more information out of him and going to tell Dominick what he'd already learned. The decision was taken out of his hands as a female scream echoed through the house.

"That's Lilith!" Philip exclaimed, glancing quickly toward the door.

"Is it? I thought someone had stepped on a cat's tail. Well, one's much the same as the other. Toddle along and see what's amiss, Philip. Someone probably hid her rouge pot. Oh, and don't forget to send in my man." The marquess's thin smile held a delight that made Philip immediately suspicious, but when Lilith screamed again, he pushed the thought to the back of his mind and left the room.

People were running from everywhere as Philip flew down the stairs to where Lilith stood in the foyer, panting to regain her breath, hugging her middle, and still loudly calling for help. Her lovely face was scratched, her hair a tangled mess, her gown dirty, as if she had fallen, fallen more than once. And her eyes—her eyes were wild. He reached her first, taking hold of her shoulders and shaking her roughly, trying to get her to calm down enough to talk to him.

"It—it's Hallie!" she got out at last, and Philip shot a quick look to Dominick, who had been working in his study all morning rather than being out in the fields. "We went for a walk. Just a short walk in the woods behind the gardens. God, Philip, you have to save her! This is my fault! This is all my fault! I wanted to know about how she was treated by the savages, what they did to her. It all seemed so exciting, so deliciously perverse . . . and her tattoos and everything—oh, don't just stand there, Philip! *Find her!*"

Brighid was beside him now, silently pressing a rifle into

his hand, a knife, before doing the same with Dominick. "Where, Lilith?" she questioned the older woman tersely. "Where in the woods?"

Lilith turned her tear-wet face to Brighid. "I don't know! Oh, Jesus, *I don't know!* We were walking . . . and talking . . . picking flowers for the nursery . . . and then I was on the ground, my head hurting like it had been split open . . . and Hallie was gone. I got up and ran. I ran and I ran. I ran *forever!*" She grabbed onto Philip's arms. "He's got her, Philip! The madman has got her!"

Without having said a word, Dominick was already out the door, turning to his right and heading, Philip was sure, to the back of the house, past the gardens and into the woods. Philip looked around and saw that Cora was determinedly leading a protesting Bryna into the drawing room, but there were two male servants, Lucas, Brighid, and Lucretia, all standing at the ready. Everyone in the house was present, everyone save Giles, who would be useless in any case.

"Listen to me, all of you," Philip ordered, his mind whirling even as his heartbeat remained slow and steady. "Lucretia, make sure Mary Catherine stays in the nursery with the children, then go to the stables and tell the men there to arm themselves and follow us. The rest of you, come with me now. We're going into the woods as quickly and with as much noise as we can make. Understand? Yell out Hallie's name. Yell anything you can think to yell. If he hears us coming, he may run off before it's too late. *Let's move!*"

Brighid had already stripped off her petticoats and pulled the rear hem of her gown up and between her legs, tucking the ends into her waistband, all so that she could run faster. She then took out her knife and slit Lilith's gown and petticoats from waist to hem, for Philip's sister was trembling so violently that there wouldn't be time for anything else, and Lilith would have to be able to run. He grabbed his sister's hand, and they all ran toward the back of the house, out the door in Dominick's study, and down the hill.

"Where, Lilith?" he shouted as they halted for a moment at the bottom of the gardens. "Where did you go into the trees?"

She looked around, pushing her hair out of her face, still sobbing, still trembling as if she had taken a bad chill. She held out her hand, pointing to the path that led to Lokwelend's cabin. "There! We went into the woods there!"

Of course they had gone into the woods that way. It was the only logical move. The woods were thick, virgin, and ten feet away from the path was as good as ten miles, for all that anyone could see through the trees and dense undergrowth that kept the sun from reaching the ground in most places.

"He won't have taken her any closer to Lokwelend's," Brighid said, gently pushing Lilith to the ground, telling her to stay there. "Lilith, what side were you walking on? To Hallie's left or to her right?"

"What? I don't—I can't—to her right! I was walking on her right! And then I was on the ground, and Hallie was gone."

"Let's go," Philip said, taking Brighid's hand. "Dominick's ahead of us, but you're the one who can read signs, Brighid, although I doubt it will be hard to follow the bastard."

But it was. They saw Dominick ahead of them on the path, about halfway along the three-quarter-mile distance between Pleasant Hill and the Lenape's cabin, standing there, looking first one way, then the other. "Everything's pretty trampled, like she put up a good fight," he told them as they joined him. "And then Lilith must have run around in circles, because the path has been crossed and recrossed a half-dozen times. Brighid?"

Both men watched as Brighid fell to her knees amid the scattering of wildflowers the two women had been picking, looking at the foot impressions. "Lilith was wearing heeled shoes, so these are her tracks. She's made a real mess of things." She rose, walked into the woods a few feet, then touched a broken twig. "There are none of Lilith's footprints here. I say we go this way, to our left, straight to our left, as he wouldn't want to move closer to either Pleasant Hill or Lokwelend's."

By now there were ten in the search party, all of them armed, all of them told to fan out within sight of each other along the path before entering the woods to the left, calling and shouting as they made their way into the trees.

Philip kept Brighid close beside him. They moved as quickly as they could, unable to run because of fallen trees and dark patches of black mud caused by the rain that had fallen during the night.

"Hallie!" Brighid called out loudly, echoing the voices of the others as everyone began the hunt. *"Hallie!"*

"Gerlach!" Philip shouted, and Dominick took up the same call. "Let her go!"

The man had to be mad, Philip thought as they kept moving, as Brighid stopped once or twice to look at twigs, at footprints, then motioned for them to continue. Only a madman would dare to snatch Hallie away in the middle of the day and so close to Pleasant Hill. Had the blood lust become that strong, that impossible to deny? And why? Why?

Unless he's done it simply to prove that he can. The thought nearly stopped Philip in his tracks and made him remember his father's smile at the sound of Lilith's scream. His knowing smile. "Son of a *bitch!*" The words exploded from him even as Brighid pulled on his arm, stopping him, so that he looked ahead once more and saw Lokwelend coming toward them through the trees.

"Grandfather!" Brighid called out, gasping for breath, as was Philip, for they had been running for what seemed like hours, although no more than ten minutes had passed since Lilith's return to Pleasant Hill. "Where's Hallie? Is she all right?"

"An old man cannot even die in peace," Lokwelend said as he stepped over a rotted log and then sat down on it, glaring up at Philip and Dominick, who had joined them along with the rest of the search party.

"You're *not* dying, Grandfather, thank God." Brighid

shot back at him without rancor, causing Philip to nearly snap his neck as he turned to look at her in amazement. "Cora told me what you were about days ago. You simply can't help being a meddlesome old man who weaves six truths and ten lies before breakfast. Now, where's Hallie? She is all right, isn't she?"

Lokwelend merely shrugged her words away. "Believe what you will, Brighid Cassidy. As your wise man Euripides said, 'Dishonor will not trouble me, once I am dead.' Hallie is just there, hunkered down behind that large oak. She is a modest young woman and would like a shawl or some other covering before showing herself."

Philip untied the sash from around his waist and shrugged out of his deerskin jacket even as he told the search party to return to Pleasant Hill with his thanks. "How badly is she hurt?" he asked Lokwelend when the others, except for Brighid and Dominick, had gone. "Was— was she raped? Was she cut?"

Lokwelend shook his head. "This was not like the others, Tauwún, and was never meant to be," he said, reaching into his sleeve cuff to pull out a scrap of paper. "Hallie was stripped of her clothes, gagged with a cloth, a sack over her head, and her wrists lashed to a tree when I found her. The man is mad, and he is no woodsman. I've heard less noise from a pig caught in a briar, which made it easy for me to find her, although your madman was long gone. Here," he ended, holding out the note. "You will not like this, Tauwún. I do not like this."

Philip took the crumpled sheet of brown paper even as Brighid snatched the jacket from him and, with a determined look that told him she'd know the contents of the note before the hour was out or know the reason why, made her way to Hallie's hiding place.

Dominick looked over Philip's shoulder as the paper was unfolded. "Execrable handwriting," he commented, then fell silent as Philip read the few lines aloud.

"'I am everywhere. I am all powerful. I am the right hand of God. Do as I say, heed my demands, for my reach is long and can touch anyone, at any time. No one you love is safe unless you obey me. No one.'"

Philip crushed the note in his hand. "The man's as cryptic as you, my father, in his own way. It has to be Gerlach, of course, and he knows we know he's the killer. Damn it! Do as I say, he tells us, but doesn't tell us what he wants us to do. This makes no sense; it makes no sense at all." He turned to Dominick, frustration tightening his muscles until his entire body ached. "He'll hide now until he strikes again, and there's nothing we can do about it. And we still don't know why. If only we knew *why!*"

"Lokwelend?" Dominick asked, looking to the old Indian.

"As I have said before, my son," Lokwelend responded wearily, looking straight at Philip. "It is possible for a single evil to take on several forms. Do we fear the knife or the man holding it? How does he use his weapon and when, for what reason? To punish or to hide? To feed his madness or to conceal an even greater evil? Or both?"

"But does it really matter why, my father?" Philip asked, in no mood for the old man's puzzles. "I'd like to know what's going on, yes, but I'd be happy to settle for having the man stopped before he kills again."

"We have a name now, a face to put to the name, a recognizable form of the evil," Lokwelend continued, as if Philip had not spoken. "You are closer. Open the door, my son. Do not listen to the Pale One, for he is mischief, nothing more, and his heart is already dead. You know the name and the face of my greatest sorrow now, have discovered what I could see only as a shadow that haunts my dreams. This is a good thing, even if you have yet to learn the depth of this evil. The soul of my son, Pematalli, the souls of all those who died too soon, depend on you, Tauwún. Only you and the Night Fire together can open the door. Hurry, my son. I am a patient man, and I love you, but I have already waited too many years."

Philip stabbed his fingers through his hair, trying to understand this new twist in an already convoluted riddle.

"You, my father? You have waited? I thought this was about these women, about Brighid. What has Gerlach to do with Pematalli, with you?"

Lokwelend stood up as Brighid led a quietly weeping Hallie from the trees, both of the women keeping their eyes cast down as they walked by the men and made their way back toward the path. "The wise chief named Euripides said, 'Fate is stronger than anything I have known.' It was the Night Fire's fate that brought her here, Tauwún, her fate that took her away for so long."

He walked over to Philip and laid a hand on his forearm. Philip felt the strength in the old Lenape's grip; he felt the love, the hope, and the determination. "It was your fate, Tauwún, that brought you to this place, that made yours the hand that gave Pematalli his fate. Between you, you and the Night Fire will also give Pematalli his revenge, his justice, and the justice of so many others. The Night Fire has all the secrets locked inside her memories. You, my son, have all the power of justice and love. One cannot succeed without the other, or the victory over this Gerlach will be hollow. Open the door to the Night Fire's memory, open your heart to love, and close the door on the treachery of the past. It is your fate, Tauwún. Do not fail those who have placed their trust in you. Do not fail to be kind and forgiving. Do not fail to seek justice. When you have gained it all, only when you balance the love with the justice, will you be all the man I have seen in my dreams."

BOOK FOUR

Communion

We know how to speak many falsehoods
which resemble real things, but we
know, when we will, how to speak true things.
—Homer

So my conscience chide me not,
I am ready for Fortune as she wills.
— *Dante*

CHAPTER 15

BRIGHID SAT ON THE WIDE WINDOW SEAT IN THE NURSERY AND watched the sun slipping inexorably toward the horizon, wondering if it would be the last she'd ever see. Certainly it would be the last she would view from the safety of Pleasant Hill.

Gerlach's words, as she had read them in his note earlier in the day, had been a direct warning to her, although she had not said so to Philip or to anyone. Either she met with Gerlach tomorrow at noon, or he would kill again. Either she gave Daniel over to him and disappeared, or the people she loved would die.

As if he would allow her to "disappear." He wanted her dead, not simply gone. It would be kill or be killed tomorrow at Lokwelend's sweathouse. And Helmut Gerlach had to be mad not to believe that she knew it.

If only she knew the reasons behind his madness, the twisted rationalization behind his personal hatred of her.

"Brighid? Will you talk to me without urging, or am I going to be forced into pleading my belly and my delicate condition in order to get some sort of truth from you?"

Brighid turned and looked up at Bryna, then smiled. Bryna was wearing her I'll-be-hearing-none-of-this-nonsense-thank-you expression on her beautiful face, the one she used on the twins when they tried to explain away the jam prints on the wall or the frog in Hallie's bed.

She should have known her cousin would seek her out, her intelligent mind stuffed full of questions. She patted the space beside her, inviting Bryna to sit down. "I can't tell you what I don't know, Cousin," she said reasonably.

"Well, then that's no help to us, is it?" Bryna responded, squeezing Brighid's hand. "Except that Lokwelend believes you know more than nothing and less than everything. Perhaps if the two of us put our heads together, we can fit the pieces together, blending the known with the unknown?"

Brighid kept her eyes averted from Bryna. Surely her friend had not told her cousin about Daniel. "Lokwelend spoke to you about me? I highly doubt that. And what has my grandfather said to you?"

"Oh, pooh! Nothing really," Bryna answered, sighing theatrically. "I just *feel* that he knows something and hoped to trick you into some sort of admission." She sighed again. "Now I'll have to think up another lie and see if that one bears fruit. Either that, or I will be a bully and badger it out of you. Because you do know *something*, don't you, Brighid?"

"I know that Helmut Gerlach hates me," Brighid admitted, feeling her head begin to pound as she recalled Gerlach's face as it pressed close to hers, smelled the rancid sweat of his body, the putrid stink of his breath. "I just don't know why."

"He hates all of the female captives, Dominick says," Bryna said reasonably. "That's why he's killing them one by one. He feels he is the Lord's agent here on earth, cleansing and then redeeming the damned. Dominick also says that

Gerlach took Hallie today because we know he's the murderer even if no one in New Eden agrees, that we've been following him, making his life miserable, and he took Hallie to prove that he could, to prove that he is stronger than any of us."

"And you believe all of that?"

Bryna shook her head, her liquid green eyes twinkling with mischief. "Only half of it, I'll admit, with only you about to hear me say the words. I would never say so to Dominick, as men must be allowed to think themselves superior at times. It makes it that much easier to go off and do what *we* want without them getting in the way. Although I must also say that Lokwelend's plea to Philip, his mention of Pematalli and all those killed in the raids, has certainly confused Dominick's theory, so that he and Philip are downstairs now in the study, working and reworking both their questions and their deductions. Me, I thought I'd come directly to you, who may actually have some answers."

Brighid laid her head against her cousin's shoulder. "I'm glad I came back, Bryna," she said softly, feeling tears pricking behind her eyes. "I'm glad you were so stubborn and made Philip come after me. I was living a dream these past five years and hiding from who I am, what I have lived, the person my life has made me. Even, I imagine, from what Lokwelend has always known about me. But from now on, I must be allowed to make my own choices, even if you don't understand or agree with them. I thought you should know that. That and how much I love you. How much I love all of you. Daniel could not have a more loving home, and I thank you for it."

She felt Bryna's arm go around her shoulders, squeezing her close. "You make things difficult, Brighid, my love. But if I have learned anything myself in these past years, I have learned that I cannot control everything, make the world turn to my order, as Dominick has so often teased. You're a woman grown, Brighid, and your life is yours to live as you see fit." She laughed then, releasing Brighid and rising to her feet. "My, but saying that hurt! Yet Dominick would be proud of me. Now, come on, dearest Cousin, and the two of us will say our good-nights to our children. Then you might go rescue Philip from Dominick—only if you've a mind to, you understand. Far be it from me to tell you what to do."

Brighid rose as well, putting her hand into Bryna's. "You'll be telling Saint Peter how to best open the pearly gates before you walk on through to collect your angel wings, Cousin," she teased, giving Bryna a kiss on the cheek. "Now, come on. We'll see if Mary Catherine has wheedled those twins of yours and my Daniel into saying their Our Fathers."

Brighid stayed away from her bed, just as she had been avoiding Philip all of the afternoon and into the evening. Both would do nothing but fill her head with dreams, dreams she both welcomed and feared.

But he would find her, even if he had to come to her room and break down her door. He would find her because he loved her and worried for her and wanted truths from her, truths she did not know and the secret she still hid.

It would do no good to hide from him, so she took up her shawl and walked outside, into the gardens, using the full moon as her guide as she wandered over to a bench and sat down, breathing in the sweet night scent of Bryna's first roses.

She looked up at the windows of the house she had grown to love, the house that held the people she loved. There were lights in Bryna's windows, where she and Dominick were probably lying close together in their great bed, talking, holding each other, and loving each other.

The nursery wing was dark, with the children all asleep these past three hours, snugly tucked in their cots, dreaming the innocent dreams of childhood. Unless, of course, Mary Catherine still laid awake, fingering her rosary beads with the sureness of great faith, a faith Brighid wished she could feel.

The only other lights on the upper floor came from the

marquess's rooms, which seemed odd, for the man usually chose to spend his evenings in the drawing room, close to the decanters.

Brighid's own room, at the front of the house, and Lilith's were also dark, she was sure. Philip's normally carefree, hey-go-mad sister had finally agreed to take the laudanum Bryna had pressed on her, for the woman's first hysterics may have faded but her guilt in having taken Hallie into the woods had left her pale and shaken. But probably no wiser, Brighid thought with a wry smile. Lady Lilith did not seem the sort to learn from her mistakes.

Do any of us? she wondered, drawing the shawl closer around her shoulders. But she would play her cards as they had been dealt to her and accept the consequences of both her lie and her solution. She saw no other choice. Not if she wanted to protect those she loved. Not if she could not—as Lokwelend had asked of Philip, of her—open the door to *all* of her past.

She looked up at the marquess's window again, the panes still glowing faintly yellow from the candlelight. Philip could not be told of the depth of his father's evil, for he would then feel honor bound to defend her and to attack his own father. That she could not allow. No more than she could allow his father to be the one who told Philip about Daniel, told him what Gerlach knew of her past. The marquess had kept silent so far, sure he held the trump card that would remove her from his life. She had to either take away his reason to play that card or regain her memory so that she could defend herself.

So she would meet with Helmut Gerlach just as he had asked. She would listen to his story and pray her memory opened to her, proving him not only a monster, but a liar. Because she had to know who she was, who she really was, what she had done during the time Johanna had begged her to forget.

And then? And then?

Brighid closed her eyes, refusing to think beyond tomorrow—when she would meet her monster face-to-face.

* * *

"You knew."

The marquess of Playden turned away from the card his valet had just laid on the table, his wince possibly for the card, possibly for his son's rude entrance into his private bedchamber at this late hour, possibly just because his stays had dug into his side when he'd shifted in his chair. "Knew what, Philip?" he asked, turning back to draw a card from his own hand and negligently toss it onto the makeshift playing surface. "Your trick, I believe, Soames, curse you."

Philip fought the urge to cross the room at a run and drag Giles from the chair, slamming him up against the wall. Only the passage of several hours and keeping a careful distance from the man had so far succeeded in calming Philip enough that he could even look at his father without murdering him. "You knew Gerlach was in the woods, probably even helped him pen the note. And it was you who filled Lilith's head with questions about Hallie's experiences with the Lenape. According to Lilith, you suggested this morning's walk in the woods. Don't bother to insult me with a denial."

The marquess tipped back his chair on its hind legs and twisted his head around to grin back at his son. "I wouldn't think to deny a word, my boy. It was, all in all, one of my better efforts. And there was no real harm done. Lilith hasn't had so much exercise since she was spreading her thighs for that satyr Holbrooke. She finally had to give him up, you know, no matter how many diamonds he showered on her. Something about a whip and leather restraints, I believe, or so I heard in the clubs."

Philip drew his hands into fists. "Why? Just tell me why."

"I believe Holbrooke has a fondness for pain actually," the marquess responded smoothly, shooing Soames out of the room as he rose from his chair and faced Philip. "Oh, you mean why did I help arrange this morning's small demonstration of Gerlach's prowess? For the tickle it gave me perhaps?" He tipped his head to one side as he glared at Philip, his near colorless eyes narrowing to slits. "Ah, but that would be a lie, wouldn't it? It's rather more than that.

To be perfectly honest—honesty can be so *rewarding* at times, I've found—I wished to demonstrate to you how much I know, how much that knowledge is worth, and how much Gerlach's trust in me is worth. I do have your interest now, don't I? Would you care to ante up again and find out what else I know?"

Philip stepped back a pace, realizing that he had nearly stumbled into doing just as his father wanted him to do. The man had knowledge all right, some terrible knowledge gleaned from Gerlach that he had shared with Brighid, that Brighid—for whatever reason—did not want Philip to learn. He had known from the first that Brighid had been fobbing him off with that business of being upset because of any possible fiancée Giles had told her about. There had been more, much more, and she lived in fear that Giles would use his knowledge to hurt her in some way. She had nearly begged him, *had* begged him, not to go to his father. And yet here he was. About to both betray his promise to Brighid and step blindly into the man's carefully constructed trap!

"No," he pronounced at last, watching in deadly fascination as Giles's smile faded, as the man's already pale cheeks went dead white beneath the twin flags of rouge. "No," he repeated firmly, slowly shaking his head. "It won't work this time, old man. I won't be the butterfly whose wings you rip off for the *tickle* of it, as you have done with my poor drunken mother, with Polly Rosebud, with Dominick and Lucas, as you've done with people all of your miserable life. I'll learn all I need to know from Brighid if she wants to tell me, or I won't learn it at all. See that your man has you both packed and ready to leave for the inn tomorrow morning at first light. I don't need your help to catch Gerlach, and I would have to be out of my mind to apply for it. Good-bye, Father. I doubt I shall see any necessity for the two of us to meet again this side of hell."

And with that and with the sight of Giles's sputtering anger to live in his memory, Philip quit the room and went looking for Brighid.

If he knew nothing else, he knew that she was waiting for him.

He dismounted from his great white stallion, walking toward her with open arms, and she lifted her hands to him, allowing him to help her to rise, so that they stood face-to-face, looking deeply into each other's eyes, into each other's souls. "If you won't go, I will stay here with you."

"I can't ask that of you," she told him. "I would never ask that of you."

"And that's why I'll stay," he answered, pulling her into his embrace. "Perhaps one day you will trust me enough to come with me as we look for safe passage home. I am content to wait, as long as I can wait with you. Let the forest grow, grow all around us, locking us here if it so desires. There is no other home for me but with you."

"But you don't know me," she protested, fighting her senses that longed for the touch, scent, and taste of him. "I am not who you think I am, what you think I am."

He reached out his hand and pressed two fingers to her mouth, gently cutting off her weak protests. "Don't talk, Nipawi Gischuch. Don't say anything. Just love me. Simply love me. Everything else will come in its time."

"Even forgiveness? Even those things I try to forget and those I long so to remember?" She looked beyond Philip, beyond her beloved Tauwûn, to the dark figure who crept closer, ever closer. "And what of the monster?"

"We'll face him together, learn his secrets, and vanquish him. For Lokwelend. For Pematalli and all the rest. We will vanquish him. Together."

She pulled free of Philip's embrace, felt the tear in her heart that came with that withdrawal. "No matter if we best him or he bests us, I'm afraid I will lose. It's hopeless, Tauwûn. Don't open this door. If you love me, don't open this door."

Brighid awoke all at once at the touch of Philip's hand on her shoulder. She struggled to sit up, her muscles tight after falling asleep across the length of the hard bench, and wiped tears from her eyes as he held out his hands to her. More real than in her melodramatic dream, more painful and more sweet, she felt the warmth of his flesh, the strength she had come to depend upon, the love she had borrowed, perhaps never to own.

"The last time I found you sleeping out here, it was on the ground. I see you've progressed," he said to her as she stood up. "Or is it that you didn't want to dirty that lovely gown?"

She blinked at him, blinked back both her tears and her surprise, realizing that he, like she, had no great wish to spend this night rehashing the problems of the day, the trials of tomorrow. For now, for this moment, he would be content to be with her, as she would be to find comfort and passion in his arms. "The yellow always seemed to be your favorite," she told him as he slipped her hand through his crooked elbow and led her down the path, away from the house. "I wouldn't wish to see it ruined."

"I prefer to see it gone," he told her, his smile turning the muscles of her legs to jelly, so that she stumbled against him. "Pegasus is waiting at the bottom of the gardens. Would you care for a moonlight ride to my house?"

"I'd rather we went to Lenape Cliff," she told him truthfully, knowing she was taking the first step toward good-bye. "I've a need tonight to be close to what I was. I can't explain it. If you don't mind?"

She rode in front of him, sitting sideways on the horse, her arms wrapped around his shoulders, her head pressed against his strong chest, the smooth gait of the Arabian nearly lulling her into believing that this was just another night, another moment in an endless circle of precious moments she and Philip would string like pearls fashioned from a benevolent moonlight.

But this was to be like no other night, for it might be their last night together, although Philip couldn't know that. She had never promised him forever, had made no more demands on him than she could prevent. And she had always wondered why. Why she could not feel secure in his love, secure in her future. Secure enough to have told him at the beginning all the things she couldn't tell him now—not before she met with Gerlach.

Surefootedly, Pegasus climbed the grassy incline leading to Lenape Cliff, to an abrupt end of the world that had been and a view of what this land had become, of Philip's estate in the distance below them, of all the land that was now English land, no longer Lenape land.

But here, here on the hillside, where Pematalli's bones rested, where she had buried the bits and pieces of her last five years, the Lenape were real again, almost palpably real, and she walked the sacred ground, wishing for the strength and blessing of all the ghosts of her two families.

She turned to look at Philip, who had tied Pegasus to a nearby tree and now was simply standing there, silent, willing to take his lead from her. He would hold her all night, silent and comforting, if she wished. He would love her all night, with his hands and mouth and body, if she so desired. He would give her his heart, his soul, his future.

"I love you, Philip Crown," she said at last, walking toward him, watching how the moonlight glinted off his golden hair, drinking in the sight of him as he stood there in his deerskins, memorizing him. "I have never been so happy or so incredibly sad. Da always said it was the nature of the Irish to be melancholy, and I feel melancholy tonight. Will you hold me? Will you lie with me here in the outstretched palm of the Great Spirit? Will you make me forget just for tonight, and give me something to remember?"

He came to her without words, without demands, without questions or answers. He accepted her for what she could give him, as he always had done, and gave her his love as he had promised in her dream.

Together, they sank to their knees on still warm ground, surrounded by the fragrance of evening. His hands cupping her cheeks, he stared deeply, searchingly, into her eyes, sighed, and lightly touched his mouth to hers. "It will be all right, Brighid," he promised against her lips. "I know you're frightened, and you have every reason for fear. But I'll keep you safe, make it all right. I won't lose you now. I can't lose you now."

"I'm *here* now, Philip," she told him, her palms burning as they stroked his shoulders, his back, through the supple deerskin. "If tonight is all we ever have, it will be enough."

"Never!" he gritted out angrily, pressing her close, lowering her so that she lay below him on the sweet grass, the weight of his upper body bearing her down, lifting her up. "Tonight will never be enough. We have our whole lives ahead of us, Brighid. Lives full of love and laughter and heartaches we'll share. Children we'll adore, brothers and sisters to be company for Daniel. I don't give a damn about Giles's plots or Lokwelend's puzzles or Gerlach's crazed schemes. This is what is important, Brighid—you and I, loving each other, tonight, tomorrow, for all our tomorrows. Nothing else is important. Nothing else makes any sense."

She reached up a hand to stroke his cheek. "There are times I believe I love you too much," she said wonderingly. "If I loved you less I might not be so afraid. I might be more willing to take the chance of losing your love."

He turned his head so that he could press a kiss in her palm. "You'll never lose my love, Brighid," he told her. "Just as you'll never lose me. Where would I go without you? How would I live?"

Her bottom lip began to tremble as she suppressed the nearly uncontrollable urge to tell him about Johanna, about Daniel, about her promise, her deceit. He'd probably forgive her. At this moment, he would probably forgive her. But what was the point? There was still Helmut Gerlach and *his* truths. The vision of that poor woman in the Indian camp, of her terrified screams, would never leave her. What had she, Brighid Cassidy, done to escape a similar fate? How had she saved her life that horrible night, all those horrible nights before she had awakened in Lapawin's loving care, her memory blank of everything that had happened after her father had first spied out their attackers?

Had she killed to please her captors? Had she become an animal, turning on her own, joining in the bloody revelry, doing the unthinkable to save herself, as she'd heard other captives had done at the urging of their captors, in order to save her own life? Why had Johanna told her not to pursue her lost memory of those days and nights?

Gerlach knew. Only Gerlach knew, although she did not know how he had come to hold such terrible knowledge. Only Gerlach and her own still wretchedly locked memory could give her the answers she desperately needed to learn.

"Brighid," Philip said softly, bringing his head down to hers, his breath warm against her ear. "Brighid, don't cry. I won't talk any more, won't push you. Please, my darling one, don't cry."

She took a deep, shuddering breath, then slid her arms around his back, pulling him closer even as, high above their heads, she watched a star flash across the sky, then die. "Love me, Philip," she begged him again, as she had so many times, with her words, in her heart.

"Always," he told her, raising his head slightly, then swooping down to capture her mouth.

Philip awoke when the morning sun threaded its way through the leaves high in the towering trees and spilled itself on his face and body, warming the naked skin of his upper torso. He lay very still for a few moments, trying to remember where he was, then sat up all at once.

Pegasus was still tied, munching at the sweet grass at his feet. Nearby, Philip saw a splash of yellow silk on the ground beside his own deerskin jacket and blue cotton shirt, the pristine whiteness of discarded petticoats, a narrow pair of heeled slippers.

But Brighid herself was gone.

Philip stabbed his fingers through his hair as he looked around in confusion, in growing fear, then squinted in bewilderment as he noticed the small mound of turned earth closer to the rim of the cliff. He got to his feet and walked to the spot, seeing that the hole had indeed been freshly dug, like a small, empty grave, and his perplexity increased.

Kneeling beside the shallowly scooped out earth, he picked up a small blue bead, the sort Brighid had worn on her Lenape deerskins—the deerskins she no longer wore. His mouth went dry, even as his heart began to slam inside his chest. Brighid had brought him here on purpose last night, here, to the place where Lokwelend had buried his son, where she, Philip could only imagine, had "buried" her Lenape past.

And now she had dug up that past, unearthed the life she had never been allowed to bury successfully, and once more put on the clothing of the Lenape. But why? Why?

She's gone hunting, he decided as he threw the bead to the ground and stood, turning about in a slow circle, trying to see what direction she had taken when she'd left him. *Hunting for Helmut Gerlach.*

"Brighid!" he called out loudly, knowing she didn't hear him, knowing if that she did hear him, she wouldn't answer. His hands balled into fists as he raised his head to the morning sky and cried out in his agony. "Sweet Jesus—*Brighid!*"

*He harms himself who does harm to another,
and the evil plan is most harmful to the planner.*

— *Homer*

CHAPTER 16

PHILIP PUNISHED PEGASUS ALL THE WAY BACK TO PLEASANT Hill, then deserted the horse in the drive before a groom could rush out to grab the reins. He devoured the steps in a single leap, barreled into the house with the front door banging hard against the white foyer paneling as he shoved it clear, and bounded up the stairs three at a time, his eyes glowing near red with rage and purpose.

"He's still here, isn't he?" he demanded of Dominick as his uncle stepped into the main upstairs hallway, still tying a multicolored sash at the waist of his deerskin jacket. "He may be a snake, but he slithers slowly."

"Who are you talking about? Giles?" Dominick asked, falling into step behind Philip, then trotting to keep close as they both turned a corner in the hallway and headed toward the guest chambers that housed the marquess of Playden. "What happened? And where's Brighid? She didn't come home last night. We assumed she was with you."

Philip didn't answer. He pushed open the door of Giles's bedchamber with both hands, then burst into the room even before the door had slammed back against the wall. Giles had sat up quickly at the sound, and only dumb luck and a faint heart had made him hunker down, the covers to his neck, before Philip's knife blade sliced into the headboard mere inches to the left of where the marquess's nightcap-clad skull had been.

"Where's Gerlach?" Philip demanded, crossing the carpet, then bending over the bed, pinning his father there with one stiffened arm on either side of the man's quivering body. "Tell me now, you pathetic, twisted bastard, or I'll have your hide hanging from the nearest tree."

"Philip," Dominick warned from the foot of the bed. "You'll never get a word out of him if you scare him to death. Now, stand clear and tell me what's going on."

Philip, knowing his eyes were wild, that his hair hung uncombed to his shoulders, and not giving a damn for any of it, as he had left civilization behind the moment he realized what Brighid must be up to, pushed himself up from the mattress and looked to his uncle. "My *father* has been consorting with the devil if you must know. He arranged that whole business yesterday—Lilith, Hallie, all of it. For the *giggle* it would give him. The same way he provided Mother with her first brandy. The same way he set you up to take the blame for what happened to Polly. And now Brighid's gone after Gerlach."

He whirled back toward the bed once more, grabbing Giles by the throat and half-dragging him to his feet, smelling the man's liquor-soaked breath and the stink of perfumed, unwashed peer. "Talk to me, old man. Talk to me now. *Where's Gerlach?*"

The marquess's eyes were near to bulging from his head before Philip pushed out with both arms and sent the man sprawling onto the bed once more. "I don't know," Giles choked out, straightening his nightcap over his thin, straggling hair, then abandoning that particular modesty in order to cover his bony knees and shins with the hem of his nightshirt. "Dominick, Brother, get this madman away from me! As God is my judge, I don't know what he's talking about!"

"God will judge you all right," Philip bit out, "but not before I do. Dominick, I know you're a forgiving man, and I've tried to shield you from this miserable piece of offal because you've a new life here now and just want the past to die. But I need your help now, even if my explanations sound far-fetched. Giles knows things Gerlach must have told him—lies or truth, I don't know or care, but things Brighid doesn't want me to learn. I've given her my promise, and I won't break it. But you gave Brighid no promises, Dominick. Do you understand what I'm asking? Brighid's life, God help us all, could depend on what this miserable bastard knows."

Dominick looked to Giles, then back to Philip, his expression bland, although his eyes were hard. "Wait downstairs, Philip," he said calmly. "I'll be with you directly. There's turning the other cheek, there is forgiving what cannot be changed and getting on with our lives, and then there is a gut-deep need for some small justice."

Philip pulled his knife from the headboard. "My apologies to Bryna for this good wood," he bit out, then quit the room without a backward look, closing the door on Giles's weak whimpers, and went downstairs to further arm himself as the foyer clock chimed out the hour.

He felt time slipping away from him, even as the sun rose higher in the sky. It had already gone eight o'clock . . .

Brighid felt at ease in her deerskins, once more free of the restraints of petticoats and stiff shoes, but there was no joy in her as she sat hunkered on the hillside, overlooking Lokwelend's sweathouse from the safety of the trees.

She had not eaten, broken her fast of the previous night, because a brave who hunted on a full stomach did not give his full dedication to the task. She did not prepare herself in the way of a Lenape warrior, for she was not going to war. She was out to find herself a rat, as she had once stalked mice in the moldy corn stalks near the end of a long, hard winter.

She wished Wulapen was here to help her plan what would come next. She wished Lokwelend was beside her to explain the mysteries behind what had brought her to this desperate point, to this lonely spot on the hillside, to this seemingly impossible to escape destiny.

But she was alone. More alone than she had ever been in her life. More frightened and less sure. She raised a hand to her mouth, feeling the slight swelling of her lips where Philip's kisses still lingered. He must have awakened by now to find her gone, to draw his own conclusions about what she had done, what she planned to do. As she hid from Gerlach, she also hid from Philip, from his love for her, from his justifiable anger.

She looked up at the summer sun, automatically gauging the hour from its height in the sky, its warmth on her face, then stared down at the sweathouse once more. Two hours or less and she and Gerlach would meet there, talk there, perhaps die there.

Built of logs and woven grasses, long and low, its only entrance just a few feet from the bank of the stream, the sweathouse was as dark and private as any cave, as secluded as any retreat, and as deadly as any room with only one door, one avenue of escape.

Once inside, there would be only the mats on the dirt floor, the circle of stones for the fire that sat in the middle of the structure, and a bucket of cold water. The water, ladled over the hot rocks, raised the steam that soothed a body looking for relaxation. But if the water was already hot? How would she manage that? Hot water wasn't much of a weapon. Not nearly as good as the knife she had strapped to her thigh beneath her deerskin skirt.

She would kill Gerlach if he left her no other choice, but all she really wanted now was a weapon that would let her escape him after he'd told her what he seemed so eager to say. She would leave his final punishment to the white man's justice.

She closed her eyes and saw herself inside the sweathouse, sitting cross-legged in the darkness at the rear of the structure, behind the steaming rocks, the smoke. Her back to the wall, both literally and figuratively.

Helmut would have to duck his head to enter, then stay on the other side of the fire, either crouched over or sitting, for the interior was low ceilinged and meant for no more than two people.

He'd grin at her for a moment, then realize that she hadn't obeyed him entirely, hadn't brought Daniel with her. This would enrage him, so that he'd be inclined to attack her at once, and she'd have to give him some reason to wait, some quick promise that would make him sit, encourage him to talk, to gloat over his brilliance. And some reason to get him back outside once more, where she would have more options of her own.

Brighid looked down at her clothing, fingering the blue cotton shirt for long moments before rising to strip off her wrapped skirt, leaving her clad only in her blue shirt and deerskin leggings, like a man, with the freedom of a man.

Pulling out her knife, she twisted around to pull at the rear hem of the sash-tied shirt, then cut off a piece of cloth that measured a good four inches wide and a foot long. Narrowing her eyes, measuring the distance between herself and the sweathouse, the pitch of the incline, she draped the brightly colored cloth over a low bush, folded her skirt so that it roughly resembled the outline of a cradleboard, sure her efforts would be visible, if not entirely recognizable, to anyone who looked up from below.

She would quickly tell Gerlach that Daniel was nearby but well hidden, that she would take him to the child once she had learned all Gerlach wanted her to know. And he would tell her, for the man was aching to explain himself and what he saw as his divine genius. She was sure of that.

And then, as they exited the sweathouse and as he looked up this way, to where she would point, telling him to see the blue cloth, she would strike at the back of his head with the heavy wooden hilt of her knife and run away to the safety of the woods. Lokwelend had already told her Gerlach was no woodsman. She'd have little trouble evading him, making her way back to safety.

Or her way to face the monsters to the south or the glittering hungry eyes to the north. Or to the west and that lonely building on the Plains, to take her place with those other sad-eyed, empty women. It mattered not where she went, which path she followed.

As long as she didn't have to see Philip's eyes when Giles or Gerlach told him about the woman he believed he knew, believed he loved.

For if Gerlach's truths unlocked her memory, if those memories served to prove her worst fears, she could not go back to Pleasant Hill. Not to Daniel, not to Philip.

Brighid sat down again, willing her heart to beat slower, her mind to concentrate on Gerlach and not on thoughts of Philip, of Daniel, of all those who loved her, of all she might lose.

"I cannot tell you what I do not know," Lokwelend said reasonably as his heavy-lidded eyes followed Philip's furious pacing in front of the outdoor fire. "A veil has been drawn over my dreams, and I can no longer see clearly. Nipawi Gischuch does not wish for me to know where she is. I am sorry. My heart lies heavy within me, but there is nothing I can do. Nothing we can do. It is her fate that she has gone to meet. You cannot change that."

Philip whirled about to glare into the old Indian's impassive face, his own a study of mingled fear and determination. "Don't tell me that! She's going to die, my father. Do you understand that? That bastard Gerlach is going to kill her, cut her heart out. Christ, Lokwelend, don't tell me there's nothing we can do."

"When I, um, *pressed* him, my brother said Gerlach has been hiding himself at the old Simmons farm since slipping free of the last man we set to watch him," Dominick told the Indian. "We saw signs of occupation, but he's not there now. We think, as you must as well, old friend, that he has somehow set up a meeting with Brighid. Upon reflection and also with a small bit of help from my brother's recollections, Philip is certain she met with Gerlach in the gardens a few nights ago, and they must have made their plans then. It has nearly gone noon, Lokwelend. She is bound to be meeting with him soon. Are you sure you can't help us?"

Philip combed his fingers through his hair, feeling time slipping away from him, his life slipping away from him. "We tried tracking her from Lenape Cliff, but she covered her tracks too well for us Englishmen to follow. Can you at least come with us to the cliff?"

"The wise chief Euripides says, 'In this world second thoughts, it seems, are best.'" Lokwelend looked up at Philip, his eyes shadowed with the sorrow of centuries. "I have looked into your heart, my son. I have seen your pain. And I have given this matter a second thought. Never has Lokwelend broken his word," he said quietly, slowly rising to his feet. "Never. But today is different, is it not? Today marks the ending and the beginning. Today I shall do as you ask. I cannot promise anything, my son. I can but try. My eyes are old and dimmed, but I was once a great hunter. Shall we see what tricks Wulapen has taught Nipawi Gischuch and what I might still be able to learn?"

Brighid, sitting cross-legged on one of the woven mats, poured one last ladle of water on the hot rocks and watched the rising steam all but obliterate her vision of the deer hide flap entrance to the sweathouse. Then she reached into her pouch and took out the mashed, bitter leaves and berries she had gathered, dropping them into the nearly full water bucket. Heating the water in the wooden bucket would be impossible. But if her aim was good, Gerlach's eyes would sting him terribly for a few moments, perhaps long enough for her to escape him.

Although she had begun to like another plan better—one that had a lot to do with a knife, quick and clean, drawn deep across the jugular, the way she would put a wounded animal out of its misery.

For she had become Nipawi Gischuch once more in these past two long, desperate hours of waiting, the civilized Brighid Cassidy nearly forgotten as she remembered the attack on Cora, Hallie's terror, and the deaths of those innocent women. How could she look into Helmut Gerlach's eyes, into his madness, and then let him go, possibly to free him to kill again?

Had she always thought this way, deep in the most secret places of her mind? Had she come here simply for the truth—or to rid the entire world of this monster?

Could she do it? Could she kill?

She looked around at the interior of the sweathouse, knowing that Gerlach would see the smoke rising from the small hole in the roof, hoping that anyone else who might see it would believe Lokwelend was taking a sweat.

She didn't want to die here.

She didn't want Philip to have to find her body here.

Somehow, she kept herself from visibly flinching when the flap was suddenly drawn back and the white glare of sunlight was rapidly replaced by the dark outline of Gerlach's hulking frame. Only a powerful exercise of will kept her from reaching for the knife she had slid beneath her right thigh.

Brighid was spared the sight of Gerlach's triumphant smile but not his growl of anger as he demanded to know the whereabouts of the child.

"We have made a bargain, Gerlach. Daniel is safe and awaiting his journey to the new life you have promised him in return for your silence," Brighid lied quickly. "And you can see by my clothing that I am prepared to leave this place forever, as you have ordered, the moment this conversation is finished. Sit down, Gerlach. Tell me what you know, as you have promised. Then I will take you to Johanna's son. That is the bargain we have made, isn't it?"

"Very well, for I am feeling generous today. 'The path of the just is as the shining light, that shineth more and more unto the perfect day,'" Gerlach quoted as he bent his frame and sat down on the mat Brighid had positioned so that she could see him most clearly. "This is my perfect day, you white bitch, you woeful whore of hell. On this day the light will shine for me, and you and your evil will be cast forevermore into the darkness."

Mary Catherine would probably have a fine Bible quote to toss back at the man, Brighid thought wildly before unconsciously dropping into the low, guttural cadence of the Lenape and biting out: "You talk more than you think, *Geptschat.* Your shining light is to plunge me into the darkness? *Quanna ta,* Gerlach—no matter if it does. You have already succeeded in killing me, even as I breathe. But I will know, Gerlach. First I will know."

The evil should not be allowed to smile, she thought, knowing she could not avoid Gerlach's eyes, turn away from that repulsive smile in disgust for even a moment.

"You really don't know, do you?" Gerlach said at last, his smile growing broader, more ghastly and loathsome. "You don't remember. Ah, but you remember enough. Enough to know that you are evil and that I have knowledge of that evil. You remember enough to have come here, to have brought me the child. I saw the fear in your eyes when we last met. You have lived with the Lenape, woman. You have seen what they can do. What you yourself have done."

"I killed no one," Brighid said forcefully, wishing she could believe her own words. Because she didn't know if what she was saying was true. "I have harmed no man, no woman, no child."

"That you still live is an abomination unto the Lord!" Gerlach all but shouted, twisting his body as he sat on the mat, clearly anxious to get on with the business of killing her and frustrated that he needed her alive in order to locate Daniel. His eyes narrowed dangerously as he spoke again, his words shocking her to her marrow. "I was there, you know. Captured along with Johanna. I saw it all, witnessed it all. The Lenape, drunk with power and strong spirits. Torturing. Killing. Painted devils, laughing as God's children screamed and moaned in the wilderness—as you drank and danced and took the knife they offered you. It was only by God's good graces that I escaped as they all lay unconscious with drink and I was able to loose my bonds and sneak off into the woods."

Brighid took a deep breath and held it. So that was how he knew about her: He had been one of the captives. That made sense. She wet her lips with the tip of her tongue, her heart hammering painfully in her chest, the screams of the woman she had seen being set upon and savaged by the Indians battering her brain. "You escaped, Gerlach? Leaving Johanna to die?"

"Judge me not, for I am the judge! She was as good as dead! She allowed her body to be defiled, even as I, tied to a nearby tree, was forced to watch. She whored herself for her life, losing forever her immortal soul. As did you, Brighid Cassidy. As did you. Spreading your legs for them, one after the other coming at you, welcomed by you, spilling their savage seed in you. Better to die by your own hand than to be so defiled. Better to chew at your own wrist until your veins opened than to join hands with the devil."

"He's lying," Brighid whispered, telling herself the truth, blocking out Gerlach's hateful words. She didn't know whether to be thrilled by this sudden knowledge or more afraid. *Philip was the first one. The only one. Why? Why does he lie?*

Gerlach looked at her quizzically. "You said something, whore? Speak up, for God hears you no matter how you try to hide."

"I—I said I had been injured during the raid, my head had been injured, and I was not responsible for what I did." Even as she spoke, feeling waves of relief continue to wash over her, she contemplated once again the evil of this man and searched for the motive behind his lies, his actions. "Surely you can understand that, Gerlach."

Gerlach spread his hands wide. "'She weepeth sore in the night, and her tears are on her cheeks: among all her lovers she hath none to comfort her.'" He looked across the smoking fire, a fire in his own eyes, and again quoted scripture, spitting it out rapid fire, as it suited his purpose. "I heard the voice of the Lord, saying, Whom shall I send, and who will go for us? Then said I, Here am I; send me.' I am your comfort, Brighid Cassidy. I will deliver you, as I have delivered the others, for you are the most dangerous. I see your lying heart and will soon feel it beat in my hands. 'And their going from us to be utter destruction: but they are in peace.' Come to me, Brighid Cassidy. Let me give us both peace."

Brighid looked toward the bucket, but only for an instant, for it was a paltry weapon. Laughable. She had been mad to come here, believing Gerlach held the secret to her past. Now she had to get away. Kill him? She would be lucky to escape with her own life. She struggled to keep him talking. "The others, Gerlach? You mean the other captives. The women you've killed?"

"I gave them peace," he said, once more fidgeting where he sat as if filled with an urging that could not leave him physically unmoved. "'Be sure your sin will find you out,' the Bible says. I am the messenger of the Lord, I am his right hand, and I will chastise you with scorpions. Your sin has found you out. I have found you out. Had they not divided the prey, to every man a damsel or two? And like the seed sown by the wayside, you have sown the wind and shall reap the whirlwind. *I* am the whirlwind."

You're as crazy as McMurty's cat, Brighid thought wildly but only said encouragingly, "Surely God forgives, Gerlach. He will probably even forgive you."

He slammed his fist into his palm. "I have no need of forgiveness, bitch. I am the Lord's, and I am protected. He understands. If I am to do the Lord's work, I must remain free. You had to die, Brighid Cassidy. The women who saw had to die. All of them, but you and Johanna most of all. Your deaths were assured the moment the English brought you to Fort Pitt."

Brighid slowly moved her hand toward the bucket. "The women who saw? The women who saw *what*, Gerlach? The women who saw you run away that terrible night rather than stand like a man and defend them? You're making no sense."

But he had gone beyond hearing her. "When you remember not the name, you still remember the face. Kill the one, find the one. Kill again. Kill more. Kill them all. Cleanse the defiled, remove the damaged soul, give praise to the Lord." He stared at her, his eyes wide so that she could see the whites of them both above and beneath their dark centers.

And as he stared at her, he rose to his knees, began loosening the buttons of his trousers. "I must not be stopped, for I do the Lord's work. The Lord saves them who protect themselves. Let me cleanse you, White Indian. Let me send you to your salvation with seed from the fertile ground."

She had to keep him talking, even though he was rambling. She had to learn, had to *know*. "So you'd kill me then, *Geptschat?* You'd kill me now, as you did Silky Wattson? As you did the others? You did kill them, didn't you, to *save* them? Or to save yourself? And what about Daniel? Think, Gerlach. You'll never find Johanna's son without me. You'll never get all that lovely money. Come with me now, and I'll show you where he is. I cannot leave him alone in the woods to die."

He shook his head, as if clearing it of the sight of Brighid's body lying beneath his, freeing himself of his mad lust long enough to answer her. "Johanna's bastard half-breed can die well enough without my knife across his neck. The sins of the father are in the son, and his suffering should be equal to the pain his father gave."

"You're quite mad, you know," Brighid said, reluctantly moving to her second plan, amazed that she was not trembling anymore, astounded that she could still think clearly, could think at all.

"Mad?" Gerlach reached into his pocket and pulled out a knife. A very long, very sharp knife that he looked at admiringly as it glinted in the light from the fire. "There is a part of me, yes, that wonders. What I began for one reason is continued for another. But I have decided that the Lord has given me this growing pleasure as reward for my years of true and faithful service. I have set the enemy upon each other time and time again, for the Lord is a man of war, and I have reaped the riches of war seven times over. Lord, my thanks to you that I am not like other men! The Lord wants me to have pleasure and has shown me the path."

He smiled at Brighid across the fire. "That path lies through you, Brighid Cassidy. You and all the others like you. But in you, I will find both safety and pleasure. In your death, I will find salvation. But before I take the soul, I will tend to the flesh."

He has to die, Brighid screamed inside her head, willing strength into her body. *He has to die now!* She felt her hands close over the rim of the bucket, the rope handle, but she never remembered lifting it, would never remember flinging its contents full in Gerlach's face. She would only ever be able to recall his scream of agony as he staggered to his feet, clawing at his eyes even as she picked up her knife and threw herself against him, knocking him through the deer hide flap and out onto the bank of the stream.

Straddling him, she had lifted Gerlach's hair in her fist and made the first cut across the top of his forehead when her wrist was grabbed by a strong hand and she was flung clear, landing on her back, to look up into Philip Crown's face.

If he lived to be a very old man, Philip knew he'd never forget the sight of Brighid straddling Helmut Gerlach's large body—Nipawi Gischuch in all her savage glory—her knife in the process of removing his scalp. And he'd never forget how he hesitated, just for the length of a single heartbeat, torn between saving her from the horror of murdering the man or allowing her this moment of what seemed to be a perfect justice.

Dominick, Lokwelend, and he had trailed Brighid from Lenape Cliff, following signs only the old Lenape could see, making their way beyond several twists, turns, and cutbacks she had taken in order to carefully cover her tracks—all while the sun had climbed higher in the sky and time slipped by too quickly.

In the end, it was such a simple thing that had given her away, such an elementary mistake that Philip could only believe she had, deep inside her, always hoped to be stopped before she could go through with her plans.

As they had come into a small clearing, Lokwelend had sniffed of the breeze; once, twice. "Hickory smoke," he'd announced calmly, then taken off at an easy, ground-eating lope toward the stream and the sweathouse.

Once Philip had realized exactly where his honorary father was leading them, he had sprinted ahead, recklessly leaping over fallen logs, all but tumbling down the hill toward the stream, arriving just in time to witness the explosion of bodies from the sweathouse—and to save Helmut Gerlach's miserable life.

Not that the man appeared grateful. Philip winced as Gerlach's moans of pain reached him from the back of the wagon Dominick had procured from the stables so that they could transport the injured man to New Eden, where Elijah Kester's wife could sew him up before Elijah threw him in the brand-new gaolhouse.

Gerlach wasn't that badly hurt, although his wound was long and remarkably bloody. In fact, if it hadn't been for the pain of his wound and the river of blood that had all but blinded him, Philip probably would have been forced to tap the man on the head with the blunt end of his rifle before he and Dominick could truss him up like a wild turkey ready for the chopping block and throw him in the wagon.

Brighid sat beside Philip on the wagon seat, her silence unable to be mistaken for any assimilated Lenape stoicism, thanks to the way her hands kept fidgeting in her lap. She had been quiet since stating flatly that Helmut Gerlach had indeed killed the captives and had attempted to murder her as well. She had thanked Philip for not allowing her to kill the man, mouthing the words with all the enthusiasm of a child reciting sums, and had then allowed Lokwelend to take her for a walk along the stream bank until the wagon had arrived.

Philip looked at her now, seeing the rusty-looking smudges of dried blood on her deerskin-clad thighs, where she had wiped her bloody hands after handing him her knife. He had never forgotten how she looked in her deerskins, had never wanted to banish that particular memory, but now he realized how much a simple change of costume could alter an outsider's perception of who and what this person called Brighid Cassidy, called Nipawi Gischuch, was.

"Maybe this isn't such a good idea," Philip remarked to Dominick, who rode along beside them, tall and straight on his favorite bay mare. "Do we really need Brighid? Hasn't she already been through enough today?"

"Gerlach tried to kill her, Philip," Dominick responded reasonably. "Elijah has to hear her evidence against him before he can lock him up. Then tomorrow we'll see about having him transported to Easton for trial."

"I suppose you're right," Philip answered, wishing Brighid would say something, anything, to prove to him that she was all right. "I only wish we'd thought to take her to Pleasant Hill for a change of clothing."

From behind them, lying on the bed of the wagon, Gerlach called out: " 'Can the Ethiopian change his skin, or the leopard his spots?' The White Indian is damned, and now you all will pay. You all will pay! Vengeance is mine sayeth the Lord!"

"Shut your mouth, Gerlach, or I might take my own knife to you," Philip warned tightly. Then he turned to Brighid.

"Sorry, Jezebel, my love. That was my lapse entirely. I didn't think to stuff a rag in his flapping avenging angel mouth," he quipped as Brighid's chest began to heave in what he could only believe to be righteous indignation.

And then, to Philip's great relief, Brighid laid her head against his shoulder and began to laugh.

A good retreat is better than a bad stand.
— *Irish saying*

CHAPTER 17

BRYNA CROWN ENTERED THE BEDCHAMBER JUST AS BRIGHID was slowly easing herself into a tub of hot water. "All right, Bridie Cassidy, you insufferable little sneak, I'll have the truth now if you please. And don't try to fob me off, for I won't be hearing any more fibs out of your clever mouth. Just what did you think you were about, going after that awful man all by yourself?"

"Never were the modest sort, were you, Brynnie," Brighid responded, deliberately mimicking her cousin as she used Bryna's childhood name. "Would you be minding to close that door behind you? Unless you've invited the rest of the household upstairs to question me while I'm in my bath? And they call *me* uncivilized. It's a pure wonder, don't you think?"

Bryna wasn't about to be deterred by Brighid's sarcasm, which she proved by slamming the door, then crossing the room in a deliberate stride, stopping only once she was directly beside the tub. "You were leaving us, weren't you, Brighid? Without a word of good-bye, you were leaving us. Philip. Even Daniel. Why?"

"Leaving? How could you believe such a thing?" Picking up the soap and making a great business of lathering her left arm so that she didn't have to look at her cousin, Brighid continued kindly, "It's because you're increasing, I suppose. Mama would always get the strangest ideas in her head when she was expecting another little Cassidy. Why, I remember the time—"

"Enough!" Bryna exploded, stamping her foot like a spoiled child in a temper. "I won't have lies from you, Brighid, and I won't have tales of your sainted mother, God rest her soul. I want the truth, and if I have to hold your head beneath the water until you're ready to talk to me, I'll do it. Do you doubt that I mean what I say?"

"As I still have the scar on my arm to remember your threat at the tender age of nine, I believe, to nip me with your embroidery scissors if I didn't tell you whether Patrick O'Connor fancied you or not, I suppose I believe you. Now, what is it you want to know that you didn't hear downstairs when Philip explained how the good people of New Eden believe me to be a savage who tried to scalp a white man, and a man of God, at that? A *white* man, Bryna. That's what they said. As if I truly had been born Lenni Lenape—not that, at the moment, I don't wish I had been. I thought both Philip and Dominick were going to explode, that's how angry they were, how angry they still are. But I am not surprised by any of it, not deep down inside me. Why should anyone believe the word of a White Indian, a woman damned by God?"

Bryna put out a hand, resting it comfortingly on her cousin's shoulder. "They're simple people, Brighid, and a few of them none too bright. But Dominick did admit that Gerlach was rather convincing, standing there with his bloody wound, calling on the people to remember that he has always been a man of God."

"Ha! A pawn of the devil, more like," Brighid shot back, shaking off Bryna's hand so that she could submerge herself, washing the stench of Helmut Gerlach's evil from every pore, every hair on her head. She surfaced moments later, sputtering, and began roughly soaping her hair. "And now he's free to kill again—all in the name of the Lord. Perhaps Gerlach isn't mad at all. It's just the remainder of the world that has gone insane."

She allowed her hands to fall to the sides of the tub as Bryna began washing her hair for her, relaxing against the rim as her cousin's gentle fingers worked the sweet-smelling soap into a lather.

Brighid was so tired, so bone weary, that she shut her eyes, her guard relaxed after holding her secrets close for so long. She luxuriated in the feel of Bryna's fingers massaging her scalp, washing away the cares of this long, difficult day.

"A pity you didn't get to kill him," Bryna offered quietly after a few moments. "And since you would have been miles away from the sweathouse by the time they found his body, you would have been safe enough."

"I know," Brighid answered absently, lulled into stupidity by her cousin's soothing fingers. "And it just might have worked."

The next thing she knew, Brighid was spitting out the taste of soap and wiping her stinging eyes as she tried to catch her breath after being pushed under the water by her amazingly strong cousin. "What did you do that for?" she protested hotly before catching a quick breath as she felt Bryna's hands on the top of her head once more and was submerged in the slippery tub yet again, only to rise to her knees in time to feel a bucket of cold rinse water slosh over her.

"What did I do that for? For not trusting me—*that's* what I did that for! I've never been so insulted, I vow it. Now hie yourself out of that tub and talk to me!" Bryna demanded, throwing Brighid a towel before she took herself off to the bed and sat down on the edge, her arms crossed over the rounded bulge of her expanded middle. "You've got a head stuffed full of secrets, don't you? And I'll be having all of them now, Brighid, every last little one, or know the reason why!"

Brighid clambered out of the tub, shivering so violently that her teeth chattered as rivulets of cold water dripped off her hair and down her bare back. She glared at Bryna as she wrapped the towel around her chilled body and was about to tear a verbal strip off the woman's hide when she saw her cousin's tears.

"Oh, Brynnie, I'm sorry!" she exclaimed quickly, going to the other woman and kneeling at her feet. "You're right, and I'm so very, *very* sorry. I've been lying from the beginning, then lying more and more to cover the first untruth. I should have told you everything at once, but I was a coward. I had heard so many stories of women being returned to their families and the families making them give up their half-breed children, the children of their shame. I was so afraid. And if you knew that Daniel wasn't really mine, that I had only promised to raise him for—"

Bryna's head shook just once on the graceful stem of her neck, as if she had absorbed a sharp slap to her cheek. "Daniel . . . Daniel isn't yours?" she repeated quietly, then pressed her fingers to her mouth as she looked down at her cousin, breathing slowly, seemingly regaining her strength with each new breath. "I—I see. I imagine Lokwelend already knows this? No, don't bother to answer me. Of course he knows. Remind me to verbally tear a strip off that old man's hide next time I see him! And you didn't tell me because you thought I'd insist you give that darling little child away?"

"To protect me, yes. To make it easier for me to forget I'd been a captive, easier for me to settle back into life here in New Eden," Brighid explained as she rose to sit beside Bryna on the bed. "And to protect Dominick. When Lokwelend came to me that first time, he told me that Dominick was an English lord. I hadn't known that, you see, when he visited us at the farm, when he sat and smoked with Da after dinner. Would an English lord want a half-breed child under his roof if his presence wasn't really necessary, if there was no blood bond between Daniel and his wife's cousin? Would *you?* You've always been a proud one, Bryna, I don't have to tell you that either. And you'd manage the world if you could."

She sighed, taking Bryna's hand in hers. "I couldn't let you manage me, Brynnie. I couldn't let anyone manage me. The Bryna I remembered from our childhoods is a far different Bryna than the one I found when Philip brought me back to Pleasant Hill, but by then it was too late, because everyone had so easily accepted my lie. I saw no reason to make things more difficult by telling you the truth about Daniel."

She lowered her head, feeling her cheeks begin to flame. "Or by telling Philip, who never would have taken me to his bed if he'd known I was a virgin. I needed him, you see, needed him so very much. Love him so very much." She looked at her cousin again, searching her face in order to gauge her emotions. "I just thought it better for everyone if I kept silent."

"And you call *me* managing?" Bryna shook her head, then gave a small laugh. "Brighid Cassidy, I would no more advise you to give Daniel away than I would ask you to cut off your right arm. That child is a part of you, and you *are* his mother. And, by the by, I doubt you could chase Philip away with a pitchfork from the stables. Now, go put on a dressing gown before you take a chill, wrap a towel around that wet head, and then you will tell me the rest of it if you please. I believe I have earned the right to know the entire truth. About your life with the Lenape, about Daniel, and about why Helmut Gerlach frightens you so much that you would do anything as woefully stupid as to agree to meet with the man today."

Brighid dropped a kiss on her cousin's cheek. "Yes, ma'am," she said, wiping at her wet eyes as she went off in search of her dressing gown. "Having been asked so nicely,

I'll tell you everything. Everything I already understand—and all that I don't."

Philip paced Dominick's study, his disenchantment with the inhabitants of New Eden multiplying tenfold each time he thought about the treatment both Brighid and her story had received at their hands.

"They as good as told Brighid her word was worth nothing, that her *life* was worth nothing!" he shouted over Dominick's offer of another glass of wine. "You know that, don't you, Dominick? Even Kester, damn him for a fool. Even *Kester* said she had to be mistaken. I'd say I miss the civilization of London, except that idiots are everywhere. Consider my father, for instance. Damn it, Dominick—why didn't they believe her?"

"The knife cut didn't help matters," Dominick answered, seating himself behind his desk once more, picking up his letter opener and balancing it between his fingers. "The townspeople found it to be, well, rather *savage*. To tell you the truth, I'm rather shocked by Brighid's actions myself. Frankly, they weren't those of a rational-thinking young woman."

Philip glared at his uncle, longing to leap across the desk and hit him, then slowly subsided into the nearest chair, letting his breath out in a long sigh. "I know it, Dominick. Damn it to all hell and back, I know it. Nothing Brighid has done has made any sense. Not since the first day she saw Helmut Gerlach on the streets of New Eden. What did that man do to her? And why, in God's name, won't she trust me enough to tell me?"

"Perhaps, my son, you simply don't inspire the finer virtues in others," Giles Crown drawled from the doorway. "Charming thought, wouldn't you say? I'd like to think you resemble me in more than your physical attributes."

The chair he had been sitting on tipped back onto the floor with a resounding crash as Philip leaped to his feet and turned to confront his father. But his angry words died in his throat when he got his first look at the man. Giles

Crown, marquess of Playden, bane of Philip's past and present existence, now owned two badly swollen, discolored eyes. His bottom lip was split, and his left cheek appeared to have made a close acquaintance with something quite hard. He was leaning heavily on his beribboned walking stick, his left arm in a sling fashioned from a triangle of pink silk.

"My compliments, Uncle," Philip said smoothly, looking toward Dominick, who still sat at his ease behind the desk.

"The pleasure, Nephew, was entirely mine," Dominick answered, then both men concentrated on the marquess once more as that man entered the room and, with only a faint wince to reveal his pain, sat himself down on the leather couch at the far side of the room. "You've a need to unburden yourself of more information, Giles?"

"Hardly," the marquess answered, touching his manicured fingertips to his bruised cheek. "And don't bother to beat on me again, Brother. You cannot, I've heard, get blood from a stone. I have told you all that I know."

Philip righted his chair and sat down once more, at last reaching for the wine Dominick had poured for him. He still did not know all of what Giles had revealed to Dominick and never would, unless Brighid chose to tell him. Not that he'd allow his father the satisfaction of knowing that. "Yes, Father, and we were careful to explain to Gerlach just exactly how helpful you were to us. I most seriously doubt he intends to remember you in his prayers."

Giles shrugged, reaching into his pocket for his snuff box. "He's locked up nice and tight. I have no reason for concern."

Philip smiled at Dominick over the rim of his glass. "On the contrary, Father. He's *not* locked up. He's free as a bird. A little the worse for wear, like you, but free to go where he wants, do what he wants, *visit* whom he desires to visit. Do you think he'll want to visit you? You, Father, Helmut Gerlach's very good friend, his boon companion and confidante."

He turned to skewer the marquess with a look. "Or do

you think he was less than overjoyed when we informed him that you'd told us where we could find him, that you'd shared the information that he'd killed all those women?"

The snuff box was never opened. The marquess returned it to his pocket and put his hand to his mouth, rubbing at his lips and chin. "He's free? He's out and about? My God, Philip, the man's mad as a hatter! He's dangerous. There's no telling what he might do next."

"We can have him locked up," Philip suggested, seeing a quick solution to their problems in this most unlikely of allies. "If you were to agree to tell the people of New Eden what you know about his involvement in the murders, agree to testify against him?"

The marquess's eyes shifted down and away from his son's. "I think not actually," he said quietly, painfully rising from the couch. "As I said, the man is mad," he continued, all the time hobbling toward the door. "Why, he might even attempt to save himself by saying outlandish, utterly false things about me, babbling on and on and on. No, no. I have nothing to say. Nothing to say at all. And I'll be leaving this benighted Eden on Monday, or so Lilith tells me, and without your help. Seems she has procured the services of some strapping young lout with a suitable carriage, and he has agreed to take us all the way to Philadelphia. What a strange girl Lilith is. She'll tip herself over for the damnedest things . . ."

Philip watched his father leave the room, then turned to grin at Dominick. "Whoever said revenge had a bitter taste never saw the marquess of Playden brought low. Hardly a *giggle* out of him, did you notice?" Then he sobered. "What do you think Gerlach told my esteemed father, Dominick? What favor did Giles ask of him in return for giving him a plan that would put Brighid within his reach?"

Dominick raised one eyebrow as he returned Philip's look, so that Philip held up his hand, waving it back and forth as if to erase his last words. "Never mind. I asked you not to tell me anything, and I won't badger you. I only wish we could have marched my father into New Eden and made him tell Elijah Kester the same things he told you. Then Gerlach wouldn't be free."

"Wouldn't he? My brother is not known for his veracity, remember. He'd probably tell everyone we'd beaten him until he told us what we wanted to hear, which would be true enough, although damning to our cause. Think about it, Philip." Dominick rose from his chair and went to the window, turning his back to Philip. "Besides," he said, looking out over the gardens that were rapidly disappearing in the dusk, "I don't know what Giles promised the man or what the man promised him. I'm still struggling with the notion that they spoke to each other at all.

"Second," he continued, turning to face his nephew, "I don't believe a word of what Giles *did* tell me he'd learned about Brighid. I will, however, tell you that neither of us want him repeating a syllable of it to Elijah Kester or anyone else. She has enough on her plate as it is, having carved up Gerlach's forehead the way she did. We should just feel lucky right now that Kester didn't have her arrested for trying to kill the bastard. People have been hanged for lesser offenses, you know. No. Giles was and is no good to us. Except, of course, for his fairly unhelpful information as to where Gerlach has been hiding himself, not that he'll go back there now. I believe the man is convinced you want to kill him, Philip."

"And he'd be right, damn him," Philip spat, then realized that someone was behind him. He whirled about, thinking Giles had returned, only to see Lucas Deems standing just inside the doorway, wringing his hands. "What is it, Lucas?" he asked, instantly on guard.

"It's Mr. Kester, my lords, and a few of the other men from New Eden," he whispered as if his every word could be overheard. "I made them wait outside, wouldn't even let them in the foyer. They say they've come to arrest Miss Cassidy, my lords. For trying to kill that madman, they say."

"Je-sus *Christ!*" Philip exploded, already reaching for his rifle. "I'll shoot the first man who dares to lay a hand on her. This gets more insane by the minute."

"Go up the back stairs, Philip, and fetch Brighid. Take her to the sweathouse and stay with her," Dominick said, already on his way out of the study. "I'll deal with these idiots. Go on—now. And, for God's sake, make her talk to you. I'll come to you in the morning."

Dominick was right. Sooner or later, things would sort themselves out and Brighid would be vindicated. But Philip would be damned if she'd spend a single night in the New Eden gaol while the sorting was going on. Nodding his agreement, he brushed past Lucas and climbed the servant stairs two at a time, moving both quickly and quietly.

Less than five minutes later, he and Brighid were on their way through the moonlit woods, hand in hand, with Bryna Crown's words echoing in their ears: "You *talk* to each other, you hear me? Or I'll be banging your two heads together!" Her message had been much the same as her husband's but more direct. And Philip believed Brighid was about to heed her cousin's threat-ridden advice.

Brighid entered the sweathouse ahead of Philip, shivering as she remembered being there that morning, being there with Helmut Gerlach. Her nemesis.

It was time, more than time—as both Bryna and Lokwelend had begged her to do—that she talked to Philip. About her past. About her fears, Gerlach's horrendous lies. About her actions of this morning and her ruined hopes for the future.

But as she sat down on the mats she quickly arranged, as Philip sat down beside her and gathered her close into his arms, her throat clogged with the tears she had been holding back for so long, and she could find no words.

"It's all right, darling," Philip told her as she sobbed, kissing her forehead, stroking her hair with his steady hands. "We're going to get through this. One way or another, we'll get through this."

"I just want to run away," she explained when she could

finally speak. "I want to take Daniel and go as far from this place as I can, as quickly as I can. But Gerlach can't be allowed to remain free." She lifted tear-drenched eyes to the man she loved, the man who loved her without question, without reserve. "He can't be allowed to kill again. My God, Philip, those poor, poor women—to have that man's fevered eyes be the last thing you ever see!"

Philip continued to hold her close, rocking back and forth with her as she would do with Daniel when he cried, soothing her quietly, making promises she longed to believe might come true, telling her she didn't have to say another word, had nothing to explain that he needed to hear.

"I don't deserve you, Philip," she mumbled against his deerskin-clad chest. "I've done nothing to deserve you."

"I am rather wonderful, now that I think on the matter," he quipped lightly, tipping up her chin so that he could wipe at her tears with the tips of his fingers. "Why, I imagine you might even want to kiss me, thank me in some small, personal way for being such a fine, upstanding English gentleman."

Brighid levered herself away from him, shaking her head. How could he be so good, so pure? How could he make her smile in the midst of all the horror? "I love you, Philip Crown," she told him honestly. "But then," she added with a grin as she pushed him back onto the mat, "I'm not known for being a clear-thinking person."

"I don't want either of us to think right now. I almost lost you today. We'll think later," he said against her ear, then rolled her over onto her back. "Much later," he promised, and captured her lips with his mouth.

She couldn't breathe for loving him. Found it difficult to swallow over the sudden tightness in her throat, her emotions rising, filling her, banishing every thought but the nearness of him, his love chasing away every fear, cleansing her of all her terror, all her anguish, all her doubts.

This was where she belonged. With this man. In his arms. In his life. There was no life away from him, no hope, no safety, no future, no past. He gave without taking, loved without restraint, trusted without question.

With Philip, she was simply Brighid Cassidy. Not Brighid Cassidy, White Indian. Not Nipawi Gischuch, hiding from her memories, existing in fear, not really living, a frightened girl who had survived on her wits for five long years.

In his eyes, she was a well-loved woman.

Once again, in his arms, she was whole.

Their clothing slipped away, and the night-chilled air didn't touch them. The rough-woven mats could have been fashioned of finest silk or gossamer or soft, fluffy clouds. For all that existed was each other, the world falling away below them as they rose up, up, into their own secure universe where love was both the only question and the single answer.

Brighid nipped at his bare shoulder with her teeth, then pressed frantic kisses against his chest, his stomach, hungry for the taste of him, allowing him to taste of her in turn. Fingers sought, found. Lips caressed, savored, worshiped, adored.

And when he entered her, filling her with a sigh, a promise, she lifted herself to him, taking him fully, loving him totally, moving in unison with him in this dance of love in which they instinctively followed each other without falter, without hesitation, each knowing what the other wanted, what the other needed, and then giving and giving and giving . . .

The monster was nearly upon her, the rankness of his breath blowing against the back of her neck as she ran and ran and ran . . . plunging into the dark woods, taking yet another path that had somehow appeared, as different paths had appeared to her over the years, taking her in new, yet always dangerous directions.

"Philip!" she cried out, knowing her scream was no more than a whisper, just as she knew her feet were not swift. For she was running with all her might, yet felt as if she was

making no progress at all, her legs somehow encased in heavy, dragging water, holding her back, exhausting her, even as she strained to move forward.

She couldn't turn back, couldn't look to see if the monster had come closer, was about to reach out his huge hands and pull her to the ground. She could only keep running, her breath burning in her lungs, her lips forming Philip's name over and over again.

Branches whipped at her cheeks, tree roots pushed up from the ground to trip her. She was battered and bruised, and her head hurt abominably. Blood trickled down her forehead, running into her eyes, all but blinding her.

She heard her brothers crying out to their mother, their father. She saw them fall.

One of the savages grabbed at her father's thick black hair and pulled his body up and away from the ground. Her da's arms hung lifelessly as the savage took out his knife and stood there, poised to lift her da's hair, to desecrate her beloved da. A bright crimson rose blossomed in the center of the Indian's bare chest as Brighid's ears began to ring with the sound of a rifle being fired close to her head. The Indian fell forward, over her da's body. She shook her head to banish the vision and ran on.

And on.

Her mother's voice came to her out of the trees. "Brighid! Da said they sometimes take children as captives."

"Never!" Brighid shouted, hating her mother for not loading the pistols. For not firing. Couldn't she see that they were lost? They all were lost if she did not load the pistols!

"Brighid! You are never a slave if your mind is free! Lay down the knife and they might spare you!"

No! No! Her mother was wrong. Nobody would be spared. Not her mother, not Mary Catherine, not Brighid herself. Didn't she understand? You could only fight and then fight some more. And then run. Run!

"Holy Mary, mother of God, pray for us sinners . . . now and at the hour of our death—"

Brighid lunged for the Indian who had appeared in front of her on the path, standing behind her kneeling mother. She cursed him as she tried to move her legs, as the weight of the water tugged at her limbs, keeping her progress slow when she wished to move quickly.

And then the water turned to blood. Her mother's blood. So much blood.

All that Brighid saw now, she saw through the red death of her mother's blood. The savages crowding the path. The war club, raised high above one of the Indians' heads and then brought down, brought down hard, exploding her world. Killing her. Killing her.

She fell forward onto the path, stunned but not dead, knowing the monster could not help but catch her now, kill her now.

But he wasn't interested in her . . . stepped over her as she lay there, her hair caked with her own drying blood, her clothes smeared with vomit . . . her mother's blood, hardened and black beneath her fingernails as she cowered in the dirt.

The monster didn't even look at her.

He was too busy looking at Johanna, laughing as the Indians lifted her, carried her, then threw her to the ground . . . laughing as he stepped forward, opening the buttons of his homespun breeches.

"No!" Brighid screamed as the monster cut Johanna's clothing from her, as Johanna screamed, as she pleaded with him to stop. "Don't touch her!"

And the monster turned at the sound of Brighid's voice.

And he smiled Helmut Gerlach's smile.

"Brighid. Brighid! Wake up, darling. You're dreaming. You're only dreaming."

Philip leaned over her and kept talking until Brighid opened her eyes, until her expression told him that she was fully awake and not still lost in the nightmare that had her thrashing about wildly, calling for someone named Johanna.

"Philip?" she asked at last, going very still, her face ashen in the pale light of dawn that entered the sweathouse through the hole in the center of the roof. "Oh, God!" she exclaimed, pressing herself against him, her face buried against his chest, her entire body trembling. "Oh, sweet Christ, Philip! I *remember!*"

He sent up a silent prayer of thanksgiving, then barely had time to tell Brighid he loved her before she sat up all at once and exclaimed hotly: "Lying whoreson! Miserable, murdering *bastard!*"

"Gerlach?" Philip prodded as Brighid lifted her chin, squeezed her eyes tightly shut, and growled—in anger? Frustration? Homicidal rage? "Tell me, Brighid," he continued in a low, encouraging voice. "Tell me about Gerlach."

She lowered her head, her eyes shining emerald hard with hate. "He raped Johanna. It wasn't at all what I thought, what he told me. It wasn't me who turned into a savage. It was *him!*"

"I think you'd better begin at the beginning, darling," Philip suggested, taking her hand and leading her outside the sweathouse, into the breaking dawn, then sat down with her beside the clear-running stream. "Who is Johanna?"

She threw him a stricken look, all her anger gone, replaced by an obvious fear that had him reaching out to slide an arm around her slim shoulders.

"You're going to hate me, Philip."

"I seriously doubt that," he assured her. "Now, we'll just sit here together, watching the sun rise, and I'll be very, very quiet while you tell me whatever you want to tell me, whatever you think I should know. All right?"

He felt her head move against him in assent and took a deep breath, releasing it slowly. He'd waited so long, wondered so long. And now he'd know. *God,* he thought, closing his eyes for a moment, *do I really want to know?*

She remained silent, and he thought she'd changed her mind about confiding in him. But at last she began to speak. Slowly at first, then with her words nearly tumbling over themselves, as if she wanted to have her confession over with as quickly as possible.

"I—I didn't know what else to do, you see. Bryna wanted me back. I knew she wanted me back—God, but that woman is a law unto herself! But would she want Daniel? Would Dominick? Would they want a half-breed child under their roof? Or would they tell me to give Daniel up, give him away, and get on with my life? I was so frightened—"

"Dominick and Bryna would never do anything of the kind," Philip told her, then stopped, partly because he had promised to remain silent, partly in confusion. "I'm sorry, Brighid. It's your story. You tell it."

"I know I'm complicating everything by starting with that day at Fort Pitt," she said, taking his hand in hers and rubbing her thumb across his palm, as if to soothe him while she searched for the correct words to continue her story. "I suppose it would be better if I started with the day I first saw Lapawin, the day Johanna and I first saw Lapawin.

"You already know that I hadn't been able to remember anything that happened to me the day of the raid. Da walked to the door to say the boys were coming up the hill and the next thing I knew I was waking up in Lapawin's longhouse with Johanna putting cold compresses on my head. Now, thanks to you, I remember the raid and remember why I had wanted to forget it. I've found peace with myself, peace with my parents' decisions. But I've never remembered the time between the raid and the day Johanna and I were sold to Lapawin."

Philip stared straight out over the stream, watching a fish leap in the water. "So you were never alone? You always had another white woman with you?"

"Yes. For all but the last few months, Johanna was with me. I never would have survived without her. Without her tender nursing of me when I lay injured and half out of my mind. Without her quiet wisdom, her courage, her gentle ways. Wulapen named her Wingenund, which means 'the Willing One.' She was so good, Philip, so pure." Brighid hesitated for a moment, then sighed deeply. "She was

Wulapen's first wife, Philip, the mother of his children. The mother of *all* of his children."

"The mother of—"

"Yes," she told him quietly. "Daniel is Johanna's child. Johanna's child and Wulapen's. I am not his mother, although I love him with all my heart."

Philip sat in stunned silence as Brighid told him how she had been taken as Wulapen's second wife in order to keep her safe from marriage with another Lenape brave who was known to be cruel. She told him how she had been treated like a beloved younger sister by both Johanna and Wulapen, how she had cared for their children, how she had been content in her new life. Content to exist, content not to think, not to remember. Content to be loved and needed by her new family.

Johanna had told her to ignore the dreams when they had begun. Johanna had encouraged her to forget her old life, to not push to remember what had happened in the days after the raid, and Brighid had been more than eager to let those lost memories remain out of reach, to tell Lokwelend to leave her where she was, with her new family.

And they had all been very happy.

Until Wulapen joined with the other chiefs who had decided to rid their land of the Yankwis once and for all time. Until Wulapen hadn't returned, and they had spent a long hard winter alone, three women and three young children, rooting through garbage for animal bones to boil, clubbing mice to survive, boiling maple bark to keep the children from crying in their hunger.

Still holding tight to his hand, Brighid told him how a few of the braves had come back to the village with blankets they had found in an abandoned Yankwi camp. They had distributed the blankets to everyone, and within days the first child fell sick. "Smallpox, Philip," she said, bitterness in her voice. "As had been done so many times before, the soldiers had put out smallpox-infested blankets to kill their enemy. It didn't matter if women died, if children died. After all, they were only Indians, less than human."

"My God . . . ," Philip breathed quietly, trying to imagine the tragedy that had struck down the already desperate tribe. "I'm so sorry, Brighid. So damnably sorry."

"We were all very sorry. The two older children became ill first and died within days of each other. There wasn't a family that didn't see death, most of them more than once." Her voice broke as she told him about the two children, told him their names, told him their ages. He felt sick. They had been babies. No more than babies. Innocents dying for sins committed by others.

"Johanna had taken ill with the smallpox, but I truly believed she was rallying—until word came that Wulapen had been killed. Then—then she just gave up. She loved Wulapen. She loved him very much."

"As you did," Philip said, lifting her hand to his lips. So this was what she hadn't wanted to tell him, what she had hidden from him: not only Daniel's true parentage, but that she had not just had a Lenape husband, but had shared him with another woman. Certainly shocking, but he didn't care. He simply didn't care. She'd had to stay alive, and he thanked God she had stayed alive. "I understand, and it's all right."

"No, Philip, you don't understand. I loved Wulapen as he loved me," she continued. "I loved him as I loved my sister, my brothers. Johanna—Johanna loved him as a wife loves her husband. When—when she knew she was dying, she made me promise not to let anything happen to Tasukamend, to Daniel. Tasukamend—the Blameless One. We all knew the Yankwis would come soon, that all the white captives would be taken to Fort Pitt, as had been done before. She didn't want Daniel to be given to the white husband she'd left behind. She made me promise on my hope of heaven not to let that happen, for her husband was a terrible man, she said, and hated the Indians. He'd make Tasukamend a slave. Destroy him. So I promised Johanna I would take care of Daniel. And then—and then I buried her beside her children, and we moved to the west, trying to outrun the Yankwis."

"So you said Daniel was yours so that Bryna would accept him and so that he wouldn't be turned over to Johanna's husband. And Gerlach knew your secret?" Philip asked when Brighid fell silent, probably to relive the events that had placed Daniel in her care, the events that had brought her to Fort Pitt, to him. "That's it, isn't it? He somehow knew about Daniel and threatened to tell everyone? You must have been half out of your mind, believing you'd lose Daniel to Johanna's husband."

Brighid's voice was hard when she spoke again. Hard and so emotionless that he knew she was very, very angry. "That day in New Eden, Gerlach recognized a birthmark on Daniel's thumb as being the same as one on Johanna's. He wanted me to give Daniel to him. He wanted to sell him to a family near Easton, a family who had lost their daughter in the raids, telling them Daniel was their grandson." She looked at Philip, her eyes mere slits. "I couldn't let that happen. And I couldn't let Gerlach tell you what he had hinted to me, what I had done to remain safe during the time I was with the raiding party, how I had tortured and perhaps even killed other captives to please the Indians, to keep myself alive."

Philip's mouth was dry, so that he had to swallow first in order to speak. "But you didn't know what happened during that time. You couldn't know if he was telling the truth. And, by damn, I'd like to know how *he* could have known the truth!"

Brighid got to her feet and began to walk along the grassy bank, and Philip followed after her. "That night, in the gardens, Gerlach said one thing that made me remember something else, made me see a scene of such horror that I knew I couldn't be imagining it."

She stopped and turned to face him. "I was beginning to remember bits and pieces of what had happened to the captives. That was bad enough, but then Gerlach told me that I had *cooperated* with the Indians, joining in the torture. I didn't know how he knew, but he seemed so sure, so certain. I knew he was the one who had killed those women, and I knew he had to be captured sooner or later and put to death. But first, Philip, I had to *know*. I had to know what I had done, what Johanna had not wanted me to remember, what I couldn't allow you to know."

She rubbed a hand across her eyes. "So I agreed to meet with him again, at the sweathouse. I would hear his story, find out once and for all why Johanna would never talk about the time I had forgotten, why I refused to remember it."

Philip pulled her close against his chest, burying his head in her hair. "You're the bravest woman I know, Brighid Cassidy. And quite possibly the most stubborn, stupid—"

She pulled away from him, giving him a shake. "You're wrong, Philip!" she protested. "Oh, not that I'm not stubborn *and* stupid, but you're wrong to think I shouldn't have gone to meet Gerlach. Because I found out that Gerlach had lied to me. When I met him here at the sweathouse, he told me he had been there in the camp, been a captive with me, and had seen me torture another captive, had seen me whore myself. He lied to me, and I *knew* he lied, even if I never regained my memory of that terrible time."

She put her hands on Philip's forearms and squeezed her fingertips tightly against his flesh. "It was all lies. I knew I couldn't have whored myself, Philip. And do you know why I know?"

"Because you're Nipawi Gischuch, and your heart and spirit would not have allowed such a thing," he answered firmly.

"Possibly," she answered, smiling at him for the first time in much too long. Her hands slipped up his arms, to his shoulders. "But that's not it. I know, Philip—and I'm half glad and half terrified to tell you this—because *you* are the first and only man I have slept with. Ever."

Philip felt as if someone had just kicked him in the gut, kicked him hard. His mind whirled back to that first time, to that fleeting moment of confusion pushed away by rising passion, to his later questions to Dominick. "My God," he said, knowing just how passionate he had been with her, how forceful, believing her to have been a wife, already a mother. Experienced. "My God."

Brighid rushed into speech. "Lapawin assured me that there'd be no pain, that riding horseback on Wulapen's mare and all the work I had done in the fields would have made it so that I'd be able to . . . to deceive you. Lapawin knows many things, and she was right that I did deceive you. She—she wasn't precisely correct about the pain. But I couldn't let you know the truth. You understand that, don't you? You couldn't know about Daniel, because I had left my explanation too late. And you couldn't know I was a virgin, or you never would have taken me to your bed. I would have died if you hadn't taken me to your bed, Philip. I knew what Johanna and Wulapen had had, and I wanted some of that happiness for myself, knowing you'd soon leave me and I would grow old alone. Can you forgive me?"

He stared at her in utter amazement. The world might see them and wonder how he could look past her life with the Lenape, look past her Lenape husband, her half-breed son. But not Brighid. She wondered if he could forgive her virginity. "I love you, Brighid Cassidy," he said, dropping to the ground and pulling her down with him. "I may never understand you, but I love you. Now, if you've done with confessions, come here and let me prove how much I love you."

She fell back against the bank with him but laid a hand over his mouth to keep him silent. "I love you, Philip Crown, but don't allow yourself to be distracted if you please. At least not yet. There's still the matter of Helmut Gerlach and how he knew anything at all about what happened during that week Johanna, I, and the others were traveling with the Indians. The week before we were sold to Lapawin."

Philip frowned. "He was one of the captives. Isn't that right? I mean, how else could he have known anything at all and then twisted the facts to suit his purpose?" Then he sat up suddenly, nearly knocking Brighid into the stream. "Christ on a crutch—that's it! That's why he's going around killing women who were brought back from Fort Pitt! *He's* the one who joined in the torture, the killing, and it gave him a taste for both. Our so-holy scripture-spouting man of God! That's the answer, isn't it, Brighid? That's why he wanted you dead—because you or one of the others could tell everyone what he'd done."

He stood up and began pacing back and forth on the bank. "And then he got to liking it more and more, *enjoying* the killing, embellishing his crimes, making it look as if the Lenape were behind the murders and satisfying his own growing madness at the same time." He whirled around to look down at Brighid. "I'm right, aren't I? And now, now that you remember everything, we can get Dominick and go back to New Eden and have the bastard locked up!"

"If they didn't believe me yesterday, they have no reason to believe me today," Brighid pointed out reasonably, as much as he hated to admit it. "Besides, you still don't have it quite right. Gerlach was there, as you've guessed, but not as a captive. He was there as an invited guest, because he was selling rifles and ammunition to the war party. And *that,* Philip, my darling, is why Helmut Gerlach wants any woman dead who was in that camp, any woman who might recognize him and have him turned over to the authorities to be hanged. That's why Lokwelend said that Pematalli and all those who died in the raids wanted justice: because Gerlach supplied the rifles and the hate that helped to kill so many innocent people on both sides of the struggle. And *that's* why Gerlach won't rest until I'm dead. Not that anyone except you and Dominick will ever believe me," she ended quietly.

Philip's head was near to bursting with all he had learned, all he knew he had to do. He went down on his knees in front of Brighid, taking hold of her shoulders as he looked deeply into her eyes. "A lifetime ago, a young woman named Nipawi Gischuch shamed me with her honest speech, made me take a long, hard look at myself, and dared me to try to be more than I was. Do you know what she said to me, Brighid? Let me remind you, all right, as I've never forgotten a word of it. She said, 'I know I can survive, Little Crown, no matter what. If I learned nothing else with the Lenape, I learned my own worth.' Do you remember that brave young woman, Brighid?"

She smiled at him through tear-bright eyes. "It's a long time since I've called you Little Crown. A lifetime. Yes, Philip, I remember. But so much has happened since then. I'm not half so sure of myself now as I was then. These are not my people, Philip, and they have no reason to believe me."

"They'll believe you. And I'll be with you every moment."

He waited, holding his breath.

At last, she nodded. "I'll go with you to New Eden, Tauwún. It is time to open *all* of the doors."

> *A man ties a knot with his tongue
> that his teeth will not loosen.*
> *— Irish saying*

CHAPTER 18

IT HAD TAKEN CONSIDERABLE EFFORT, BUT DOMINICK, AN acknowledged leader in New Eden, had finally arranged for a community meeting in the common room of Crown Inn and Stores for noon of the next day.

Helmut Gerlach had been easy to locate, as he had taken a room at the only other inn in town, then set up preaching on the wide front porch, calling on all good Christians to listen to his words, to heed the Lord's will in casting out the demon creature among them. With a wide white bandage on his head and his Bible in his right hand, he had preached hour after hour, drawing his sermons mostly from the Old Testament, calling up visions of fire and brimstone and an avenging Lord and generally damning Brighid as both a whore and a murderess.

Giles Crown was already in residence at Dominick's inn, very agreeably under lock and key, as a matter of fact, waiting impatiently for the coach that would take him to

Philadelphia and away from Helmut Gerlach—and without more than one hundred pounds in his pocket.

Lady Lilith, who had indeed found herself a brawny, if somewhat dim lover in the form of the owner of the coach that would transport them back to the Philadelphia docks, was also staying at the inn and doing her best to prove her father correct in his pronouncement that his daughter was no more than a common strumpet. Although she had found time away from her lover to sit at the back of the common room beside Cora and Hallie. Her hair was powdered, her dress of satin and striped a merry green, yellow, and orange, her bosom a creamy white expanse above the low-cut bodice.

Three black beauty patches—two stars and a crescent moon—accented her cheekbones and the left corner of her coyly smiling mouth. She looked very much the exotically plumed bird perched between two brown wrens. She smiled at everyone who entered, then snapped open her fan and employed it to outrageously flirt with a few flustered gentlemen who were quickly given none-too-gentle nudges in the ribs from their straight-backed, tight-lipped wives. And she had considerably more than one hundred pounds in her reticule and a letter to Philip's solicitor as well, setting up an ample quarterly allowance in her name.

At ten minutes to the hour, all of the Crowns, excluding Giles, were gathered in the common room. Brighid, dressed in her yellow gown, her hair drawn back from her face and curling to her shoulders—looking as Irish and as white as Bryna could make her—sat stiffly beside Philip, her hand in his, her face pale, her eyes bright. Dominick and Bryna sat on either side of them, lending them their support, silently warning everyone to keep their distance, to keep their opinions to themselves, until Philip had spoken on Brighid's behalf.

One by one, townspeople continued to straggle into the room. Husbands and their wives, dragging along small children who had no idea why they were there but had been told they were to have an "edifying experience." A few trappers in town for provisions. Eunice Wright and her milksop of a husband.

And, lastly, Helmut Gerlach, striding into the room with the confidence of a man among friends, his Bible in his left hand, his right outstretched, pointing at Brighid in accusation as he pronounced loudly: "Behold the Jezebel!" Then he turned in a full circle, looking straight into the eyes of everyone in the room. "'Who is on the Lord's side? let him come unto me.'"

Philip felt Brighid's fingers digging into his hand and squeezed hers in return. "It's all right, darling," he whispered, bending close to her ear. "We'll let him talk. Given enough rope, he may just hang himself and save us the trouble."

"But what if they don't listen to you, Philip?" Brighid asked, turning away as Gerlach was helped to a chair, complaining that his head wound pained him. "What if they refuse to do as you ask?"

Philip hated to see Brighid so frightened. He hated that she was even here, forced to face her accuser, forced to confront the past she had tried so desperately to forget. She was a strong woman, incredibly strong, but her particular strengths did her no good in this setting.

Now it was time for *his* particular strengths. He might not know how to track a bear through the woods, but he could verbally bring down a hyena at ten paces in any London drawing room. He had enough of his father in him to easily find his way around a complicated plot and enough anger in him to destroy Helmut Gerlach with a few well-chosen words. Of this, Philip was confident.

"We have the truth on our side, Brighid. And after what you told me last night, we have nothing to worry about. We'll just sit here and listen"—he looked to his sister, who took time out from leering at a young farmer to wink at him—"and wait for Lilith to do her part."

"I can't believe she volunteered," Brighid said, nodding to Lady Lilith as the young woman smiled and then gaily waved to her with her fan.

"I know. I'd like to think she's doing it because of some great love of justice or of me, but I believe she's only being so amenable in order to tweak our father. And for the money, of course." Philip could have said more, could have told Brighid what he had told Dominick, told her that Lilith felt sure their father had only engineered his odd relationship with Gerlach in order to be sure Brighid died before Philip "threw himself away on a penniless nobody."

But Brighid had enough on her plate without adding to it with that particular bit of information. It was enough, had to be enough, that Giles Crown was leaving New Eden, never to return. And never to see another penny of Philip's money, not if the marquess of Playden ended his days rotting in debtor's prison!

Once Elijah Kester—the only other person in the room privy to the information Brighid had imparted to the Crowns late last night—had closed the door to the common room and positioned himself in front of it, his large, muscular arms crossed against his massive chest, Dominick stood up and walked into the cleared area in the center of the room.

He was dressed in his finest clothes, a none too subtle reminder that he was, indeed, Lord Dominick Crown. He looked both handsome and impressive, and all the low murmuring stopped when he opened his mouth to speak.

"Ladies and gentlemen," he began, touching a hand to the sapphire pin nestled in his lace jabot, "I want to thank all of you for coming here today. As you know, Mr. Helmut Gerlach has charged my ward, Miss Brighid Cassidy, with an attempt on his life. My ward has already admitted to being the person who did, in fact, strike at Mr. Gerlach with a knife, as you also know. But she additionally states that she acted in abject fear for her own safety, that Mr. Gerlach is responsible for the death of Silky Wattson and the murders of several other poor unfortunate women we have heard about, and that he wishes to kill *all* of the female captives lately returned to us from Fort Pitt."

He turned in a slow circle, looking into as many avidly

interested eyes as possible, then walked over to Gerlach and smiled down at him. Kindly. Encouragingly. "Mr. Gerlach? As you have brought the charges against my ward, I think it only fitting that you speak first. You may take the floor, remembering that Miss Cassidy's representative, the earl of Ashford, will then have the opportunity to refute your charges. Oh, and I trust you will be brief and remember that there are ladies and young children present." And then he turned his back on the man and returned to his seat.

Gerlach slowly rose to his feet, adjusting the bandage on his head as he positioned himself in front of the roomful of interested listeners. "My brothers and sisters, I come here today, as I have come to you these past years—as I have come to so many small towns and villages throughout the colony—as a man of God," he began quietly, almost modestly.

But his modesty didn't last past a second opening of his mouth. "I have prayed with you, my people, and have taken the word of the Lord into the wilderness. I have nursed your spirits and done my best to save your souls for the Almighty. I am one of you. Listen to my words, and heed them, even as I admit to my own failing and beg your forgiveness even as the Lord has forgiven me."

"What's he up to?" Dominick asked Philip quietly. "He's admitting he went after Brighid? I don't get it."

Perhaps his uncle didn't understand, but Philip did and at once, so that he squeezed Brighid's hand in warning, silently begging her not to interrupt when Gerlach spoke again.

"As is written in the Lord's good Book, 'Now the serpent was more subtile than any beast of the field.' And, indeed, that serpent did beguile me. And, indeed, my people, I did think to eat." He hung his head, his hands at his sides, a man humbled and obviously in deep personal agony of spirit. "And I did think to eat," he repeated, raising his head, his eyes shining with tears, with religious fervor.

"She beguiled me!" he shouted as he whirled to point an accusing finger at Brighid. "For all my strong faith, for all my years of service to our Almighty Lord, she beguiled me! 'For the lips of a strange woman drop as an honeycomb, and her mouth is smoother than oil,'" he quoted, his voice lifting to the ceiling, banging against the wooden beams, "'but her end is bitter as wormwood, sharp as a two-edged sword.' Yes! I say to you, more bitter than death is the woman. 'Her heart is snares and nets, her hands as bands.'"

"I should have used my knife lower, on his lying throat," Brighid muttered as Philip slipped an arm around her shoulders, felt the growing tension in her body.

Gerlach punched his fist into the air. "But the Lord looked down, my brothers and sisters!" he shouted, his voice rolling like thunder. "The Lord looked down and saw this poor sinner, and He saved me. He gave me the strength to cast off the devil who had taken human form. He gave me the will to resist this Jezebel's comely lures. And so I sank to my knees in prayer, thankful to the Lord my God, and I bade the Jezebel to do likewise. And then," he ended, lowering his voice so that those in the back of the room leaned forward as one, the better to hear him, "and then she struck out at me in her evil. She struck out at me with her knife in the way of the savage. And I did fall."

That was that. Gerlach had admitted to having lusted after Brighid but then blamed her for trying to kill him after he had come to his senses at the last moment, remembered that he was a Christian man, and spurned her advances. Very neat. Very believable, as he had been the Lord's minister to most of these simple folk for many, many years.

Philip's slow clapping broke the awed silence in the common room as he rose to his feet and cried out, "Bravo! Bravo! A sterling performance, I am sure, Mr. Gerlach. Truly inspired!" Then he turned to Gerlach's captive audience. "And now, ladies and gentlemen, perhaps we might hear the truth?"

"The whore has nothing to say that God-fearing souls wish to hear," Eunice Wright exclaimed, hopping up from her seat. "She lost her soul the day she turned from God and took on the ways of the heathen. A godly woman would have died by her own hand rather than submit. She should have strangled her half-breed bastard at birth! And so we all say, isn't that right?"

Philip tried to take hold of Brighid's arm as she leaped to her feet, but she pulled away from him and advanced toward Eunice Wright, her hands drawn up into fists at her sides. "Who *are* you?" she demanded as Eunice sat down again, cowering against her husband. "Who are you, *any* of you, to judge me? To judge my mother?"

"Brighid, love, sit down," Bryna said, patting the empty place beside her. "Please, let Philip handle this."

"No!" Brighid exclaimed hotly. "I am not ashamed of what I did, what my mother did. Think, Bryna. I wouldn't be alive if my mother had done as these people think should be done. Mary Catherine would not be alive. The greatest sin is to give up. The greatest sin is to die. *Life!* This is the Lord's most precious gift. To kill another is a sin, and to kill oneself is a worse sin—against God, against life itself. How dare these people hate me because I chose to survive? Who gave them the right?"

Gerlach shot to his feet. "'Can a man take fire in his bosom, and his clothes not be burned? Can one go upon hot coals, and his feet not be burned?' So it is with the Lenape, my brothers and sisters. She took the savage to her bosom, walked the path of the heathen. And the fire has burned up her soul!"

"Oh, shut up," Philip said baldly, putting his hand flat against Gerlach's chest and rudely pushing him back into his seat. "Miss Cassidy," he continued, angling his head toward Brighid, "may I remind you that you have agreed not to speak in this forum? That I, as your representative, will speak for you. Please, take your seat."

"Geptschátschik!" Brighid pronounced very loudly and most unhelpfully lapsing into the language of the Lenape to label the entire assemblage fools, then finally heeded Bryna's continued pleading and left Philip's side to once more sit beside her cousin.

Philip slowly counted to ten, waiting patiently as the

audience—he could only think of them as his audience—mumbled and grumbled their way back to silence, then lifted a hand to his mouth and politely cleared his throat.

"Did Miss Brighid Cassidy attempt to kill Mr. Helmut Gerlach? Yes. Yes, she did. And it is my job, my responsibility, to tell you *why* Miss Cassidy acted as she did. I promise not to take up too much of your time," he continued over the murmurings that had begun again, deliberately smiling at Eunice Wright, "but I do have a small story to tell you. It begins, as all good stories should, with the words 'once upon a time,' although, I assure you, this is no fairy tale."

He began walking up and down in front of the rows of chairs, knowing his clothes were impressive, knowing his title was equally weighty, knowing that half of his audience respected his title while the other half resented everything about him. He was about to give the most important speech of his life, of Brighid's life. And strangely, he felt entirely calm.

He stopped, midway along the front row of chairs, and smiled at the small child perched on her mother's lap, her thumb stuck in her mouth. "Once upon a time, there were two little boys and their sisters—one just about your age and one nearly grown. They were very happy. Very happy. But one day something terrible happened, and the little boys went up to heaven. The little girl was saved, her mother's bravery and sacrifice saved her, and the almost-grown girl was taken off by wild Indians, never to be seen again for five long years—until she was all grown up and found her way home. How happy she was to be home again!"

The little girl smiled around the moist thumb in her mouth and Philip patted her head, then began to pace once more, careful to make eye contact with as many people as possible. "But that happy homecoming didn't last. It couldn't. For word came to her that somebody was killing other white women who had been returned to their homes. Why, somebody had even killed Silky Wattson, who also had once been a captive of the Lenape. And that *somebody*, that crazed killer, was now after her!"

"The Lenape killed those women," a man called out from the back of the room. "Everybody knows that. The Lenape didn't want the women to tell anyone of their plans to come back here, to the east, to kill all the white men and steal their land."

"If that isn't the most ridiculous thing I've ever heard!" Brighid exclaimed, hopping up from her chair once more. "The Lenape are on the run, trying simply to survive. While the white man gives them diseases and rum and steals *their* land!"

"For God's sake, Brighid, this is difficult enough. Don't help me," Philip whispered out of the corner of his mouth as he walked past her, put a hand on her shoulder, and pushed her back down beside Bryna.

"It's *my* life, Philip," she shot back at him.

"Yes, love, it is, and I'm trying to save it, all right?"

She lifted her chin and looked away from him, even as the voices behind him threatened to break into angry shouts.

"If I might continue?" he asked, turning around once more, spreading his hands and again appealing to his audience for silence. "Thank you. Now, on with my little story. Did I mention that this young woman had been struck on the head during the raid at her parents' farm? Yes, it's true. And that because of this horrific injury, she had no recollection of the raid or of the days following that raid when she and other captives had been on the run with the Indians, moving ever westward? No, I don't think I did. I'm so sorry. Forgive my lapse, for this is most important to my story, as what happened during those days after the raid are very much the heart of my story and explain the murders. And is it any wonder Miss Cassidy could not remember her time in the Indian camp? Is it any wonder any sane person would wish to forget the horrors she saw, the suffering she deplored, but could not stop?

"You see," he went on, knowing he now had everyone's full attention, "Brighid Cassidy and all the women who had been captives of that raiding party had seen the man who rode into the camp every day, bringing information to the savages. Information . . . and weapons. Telling them of the most vulnerable targets for their raids, providing them with the ammunition to shoot defenseless farmers and their families."

"Who?" Lady Lilith called out, right on cue. "Who did this terrible thing?"

"A good question, madam, and with a terrible answer. It was a *white* man, ladies and gentlemen. Our culprit is a foul, vicious, soulless, heartless man who deliberately foments hatred and fear both of and in the Lenape, then supplies those Lenape with the weapons to slay their white enemies. A man so vile, so base, that he gleefully joins with those Indians in torturing their captives. Night after night, raping innocent, helpless women. Killing the weak, the troublesome. We already know that over those horrific days Brighid Cassidy was with the Indians, all the male captives were killed, one by one, both man and boy. And all while the women watched. While Brighid Cassidy, wounded and too weak to fight but too strong willed to die, also watched. And the man laughed."

He had them now. Nobody moved, nobody spoke. He held them all in the palm of his hand. All except the man he most wanted to have. He didn't look toward Helmut Gerlach but didn't need to in order to feel the man's smile. "This man is very clever. He travels through white villages and Indian camps with impunity, without suspicion, for he pretends to be a man of God, welcomed everywhere, suspected nowhere. On the blood of innocents, he makes his fortune and satisfies his own growing bloodlust. In the word of God, he butchers and provokes and breaks all the Commandments again and again and again."

The moment had come. He spun around on his heels to point an accusing finger at the smiling man. "And Helmut Gerlach would still be free to wreak his destruction!" he shouted, startling the little girl in the front row so that she began to whimper. "He would still be free to travel the countryside, murdering any woman who might recognize him for what he is! He would still be free—if it were not for Brighid Cassidy and the return of her memory of that horrific time. Those terrible days when Helmut Gerlach took those poor women from New Eden into hell with him and laughed at their pain!"

Amid the uproar that followed, Philip sat down beside Dominick and waited for Gerlach to speak. He looked to Lilith, wordlessly telling her to be ready, and then sent up a quick prayer that his melodramatic speech would bear fruit.

He didn't have long to wait.

"Is this true, Gerlach?" someone cried out.

"My God—my sister died in the raids! Her two babies!"

"My brother's son was taken and never returned! He was only twelve years old!"

"Gerlach *was* free to travel. He could have done it."

"Certainly doesn't make his money on that miserable farm of his. Speak up, Gerlach. Let's hear what you have to say for yourself!"

Gerlach allowed the comments to pass over his head without giving answers as he glared at Philip, then stood up to speak. "'They brought Daniel, and cast him into the den of lions,'" he quoted, spreading his arms wide as if to make a sacrifice of his worldly body. "How can you believe the words of this fornicator, my brothers and sisters, this man who has obviously been bewitched by the Jezebel? Is this why I have labored for your souls? So that you could cast me to the lions?"

And that's when Lady Lilith proved that she most certainly could have done quite well if she had been able to trod the boards in London as an actress. In clear, easily heard tones, she shouted from the back of the room, "And to think—his own wife died in the raids! His own dear Johanna! When I asked him to pray for me, he told me of his dear wife. How can this be true? I am shocked, shocked beyond belief, and think I may swoon." And then she did, most gracefully—and most conveniently—into the arms of a visibly pleased young farmer.

Philip watched as Gerlach lost his smile and his florid color. Clearly the man did not wish anyone to visit upon the subject of his wife, of the well-tended grave at his miserably neglected farm.

"Your turn again," Dominick whispered to Philip, who was already rising, holding firm to Brighid's hand as he assisted her to her feet. "And your trick, I imagine. You're doing very well, Philip."

"Ladies and gentlemen," Philip shouted above the dozen frantic conversations now taking place in the room. "Ladies and gentlemen, I ask your indulgence while you listen to Miss Cassidy. Please allow her to tell you about her friend. About the woman whose own husband sold her to the Indians. About that same woman who kept her new friend Brighid Cassidy alive even as she was routinely being tortured and raped by her captors. About that sainted woman, dead now, whose child Brighid Cassidy has taken to raise as her own. About the woman given the Lenape name of Wingenund. The woman, ladies and gentlemen, Brighid Cassidy first knew as *Johanna Gerlach!*"

Now the room exploded in sound, led chiefly by Gerlach's shout of "Lies! Lies!" before he pushed his way toward the door, saying he refused to breathe the same air as a godless strumpet who would say anything to save her miserable life. "Hang her! Hang her for the lying, scalping heathen she is! I wash my hands of all of it!"

But Elijah Kester waited at that door, barring Gerlach's exit. "You're leaving all right, Helmut," he said, "but you're going to your farm. *All* of us are going to your farm. And we'll be taking shovels."

The grave was empty.

Brighid watched as Elijah Kester and two other volunteers began to dig in the earth in front of the cross Gerlach had used to mark the grave: Johanna, Beloved Wife of Helmut. The grave he used to show that he was one of the many victims of the Lenape raids. She stood with her family, Philip's arm around her, as the men dug down three feet, then four, then six.

It hadn't been until late the previous evening, as they had all sat together in the drawing room at Pleasant Hill, that Dominick had said the words that put all the pieces of the puzzle together: "What a bastard Gerlach is. And to think—his own wife died in the same raid in which you were taken, Brighid. His own wife is one of his victims."

Brighid had been confused at first, then quickly realized that although she had now told everyone about Wingenund, about Johanna, about Daniel, she had never identified Johanna's hated husband by name. Within five minutes, everyone understood the remaining duplicity of Helmut Gerlach, and within ten, a plan to unmask him once and for all had been formed.

Lilith had done her part, and Elijah Kester had done his. But Philip had been absolutely brilliant! There was no way out now for Gerlach. He would be taken to Easton, tried, and hanged.

And Johanna Gerlach and Pematalli and all those who had suffered at the hands of this evil man would be able to rest in peace.

"There's no sense in digging deeper," Elijah announced, taking Dominick's offered hand and climbing out of the hole he had dug. "There's no body there. Never was no body in there. Gerlach, you about ready to talk to us now?"

Gerlach remained silent, but the sound of a low, guttural voice had everyone turning as one to listen to a new speaker.

"As is written in your Holy Book that the Moravians gave to me, as I have read in that part you call Revelations, 'Behold, I stand at the door, and knock.' He has much to say, this man, and he will say it, for the last door is now open. He will say it, and we shall all hear. Only then shall we have real peace and understanding between our two peoples."

Brighid pressed her hands to her mouth as Lokwelend

finished speaking. He seemed to have materialized out of nowhere. He walked slowly into the clearing, his posture straight and tall, his daughter Cora by his side and dressed in the Lenape way, proud of her heritage, her chin lifted high as if daring anyone to question her reasons for being there. The crowd parted before them, respectfully, fearfully, some even shamefaced, giving them freedom of passage.

"I am happy to see you here, my father," Philip said quietly as the old Indian paused in front of him.

"And I am happy, Tauwún, that you and Nipawi Gischuch have at last fulfilled my dream. You have done as this old man asked, what I have waited for all these long years. You have opened every door, those to the past and those to the future. The evil is all but over now, and we wish to witness what happens and take word of what we see to Pematalli," Lokwelend said, then moved on, leaving Cora with Brighid.

His passage took him past Gerlach, and the man made short work out of lunging at Lokwelend, stripping him of his knife, and placing its tip just below the old Indian's right ear. "Move, and I'll slice his heathen throat!" he shouted, and Brighid grabbed hold of Philip's forearm to keep him from running at Gerlach.

"Forgive me, my son," Lokwelend said as everyone stepped clear of the two men as Gerlach's forearm tightened around the Lenape's throat. "I grow old and slow. Time was, this would not have happened."

"You're not going anywhere, Gerlach," Philip told the man calmly as he pried Brighid's clinging fingers from his sleeve. "There's nowhere to go that you can outrun word of your crimes. You'll soon be the most hated man in the colonies. And the most hunted. Unless you can convince us of the rightness of your behavior? Yes, there's a thought. Dominick? What do you say? Should we give Gerlach here a chance to explain?"

Brighid held her breath as Dominick stepped forward a pace to stand next to his nephew. "It seems only fair. After all, Gerlach says he's a man of God."

Philip smiled, spreading his hands to show he was unarmed. "Hear that, Gerlach? Now, why don't you put down that knife, and we'll talk about what you did and why you did it. Why you most probably *still* do it. Perhaps you can explain your reasons, and we can let you go? You might want to start with the reason you sell rifles to the Lenape."

The knife never wavered, its sharp tip pressing a small dimple into Lokwelend's skin as Brighid took Bryna's hand and stayed very still, so as not to startle Gerlach in any way.

"'The Lord is a man of war,'" Gerlach began, his eyes shifting first toward Philip and then to Elijah Kester, who stood to his left and partially behind him, his shovel poised and ready for attack. "And I am a soldier of the Lord. It is the will of the Lord to strike down the savage, those who do not recognize the Lord our God as their savior. If the whites will not make war on the heathen, I will give them a reason to make war."

"And make yourself a fair amount of money in the process, selling rifles to the Lenape. You still do, I imagine," Philip interrupted, his tone not threatening but conversational, almost conciliatory. "Possibly even taking your *share* of the jewelry and other booty an attacking war party might carry away with them after killing and scalping women and children? You must see this as your small reward for doing the Lord's work?"

Gerlach pushed out his tongue to moisten his lips. "I sell my share of scalps, yes," he admitted, almost boasted. "My work is not yet done, and won't be until the savages are destroyed. I need money to buy arms, to spread the word of God in the west, to the north. The farmers who die are welcomed into heaven as martyrs. Martyrs to the will of our Lord."

"Martyrs? Really? Is that how you see it? That's very interesting. You even sold your own wife to the Lenape," Philip offered. "Why? Had she discovered what you were doing?"

"Johanna was a fool," Gerlach spat out tightly, beginning to back toward the woods, dragging Lokwelend with him.

"All women are fools and vessels of the devil. She threatened to block the path of righteousness."

Brighid couldn't stand the tension any longer, could not remain still while she watched Lokwelend being pulled inevitably toward the dense woods, toward his certain death. "You're the fool, Gerlach, and a liar into the bargain," she told him, speaking through gritted teeth. "All those innocent women you've killed—and all for nothing. There's nowhere you can go now, nowhere that you'll be safe. Lenape and white man alike will hunt you down. Because you won't stop killing. And God has nothing to do with it! You *like* the killing. You *enjoy* it, don't you? What did you say to me? Oh, yes, I remember. You said, 'What I began for one reason is continued for another.' Do you remember that, Gerlach? You began your killing to keep from being discovered, being found out for the villain you are, but you continued it because you *like* it. Don't you, Gerlach? You like it so much, you killed Silky Wattson— butchered her—a harmless old woman who couldn't possibly have been any threat to you."

Philip took another step forward as Gerlach kept his eyes and attention on Brighid. "Yes. I think she's right, Gerlach. You *like* it. A very wise man told me something not so long ago, something that confused me. But now I understand. Dominick, you remember what that wise man said, don't you? 'It is possible for a single evil to take on several forms. Do we fear the knife or the man holding it? How does he use his weapon and when, for what reason? To punish or to hide? To feed his madness or to conceal an even greater evil? Or both?' This wise man begged me to open the door, to see what lay behind it. And now, Lokwelend, thanks to you, to Brighid, the door is open. Now we all can see, we all can hear. Tell us, Gerlach. Tell us all. You killed those women, didn't you? Not just to protect yourself and your secrets, but because you *liked* it. You hunted them. You raped them. And then you killed them. Cutting out their hearts, feeding your madness with their blood. *Didn't you?*"

Gerlach licked his lips again, his eyes burning hot with

the sickness he could no longer hide. "'The word of God is quick, and powerful, and sharper than any two-edged sword, piercing even to the dividing asunder of soul and spirit, and of the joints and marrow,'" he said, almost babbling as he stumbled over the words. "I am the Lord's soldier, and I divide the soul and the spirit, I cleanse with new seed and purify the soul." He shivered, the point of the knife moving so that Brighid could see a small trickle of blood begin running down Lokwelend's throat. "I cannot be persecuted for doing the work of the Lord!"

Out of the corner of her eyes, Brighid could see Elijah Kester moving with a slow grace difficult to believe the massive blacksmith possessed, moving slowly, quietly to his left, slightly behind the now incensed Gerlach. *Keep him talking, Philip,* she urged silently as Elijah nodded and took another step. *Just keep him talking.*

"Well, now," Philip said almost kindly, so that Brighid looked to him in surprise, baffled by his careless tone. "That explains everything. Dominick, doesn't that explain everything? Gerlach here was doing just as he always claimed. The Lord's work. Who are we to judge him? Who are we to say if he is mad? Gerlach, as far as I can see, you're free to go."

"Free to . . . free to go?" Gerlach questioned him, the hand holding the knife going slightly slack, so that Lokwelend closed his eyes in quiet relief.

"Free to go," Philip repeated, looking straight into Gerlach's eyes. "So go. Go *now!*"

Elijah Kester lifted his shovel, but Gerlach moved quickly to avoid the blow, pitching Lokwelend forward, toward Philip. Then, instead of running away, he gave out with a terrifying yell and launched himself at Philip, his main accuser, his chief tormentor.

As Dominick pulled Bryna's head protectively against his chest, blocking her sight, and as Brighid watched a struggling Lokwelend tumble facedown into the dirt, Philip sprang forward, grabbing Gerlach's wrist in an attempt to wrest the knife from his hand.

Together they fell to the ground, still fighting over the knife, rolling over and over in the dirt before they both disappeared into the open grave.

"Philip!" Brighid screamed, running to the edge of the deep hole. *"Philip!"*

A moment later, a lifetime later, Philip reached up a hand and Elijah pulled him out of the grave. "Thank you, friend," Philip said, dusting off his ruined satins as Brighid watched, trembling so violently she was surprised to realize that she could still stand upright. "If you've nothing better to do for the next hour, I suggest we fill in this hole. After all, I suppose every man deserves some sort of burial."

"I could murder you, you know," Brighid said when the burial was over, after most of the residents of New Eden had long since gone back to their homes, when she was fairly certain her voice wouldn't tremble and betray her fear. "You said no one would be in any danger. We'd simply let Gerlach talk and then tell everyone about Johanna and then—"

He pulled her into his arms. "Well, Brighid, now you know the truth about me. I'm not infallible. Disappointed? Do you believe you can possibly abide being married to a fallible man? With you and all your own plans for Gerlach being so perfect, you understand."

She looked up into Philip's laughing blue eyes and shook her head. "You'll pay for that, Little Crown," she said, melting against him. She took one last look at the new grave and shuddered. "Now take me home."

"With pleasure, my darling," he said, lifting her high against his chest and walking toward Pegasus. "With the greatest of pleasure. Dominick, don't bother putting a candle in the window. Your ward will not see Pleasant Hill tonight."

"You have my cousin back first thing tomorrow morning, Philip Crown," Bryna called after them from her seat in Dominick's open coach, both relief and laughter in her voice. "We have a wedding to plan!"

"Geptschat," Brighid muttered against Philip's neck as he helped her onto Pegasus's back. "Now we'll be poked and prodded and dressed up like pet monkeys just to make Bryna happy."

Philip mounted the white stallion behind her and reached forward to take hold of the reins. "And we'll be glad to do it, my darling. If it weren't for Bryna and her stubbornness, we'd never have met."

Lokwelend's brown hand closed over Philip's. "Believe what you will, Tauwún," he said, and Brighid drew in her breath sharply as she saw tears in the old Indian's eyes. "But in the words of the great chief Euripides, 'Slow but sure moves the might of the gods.' You only but go to live out the remainder of your destiny, one that is full of love and children and a good old age. Go in peace and with my thanks. Pematalli has been vindicated, and at long last my heart is at rest."

Brighid leaned down and pressed a kiss against Lokwelend's weathered cheek. "I love you, Grandfather, and I will always be grateful to you."

Lokwelend's smile, so rarely seen, shone bright in his dark face. "You'll stay here until I am gone, Nipawi Gischuch, and give me time to teach Tasukamend the ways of the Lenape. That will be your thanks to me."

"We promise," Philip said as Lokwelend stepped back from the horse. "We will stay here until you are gone. Unless you decide to keep us standing around when all I can think of is getting this woman to myself—in which case I might be tempted to speed your departure."

Lokwelend's hearty laughter and his slap to Pegasus's rump sped Brighid and Philip on their way to his estate. On their way home.

EPILOGUE

Completion

If ever two were one, then surely we.
If ever man were lov'd by wife, then thee;
if ever wife was happy in a man,
compare with me ye women if you can.
—Anne Bradstreet

*Once a woman has given you her heart
you can never get rid of the rest of her.*
        — Sir John Banbrugh

"K'DAHÓLEL. NOW, TRY IT AGAIN."

Philip shook his head. "I cannot believe that means 'I love you.' Wouldn't you rather hear how it's said in French? Whispered in your ear as I nibble on your soft skin perhaps? Trust me in this, Brighid. French is sweet, musical. The Lenape language, frankly, sounds more like you're having trouble clearing your throat."

"Geptschat!" Brighid countered, falling back on the bed but unable to keep a smile from her face as she looked up at the fresh, fragrant grasses Philip had hung from the ceiling. "But I must agree with you, I suppose. Lokwelend told me the Iroquois call the Lenape Akotshakane, which means 'the stutterers.' Lokwelend considers this a vicious insult."

"How rude of them," Philip said, rolling onto his side to begin nibbling at his wife's slim throat. "My poor, insulted father. Remind me to go out and slay a half-dozen Iroquois first thing tomorrow morning. But as for the remainder of the night?"

Brighid giggled, for Philip's kisses tickled as much as they aroused, and pushed him away, because she wanted to talk. "If you could be serious for more than a moment, Husband, I have a few things to say to you. First, I have to explain why you found most of your clothing on the porch when you came home this evening."

Philip began playing with the ribbons of Brighid's nightgown. "I already know why, for I've learned at least something about the Lenape culture. For one, marrying you has made me a member of your family and, in the Lenape way of things, women are now totally in charge of my life—not that I mind. And second, Lapawin has decided that you should divorce me. Again. She ruined my new blue satin last week, remember, tossing it into a puddle—and all because I said she couldn't bring a goat into the house. What did I do wrong this time, if I might ask?"

Brighid sighed as Philip's hand made its way inside her bodice, his fingers instantly busy, instantly waking a need in her she had thought satisfied only a half hour earlier when they had first come to bed. "It's what you haven't done, darling," she told him, doing her best to ignore the delightful tightening deep in her belly. "You haven't convinced Lokwelend to leave his log house and come live with us. It has been three months, Philip, and Lapawin grows impatient."

"She'll grow whiskers before Lokwelend allows himself within a mile of that woman's wiles. But—just a moment—she already does have whiskers, doesn't she?"

"You're an evil man, Philip Crown," Brighid scolded, once again trying not to giggle. She had done little but laugh and love and enjoy life ever since their marriage. It was as if Philip were intentionally trying to fill her life with such happiness that she would have no time to remember the past, to remember the horror that preceded the joy she had found with him. "Now stop teasing me and let's get to sleep.

There will be dancing all day tomorrow at Cora's wedding, and I mean to dance until I drop to the ground in exhaustion. Lokwelend says Lucas has promised to wear full Lenape regalia for the ceremony, if you can believe it."

"With those bandy legs of his?" Philip slung a leg over Brighid's and moved half on top of her, pinning her to the bed. "Well, I suppose Lucas can be stark, staring naked for all I care at the moment," he said, easing her nightgown off her shoulders before blazing a trail of kisses from the base of her throat to the sensitive skin between her breasts. "I'd rather concentrate on giving Daniel a brother or sister. Seeing Bryna's beautiful little Felicia and Dominick's obvious pride in his daughter have made me realize that I'd like us to have a veritable clutch of little lords and ladies."

Brighid wrapped her arms around Philip's bare back, stroking his heated skin. "Lords and ladies," she said, sighing. "I still can't believe I'm actually the countess of Ashford, someday to be marchioness of Playden. Less than a year ago, I was Nipawi Gischuch, scrabbling in the dirt, simply trying to survive. It's a strange world, Philip. A strange, strange world. I only wonder if Daniel will ever find his place in it."

She frowned as Philip suddenly rolled onto his back, taking her along with him, so that she was above him, looking down into his beloved face. "I didn't tell you, did I?" he asked, and she could see from the sparkle in his eyes that he had been waiting for the proper moment to say whatever he had to say. "With help from Lokwelend, in the naming of it, and from Dominick, who took care of the legalities, I have done something I hope will please you."

"What have you done?" she asked, knowing he had already done so much. He'd saved her life. He'd rid New Eden of its greatest evil. He'd given Pematalli peace at last. He'd taken Daniel as his own. He'd even allowed Lapawin and her pipe and her assorted silliness into his beautiful new house. "I can't think of anything you could do that would make me happier than I am at this moment."

He reached up to kiss the tip of her nose, then motioned for her to sit back against the pillows as he did likewise. "Brighid," he began, his tone now so serious that she became frightened, "we're going to have to leave here one day."

She bent her head, toying with the ribbons he had so lately untied. "I know. I heard you arguing with Dominick the other day when I rode over to see Bryna and the baby. Dominick's loyalty is to the colonies, and yours is to England. Do you think Dominick's right—that one day the talking will stop and the colonies will rebel?"

"I don't know, darling," he answered. "But I certainly hope not. They don't stand a chance if they do, not against the full weight of the British military. I do know that our time here is limited, both by the problems with the colonists and my responsibility to Playden Court when my father finally sticks his spoon in the wall. We promised Lokwelend we'd stay here, that we'd allow him to teach Daniel the ways of the Lenape, about his Lenape heritage. But the day will come when we have to leave. Which is why," he ended, smiling once more, "I have deeded Enolowin over to Daniel. When he is grown, when he can make his own decisions, he can either stay with us at Playden Court or he can come here to Enolowin. For, no matter how I love him, no matter how we both love him, Daniel is still Wulapen's son."

Tears stung Brighid's eyes. "Enolowin. Standing Guard. What a perfect name, Philip. You and Lokwelend chose well." She pressed her head against his chest. *"K'dahólel, Philip. K'dahólel."*

"Hmmm," he said, sliding his hands beneath the twisted hem of her nightgown. "I'm beginning to like the sound of that. *K'dahólel,* Brighid Crown. I love you. And I will love you forever. Remember, I'm yours to command."

As he pressed her against the mattress, before his mouth

could claim hers, she teased, "Then you'll agree to help Lapawin in her pursuit of Lokwelend?"

"Not on my life," he mumbled against her lips. "Now, stop talking and kiss me."

"Yes, my lord," Brighid said, smiling, and did as her husband bid her. After all, it wouldn't hurt to let him have his way every once in a while . . .

Kasey Michaels

Kasey Michaels is "one of the romance genre's most beloved authors....a powerhouse writer."

— *Romantic Times*

The Promise

Coming soon from Pocket Star Books

POCKET STAR BOOKS
PROUDLY PRESENTS

THE PROMISE
Kasey Michaels

Coming soon from
Pocket Star Books

The following is a preview of
The Promise . . .

When Daniel Cassidy Crown entered a ballroom, conversation stopped, then began again, quickly, nervously, as he stood in the doorway and employed that easy smile that never quite reached his heavy-lidded, storm-swept dark eyes.

He was tall, Daniel Crown was, taller than most, with broad shoulders and a narrow waist above long, straight legs. And he was dark. Dark eyes, dark hair, dark past. Mysteriously dark. Arrogantly dark. Frighteningly dark. Intriguingly dark. And handsome as sin. A living, breathing invitation to sin, that was Daniel Crown. A good-looking, marvelously titillating, mouthwatering, definitely dangerous invitation to sin.

All sorts of sin.

Women, young impressionable debutantes as well as dashing matrons, envisioned the torment in his soul and longed to explore the depths of his unknown passions. To a woman, they all ached to be that one very special woman who might someday unleash his passions, touch his heart.

Men, especially young, rather jealous men, were intrigued in a much different way than their female counterparts. They sensed the leashed power in Daniel Crown, the darkness in him, and feared his intensity even as they envied his rapier wit, his physical abilities, his cool self-assurance. They courted him, because it would be fruitless to oppose him. They called him their friend yet, as with the women of London, they were aware that they did not really know him.

No one dared.

It wasn't enough to show the world a dark countenance, a quick wit, a hint of mystery, a dollop of hidden sadness; and Daniel Crown, who was totally unaware of his effect on his fellow creatures, had not consciously done anything to create his quite fearful and provocative reputation among the members of the *ton*. Not consciously. However, one vision of his banked fires bursting into flame, early in his first season, when a supercilious young leader of society dared to insult Daniel's Lenni Lenape father and was summarily dealt with, had proved to be enough to keep a smart enemy well hidden behind a smiling face.

For society had learned quickly that there was no winning against Daniel Crown. There was no victory to be found in verbal sparring, no thrill in whispered insults, no reward in sly jokes about the dark, savage Crown, the half-breed adopted son of the marquess of Playden. No, there was only the fear of discovery and swift, total annihilation. After the disgrace and removal of that one supposedly all-powerful enemy two years ago, there were none in the *ton* who ever again openly risked a similar fate. After all, hadn't Addison Bainbridge's disgrace been lesson enough for them? And where was Bainbridge, society's once-acknowledged leader, now? In America, that's where—probably still figuratively nursing his wounds and wondering what had happened to him.

Yes, it was much easier and safer to be Daniel Crown's friend. A man could enjoy him as they played at cards, rode hellbent-for-leather across country, drank themselves beneath the table in low dives, or talked the night away, discussing the merits of a good wine, a loose woman, or the poetry of John Milton.

So that was Daniel Crown. Adopted son of a marquess. Privy to one of the finest fortunes in all England. Handsome. Intelligent. Boon companion. Welcomed into society. The envy of many, the dream of more. All in all, Daniel Crown's reputation, his physical perfection, his connection to the marquess of Playden, would seem enough to make any young man happy.

Which did nothing to explain his dark scowl when his younger adoptive brother, Michael Crown, ran him down in the card room of Lady Cornwallis's townhouse, pulling on his arm, begging him for a few minutes alone.

Daniel gently removed the young man's hands from his finely tailored sky-blue jacket. "There you go again, Michael, creasing my satins with your clutching paws. And why so serious? What is it?" he then asked as he steered the younger man out onto the balcony, away from interested ears, for he had a fairly good idea what was bothering his brother. "You haven't outrun your allowance, have you?"

Michael colored beneath his liberally powdered hair. "Don't tease, Brother. I've never been so foolish, and you well know it. Leave that to our idiot sibling, Joseph, who has discovered the myriad joys and pitfalls of cockfighting this past week. He'll be rusticating well before June, hiding from duns back in

Sussex, if he keeps it up. No, this is not about me. This is about *you*. Mama tells me you're sailing to America next week on one of Uncle Dominick's ships. Why? And why now, just as the season is getting underway? Say it isn't so, Daniel! And if it is, say I can go with you. Mama will listen to you. She always does."

Daniel looked at his brother, younger than he by less than two years, but so very much younger in experience. Michael had been little more than a baby when Brighid and Philip Crown had packed up and left New Eden, departing from their sprawling estate of Enolowin in the Pennsylvania Colony before the rebellion could reach them, returning to the safety of Playden Court and to the title of marquess that awaited Philip upon the death of his miserable, unloved, and unloving father.

"How old were you, Michael, when we left New Eden? Not quite six?" Daniel asked now, keeping his hand on the younger man's elbow as they went down the steps and into Lady Cornwallis's garden. "What do you remember of Enolowin?"

"Less than I should, I imagine," Michael said, frowning. "I remember a large stone house, a multitude of tall trees, and an old Indian woman who talked gibberish as she bounced me on her knee. God, she didn't have any teeth, did she? And there was a man. Another Indian. Old and gray. Lokwelend, wasn't it? But he was yours, as I recall, not mine. Joseph remembers even less. I asked him one time, and all he could tell me about was the trip home and that storm we encountered. Poor Mama, being pregnant with Johanna and all. It wasn't a good crossing. I suppose you remember more? Tell me."

Daniel sighed, shaking his head. How could he explain to Michael, explain what even he did not understand. Daniel's memories of Enolowin were still clear, etched into his brain. He remembered every room of that wonderful house, every path he had walked with the old Lenape, Lokwelend, the man he had called Grandfather. And yet, there were times when he felt as if he had forgotten everything of real importance.

He looked at his brother. "You have no real urge to return then, do you, halfling?"

Michael colored again. "Don't call me that, Daniel. I'm not that much younger than you, for all you've been walking around looking as if you wear the worries of the world on your shoulders these past few years, ever since you reached your majority, now that I think on it. And, no, I'll admit that I see no reason to visit the place, except to accompany you. America's probably going to side with the French in this mess, you know. Rebels are rebels, I suppose. And I also suppose they both think they have good reasons for what they did, what they're doing. But that don't make me like them any the better. You'd best be careful, Brother. What's to say the Americans won't set up their own guillotine and slice off the heads of any Indians they might find wandering about."

"They're teaching you this drivel at university, Michael? Now, why do I doubt that?" Daniel stopped on the path and looked up into the night sky. Lokwelend had taught him about the sky, the clouds, the positions of the stars. "I suggest a closed carriage if you're doing any more carousing after this deadly dull party. We'll have rain before morning."

"Devil take the weather! And devil take all this talk about you leaving us. You know that Mama has been crying most of the day, don't you, and Papa was locked in his study when I left, fiddling with estate work, he says, but I know better. I believe neither of them think we'll ever see you again." He turned and grabbed onto Daniel's sleeve with both hands. "Don't go, Daniel, please. There's nothing for you there. We're your family. We've always been your family. You're our brother in everything but blood."

"I'm sorry, Michael. I really am. But I have to do this." Daniel stepped back and, with a wave of his arm, indicated all of London. "This is a vacuum, Michael. I cannot exist here. I can't *breathe* here. Powdered, bewigged, rigged out in satins and jewels. Spending the day waiting for the evening and the evening searching for amusement. Playden Court is yours, Michael, not mine. Enolowin could be mine. Papa has made me a bargain. If I live there for a year, work the land, the estate is mine. If I live out that year and want to come back to England, he'll sell Enolowin to Uncle Dominick and use the proceeds to buy me my own land in Sussex. I am a Crown by name, little brother, not by birth. I am not entitled to take anything from you and Joseph and Johanna. I need to make my own way."

And I need to know who I am. What I am. What I will become. But he did not say these words, for Michael couldn't understand. Not when he himself did not understand. All Daniel knew was that he was not happy. He wasn't settled. He didn't belong, trapped in England, trapped inside his stylishly clad half-breed body whose mind told him he was a civilized white man but whose tortured soul cried out for the more earthy yet mystical life of the Lenni Lenape. His father's people.

"I've got to go, Michael," he said at last, turning back toward the well-lit house and the sound of violin music being sawed out by an energetic if not talented lot of musicians. "If you can risk a bit of poetic nonsense, I believe I have to find out who I am."

"But you'll come back to us," Michael pleaded. "You *will* come back to us, Daniel."

Daniel smiled, giving his brother's shoulders a

quick squeeze. "Of course I'll come back, Daniel. I'm not going out of your life forever."

"No? Then where *do* you think you're going?"

The smile that had not reached Daniel's eyes slipped away to be replaced by the dark look that obscured his deep-running emotions. "I don't know, Michael. Could I possibly be going home?"

There was a smell to summer that was unequaled by any other season. The smells of growing wheat and corn; the soft breeze that carried the perfume of wildflowers. The clean fragrance of growing things. And in the morning, with the dew still wet on the grass—ah, then it was most wonderful of all!

Especially when one was racing that summer breeze, cutting through it on the strong back of Freedom's Lady, Brianna Cassidy Crown's huge bay mare. The horse's long mane and tail both flew in that part natural, part speed-generated breeze, as did Brianna's own long chestnut curls. Riding with her knees lightly controlling, her hands loose, yet steady, on the reins, her head bowed low over the mare's ears, Brianna watched the ground flying by beneath her, kept one emerald green eye on the horizon that rapidly approached, the fence that would fall away beneath Freedom's Lady's hooves and take them both onto Enolowin land.

Her land. Or so she had always seen it. Until last night.

Brianna's hands tightened on the reins as she glowered into the distance, remembering her father's words of the previous evening when he had taken her into his private study to "discuss" something with her.

She dreaded these "discussions," for they never boded well for her. *Lectures* was a better word for those uncomfortable interviews during which her papa would talk and she would listen. Quietly. Respectfully. Agreeably. And then escape the study to go do exactly what she pleased!

Her papa knew this, knew he was talking to a pleasant, smiling young woman whose iron will, if not exceeding that of her mother's, certainly matched it. But they both kept up the pretense, both played the small game that seemed to satisfy her mother, who had long ago learned that attempting to reason with Brianna was about as fruitful an exercise as trying to hold back the wind.

But her mama would order a "conference," and her papa would obey. Brianna would trail into the study, dutifully listen to every word, every suggestion, every warning, and everyone would be happy again.

Her older brothers, all four of them, had seen their own share of "discussions" in their youth but, Brianna was sure, if they had counted them all up and totaled them, they would not come within a mile of the talks she had been forced to endure. Not even if her sister Felicia's trips to Papa's study were added into the figure.

Of course, Felicia had been a dream of a child, quiet, biddable, never a bother, and since she was long married and living in Virginia with her gentleman-farmer husband, that left only Brianna to suffer the tender mercies of her mother's notion of the correct behavior of a proper young lady.

Being the youngest of a family was simply not fair, that's what it was, Brianna had long since decided. And, with all four of her brothers gone to sea for the summer and Felicia nowhere to be found, her parents seemed to have nothing better to do with their time than to fill it by doing their best to bring their youngest, their *baby,* up to snuff.

Which explained Brianna's most recent trip to Dominick Crown's oak-lined study. Which explained his lecture on the folly of wearing her brother's cast-off breeches and riding Freedom's Lady neck-or-nothing all over the countryside. Which explained why she had been told in no uncertain terms that now that her cousin Daniel Cassidy Crown was about to arrive to tend to the Enolowin estate, she was to no longer race helter-skelter all over the fallow fields as if that land was her own property.

Which, alas, also explained why Brianna Crown, after listening to this latest lecture and agreeing with her papa's every word, was out and about early, clad in her brother Rory's old white shirt and fawn breeches, riding astride Freedom's Lady as the mare took the five-bar fence with ease and began racing across the newly planted fields on her way to visit Winifred and Otto Bing, who were caretakers for the long-abandoned property.

The chimneys of Enolowin appeared above the treetops as she slowed Freedom's Lady to a walk before entering the tree line that separated the fields from the more private grounds, and she smiled as she caught the aroma of baking bread. Winifred always baked on a Friday. She did her washing on Monday, her ironing on Tuesday, her cleaning on the following days—Wednesday "up" and Thursday "down"—and her baking on Friday. Potato bread. Small white loaves stuffed with raisins or currants. Lovely sweet buns drizzled with sweet white icing. And if Brianna was very lucky, a wet-bottomed molasses pie with buttery crumbs on top for her very own.

Her mouth already watering, for she had run off before breakfast, before her mother could espy her in Rory's breeches and send her back to her room to change, Brianna guided Freedom's Lady through the stand of trees and out onto the sweeping, well-scythed lawns to see three smart traveling coaches lined up in the circular drive.

"Well, would you look at that mass of grandeur, Lady," she muttered under her breath, knowing that her cousin had arrived, and in some style she was forced to acknowledge, watching as a half-dozen servants she didn't recognize busied themselves unloading the three coaches and carrying box after box inside the house. "So, he's here. Cousin Daniel. Sweet heaven protect us, Lady. I'll wager he wears red-heeled shoes . . . and minces."

Deciding to investigate and uncaring that her mother would be mortified to see her daughter approaching Enolowin looking more like a stable boy than a well-bred young lady of means, Brianna urged her mount forward, riding straight up the drive, fully intending to be polite and welcoming—and then wheedle permission to ride Enolowin's fields out of the English dandy before he could figure out a way to deny her.

She had kicked her feet free of the stirrups and was just levering her right leg over Lady's head—for she dismounted Lenape style, gracefully jumping to the ground—when a pure white stallion came galloping around the corner of the house.

After that, things happened quickly. Freedom's Lady lifted her head, aware of the stallion's presence, and seemingly forgetful of her mistress's momentarily precarious presence on her back. The stallion was pulled to a plunging, dancing halt by its rider. Freedom's Lady swiveled in place, then lifted her front legs and pawed at the air.

And Brianna Cassidy Crown, who above all things prided herself on her horsemanship, landed butt down in the gravel drive, her legs sprawled out in front of her and her wind gone, knocked straight out of her. She sat there, dazed.

"You, boy! Are you all right?"

The voice was deep and cultured and definitely English. And definitely laced with humor at Brianna's expense. And if she could only catch her breath—and stop those silly blue stars from circling around her head—she'd give the man a piece of her mind! "Boy," indeed! It was one thing that the rider had no brains. Did the man also have no eyes in his head?

But all she could do was sit there, feeling foolish, trying to make her mind order her body to, for heaven's sake, *breathe* and stare up at the man whom, she decided with a fatalistic sinking of her heart, just had to be her adopted cousin.

Lord, but he was a handsome specimen! Tall—she could see this clearly, as he had dismounted to stand in front of her—with thick black hair casually tied back at his nape, a pair of devil-dark eyes, and a distinctive, hawkish face that shone with intelligence and humor. The humor, of course, was all directed at her and her predicament, a circumstance that precluded Brianna from lingering long on her cousin's attributes and urging her to center on the fact that she didn't want the man here, probably did not like him very much, and wished he would go away and leave her alone to suffocate.

"Good Lord, you're no boy, are you?" Daniel Cassidy Crown exclaimed, bending over and putting out a hand to her, offering his assistance. "Here, let me haul you up on your feet. Your breath will come back soon enough. Don't fight it."

"I'm . . . not . . . *fighting* . . . it," Brianna gasped out, the stars circling her skull gratefully fading as she swayed on her feet and took a few short, painful breaths. "But . . . I'd like . . . to see . . . your horse gelded."

"Never blame the horseflesh for your own inabilities, young lady," Daniel responded, dusting her off with more energy than concern for her possibly broken bones, Brianna thought nastily, knowing her anger came from her embarrassment at having been unseated like a raw novice. His blithe condemnation of her expertise only doubled that anger.

"But I will apologize for riding on my own land if that soothes your ruffled feathers at all," he went on, obviously not noticing or caring that she was not merely chagrined, but mad as fire. "Leaving us with one question, I suppose. Delighted as I am to make your acquaintance, what are *you* doing on my land?"

Brianna wrinkled her nose, already anticipating the tongue-lashing she was bound to receive from her mother when she returned to Pleasant Hill. "Then you are him, aren't you?" she asked dully, doing her best not to be overly impressed by her cousin's handsome, fairly exotic face. "Daniel Cassidy Crown? Uncle Philip and Aunt Brighid's adopted son?"

"Uncle Philip?" Daniel looked blank for a moment, then smiled broadly. "My God, you must be Brianna! The unexpected jewel in the Crown family, I believe your mother called you when she found out she was increasing again. I don't believe it! I helped deliver you, you know, no more than a month before we left for England. Uncle Dominick was away playing at soldier, and Mama and I were the only family handy when you decided to come into the world at midnight in the midst of a terrible thunderstorm, as I recall. I was very young, not yet eight, and your arrival made quite an impression, you understand. A few pains, a bit of bother, and then there you were—all red faced, clench fisted, and squalling."

He paused a moment, then added, still smiling: "And, by the looks of things, seventeen years haven't served to change you much."

"How very droll, I'm sure. I, of course, have no recollection of the matter," Brianna answered tightly, turning to mount her mare before her cousin could see the blood rushing into her cheeks at his description of her birth and his joke at her expense. Once on Freedom's Lady's back once more, she looked down at Daniel Crown—not very far down, for he was extremely tall—and counted to ten, attempting to control her temper.

She smiled politely and summoned up all the training her mother had instilled in her, saying, "It has been a delight, truly, to see you again, Cousin. But I fear I must leave now to return to Pleasant Hill and inform my parents of your arrival. You will drive over for dinner this evening, I assume? We dine at six. Otto Bing, your caretaker, can be counted upon to give you our direction. My parents doubtless will be delighted to see you."

Daniel reached out and took hold of Freedom's Lady's bridle. "Yes, I imagine they will, as I'll be delighted to see them. Tell me: Do they allow you at table? Or are you still in the nursery?"

The man was deliberately goading her, as if he knew just where to stick his pins in order to prick her temper beyond its limits. Brianna's tongue would soon bleed, in fact, if she had to bite it any harder. "La," she fairly trilled, hating herself, "I'm nearly eighteen, Cousin, with my nursery days far behind me. So, yes, I will be at table tonight. Why, I may recall how to use the silver and even refrain from spitting in my soup. You might, in fact, be surprised at my accomplishments since last you saw me."

He looked her up and down as she sat astride the horse, and suddenly she felt, for the first time in her life, uncomfortable under a man's gaze, uncomfortably aware of the tightness of her breeches, the way they hugged her thighs, her calves. "I am already surprised, Brianna. And fairly impressed. Until this evening then?"

Her mouth was so dry she couldn't speak, and so she only nodded her agreement. Then, digging her heels into Freedom's Lady's flanks as she pulled on the reins, she and the mare wheeled about smartly and broke into an immediate gallop, heading away from Enolowin, from that great white stallion, from Daniel Cassidy Crown—just as fast as the horse could move.

Which was fairly self-defeating for them both, Brianna concluded nervously, as she and the mare, it seemed, were both almost painfully aware that they were suddenly and most foolishly looking forward to the dance and whirl of the mating season.

Look for
The Promise
Wherever Paperback Books Are Sold
Coming soon
from Pocket Star Books

The author of more than forty novels, KASEY MICHAELS has won a vast and devoted audience, making her one of the most celebrated romance writers of our time. In addition to *The Untamed*, her work for Pocket Books includes *The Homecoming*, *The Passion of an Angel*, *The Secrets of the Heart*, *The Illusions of Love*, *A Masquerade in the Moonlight*, *The Bride of the Unicorn*, and *The Legacy of the Rose*. Ms. Michaels resides in Whitehall, Pennsylvania, with her husband and four children. She appreciates hearing from readers; you may write to her c/o Pocket Books, 1230 Avenue of the Americas, New York, NY 10020.

Hailed as "a master storyteller" by *Romantic Times,* Kasey Michaels has captured the hearts of millions, and now holds them spellbound with a tale of unforgettable love born in the rugged wilderness of the American colonies....

THE UNTAMED

It has been five years since a brutal Indian raid claimed Brighid Cassidy's family. But with the resilience and generosity of a young girl, Brighid has grown accustomed to the beautifully simple life of the tribe that took her hostage, then loved her as one of their own. Now a peace treaty is forcing her to return to civilization, and a society that she is sure will never accept her. She wants to despise dashing, blond Philip Crown, the distinguished English peer who escorts her back to Pennsylvania, yet even this desire is undermined by his warm smile and gentle manner....

When the young Earl Philip Crown promised to fulfill a family obligation by showing the long-lost captive home, the last thing he expected was to fall in love with her penetrating aquamarine eyes. As wild as the Indians she's lived with, and as stubborn as her Irish ancestors, Brighid remains as irresistible to him as she is unfathomable. But there is one thing Philip knows for certain: he must convince the spirited Brighid that happiness *can* be found beyond the wild life she has known...in the arms of an English nobleman.

ISBN 0-671-50115-1

50115>

UPC

0 76714 00599 0

$5.99 U.S.
$7.99 CAN.

PRINTED IN U.S.A.